Acclaim for Suzanne Adair

Deadly Occupation

"Thick with intrigue and subplots to keep readers guessing."
—Caroline Clemmons, author of the "Kincaids" series

Regulated for Murder

"Best of 2011" from Suspense Magazine:

"This is mystery writing at its best."
—Great Historicals

A Hostage to Heritage

winner of the Indie Book of the Day Award:

"Suzanne Adair is on top of her game with this one."
—Jim Chambers, Amazon Hall of Fame Top 10 Reviewer

Books by Suzanne Adair

Michael Stoddard American Revolution Mysteries
Deadly Occupation
Regulated for Murder
A Hostage to Heritage
Killer Debt

Mysteries of the American Revolution
Paper Woman
The Blacksmith's Daughter
Camp Follower

Killer Debt

Suzanne Adair

A Michael Stoddard American Revolution Mystery

Acknowledgements

I receive help from some wonderful and unique people while conducting research for novels and editing my manuscripts. Here are a few who assisted me with *Killer Debt*:

The 33rd Light Company of Foot, especially Ernie and Linda Stewart

Terry Gray Chandler

Larry Cywin

Mike Everette

Nolin and Neil Jones

Valerie Stein

JJ Toner

Executive producers: Robert and Heather Gruber

Special thanks to Ava Barlow for cover photography; Author's Assembler and Jennifer Soucy for cover design; and Author's Assembler for interior format.

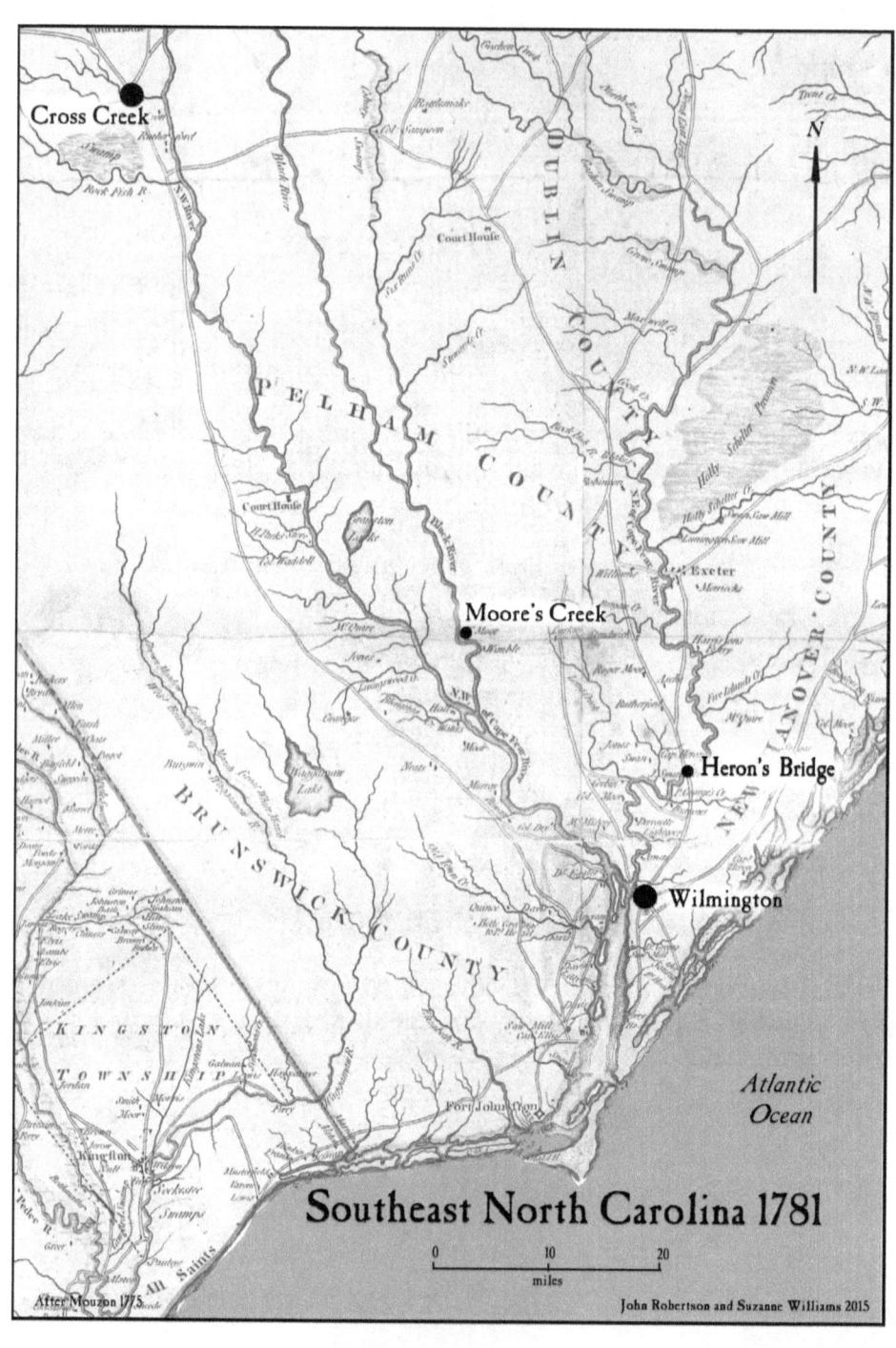

Cross Creek

Moore's Creek

Heron's Bridge

Wilmington

Atlantic
Ocean

Southeast North Carolina 1781

0   10   20
miles

After Mouzon 1775

John Robertson and Suzanne Williams 2015

Chapter One

THE FILMY, GRAY quality of the smoke column rising to the southwest told Captain Michael Stoddard that they were too late. The residence was gutted. He and his patrol of six redcoats from the Eighty-Second Regiment could render no aid.

He'd seen far too much of arson's smudge upon the sky during his six months in North Carolina. Nevertheless, he pressed his mare toward the smoke through summer's swelter. A loyalist financier named Jasper Bellington owned the house and surrounding land. Bellington's business partner hadn't seen him since Friday, July twentieth, four days earlier. Tension knotted Michael's stomach. Had the loyalist and his three slaves perished in the inferno of his house?

Clear sky arced above the soldiers, a hot, hard awning of lapis. The road ribboned south through stands of long-leaf pines and live oaks, sand and shells sighing and crunching beneath horse hooves. Aside from the squawks of crows, the only other sounds keeping Michael and his men company were the ebb and swell of cicada-song in the brush, and the occasional dull clack of a leather-and-wood canteen lifted to the lips of a thirsty soldier.

A breeze blew the smell of sweaty horses away for a second. Michael, riding in front, got his first whiff of burned wood. He sat taller in the saddle, blinked sweat from his eyes, and spotted the entrance to Bellington's drive an eighth mile ahead. "There it is, lads. Come along." He urged his mare forward.

On the drive, trees shaded the men, and the sharp stench of charred wood blanketed them. Michael's gaze raked over the surrounding foliage for anything suspicious or dangerous. Rainwater from a thunderstorm two nights earlier had evaporated, and he spotted recent wheel ruts and hoof prints leading up the sandy track—potential evidence being obliterated by the passage of his patrol. He ordered his men off the drive, single-file behind him in the grass and low brush.

The smoking, blackened skeleton of Bellington's two-story house awaited them at the top of the drive, in a clearing ringed by singed trees. Heat oozed off the devastation. Whenever the breeze died, Michael heard the creak and shift of burned timber. Anyone trapped in the house after it was ablaze was surely dead.

Sweat dribbled from his scalp through his dark hair, down the sides of his face and into his neck stock. He removed his hat long enough to blot his forehead with a handkerchief, then signaled his men to dismount. For several seconds, everyone studied the ruin, and Michael sensed the men's apprehension over what they'd find.

Private Henshaw's voice was subdued. "Looks like the Reverend's work again, sir."

It did indeed. At the helm of a band of slippery, self-appointed dispensers of rebel "justice" was the Reverend Paul Greene, weapons smuggler and thorn in the Eighty-Second's side since January. In late May, he and his band began roaming the Cape Fear area, terrorizing the King's Friends, burning homes, and stealing slaves and other property.

Private Jackson cocked a fist on his hip. "Poor losers, every one of Greene's band."

Michael grunted and fanned away a cloud of gnats. "Desperate losers. All right, men, let's check those outbuildings and the stable over there for survivors."

With Henshaw watching the horses, Michael and the remaining soldiers fanned out, firearms loaded. By his order, the men avoided tromping through the crisscross of wheel ruts and hoof prints in the clearing. As he approached the stable, a horse from his party snorted. From the stable came a nervous whicker in response.

Michael and the two men nearest him, Ferguson and Wigglesworth, froze and studied each other. The same logic must be going through all their heads. Why would rebel arsonists leave a horse behind?

Was this some sort of trap?

Memory provided him with ghastly examples of the traps that rebels set and affirmed his caution. He motioned Ferguson and Wigglesworth forward with him and signed for the others to hold position. Heart thudding against his ribcage, he stepped to the hinge side of the right stable door and pressed his back to the outer wall. Ferguson sneaked to the hinges of the left door, with Wigglesworth just beyond him. All three held their firearms at half-cock and ready.

Michael rapped the door with his knuckles. "Hullo! Anyone in there?"

No human answered, but the horse rustled about and snorted once. "Hullo, we're from the Eighty-Second Regiment, here to help." No response. Seconds ticked by in Michael's waistcoat watch, in the creep of sweat down his back.

"We're opening the door now." With the end of his fusil, he unlatched the right side of the door. It swayed ajar an inch or two with a soft squeak of hinges.

The wind shifted and blew the bitter, charred-wood stink over them, along with some ash. Wigglesworth and Ferguson fanned away the smoke, and Wigglesworth coughed. Michael motioned for Ferguson to push the door open with his musket, and the door yawned wide on its hinges. "No need to be alarmed. We're coming in now to help you." Before he could lose his nerve, Michael darted through the opening, fusil raised.

He expelled a pent-up breath and lowered his weapon. The only occupant of the stable was one nervous horse, a gelding tucked into a stall, his water pail empty. Wigglesworth entered behind him. He soothed the horse, backed him from the stall, and checked him over, then shrugged at Michael and shook his head. No sign of injury on the animal, but he looked thirsty.

From the droppings in the adjacent empty stall, another horse had been housed there as recently as a day ago. Why would rebels steal one horse and leave the other healthy beast behind?

He sent Ferguson to check the kitchen building for survivors and assigned Wigglesworth to water the gelding and ready him for transport back to Wilmington. Then he examined Bellington's two-wheeled gig. Sand clung to both wheels but crumbled off when he flicked it with a forefinger. The gig hadn't been driven in at least a day.

Was this the only vehicle to make those wheel tracks in the clearing and on the drive? Curious, Michael used the length of his booted foot to measure the distance between the gig's wheels. Outside the stable, two of his men held position across from him, awaiting his orders. "Search around the house," he called out before giving attention to the maze of wheel ruts, hoof prints, and shoe prints before him.

He walked out into the clearing, even though doing so muddled evidence. In addition to tracks from Bellington's gig, he recognized those of a four-wheeled vehicle. Not a wagon: the wheel ruts weren't thick enough. A passenger vehicle, then, perhaps a small chaise. The distance between the back wheels of the vehicle was almost a foot wider than the wheels of Bellington's gig. With a swirl of ruts, the chaise had halted before the house within the past two days. A man had exited on the left side and walked toward what had been the front door.

Michael cocked his head, gaze sweeping the trail of shoe prints up to the house. There was a round indentation in the sand to the outside of every right shoe print. Whoever Bellington's visitor had been, he walked with a slight limp in his left leg and used a cane but didn't lean heavily on it. From the length of his stride, Michael judged him of medium height, like himself.

"Mr. Stoddard—sir!" That was Jackson, at the rear of the house. The short soldier's voice quavered. "There's—there's someone inside!"

Michael's pulse kicked. He sprinted across the clearing for the back of the house. Rounding the corner, he huffed up to the soldier, who stood near a singed bench and several potted banana and citrus trees in the dirt behind the house. "Someone alive?"

"N-no, sir, it—it—" Jackson pointed into the charred timbers, his complexion greenish.

Michael faced the house. Over the stink of blistered beams, he got his first deep whiff of burned flesh. He coughed, grimaced, and swung his gaze back and forth before it probed deep into the tumble of timber and the wreck of books and furniture, into what had been the study. It lodged on the blackened, standing figure of a man.

No, not standing. The corpse was hanging—arms overhead, wrists apparently strapped together—from a beam. His shoes were flat on the burned floor. His head and crispy wig lolled forward, and to one side.

It was Bellington. Good gods. The clothing on his upper body was gone, and his chest—

Eyes bulging, Michael recoiled one step from the house. Horror and revulsion ground through him with a queasy grab at his gut. He closed his mouth on the smell, the taste, of violent death and incineration. The private staggered into the brush behind him and retched. Michael couldn't blame him.

Bellington's ribs protruded starkly, like some sort of roast. Before the house was set afire, and the man's body had burned, long slabs of flesh had been skinned off his torso. They'd since baked against his breeches. His murderer must have counted on arson obscuring how the victim had been tortured beforehand, flayed—

Flayed. His breathing shallow, Michael backed another step. Incredulous, he glared eastward, as if he could see across the Cape Fear River to Wilmington and the regiment. Outrage swelled in him and chased away his queasiness. Ye gods, this could not be so! But moments before in the clearing, he'd seen with his own eyes the evidence that a man with a left-leg limp and a cane had visited Bellington in the past day or so.

Maybe rebels hadn't murdered the financier and set his house ablaze. Maybe the true criminal was an officer and wore His Majesty's scarlet. Michael felt a sneer of determination peel his lip off his teeth. His breath hissed out, and he whispered, "Damn you, Fairfax!" It was long past time that Michael saw that devil hanged for indulging in his depravity, his *sport.*

Leaves and twigs exploded behind him with the discharge of a firearm, followed by Jackson's scream. From the front of the house, Henshaw hollered through the firearm's echoing report. With nowhere else to hide, Michael dove behind the potted orange trees, then sought better cover from the big-leafed banana trees beside them. The rotten-egg stink of black powder smoke rolled over him. Debris rained on the foliage not far away.

He could hear Jackson's ragged breathing somewhere out in the brush plus the running approach of soldiers through dead leaves. He turned his head and jutted his chin. "Stay back, men!" His own fear and hammering heartbeat hiked the pitch of his voice. "Take cover!" They fell back, around the side of the ruin.

Clearly this was an undesirable situation. Potted trees as a shield, heat from the house slowly simmering Michael's arse. Plus the color of his coat made a rebel marksman's job easy. Michael worked on calming the rabbit in his pulse and hoped his clothing wouldn't ignite. Fusil gripped in both hands, he peered between banana leaves. His gaze scoured the ground and lower trunks of trees. He spotted Jackson's musket lying on the ground.

Seconds thudded by. No more shots were fired. Where was the marksman? Where, for that matter, was Jackson? It sounded like the private had been hit. Had he lost consciousness?

"Mr. Stoddard, sir. Can you hear me?" Jackson's voice still quavered.

Michael squinted. "Yes, I can hear you, lad. Stay down. Are you hurt bad?"

"I—I think the ball skimmed my scalp, sir. Top of my head's bleeding. Hurts like the devil. A-and I think I'd be dead if I were a taller fellow."

Why hadn't the marksman fired again? Michael wasn't that difficult a target, and it sounded like Jackson wasn't, either. He stuck his hat on the end of his fusil's barrel and jiggled it to the side, beyond the banana leaves. Nobody shot at him.

Jackson's voice firmed. "While I was puking, sir, I tripped some kind of trap with a loaded pistol and a snare. Might you please help me down?"

Loaded pistol? Snare? "Help you *down*?" Fusil in hand, Michael rose, planted his hat on his head, and walked away from the potted trees and overly warm house.

From a sturdy sapling, Jackson hung upside down about five feet off the ground, one lower leg tangled in the rope of a snare. Blond hair on the top of his head was matted with blood. Nearby, a spring-gun—a lock, stock, and shortened barrel with a post—was mounted on a stump. Rope from both gun and snare lay mostly hidden in dead leaves.

The private made eye contact with Michael and wobbled out a salute. Michael propped his fist on his hip and heaved a sigh. "Ah, bloody hell."

Chapter Two

MICHAEL CLOSED THE gun, rope, and peg that had comprised the snare and trap into a canvas sack and hooked it onto his mare's saddle for later study. The patrol found no other snares, but their search of the grounds turned up one dead slave with multiple stab wounds and a slit throat. They also found three hounds, all dead, an entrance and exit hole in each torso suggestive of a firearm ball passing clean through the heart. No dog was closer to the house than two hundred feet. They weren't together in a pack. The dead slave hadn't been with any of them.

While soldiers buried the dogs, Michael returned to the clearing and reexamined the wheel grooves and cane marks. In the past day or so, a man with the height and limp of Fairfax had arrived in a chaise for a visit with the financier. Bellington's dogs would have greeted him when he alighted. By the time he left, the visitor would know how many dogs and slaves Bellington had.

Michael stared into the dense woodlands on the estate and tried to make sense of what he'd seen. If the murderer had sneaked onto the property, wouldn't the barking and growling of three dogs have generated enough clamor to alert the people for defense? Wouldn't the killer's first shot have summoned the remaining two dogs?

Perhaps the killer hadn't sneaked around. If Bellington knew him and let him into the house, that might explain how the financier had been murdered in the study. But did that mean the dogs were shot during the criminal's departure?

A soldier tripped and went down with a crash, then stood and brushed himself off. Michael glanced at the sky, startled at how the afternoon had advanced. Lengthening shadows reduced visibility.

Even though Bellington's two other slaves were unaccounted for, Michael called off the search to make sure his patrol returned to town before dark. Heat from the house would discourage scavengers overnight. In the morning, the light would be better for spotting evidence, and the house would have cooled enough for them to retrieve the financier's body. There'd also be time to question neighbors about what they'd witnessed.

The patrol reassembled in the clearing, swatted off gray ash nestled in the creases of their scarlet uniforms, and mounted their horses, Bellington's gelding in tow behind Michael's mare. As they set out on the drive, he ordered them to keep silent about the murder's grisly details, to not discuss it, even among themselves, while the investigation progressed. Leaking the particulars of such a killing might foul the investigation and cause civilians to panic.

In Wilmington, after dropping the gelding off at the regiment's stables, he sent Henshaw to the financier's office with the bad news and escorted Jackson to the infirmary to have his wound treated. Then he strode for Second Street. At the house where he and several officers, including Fairfax, were billeted, he headed straight to the stable at the rear of the property.

Parked inside was the four-wheeled chaise that Fairfax had been driving since his broken leg had healed enough to restore mobility. Using his booted foot, Michael took a measure of the distance between the two rear wheels—a match with the wheel tracks in the clearing before the burned house. Fairfax must have driven the chaise out there and called on the financier not long before the murder.

For a moment, Michael indulged in the pump of sick exhilaration through his veins. His lips thinned, and he gritted his teeth. Since the summer of 1780, when Fairfax had tortured a Spanish assassin to death and framed Indians for the murder, then tried to kill Michael for solving the crime, Michael had dreamed of catching Fairfax in his own lies.

What a pity the evidence he'd uncovered that afternoon was circumstantial. None of it proved that Fairfax had murdered Bellington. Michael swept his hand once across the top of a wheel, then studied fingers free of sand. Evidence could be tampered with, manipulated, misinterpreted. His personal bias put him at risk of all that, in addition to missing clues. Fortunately he knew where to find assistance from an impartial expert in death.

Carrying the sack containing the snare and trap, he returned to the infirmary, converted from one end of the stables. A little bell over the door tinkled to announce his arrival. He removed his hat and proceeded to the horse stall that an army surgeon, Clayton, had dubbed his surgical room. In the opening to the stall, he looked in on Jackson, sitting on the table, the top of his head bandaged. Dark-haired Clayton said to the infantryman, "Muscle strains in your neck, shoulders, and ankle. A one-inch scalped spot on your head. You'll live. But all that calls for light duty through Thursday morning." Clayton hiked his thumb toward the entrance to the horse stall, where Michael waited. "Off you go, lad."

The private slid from the table, limped a few steps toward Michael, then frowned over his shoulder at Clayton. "I was scalped? You mean like what the Indians do?" He fingered the bandage. "Is my hair going to grow back?"

"No, you won't be growing hair in that patch again." Clayton flicked a dried leaf off the wooden table, clean but mottled with old bloodstains. "From now on, it's up to you to make sure the ladies don't bother checking the top of your head." He fanned the air before his nose and grimaced. "And you'd best do something about that fire-pit aroma on you."

A gust of laughter escaped the infantryman. He stood taller and lifted his chin, accepting the challenge. "Thank you."

Michael waved off the private's salute, shifted aside to allow him to exit, and resumed his place. Clayton leaned against the table and nodded at him. "A messenger stopped by right after you brought Jackson, sir. The major wants to see you."

Naturally. Whenever anything bizarre happened to one of Michael's patrols, Major Craig managed to get wind of it before the soldiers returned to town. Craig would want a full report on the incident.

The tinkle of the bell informed them that Jackson had left. Clayton continued, "So it's another adventure for Major Craig's lead criminal investigator. You do make my life interesting. I get bored with stitching men up and cutting off their limbs."

Michael rolled his lips inward a second to seal in a bleak smile. "Jackson reckons that being short of stature saved his life."

"Well, if that trap was set up the way he described it, he's probably correct." Michael lifted the sack. "Here it is."

The surgeon straightened and motioned him in. "Excellent. Let's have a look, sir."

Michael entered, pulled the items from the sack, and recreated the snare and trap assembly using the table as a substitute for the stump. "Imagine you have a sapling bent over here." He pointed out the loop of rope on the floor. "Notice how I've tied the trip for the spring-gun to the loop. Jackson steps in. Rope tangles around his ankle. Up he goes, courtesy of the sapling." Michael yanked the circle of rope off the floor and suspended it as high as he could reach. "At the same time, the gun fires, and the ball grazes his scalp."

Clayton examined the spring-gun. "We used one of these guns in Williamsburg a few years ago to shoot thieves raiding a magazine."

"Yes, we did."

"How high was the stump, sir?" Michael dropped the rope and measured a distance off the floor with the flat of his hand. The surgeon nodded. "Then I'd say Jackson is correct. Even another half inch on him would have been deadly. Most men's skulls aren't as thick as their womenfolk believe."

Michael shoved the parts of the trap into the sack. "So the snare and trap were intended to kill a man—someone who arrived to look for Bellington."

"Yes, quite probable." Clayton's brows pinched downward. "Have you an idea why the criminal set up the snare and trap in that particular location?"

Michael thought back to his observations and felt his expression darken.

"Possibly to catch someone who saw the condition of Bellington's body, then backed away in shock."

The surgeon's lips tightened. "Then you've a demented criminal on your hands, sir. The sight and smell of a burned human body is shocking enough to make almost anyone recoil—pivot away and retch. Even soldiers."

"Which is exactly what Jackson did." Demented criminal, indeed.

The surgeon shook his head. "Did you find anyone else on the property, alive or dead? I understand that Mr. Bellington owned three slaves."

"We found one dead, murdered. As soon as I get descriptions of the others, I'll post notice." Had any of the slaves witnessed the financier's death?

"Where is Mr. Bellington's corpse?"

"We must allow the wreck to cool overnight before we fetch it. Don't want to jeopardize the men's safety unnecessarily."

Internally Michael chafed at the delay. He had to close this investigation quickly. If Captain Dunstan Fairfax was behind this murder, by waiting even one extra day, Michael ran the risk that Fairfax's lust for bloodshed would gain momentum, and he'd torture and kill again.

Fairfax had been convalescing in town since early April, along with Lord Cornwallis's other soldiers injured in a battle in March. As the regiment numbered few more than two hundred regular soldiers, and Major Craig had had no luck obtaining more from South Carolina, he was doing his best to hang onto every one of Cornwallis's men. That meant Craig wouldn't turn loose an officer unless he was convinced that the man was a liability.

Michael must use the extra day to substantiate evidence against Fairfax. He said to the surgeon, "I need you to keep quiet about this investigation for a while."

"Of course."

"Good. I'd like you to ride out to the site with us on the morrow and have a look at the body. I've a feeling the arsonist set fire to the house to cover up the true way he'd murdered the man."

Clayton's eyebrows rose, and his neck lengthened. "True way? Wasn't Mr. Bellington burned alive?"

"From the looks of things, I question whether he was alive when the criminal set fire to his house." He saw Clayton's lips form a little "o" and knew the surgeon was intrigued. "The patrol will assemble in front of the barracks at dawn on the morrow. Are you with us?"

The surgeon's eyes sparkled. "I'll be there."

* * *

On the porch of the three-story house at Third and Market, the provost marshal's guard waved Michael up ahead of nine people queued in the July sun to see Major Craig. Whenever the guard signaled Michael forward like that, it meant something big was afoot. What a relief this time that Michael wouldn't be guessing about the assignment while standing in Craig's study, waiting for his commander to get to the point. Jasper Bellington had been a prominent local businessman and supporter of the King. Craig would place priority on solving the murder.

Musing over the snare and trap, he strode past petitioners. A whiff of violet perfume snagged his attention. At the head of the queue, goodwife Alice Farrell, bearer of a pale purple parasol, lowered her shade and smiled.

His attention hopped over Mrs. Farrell's gossip-bright grin to the blonde widow in her company. Their gazes met, and his heart leapt with the memory of one kiss in a grain shed four long months ago. Then his heart shivered, as if pierced by needle-slender rapiers. Without breaking stride, he gave the ladies a quick nod of greeting, yanked his gaze forward, and mounted the steps.

There could be only one reason for Kate Duncan to add her voice to that of Mrs. Farrell. The Wilmington ladies must have become determined to schedule that festive supper honoring the Eighty-Second. But the fête was never going to happen. The regiment was simply too busy keeping order in the lower Cape Fear.

He stomped onto the porch, realized that he'd forgotten to exhale most of the way up the stairs, and shoved out a hard breath that rattled his ribs. A muscular man in a dusty hunting shirt and riding boots exited the front door. He was Michael's age, twenty-six, and after taking two steps out onto the porch, he dropped his wide-brimmed hat over a head covered by a silk handkerchief. Michael saluted him. "Colonel Fanning. How good to see you again, sir."

David Fanning, appointed by Craig as commander of loyalist militia in several counties, returned the salute. "Likewise, Mr. Stoddard. I hear congratulations are in order." A smile flitted over his face. "Your promotion is well-deserved." He accepted the return of his rifle from the provost's guard.

"Thank you, sir." Michael nodded to acknowledge the praise. "Headed out of Wilmington again?"

Fanning's gaze hardened. All traces of a smile vanished, and he lowered his voice. "I've learned the whereabouts of a leader of rebel scum, Philip Alston." He shifted the rifle from one hand to the other in a crisp motion. "He's skulking about the Deep River."

In February, Michael had traveled nearly that far west. He considered the distance between Wilmington and the Deep River. "You've a solid five-day ride ahead of you, sir." He stepped out of Fanning's way. "Good hunting."

Fanning touched the brim of his hat. "And you, too, sir." Down the steps he thumped.

The guard pushed the front door open. Michael swept off his hat, wiped his boot soles on the mat, and entered the shadowy foyer of the house. The study was closed, so he nudged open one side of the double door and, after drawing the door to behind him, continued all the way in.

As usual, he found Major Craig sitting at the table facing the doors, his quill scratching paper while he caught up with correspondence. A curtained window was at his back. In fact, curtains shrouded all the windows, darkening the room, sealing out most of the heat. Flame from a candle near Craig's wrist stood at attention in the dead air. The major acknowledged Michael's salute, then blotted his temple with a handkerchief and peered past him. "Let's keep the heat out there. Spry, do make certain the doors are closed all the way."

Spry? In surprise, Michael swiveled around to spot his six-foot tall, blond assistant investigator striding to the doors, his lips tense and down-turned in a face meant for laughter. But Spry had been on assignment ten miles north, at the Herons Bridge post—

Corner shadows convulsed, seizing Michael's gaze. An officer rose from a chair, and Michael's heart banged a few beats out of rhythm. Finally he understood his assistant's gloom. Fairfax. What was that murderous demon doing here?

The handsome, russet-haired officer had gained his feet in a smooth movement, with little assistance from the cane in his right hand. A sneer twitched his lip, then vanished. His nod of greeting was almost imperceptible. The coldest spot in the room was his eyes: green hoarfrost.

Spry stepped forward and assumed position near Michael's right side. Michael whipped his attention back to Craig. Instinct blared a dire warning in his gut.

The commander of the regiment set letter and quill aside and capped the inkwell. After pushing away his correspondence pile, he interlaced his hands on the table before him and studied Michael. "Your report on the fire at Mr. Bellington's estate?"

Not while his nemesis listened was Michael going to admit all he'd seen. If Fairfax were responsible for that atrocity off the road to Brunswick, hearing Michael's impressions of his handiwork would delight and entertain him. "The outbuildings are intact, sir. We found an uninjured horse in the stable and brought him back with us. But the house was destroyed, and I saw Mr. Bellington dead within the ruins—murdered."

Craig winced, and Michael continued. "We found one slave, also murdered. I shall post a notice about Mr. Bellington's two missing slaves."

Craig nodded, a curt motion. "You brought back Mr. Bellington's body for a proper funeral?"

"No, sir. The structure was too hot for us to venture within. I've scheduled a patrol to return early on the morrow so we can retrieve his body and search longer on the property. And I plan to question the nearest neighbors about what they might have witnessed."

Another nod from Craig. "I heard that Jackson was injured. How?"

"Sir. He stepped into some sort of snare coupled with a spring-gun in the woods behind the house." He glanced at Fairfax. The other officer stood still as marble, displaying no reaction to Michael's account. If Fairfax had been the one to set it up, he was concealing his response well.

The major's eyebrows rose. "Was the trap created by Mr. Bellington?"

Hmm. Michael hadn't considered that. Neither time he'd met Bellington had the financier impressed him as being the sort of man to set up such a complicated trap. Nevertheless, wealthy men sometimes acquired enemies. Desperate men used extreme means to rid themselves of their enemies.

Had Bellington been desperate about something? Michael needed to find out. And he needed to ignore Fairfax and focus. He should have already thought about the angle that Craig had suggested.

He addressed his commander. "I doubt that Mr. Bellington set it up, sir. Possibly he commissioned it. Or perhaps his killer assembled it. We found no additional traps."

Brow lowered, Craig digested Michael's words a moment. "Do you believe this incident of arson and murder was the result of Reverend Greene's activities?"

"Not necessarily, sir. When Mr. Greene's band visits arson upon loyalists, they do so after first evicting the occupants from their dwellings. Mr. Bellington was not evicted. He was murdered in his home. Thus I suspect a personal motive at work."

"I see." Handkerchief gripped in one hand, Craig shoved himself up from the chair, turned to the window behind him, and pressed the curtain aside with his forefinger. After peering out in the direction of an overcrowded, outdoor pen of rebel prisoners, he let the curtain fall into place. His back to the men in the room with him, he mopped his neck and brow. "Well done, Mr. Stoddard. Turn your notes and evidence over to Mr. Fairfax by eight o'clock tonight. He will complete the Bellington investigation."

Chapter Three

FAIRFAX COMPLETE THE Bellington investigation—what? The order felt like a fist of lightning rammed into the pit of Michael's stomach—without warning, paralyzing. His gut tensed. Sensing Fairfax's pleasure over his distress, he firmed his shoulders and jaw.

"Conflict of interests" didn't begin to describe this reassignment. The previous summer, in the town of Alton, Georgia, Fairfax had flourished in the environment of investigating murder—the Spaniard's murder that he himself had committed. How could Michael allow him to do something similar in Wilmington?

The major swiveled his neck and offered his Roman senator's profile to Michael. "Mr. Stoddard?"

Michael coughed to loosen his throat. "Sir. I've already begun this investigation. Transferring it to Mr. Fairfax will lose time while Mr. Bellington's killer roams free with the opportunity to kill again."

Craig faced Michael full on, his eyes narrowed. "Are you questioning Mr. Fairfax's competence as an investigator?" He tossed his handkerchief to the tabletop.

"No, sir, but he's still recovering from a broken leg. Recall that Lord Cornwallis's surgeon originally advised amputation because the break was severe."

He spared another glance at Fairfax, who put weight on both feet without appearing to favor the left leg. He'd crossed his arms above his chest and balanced his cane against his right leg. As if to prove Michael doubly wrong, Fairfax swelled his chest and smirked. From the musculature filling out his scarlet coat, he'd been successful at gaining back much of the weight he'd lost while convalescing.

Bum fodder. Michael whipped his attention back to Craig and made his tone even. "Mr. Bellington's estate is primarily woodland, sir. Excluding the possibility of additional traps, the terrain surrounding his house is treacherous and uneven for a man walking with a cane. For the past two months, Mr. Fairfax's analytical skills have been expertly put to use sorting through county revenue records for evidence of fraud. It's my recommendation that he continue that work and not venture into the wilderness, where he may re-injure his leg." Especially since the Almighty Himself would have difficulty making sense of those county records, damaged by water when the regiment confiscated them in January.

Craig's head bobbed. "Your concern for your fellow officer is commendable. As you can see, Mr. Fairfax has made remarkable, even miraculous, progress at regaining use of his leg. In fact, Clayton has cleared him to begin retraining on horseback next week."

Bloody hell. How could this be happening?

Craig strutted out from behind the table. He was the shortest man in the room, and no one dared comment on it. "Don't be concerned that progress on the revenue records will stall while Mr. Fairfax works on the investigation. He's isolated several business accounts—rebel business accounts, he says—that appear associated with delinquent taxes, and he's assured me that he's eager to continue investigating them."

Bloody hell. How could this be happening, too? Fury, frustration, and fear swirled in Michael's belly. He let out a stifled breath slowly.

Criminal investigation probably wasn't his ultimate career, but it was certainly an improvement over the dull duty assignments that officers usually received. For weeks he'd watched Fairfax buff Major Craig's arse. Now Fairfax, who might have murdered Bellington, had stolen the investigation from beneath Michael's nose. Damnation.

Sweat trickled an itchy path down the hollow of his back. How could he regain control of his investigation? Behind him, he heard a soft exhalation from Spry, like a sigh of dejection. Where did this reassignment leave Spry? Had Craig dragged Spry back from Herons Bridge to assign him to the investigation with Fairfax? Christ Jesus, Spry would hate that. In February, in Hillsborough, Nick Spry had also been on the receiving end of Fairfax's brutality.

The major leaned against the front edge of the table, one hand on his hip, the other braced on the table's surface, and one ankle crossed over the other. "From your expression, I know exactly what you're thinking, Mr. Stoddard."

No, you don't, thought Michael.

"Since January it's been my good fortune to have your excellent investigative skills at my service." Craig flicked Spry a glance. "And those of your assistant. I'm now in a position to expand your skills into another arena. And that's why I've transferred the Bellington investigation to Mr. Fairfax."

From the preamble, Michael realized that Craig was about to hand him the rare opportunity to diversify his experience. Peripheral vision alerted him to the shift in Fairfax's posture, the sharp way he focused on Major Craig, and a jolt of comprehension shot through Michael. In advance of Michael's arrival in the room, Craig had told Fairfax that he'd transfer the Bellington investigation to him; that explained Fairfax's gloat earlier. Only now did Fairfax realize that the "plum" he'd wheedled out of Craig wasn't the best the major had to offer. No, Craig had offloaded the investigation onto Fairfax so he could present Michael with a greater challenge, a way to deepen his value as a military professional.

Fairfax must be enraged. The turnabout would have elated Michael had he not known Fairfax's history, the way he'd flayed alive that spy the previous summer. Could Michael accept whatever grand assignment Craig had picked for him while knowing that the criminal investigator assigned to solve Bellington's murder might very well be guilty of the crime? Could Jasper Bellington be guaranteed to get the King's Justice with Fairfax investigating his murder?

How Michael longed to question Fairfax while Craig listened, find out why he'd driven to see Bellington shortly before the man was murdered and his house set afire. But he kept his lips sealed. This wasn't the time for those questions. Not yet.

Craig said, "I presume you ran into Colonel Fanning as you arrived? I'm grateful to have such proficiency at my disposal. However, Mr. Fanning brought with him to Wilmington a number of prisoners." Craig rubbed his eyelids. "The pen is full of rebel prisoners. The prison ships are full of rebel prisoners. The rebels are holding our people. We need a prisoner exchange, and we may now have that opportunity."

Michael stood taller. "Sir. You wish me to negotiate with rebels for our captive men?" Well, now, that would present quite a challenge. His negotiation experience was on a much smaller scale.

"Oh, no. I'll be doing the negotiation—if it comes to that." He twisted back to retrieve a letter off the table. "I have here correspondence from Mr. William Hooper, one of the signers of the Declaration of Independence. He wishes to come to Wilmington under flag of truce and negotiate for prisoner release."

Negotiate. Michael cocked an eyebrow. "He'll use the opening to check on his family, perhaps remove them." In January, desperate to gallop away to the west and escape the approach of the Eighty-Second, Hooper had been forced to abandon his estate on the Sound and leave his loved ones behind in Wilmington—trust his household's safety to Craig's mercy.

A brief smile crossed Craig's lips. "Precisely." He dropped the letter back on the table and folded his arms over his chest. "I shall be delighted to provide a flag of truce for Mr. Hooper and allow him to stay with his family while he's here." Craig's smile soured. "To the extent that I also receive detailed instructions about the prisoner exchange from Mr. Burke—that pompous ass whom the rebels now call 'Governor' of North Carolina—I shall negotiate with Mr. Hooper for our prisoners of war. But I shan't release his family."

"Sir."

William Hooper's wife and children were hostages in Wilmington. Hooper should thank his lucky stars that they'd been under Major Craig's protection, not savaged by loyalists.

"As for your role, Mr. Stoddard, you will organize Mr. Hooper's bodyguard while he is under the flag of truce."

Michael frowned. "His bodyguard, sir? But a flag of truce—"

"Fanatics care nothing for a flag of truce. I'll not have one of Mr. Greene's minions martyr a signer under a flag of truce during my command. It would make us look incompetent. Is that clear?"

"Sir."

"I expect Mr. Hooper to visit for several days. You will select a team of men, including Spry, to assist you at protecting him during that time. The resources of the Eighty-Second are at your disposal to help you develop watch schedules and devise security measures appropriate to ensuring that Mr. Hooper comes to no harm. At nine on the morrow, bring me a draft of the measures you intend to enact."

"Sir."

Fairfax spoke for the first time. "Major Craig."

The major inclined his head. "Mr. Fairfax."

"Sir, while I was under Lord Cornwallis's direct command, I served as a bodyguard for one of General Nathanael Greene's emissaries who arrived in camp to discuss a prisoner exchange. I coordinated security measures to ensure his safety." Fairfax lifted his chin. "As Mr. Stoddard has no previous skill in this capacity, I offer to take his place *and* investigate Mr. Bellington's death while continuing my work on the tax records."

That damned snake. Michael clenched his jaw.

"Thank you, Mr. Fairfax. I appreciate your apprising me of your knowledge and previous experience. But two simultaneous investigations are enough for any man, especially a man who is still convalescing. Besides, Mr. Stoddard has worked for the better part of the year with the men of the Eighty-Second. He knows without a doubt on whom he can rely for his team. I consider that knowledge and experience of the greater importance.

"Ensuring Mr. Hooper's safety will take priority over solving Mr. Bellington's murder. Thus while Mr. Hooper is in town, you will render assistance to Mr. Stoddard, should he call upon you. Considering your vast experience, I've no doubt that you will be an asset to him."

Craig returned his regard to Michael without waiting for Fairfax's response. He didn't see the cold fire that widened Fairfax's eyes or the way his lips smashed together. Fairfax had been placed under Michael's command—even though he had seniority by five months.

Fairfax was spitting nails. Now he'd wield the Bellington investigation for self-aggrandizement. A killer would likely go free, and the murdered financier would get no justice.

To hell with Fairfax. Michael knew his duty. He must solve Jasper Bellington's murder. It was the only way the financier would receive evenhanded treatment. And if Fairfax had killed Bellington, oh, the pleasure it would give him to arrest that son of a mongrel.

He focused on Craig and thrust out his chest. "I'm honored by your confidence in me, sir. You may rely on me to ensure Mr. Hooper's safety."

"Excellent." Craig handed him a slip of paper. "Here's information about the location where you'll assume his escort to Wilmington on the twenty-sixth. That gives you two days to prepare."

"Sir. Shall I inform his wife of your plans?" Michael pocketed the paper in his waistcoat.

"Yes, do so. You seem to have developed a rapport with her." He drummed fingers on his thigh. "Gah. One more thing. Those annoying Wilmington ladies." He pressed his lips together and expelled a breath through his nose. "Nagging me about scheduling that celebratory supper. It occurs to me that I can get them off my back by telling them to plan it for Friday night. I shall make certain that Mr. Hooper and his wife are invited." He clapped his hands once. "Yes, indeed. That will please the women who are waiting out there in line to pester me today. And remember that those women insist upon presenting some sort of symbolic matrimony at the head table between the local business owners and the regiment." He rolled his eyes to the ceiling. "They partnered you with the widowed owner of White's Tavern for the evening. You'll have to put Spry in charge of security that night."

Michael's heart writhed again, the imaginary needles driving in deeper, but he kept the muscles of his shoulders relaxed. From the corner of his eye, he'd registered the sharp tilt of Fairfax's head at Craig's news. He knew damned well that if Fairfax suspected Kate meant something to him, he'd find a way to torment both of them.

Kate and her brother Kevin owned and operated White's Tavern. They also ran a whiskey still ten miles north of Wilmington and evaded taxes on the sales. Call it instinct, call it cynicism over human nature—Michael suspected that they'd ignored his commands to shut down production.

Their whiskey business was a perfect example of the kind of operation to catch Fairfax's eye during his scrutiny of tax records. If he found out that Michael knew of such an operation without penalizing the perpetrators, he'd drag Michael's credibility through the latrine. For that reason, Michael had kept his distance from Kate and Kevin since spring.

But surely he and Kate could sit at the feast table together Friday night and pursue cordial conversation for however long the meal lasted.

He stood at attention and maintained a straight face with his gaze on the commander. "Sir. Partnered with a widowed business owner for the evening. For King and country, yes, sir."

Craig laughed, as Michael had hoped. Cold silence yawned from Fairfax's corner of the room. Fairfax had no sense of humor.

The major glanced back and forth between the two officers. "Any questions on your assignments, gentlemen?"

At the same time, both Michael and Fairfax said firmly, "No, sir."

Craig pushed off from the table and swaggered back behind it, to his pile of unanswered letters, and yanked out his chair. "Very good. Mr. Fairfax, a quick summary from you of those business accounts you suspect of delinquent taxes. Mr. Stoddard, you and Spry are dismissed."

Chapter Four

OUTSIDE, THE LATE afternoon sun pounded Wilmington's wood and brick buildings, rippling heat over the dusty streets of a town denuded of trees back in January by the soldiers. Michael waited for the passage of a lumber wagon, its horse team and driver drooping in the warmth. Then, with Spry at his side, he crossed Market Street, dodging between three dockworkers and a goat.

The two men paused in the shade of a house. A few feet away, an orange tomcat toyed with a tailless mouse. Michael regarded the pair as he blotted sweat off his neck and forehead with his handkerchief. Part of him wished that he could have lingered to eavesdrop on the conversation between Fairfax and Craig. But that would waste time.

He had work to do ahead of Fairfax, whose next stop would no doubt be Bellington's office for a chat with the financier's business partner, Jonas Hickory. Michael must get there first. He settled his hat on his head and withdrew his watch long enough to check the time. "A quarter to five."

"Sir?"

Michael gave Spry an up-and-down glance, then a clap to the shoulder. "Good to see you, lad. You're looking well." He waved for his eighteen-year-old assistant to accompany him south, toward the Cape Fear River. "Not much sunburn, at least."

"Thank you, sir. Likewise. And congratulations. Promotion clearly agrees with you."

Michael dipped his head in brief acknowledgement. His captaincy had come through on the nineteenth of July, but he wasn't weary of hearing the good wishes. For years he'd struggled as a lieutenant with no means of purchasing advancement.

In early April, his heroism in the line of duty had caught the attention and gratitude of two English peers, who became his benefactors and purchased his captaincy. Afterwards they'd struck a bargain for him to advance from captain to major. Michael stayed busy to keep from dwelling upon that bargain and the black barb it had lodged in his soul. Sometimes it kept him awake at night. Literally.

A gaggle of chatty goodwives passed them. After a glance around to make sure none of them was close enough to hear, he pitched his tone low. "This afternoon, I led a patrol out to investigate the fire at Jasper Bellington's estate. In the dirt before his burned house, I identified the wheel tracks of Mr. Fairfax's chaise as well as imprints from his cane. No more than two days ago, our 'friend' called upon Mr. Bellington."

Michael studied Spry's grasp of the details. His assistant's eyebrows rose. Michael continued. "And not long after Mr. Fairfax came calling, Mr. Bellington was tortured. His chest was flayed to the bone. Then his house was set afire."

The private's eyes bugged. "God Almighty!"

"Jackson was first to spot him, still dangling from a beam in his study." An image of the grisly sight shot through Michael's memory. A chill scurried his spine. "Somehow the rope hadn't burned through. Jackson turned away to puke and stepped into a trap that nearly killed him." Michael described the snare and spring gun setup for Spry. The two men walked for a quarter minute without talking.

Spry said softly, "Sir, I recall you telling me that Mr. Fairfax flayed alive a Spaniard in Georgia last summer. And before you stepped in, he'd been assigned to investigate that murder."

"Correct."

"You suspect him of murdering Mr. Bellington, sir." They arrived at Front Street, and Spry followed his commander to the right. "If he did so, then he has again been assigned to investigate the murder of his victim. Quite a conflict of interests."

Michael's lips twisted. "Yes, life is full of little ironies, isn't it?"

They halted in the street before the financier's office. Spry propped both fists on his hips and nodded at the business sign. "Well, sir, it's a good thing that we don't need to work out details for the protection of Mr. Hooper quite yet." He caught Michael's eye. "As I'm guessing that we don't have much time in here, specifically what are we looking for in the office?"

"I will be looking for anything that might implicate someone—including Mr. Hickory and Mr. Fairfax—in the murder. You will be looking out a front window for Mr. Fairfax while listening to the conversation I have with Mr. Hickory. And when you spot Mr. Fairfax headed our way, remind me that I have an appointment or some other such balderdash. We'll leave from the rear entrance."

"Yes, sir."

They trotted up a few steps and arrived on the building's porch as a slender man in his late thirties exited the office, hat on his head, and a padlock in hand. He paused in the half-open doorway to regard the soldiers, dark eyes hollowed. "Mr. Stoddard." He squared his shoulders. "Private Henshaw gave me your message. I'm closing the office for a few days." A sign tacked to the front door read *Closed due to bereavement. Will reopen Monday 30 July.*

"I understand. My condolences, Mr. Hickory."

"Thank you." The man's gaze traveled to Spry, then back to Michael. "This is such a shock."

Michael gestured inside the office. "Before you leave, might I have a word with you?"

"Of course." Hickory waved them into the stuffy front room. "I always have time for Major Craig's investigators. Perhaps you can get to the bottom of this tragedy." All three men removed their hats. Hickory set down the padlock, closed and barred the door, and gestured them to an elegant sofa.

Michael nodded to Spry. "Enjoy the view." His assistant went to the nearest window.

Hickory watched the way Spry assumed his post. "Is Spry standing guard?" He swiveled to Michael and frowned. "Am I in danger, Mr. Stoddard?"

"I hope not, sir." Michael took a seat on the sofa and motioned to a nearby chair. The financier perched on the edge of it, tossed his hat to the other end of the sofa from Michael, and rested hands in his lap. Then, with a cough of dismay, he whipped out his handkerchief and scrubbed at an ink stain on the outside edge of his right hand, his movements jerky. Michael waited for him to calm down and stuff the smudged handkerchief back in his waistcoat pocket. Then he made his tone easy. "Just after noon today, you told me that you saw Mr. Bellington in the office four days ago." Hickory dipped his head in acknowledgement. "When was the last time you saw him?"

"Four days ago, on Friday, here in the office." Hickory held his gaze.

"Yet you didn't report him missing."

"I didn't think anything was amiss." Hickory looked away and spread his hands. "He's the senior partner and works from his estate a good bit." A strand of his straight, dark hair had loosened from its tie. He tucked it behind his ear. "Often I see him only two days out of a week."

"How long had you been business partners?"

"Eleven years."

Michael rubbed his chin a second or two. "Who else works in the office with you?"

"Jasper's nephew, Sam." Hickory glanced from Michael to the door. "But he's been in Brunswick for a week with his ailing mother."

Michael made a silent note to check on Sam. "Where were you all day yesterday and last night?"

"Well, during the day I was here, of course. And after I closed the office, I went home."

"You've witnesses?"

"Yes, sir." Hickory eyed him straight on. "Several clients stopped by the office yesterday. At home, my housekeeper and manservant will confirm that

I was there all night."

Not every business partner could resist the lure of prosperity. Eleven years was a long time to wait for seniority. Michael instructed Hickory to provide him with the clients' names as well as those of the housekeeper and manservant. "Oh, and as of this morning, how many active clients have you?"

"Fifteen."

"So fifteen people currently owe money to your business." Michael eyed the financier. "Debt, especially debt with interest, puts strain on a man, makes him tense, angry. Which of your clients are angry enough to kill Mr. Bellington?"

Hickory's head drew back. "I've never seen any of our clients angry with Jasper. He puts them at ease." His shoulders sagged, and his gaze drifted away. "At least, he used to put them at ease."

Michael made noises of sympathy. "Have you witnessed anyone arguing with your business partner lately?"

Hickory's attention snapped back to him. He scowled. "Yes, indeed. Last Friday, the twentieth, Captain Fairfax came here. He claimed that he'd been conducting a criminal investigation for several months and demanded access to our client records."

Victory fired Michael's pulse. He and Spry shot each other a glance. His assistant's expression hardened. "Did Mr. Bellington give him access to those records?"

"Absolutely not. He reminded Captain Fairfax that our client list is confidential and that you and Spry are Major Craig's only official criminal investigators. That's when Mr. Fairfax became angry, and they argued."

Hickory's fists balled. "He tried to intimidate Jasper, but Jasper dismissed the threats and reminded Captain Fairfax that we're loyalists. Plus he has two cousins in the House of Commons. He insisted that Mr. Fairfax must have personal reasons for wanting access to our client list."

Personal reasons, indeed. Easy enough to figure why Fairfax was after those records. If any of Bellington's clients were also business owners who evaded taxes, Fairfax could build a case against them by showing that they'd needed a loan.

Fairfax considered anyone who wasn't a staunch loyalist to be a rebel. That included neutrals, like Kate and her family. Michael would have a look at Bellington's client list before he left—not merely to ascertain who owed the firm money and might be motivated to murder, but to see whether Kate, her brother, or their aunt were clients.

"Jasper told him to be off. Bring a signed letter from the major if he wanted to see the records."

Michael winced. That moment might have provoked Fairfax to approach Major Craig about dubbing him a temporary but official criminal investigator.

Hickory babbled on about his outrage over Fairfax's anger. Michael studied his high-cheekboned face and dark eyes. The financier had Indian in him several generations back. He'd been fortunate to land such a prestigious position. Most colonists considered the Indians savages, untrustworthy.

The financier stabbed a forefinger at Michael's chest. "And then Captain Fairfax said to Jasper, 'I'll be back. And you'd better have those records ready for me when I return.'" While he quoted Fairfax, Hickory's expression and voice shifted, chameleon-like, his eyes adopting an angelic radiance in a disturbing imitation of the other officer.

Michael repressed a shudder. He'd seen that look on Fairfax's face right before he killed. To stand up to that, Bellington had had stones, no doubt about it. "Did Captain Fairfax return?"

Hickory's eyes flashed. "Early yesterday afternoon, he presented me with a signed note from Major Craig."

Typical. After Fairfax picked up a scent, he never gave up the chase. Michael's stomach soured. "So now he has your client list and records."

"Oh, no." The financier's voice dropped. "I lied, told him that I thought Jasper had taken the records home with him on Friday."

The chill squirmed up Michael's backbone. "Christ," muttered Spry.

"Captain Fairfax sneered at me and said, 'Well, then, I shall pay him a visit at his home.'" Hickory stared at the ink stain on his hand, much faded after he'd rubbed it with the handkerchief. "Mr. Fairfax hasn't come back here. Maybe he thinks those records burned in the fire."

Fairfax wouldn't make that assumption. Soon, possibly within minutes, he'd arrive to plague Jonas Hickory about the records. The financier hadn't yet voiced a suspicion that Fairfax murdered his business partner. Perhaps the thought would come to him when the initial shock of the news had passed, and he'd mulled over the sequence of events.

Michael pushed up to his feet, walked over to Spry, and signed for quiet, a reminder that his assistant not give away any information that might influence Hickory's thinking. Then, hat in hand, he crossed his arms and studied the financier in the lengthening shadows of the day.

From the sound of it, yesterday afternoon, Fairfax drove out to Bellington's estate with Major Craig's note of permission. The financier would have denied that he had the records, even if Fairfax bullied him around. Had not finding the records made Fairfax angry enough to torture Bellington to death and burn the house?

The narrative Michael constructed in his head yawned with holes. He didn't yet have enough information to make the sequence hold together. Had Fairfax searched the house for the records? Did he know how to set up that snare trap? And where were Bellington's slaves?

"Mr. Hickory, you've met the slaves over at the estate, haven't you?" The financier's head came up with a nod. "We found one murdered. The other two are missing."

"Murdered—no!" Scowling, Hickory rose quickly, hands at his sides, and faced Michael. "Then do you believe the other two somehow escaped—the—the fire?"

"Well, we haven't found their bodies. Give me the names of all three slaves and their descriptions. I shall search for the other two on the morrow."

Tension ebbed out of Hickory's shoulders. "Uno is about forty years old, rather stocky and powerful. He cooks for Jasper, tends to him, cleans the house. Otis is in his twenties, a tall and burly fellow. He takes care of the horses and gig and lends a hand when his twin brother, Tucker, needs help with grounds keeping."

It didn't sound as though Bellington had owned feeble slaves. These were men who could physically defend their master. Another chill teased the hair at the base of Michael's neck. The hounds had also been powerful, capable of protecting Bellington. Yet the murderer had dispatched them with ease.

From Hickory's descriptions, Michael's patrol had found the body of either Otis or Tucker that afternoon. Were Uno and the other brother dead or hiding? And what, if anything, had they seen yesterday?

Michael glanced at Spry, who shook his head to communicate that there was no sign yet of Fairfax. Still, he'd best not dawdle. He returned his attention to the financier. "Show me your client records."

"Of course, sir. Do you suspect one of our clients of Jasper's murder?" At Michael's shrug, he headed for the back room. "Well, I suppose you can leave no stone unturned at this point."

With Spry monitoring the view from the front window, Michael followed Hickory into a small back room that smelled of dust and old tomes. Shelves lined the walls, floor to ceiling, and sagged with the weight of dozens of bound volumes. While the financier unlocked a fortified chest, Michael pushed back the curtain over a window on the west wall to let in the remaining daylight, then waited by the building's rear door.

Hickory withdrew a leather portfolio, closed the trunk, and extracted several large sheets of paper from the portfolio. He then fanned the papers over the surface of a fine, mahogany table. "Once a month Jasper has me create a single summary page of all active accounts from the data in the individual client files. Here are the most recent six months of summaries. This may be enough information for your investigation, but if you need more, I shall pull out the original client files."

"Thank you, Mr. Hickory." Michael set his hat on the corner of the table.

The other man fidgeted and frowned. "Mr. Stoddard, a terrible thought has occurred to me. Mr. Fairfax said he was going to visit Jasper at his estate yesterday. What if he was so enraged at not finding the records there that he killed Jasper and set his house afire?"

Finally. "What threats did Mr. Fairfax make to your business partner?" Usually Fairfax wouldn't do that in front of a witness.

Hickory's gaze slanted off. "Well, I'm not sure about threats. But I do know that he was much too forward."

"Mr. Fairfax is a rather forward man."

Hickory bit his lower lip for a second. "Maybe if I'd given the records to Captain Fairfax yesterday morning instead of lying to him—"

"Sir, your regrets won't assist me in progressing with the investigation. Give me a few moments with these summary sheets." Michael guided the financier by the elbow to the doorway. "There's a list of names you owe me. And do consider any conversations you've heard in the past week that might have bearing on the crime."

Hickory's shoulders bowed. "Very well." He left the room, footsteps soft.

Michael returned to the table, pushed the nearby chair aside, and arranged the half-year of debits and credits chronologically on the tabletop. He checked the portfolio to make sure that there were no more pages inside, then leaned over the table to study the clientele. Every name was accompanied by information about the original date and amount of the loan, how much had been paid off, how much was owed, including interest, and what was provided as collateral. For the month of July, there were fourteen debtors—not fifteen, as Hickory had claimed. Michael memorized each person's name.

William Hooper's wife, Anne, was on the list, her name first appearing in July. The amount she'd borrowed was nominal—likely funds to help her get by with household expenses. Her husband would probably bring her some money. It didn't surprise Michael that she'd given her business to a loyalist—not when any rebel financiers would have fled town ahead of the Eighty-Second in January.

Everyone else on the list had also borrowed a prudent amount of money—except for Kate's brother, Kevin Marsh. His name also first appeared in the July summary. Michael couldn't help but gawp at the amount of money that the manager of White's Tavern had borrowed, a sum the size of what was needed to start a business or purchase a building. For collateral, he'd offered—hmm, that portion of the entry had a smudge of ink on it.

Michael held the paper up to the sunlight and verified the collateral. It was the house on Third Street where Kate, Kevin, and their Aunt Rachel lived—collateral to turn a decent fellow into a desperate debtor. His gut sank. What had Kevin done, and why?

Spry's determined step across the wooden floor yanked his gaze off the summary sheets. His assistant, hat already on his head, bustled into the back room and said in a brusque tone, "Don't forget that appointment you have this evening, sir. Time to go."

That was Spry's signal that Fairfax had arrived. "Thank you, Spry." Michael motioned toward the rear door with his head, raked six months of summaries into a pile, and shoved the pages into the leather portfolio. While Spry lifted the bar across the door, Michael attempted to jam the portfolio inside his coat. But Hickory appeared in the doorway. With a noisy exhalation, Michael set the portfolio back on the desk and donned his hat.

"You're leaving, Mr. Stoddard?" He handed Michael a piece of paper with names scripted on it.

"Yes. We appreciate your time, sir." Michael shoved the paper in his pocket, then closed his hand over one side of the leather. "May I take this portfolio with me for tonight?"

"No, sir. Client information stays in the office, except if Jasper removes it."

The inside of Michael's mouth tasted bitter. He pressed his lips together,

then willed his hand to open. "I need more time to examine the summaries."
Was that true? Or did he just want to keep information away from Fairfax?

A sharp rapping on the front door heralded a visitor who didn't give a damn
about the message posted on the sign. Hickory threw a quick glance over his
shoulder, then blanched and stepped into the back room. His words tumbled
out. "I cannot give them to you this moment. Mr. Fairfax has returned." At the
announcement, Spry pushed the back door open and stepped out. "And it's
those summaries he's after." The financier massaged his temple and gritted
his teeth.

Michael didn't want to irritate Hickory, just to obtain information. Since
he was technically off the Bellington investigation, and Fairfax was champing
at the bit twenty feet away, he probably wouldn't be able to finagle another
look at the records. Not today, at least. "Then, Mr. Hickory, I shall take my
leave." He strode after Spry.

"Why are you leaving out that way instead of the front door?"

"It's a shortcut to my next appointment."

"But—but won't you stay and listen? What if Captain Fairfax is the one
who killed Jasper?

Hickory wanted Michael and Spry as mediators, witnesses. Despite the
heat of summer, coldness bathed Michael. "I suggest that you cooperate with
him." Fairfax demanded admission again, this time as if he had hammers
for knuckles, a condition with which Michael was all-too familiar. Ignoring
Hickory's wide eyes, he gained the back step and reached for the handle. "Good
night, sir. Don't forget to lower the bar after us."

He shut the back door, muffling the financier's protest but not the sound of
Fairfax rattling the front door, then skipped down the steps after his assistant.
They crossed the next lot, that of a grocer, and maintained their bearing until
they'd put two lots between them and Bellington's office. Michael held out his
hand to halt Spry.

His assistant said, "It was a clever gambit, sir. Did you learn anything from
those records?"

Michael's lips tightened for a second. "I learned that I need to have a word
with Kevin Marsh at White's Tavern." Spry cocked an eyebrow. "And I want
you to return to that office for surveillance. When Mr. Hickory leaves for the
day, follow him. Report to my room at eight tonight. Tell me where he's been."

"Yes, sir."

Michael spun about and headed for Market Street. As always, he was
grateful for Spry's discernment and quick mind. Few words were necessary to
get a job done. And in this instance, he'd seen in his assistant's expression that
he acknowledged the secondary purpose of his surveillance: to make sure that
Mr. Hickory left his office unharmed.

Chapter Five

MICHAEL POSTED DESCRIPTIONS of the missing slaves on several boards about town. Unwilling to turn loose of the Bellington investigation just yet and surrender his notes to Fairfax, he procrastinated with a trip to William Hooper's law office on Third Street, where the signer's family had taken up residence. One of two tall, brawny fellows who always answered the door when he called on Anne Hooper escorted him as far as the doorway of the tiny parlor lit by open windows. Inside, the Hoopers' young slave woman was cleaning the mantle with a feather duster. Expression sour, the man said, "Mrs. Hooper is dining. Wait in there."

Holding his hat, Michael entered the parlor. He waited for the slave to finish at the unlit fireplace before he walked over and took a stance there facing the doors, which his escort had left open. The Negro, who'd moved on to a small table between the sofa and chair, paused work for a few seconds to regard him. In his peripheral vision, he saw the feather duster quiver. He swiveled his head to return her gaze, but she dropped her attention to the table and resumed her work.

Faint aromas from the dining room meandered in to him: fried fish, rice, green beans with bacon, possibly a blackberry tart. His stomach rumbled, and he swallowed a mouth of saliva. How he missed the cooking of the Welsh housekeeper who used to live at the house where he slept. But she and her mistress, Helen Chiswell, left Wilmington early April in advance of the arrival of Lord Cornwallis's army, headed to a place where Michael hoped they'd be safe from Fairfax.

Shoes pattered the wood floor outside the parlor. Michael squared his shoulders. A woman entered, petite, plain-faced, about ten years older than he was. "Mr. Stoddard." She dropped a short curtsy.

Michael bowed his head. "Madam."

She turned to the slave. "You can dust that later, Lavinia. Leave us, and close the doors."

"Yes, Miz Hooper." The young woman curtsied and did as she'd been bidden.

As soon as the doors shut, Anne Hooper extended her hand toward the sofa. "Would you care to sit, sir?"

"Thank you." He took a seat on the edge of the sofa, and she sat across from him in the chair, back straight, hands clasped in her lap. Light coming in from the window allowed him to see how faded her gown had become. Her face looked pinched, her knuckles knobby—and her eyes were puffy, rimmed by bags the color of old bruises. He frowned. "Are you well, Mrs. Hooper?"

Her lips tightened, and she gave a short laugh. "As well as I can be under such circumstances, sir." She lowered her gaze to her hands.

His heart wrenched, even though he reminded himself that he must look upon her with indifference. After all, she was the wife of a signer of the Declaration of Independence, a rebel, an enemy of the King. But seldom was war so black and white. The Eighty-Second had managed surveillance of the law office since the occupation in January. Never had they spotted suspicious activity. The entire occupation, Anne Hooper and her household had kept their heads down in quiet anguish.

He didn't have to feign a soothing tone. "Then you'll be pleased to learn that two days hence, I shall meet your husband under a flag of truce and escort him to Wilmington for diplomatic discussion with Major Craig."

With a gasp, her head came up, her eyes enormous. Color flushed her cheeks. Then she turned aside almost in time to hide a shimmer of tears and blinked rapidly. Her fingers kneaded the fabric of her petticoat for a second.

A smile brushed Michael's lips at her joy. "I thought you'd want to know so you could prepare."

"Thank you for your consideration." She sniffed once and met his gaze again, the guard returned to her expression. "Is Major Craig releasing us, then?"

His expression sobered. "No, madam."

Her lips sealed. Steel found its way into her backbone. The tears vanished. "How long will my husband be here?"

"Several days, but not as long as a week. Major Craig has also charged me with ensuring Mr. Hooper's safety while he's here. And when they've completed their business, I shall escort him back to a designated meeting place, also under flag of truce."

"The Eighty-Second will let him go?" She stared at him, as if her gaze could drill through his face.

"Yes, madam. Major Craig will honor the flag of truce."

"Major Craig. Diplomatic discussion." She snorted, crossed her arms, and continued to impale him with her gaze. "Tell that to Cornelius Harnett and John Ashe."

Back in the spring, the Eighty-Second had captured rebel leaders Harnett and Ashe. Both men had died as a result of their imprisonment. Testiness wound through Michael's response. "Neither of them had a flag of truce. Nor did they have bodyguards from the regiment." He caught himself and made his tone even. "I've never lied to you."

She shifted her scrutiny over his shoulder and out the window. Her voice smoothed. "No. You haven't. And I thank you in advance for my husband's safety."

He studied the bony angles of her face and fingers again. The money Bellington loaned her must have been used for food. Judging from her thinness, the meal she'd been eating when he arrived was probably the first substantial food she'd consumed in days, so he needed to let her return to it. "Earlier this month, you borrowed money from Mr. Bellington's firm." She winced, and he hurried on past her awkwardness. "Before we leave the meeting place on Thursday, I shall ensure that your husband has brought money to give you."

"How considerate of you, Mr. Stoddard."

He regarded her a few seconds longer. She'd been one of three clients to visit Jonas Hickory at the office yesterday. "Have you heard the news about Mr. Bellington?"

"Yes, just after noon today." She frowned. "Lavinia told me he'd been murdered and his house set afire. Horrid. Who would do such a thing?"

Michael's suspicions vibrated. Just after noon, he and his patrol were *en route* to Bellington's estate to discover what had happened. How had the slave learned about it before they had? He cocked his eyebrow at Mrs. Hooper. "Indeed. Who would?"

She hiked her chin. "Surely not the Reverend Greene. I don't condone his methods, but to my knowledge, he hasn't resorted to murder."

"Yet."

She ignored his bait. "I've confidence that you'll discover who committed this atrocity. You're very good at investigation."

"Thank you, but my time on that particular investigation will be limited in the next week, as my duties have shifted to ensuring Mr. Hooper's safety."

"Oh, but surely you won't let the investigation languish during that time, just because Mr. Bellington is neutral? He deserves justice, too."

Most merchants left in Wilmington were loyalists. Interesting that she considered Bellington neutral rather than a loyalist. Perhaps he'd been a moderate loyalist rather than a firebrand, one who advocated leniency toward the rebels. There were plenty of those around. "Patriots" such as Mrs. Hooper might interpret such a stance as neutrality.

He recalled the way Bellington's chest had been flayed open, and a little spike of horror ran up his back. Fairfax considered people who proclaimed themselves as neutrals to be rebels. "Another officer will work on the investigation." Michael pushed up from the sofa. "And you'll likely be dealing with Mr. Hickory for payment of that loan."

As she rose, she made the soft sound of having tasted something rotten.

"Then I'd best pay it off quickly."

He studied her. "You aren't fond of Mr. Hickory."

"He hasn't the business acumen that Mr. Bellington has." Her eyes flinched shut for an instant. "*Had.*"

Michael hadn't received a warm impression from Hickory, either, but that didn't make the financier a killer. Perhaps her resistance to Hickory stemmed from his Indian heritage; many rebels looked down on them. "What time did you visit the office yesterday and speak with Mr. Hickory?"

"Just before noon."

So the financier had an alibi for at least part of the day. "He tells me that Mr. Bellington's nephew, Sam, works in the business. Have you met him?"

"Oh, yes. He's the son of Mr. Bellington's brother in Charles Town. In fact, I saw him at Market yesterday with Mr. Bellington's slave Uno, purchasing groceries to take out to his uncle."

Michael squinted at her. Had Sam returned from Market in time to meet Fairfax yesterday? Was Sam at the house when his uncle was murdered? Why had Hickory told him that Sam left Wilmington a week ago to care for his sick mother? "Does Sam Bellington have a mother in Brunswick?"

"Not anymore. She died three months ago."

Hair stood up on the back of Michael's neck. Hickory had lied to him. "Describe the nephew for me, please."

"He's in his early twenties, about your height, but heavier in build. Blond hair, blue eyes." The corner of Anne Hooper's mouth crimped. "It sounds as though I've provided you with a clue."

Michael bowed and settled his hat on his head. "Thank you, Mrs. Hooper." He strode to the doors and opened them. Both strapping fellows waited outside, as did Lavinia. When he oriented his gaze on the slave, she regarded the floor, the feather duster still in her hands. "Lavinia, where did you hear about Mr. Bellington's murder?"

Her grip on the duster tightened, and she sucked in a breath. "From another slave while I was out on an errand, Mistuh Stoddard."

One of Bellington's slaves, perhaps? "Which slave?"

She shrugged, gaze still pasted to the floor. "Don't know his name. Didn't recognize him. I guess he was from a plantation."

The slaves' grapevine was vast. It was possible that a plantation slave could have heard about the crime before Michael and his patrol reached the estate. Maybe Lavinia didn't recognize every slave from the surrounding plantations. But instinct nagged Michael that she did know her informant, and she was protecting him. He softened his voice. "Lavinia, I'm interested in hearing that slave's story from him. If you can recall his name, please get in touch with me. You know where I'm lodged." She nodded, still not making eye contact.

Where were Sam Bellington and the two slaves? Had they escaped Jasper Bellington's doom? What more did Lavinia know of the murder and arson? Had Bellington really been a neutral?

Michael pivoted to find that Mrs. Hooper had come to the doorway of the parlor. She studied everyone there, hands on her hips. After wishing her a pleasant evening, he took his leave of her company. He had much to ponder and couldn't wait to run what he'd learned past Spry.

* * *

Outside he checked his watch—seven o'clock—before heading back to the house on Second Street. He and the officers lodged there had hired a woman to cook and clean for them. When he arrived, he smelled beef stew simmering in the kitchen building out back. His stomach rumbled again.

Back in April, Fairfax had cited his broken leg as qualification for him to claim the spacious first-floor study for his living quarters. Michael paused at the closed study doors and listened but discerned no movement behind them. Fairfax might be in there practicing his preternatural stillness. However, Michael suspected that he was out thrashing the brush for evidence.

That meant Michael had less than an hour to draft his report about Bellington. Fortunately he wouldn't need that long to scribble out the bare bones of the investigation—minus a few crucial details, such as what he knew about Jasper Bellington's corpse and his nephew, Sam. Leaving out those particulars might qualify him for insubordination and obstruction of the King's justice. But as long as Fairfax was a suspect in the financier's murder, it was dangerous and morally wrong for Michael to hand him all that he'd uncovered.

He took the stairs two at a time and lit a candle on the desk in his room on the second floor. The hired woman had placed several letters in the center of the desktop. Michael pushed them aside unopened, grimacing at a note on top from his benefactors, annoyed because he already knew the content and didn't have time for their company that night. With quill, ink, and paper, he got right to work outlining his patrol's activities at Bellington's estate.

At seven-forty, he folded up his report, trotted downstairs, and rapped on the study door. Fairfax didn't answer. For half a second, Michael considered entering and placing the report on his desk. Then he dismissed that idea. If he didn't hand it to Fairfax in person, Fairfax would destroy the report and deny receiving it, just to make Michael look uncooperative. He shoved the notes in his waistcoat pocket instead. He'd return at eight o'clock, the deadline established by Major Craig.

Suppertime clawed at his gut. Outside the sun blistered the horizon, and he could feel the din from White's Tavern an entire block away. When he arrived there, every window was thrown open, as was the front door—feeble solicitation for a breeze. Soldiers enjoyed their beer in the shade of the porch and saluted Michael. Inside three fiddlers sawed out a tune above the cacophony of camaraderie. The yeasty, lanolin-sweaty funk of off-duty redcoats on a summer night—almost as rank as the barracks—grabbed him by the throat. Even before his eyes adjusted to the primordial murk, he knew that there were no seats available around the tables and precious little standing room. And that was unreal in a most troubling way.

Since January, when the Eighty-Second had occupied Wilmington, the price of food and drink in town had been increasing, thanks to peril that those who brought food into town for sale found from rebels on the road farther out than fifteen miles from Wilmington. Yet Kate Duncan was one of the most prosperous business owners in town, as if there were no price increases. Competing taverns had less than ten percent of the business that White's had. Uneasy over what he'd seen in Bellington's ledger earlier, Michael was now certain that Kate was making investments of the wrong kind to maintain the solvency of her business.

A flock of wilted serving wenches circled the room with trays of tankards and pitchers. Through the tobacco haze, he spotted Kate and Kevin's aunt, Rachel White, at a side table gesturing to a customer. Neither Kate not Kevin was present in the main room.

The nearest wench carried an empty tray. He waved to get her attention. She bore down on him with a toothy smile. When he bent over to holler "Kevin Marsh" in her ear, her free hand squeezed his buttock and snaked around to his inner thigh.

Mouth firm, he backed off and gave her what he hoped was a reproving look. "Mr. Marsh! Where is he?" Still grinning, she signaled him to follow her.

Jollification bumped and buoyed them across the tavern to the open door at the rear. "Kitchen" was all Michael could discern from the barmaid, even when she pressed herself against him. Massaging his upper arm with her breasts, she pointed him out the door, then dove back into the sea of customers.

Was Kevin the cook now? This Michael had to see. He jogged down the steps for a cluster of white wooden buildings behind the tavern. *En route*, he passed a sweaty barmaid, tavern-bound and carrying a tray of bowls filled with what looked like vegetable soup. He hoped the soup wasn't hot.

Two boys were up to their elbows in a soapy tub of bowls and tankards. He walked past them and stepped up through the open doorway into the kitchen— overheated, even with all windows open, and redolent of chicken broth and bread. Immediately he hopped out of the way of another server with a laden tray. She bustled out the door.

At a nearby table, an older woman ladled soup from a pot into bowls, perspiration glistening on her face and neck. Another barmaid loaded the bowls onto a tray, and a boy sliced a loaf of dark bread. There was no sign of Kevin Marsh.

At the brick hearth, Kate was bent over a steaming cauldron, using a large spoon to taste the soup within. She'd changed from the silk polonaise gown worn for her audience with Major Craig a few hours earlier into an old gown with a food-stained apron. She set the spoon on a platter beside her, straightened, and faced away from the doorway. "It's missing something," she said to the Negro cook beside her. "Did you add thyme?"

His expression fell, and he blotted his forehead on his shirtsleeve. "No, Miz Duncan. I forgot."

The white of Kate's mobcap bobbed. "I know you're worried about your cousin, but we have all those mouths to feed in the tavern, Eli."

"Yessum." His gaze hopped past her to Michael. "You got a visitor. A soldier."

She swiveled, and when she recognized Michael, some of the tension on her face eased. She thrust a small bag into the hands of the cook. "Start with two teaspoons. Don't forget to taste it after five minutes. I'll be back shortly with more rice."

Without waiting for his response, she pivoted and walked for Michael. Blonde hair escaped her mobcap in limp strands. Sweat glistened on her throat and brow. The skin beneath her eyes was taut, darkened, as if she wasn't getting enough sleep. Yet mostly what Michael saw was her trim waist, the curve of her bosom, and the glow of her skin. He reminded himself to breathe.

"Good evening." A smile plucked at her lips. "What can I do for you?"

He cleared his throat. "I'd like a word with your brother. Where is he?"

"Oh." She rolled her eyes and wiped her hands on her apron. "You want to see Kevin." Kevin, not her, was the implication. Michael frowned and opened his mouth to protest that he hadn't meant it that way. "I've missed your patronage in the tavern, sir." Her blue eyes glittered, and she fanned her face with the apron. "Don't you care for the claret anymore?" With a tart smile, she sashayed past him out into the twilight trailing her faint cinnamon scent.

A flush crept from beneath Michael's neck stock. By then, everyone in town knew he'd been paired with Kate for the upcoming party. The women and boy working at the table gave him sly smiles. He exhaled, hard, and hastened after Kate.

As soon as he paced beside her, she produced a ring of keys from her pocket. "Now I suppose you'll tell me that you've been busy, and that's why I haven't seen you at the tavern for several months."

From her trajectory, she was headed for the grain shed. *That* grain shed. The rapiers pierced Michael's heart again, and despite those months of resolve, his groin stirred. No. He had to keep this strictly professional, not personal. "I *have* been busy."

"Major Craig keeps you too busy." She kept her attention ahead, on her destination. "Must be that rank advancement. Congratulations, incidentally."

"Thank you." The summary page flashed through his memory. He used the figures he'd seen there to refocus his thoughts. "I need to ask your brother a few questions."

"Ask me those questions."

She was putting him off Kevin. Why? They halted in front of the door to the grain shed. Kate aimed a key at the padlock. He caught her hand and forced her to look at him. "My questions are for Mr. Marsh, not you."

At the physical contact, the bloom on her cheeks deepened. Her tone softened. "This time I do need rice, and I'd appreciate it if you carried it back to the kitchen for me." She slid her hand from his and unlocked the door.

A blend of irritation and intrigue scuttled about in his chest. He followed her in and closed the door, cutting off much of the light. She turned to face him with a soft smile. He heaved a sigh. "Cease the dodging, Kate. Where is your brother?"

"Gone to New Berne," she whispered.

Sweat beaded on her skin in the cleavage that peeked above the top of her shift. He smelled salt and cinnamon. His groin tightened, and his hands ached with restraint. "When did he leave?"

"Shhh. Not so loud. Yesterday."

New Berne was four days travel away. "Why all the secrecy?" he whispered back.

Her smile flashed with teeth. "Kevin and I don't want our competitors to know. We've bought some property in New Berne. We'll be opening another White's Tavern there before the end of the year."

"That's ambitious." Again, Kevin's Marsh's entry on the summary sheet jogged his memory. "I know that business has been robust for you here. Were you able to make the purchase all by yourselves?"

"No, even after we used all our savings. So Kevin talked Alice Farrell's brother into becoming a co-owner."

Alice Farrell's brother did have money. He was also an owlish astronomer who spent his nights hunting binary stars with a telescope. Michael couldn't imagine him with an interest in something as mundane as a tavern. Either Kevin had lied to Kate about his source of funding, or she knew about the loan from Bellington and was lying to *him*. Had there really been a property purchase in New Berne?

He couldn't shake the gnawing in his head that there was no tavern in New Berne—that instead, the huge loan had funded another venture. More whiskey production north of Wilmington, perhaps? If his hunch was correct, the extra income from the whiskey might be what was keeping White's Tavern afloat. And why Kate was lying to him. Of course she was going to cover up a business that was under the table.

But she'd lied to him. After all they'd been through together, especially after the peril they'd experienced in Hillsborough in February, he'd cultivated the impression that she considered him in terms warmer than a mere acquaintance. Disillusionment soured his arousal, resounded in his soul. He may as well continue the game. Eventually she'd slip up. "When will your brother be back in Wilmington?"

"Late August." With a chuckle, Kate backed off two steps and ran her tongue over her lower lip. "We haven't told our employees or Aunt Rachel yet. This must be our secret, Michael. I'm trusting you."

Aye, what a trustworthy fellow he was. She was reinforcing the impression that he was her special friend. Now that she'd retreated, he could no longer see the sweat between her breasts. But he could imagine it. With effort, he shoved the image out of his thoughts. "Let's be clear about something, Kate. You and your brother did shut down the whiskey production in the spring, didn't you?"

She tossed her head. "Of course. Why do you keep asking me about it?"

Her question was meant to be snappish, but he heard the quaver in her voice. "I'm asking because another officer has been studying county tax records prior to this year. He's isolated several businesses that appear suspect of delinquent taxes."

"Pfft. Those tax records were for Wilmington's government under the patriots. They don't apply during this occupation."

"That isn't why I'm concerned." He clenched his fists. "You claim neutrality. This particular officer, Captain Fairfax, doesn't believe in neutrals. You're just another rebel to him. So if you're still operating that whiskey business, you're a rebel who flaunts the fact that you've evaded taxes. In his eyes, that makes you worthy of being singled out for his harassment, sanctions leveled against your tavern business—"

"Sanctions? Bah! Did you see all the soldiers in the tavern? Most of them are regulars, patrons since the Eighty-Second arrived." Kate crossed her arms and tapped her foot. "Not even when our competitors lowered prices did customers stop coming to us. They're loyal. Sanctions would make White's Tavern an exotic local legend and twice as appealing to them."

"That awfully presumptuous of you." He wondered whether her competitors' businesses lacked the padding of income from illegal whiskey to fall back on.

She screwed up her expression at him, faintly visible. "See here, I've met Captain Fairfax. I can manage him just fine. Kevin and Aunt Rachel are the ones who don't get along with him."

Manage Fairfax? Her overconfidence drove ice up Michael's spine. She no longer sounded like the woman he knew—or thought he knew several months ago. What the devil had happened to her? He relaxed his fists. "There's no way on this earth that you can manage Captain Fairfax. Watch your step with him, Kate."

"Oh, pooh. I think you're envious because he's so charming."

Charming? Michael felt his jaw drop. Heat rushed into his brain and steamed out his ears. Kate and Fairfax—no, this couldn't be.

"And you're so tame."

Tame? Black spots danced at the edges of his vision, and his pulse jumped about. In two steps, he was upon her and grasped her upper arms. His voice hissed out. "Stay away from him! He's dangerous!"

She grinned again. "And you're provincial, just like Kevin."

Kate was comparing him to her brother? Damnation! Scowling, he shook her once. "He tortures people to death for sport!"

She laughed and tried to twist free of him. "Oh, for goodness' sakes—"

"Listen to me, Kate. Do you know why Mrs. Chiswell was in such a hurry to leave town in April? In January, out in the hinterlands of South Carolina, your charming Mr. Fairfax kidnapped her and forced her to witness his torture of two spies. He usually kills witnesses, but she managed to escape him. She left Wilmington ahead of his arrival in April to avoid endangering her life—"

"What an absurd story!" Kate laughed again. "He's never been anything other than courteous to me. And I know something about him that casts serious doubt on your story of Mrs. Chiswell. Back in November, he came to White's in civilian clothing looking for a spy—and he wound up saving Mrs. Chiswell from persecution at the hands of the Committee of Safety. Why would he then be cruel to her?"

Michael growled. "Because it's a game to him. I shall tell you a more personal story, then. Hillsborough, the night of February the thirteenth. Do you recall how bruised and battered Spry and I were?"

She cocked her head, and her eyes twinkled in the dusk. "Oh, yes. You said the sheriff's men assaulted the two of you."

He snorted. "Captain Fairfax believed I was a spy and planned to torture Spry and me to death. He'd just gotten started on us when the sheriff's men attacked us. We had to join forces to fight our way out. And that wasn't the first time he'd tried to kill me."

Kate's grin subsided. "If Mr. Fairfax is really so evil, why have you never reported him?"

"What makes you think I haven't tried?" He released her, stepped away, and exhaled a ragged breath. "Last summer in Georgia, he tortured a Spaniard to death, then made it appear that the local Indians did it. When I solved the murder, I reported Mr. Fairfax to my commander. And because he's an officer and a gentleman, Captain Fairfax escaped any punishment." By then, Michael no longer saw humor in Kate's expression, but he was unsure whether to feel relieved.

"This makes no sense, Michael. He's always been courteous to me."

He glowered. What was it about that son of a jackal that appealed to her? His handsome features? His money? If her judgment was that poor, what did it say about Michael that his heart felt like pulverized cabbage that moment? A sickly glorious sensation. How bizarre, how wretched.

He straightened his uniform coat. "It's up to you if you wish to dally with such a monster. Just remember that only three people alive can bear witness to his atrocities. Spry, myself—" He pressed his lips together for three heartbeats. "—and Mrs. Chiswell."

He swept a glance over the floor. "You asked me to fetch rice. Where is it?" She pointed to a sack near the door. He hefted it to his shoulder, toed the door open with a crash, and stomped out for the kitchen. Behind him, he heard her call his name, but he kept walking.

Women. Damn it all.

Chapter Six

"YOU'RE TWO MINUTES late." The watch clicked closed in Fairfax's hand, and he slid it back into his waistcoat pocket without removing his glacial gaze from Michael's face.

Before knocking on the study door, Michael had ensured that he and Fairfax were alone in that part of the house. He pulled his lips into a smile without involving his eyes. "I was here at seven-forty. Where were you?"

Fairfax curled his lip. Framed in one open side of the study's doorway, backlit in the faint jaundiced glow of a lamp, he looked huge, dark, and demonic. "Ah. You're blathering. You don't have the report ready, and you've come to grovel for more time."

Without breaking his stare or his smile, Michael tugged the folded report from his pocket and handed it to him. "I hope it gives you a bellyache."

"What's wrong, Stoddard? Did I steal your assignment?"

"What's wrong, Fairfax? Was I awarded the more challenging assignment?"

Fairfax chuckled like a canebrake rattlesnake. "You were removed from the investigation this afternoon. Why were you in Mr. Bellington's office a few minutes later?"

Michael shrugged and feigned nonchalance while wondering whether Fairfax had intimidated that information from Hickory. "Expressing my condolences to his business partner. Best of luck on the investigation. You'll need it." He lifted a forefinger. "And don't forget about the return patrol I scheduled for the morrow. The men will assemble at dawn outside the barracks—"

"I don't need a pustule like you to schedule a patrol for me."

"Suit yourself. But this one's already set to go, and I'm sure that even you are sensible enough to prefer the early morning for work among those still-warm timbers." Although Fairfax continued to sneer, he drew his head back and narrowed his eyes in a gesture that Michael had learned signified his assent. Yes, indeed, he'd be leading that patrol at dawn.

A vision of Kate in Fairfax's arms snaked through Michael's thoughts. He felt his fists burn with the urge to pummel Fairfax's face. Instead, he doused his smile and replaced it with a mock frown of puzzlement. "Say—weren't you supposed to have been promoted to major by now?"

Fairfax lost the lip-curl and said nothing for several seconds. Michael stifled glee and maintained a straight face. That anticipated promotion must have been lost or tangled in the cogs of the Army. It happened all the time, especially to young officers who'd risen rapidly through the ranks.

Then angelic radiance swelled in Fairfax's eyes—his killing face. A wave of chilly sweat swept over Michael's body, bringing with it the wrench of nausea. He resisted the urge to recoil.

Fairfax's murmur was low and seductive. "You're such a imbecile, cluttering your tiny mind with unrelated matters. You've a worthless rebel's life to guard for several days, and the knife could come from anywhere." He dissolved into the study's shadows and drew the door closed behind him.

Michael stared at the darkened doors, gulped, and swiped damp palms on his trousers. Needling his nemesis had been foolish as well as unnecessary. What had gotten into him?

Obviously it hadn't been a good idea to talk to Fairfax right after that clash with Kate. He expelled a breath that loosened knots in his gut, then rubbed his eyes and rolled back his shoulders. Time to focus on drawing up a plan to ensure William Hooper's safety. Since Major Craig expected a report at nine on the morrow, and it could take several hours to construct, he'd best hop to it.

In the dining room, he lit a candle from the supply there and trudged upstairs to his bedroom. At the top of the stairs something moved, and he jerked his attention to the right. Spry emerged from the shadows, his expression neutral. A sigh of relief left Michael.

His empty stomach rumbled. He opened the door and entered. "Have you eaten yet?"

"Yes, sir."

If Spry had had time to sate his vast appetite, maybe Hickory hadn't made too many stops after he left the office. Michael tossed his hat on his bed and lit the candle on his desk. "I've not yet dined. Fetch me something from the kitchen while I prepare for our chat." He handed Spry the second candle.

"Sir."

Michael closed the door after him and listened to the private's shoes tap a retreat downstairs. After opening his bedroom window to dispel stuffiness, he draped his uniform coat over a bedpost, poured fresh water in the washbasin, and cleaned the day's dust off his face and hands. Then he readied writing implements, drew from his trunk the copy he'd made of the Bellington investigation notes, and set everything off to the side on the desk surface.

The unopened correspondence beckoned. He sat and discovered his older sister's missive third down in the stack. Since early April, when he'd queried Miriam, he'd been awaiting her response with a mixture of keenness and dread. He set the other letters aside and opened Miriam's first. And there it was, her confirmation of the story his benefactors had told him:

> *Yes, you are our Family's last direct male Descendent of a trea-sonous Jacobite Baron, our great-grandfather, Ewan MacKenzie. The Crown holds in attainder his Estate in the Scottish Highlands. Father finally told me the whole Story a few Days before he died. Grandfather Andrew had called the Estate "An Taigh mo Cridhe." That means "House of My Heart" in the Scottish Tongue. Of course, he'd been a young Boy when he was smuggled away to safety in Yorkshire. Who knows whether that was the Name MacKenzie originally gave the Estate or an affectionate Name from a lost and frightened Boy?*

Miriam went on to describe how their father Abraham, eldest of three brothers and a stonemason, was ridiculed as an opportunist when he sought to petition the King for removal of the attainder. The family had next pinned its hopes on the middle brother, Gideon, a corporal serving beneath the great General Wolfe in America. But Gideon died in battle with his general. Abraham and the youngest brother, Solomon, a blacksmith, approached a local nobleman with their plight and found him willing to help them on behalf of Michael.

The nobleman, Abraham, and Solomon had purchased his first two commissions. They'd kept the family history from him to allow him to distinguish himself in military service to the King without a hint of guile. In her letter, Miriam had ceased suggesting and outright ordered him to find a respectable wife.

A spark of anger hit his heart at how the family was wielding him. Yet even he had to admit that not being burdened by knowledge of his heritage had conferred a squeaky cleanness to his conduct during his decade of military service. Major Craig had commented on his good character in at least one note attached to his record.

Mr. Honest Face, people called him.

He dropped Miriam's letter atop the others, leaned an elbow on the desk, and rested his forehead on his palm. According to his sister, the family was determined to do whatever it took to support him and reclaim the title, even if it meant selling everything they owned in Yorkshire. So many people had set him on this path, and he would follow through for the sake of his loved ones in Yorkshire. But how unsettling it was that a man could go to bed a commoner one night and wake up the next morning a nobleman with all manner of responsibilities.

A night breeze unfurled the curtains in a sticky puff that stank of rotting fish and tar, Wilmington's ubiquitous odors. Michael fumbled Lord Faisleigh's note from the pile and broke the seal. *My dear Mr. Stoddard*, it read, *we've a certain Matter to discuss. Please see me at your earliest Convenience. Discretion and Hour as usual. Faisleigh.* Eyes widened, Michael sat taller in his chair and reread the note. Not at all what he was expecting from his benefactor. Could he finally have given them everything they wanted? For the first time in months, he felt something akin to relief unfold in his breast.

A soft knock came upon the door, followed by Spry's voice. "Sir, I've brought your supper."

"Come." Humming "Rule, Britannia!" he shoved Faisleigh's note beneath Miriam's and sat back in his chair, his expression easing into a smile. On the morrow, he'd stop by the house that the Earl, his lady, and their household temporarily occupied down the street and learn about the "Matter."

Spry set a cup of coffee, a bowl of beef stew, and a plate of sliced cucumber and dark bread before Michael on the desk. No wine or fruit. Considering the inflated price of food, the officers who were billeted in the house had agreed on frugality. How elaborate would the Friday night fête be?

While his captain dispatched the meal, Spry stood near the door holding a tray. When Michael was finished, the private collected dishes and opened the door far enough to set the tray outside. Michael walked over to the window, stretched his arms over his head and yawned, then ambled back toward his assistant, voice low. "Before we plan for Mr. Hooper's security, tell me what happened with Mr. Hickory."

"Sir. Mr. Fairfax left the financiers' office about ten minutes after we did." Keeping his voice down, Spry met him midway in the room. "Shortly after that, Mr. Hickory left carrying a wooden crate about two feet long. He walked to the tannery on Front Street, knocked on the door, and entered as soon as someone admitted him."

"The tannery? No one's occupied that building since early March." Michael pondered a moment. "I thought we'd accounted for all the keys back then. Who let Mr. Hickory in?"

Spry shook his head. "I couldn't see, sir. Not without risking that they might spot me. Mr. Hickory fidgeted while he waited to be let in—like the crate was heavy, like he knew he shouldn't be there because the shop isn't occupied."

"Apparently it's more occupied than we realized."

"Yes, sir." Spry cocked an eyebrow. "You'll want to search the place on the morrow, yes? Then I shall send a locksmith round to open it for us. What time?"

"Eight-thirty. How long was Mr. Hickory in the tannery?"

"Not above five minutes, sir. I tried to glimpse his host when he left but couldn't do it. Mr. Hickory departed the tannery empty-handed. No crate."

Michael sighed. "And where did our financier go next?"

"Home, sir. I waited outside for about two hours, but he didn't venture back out."

"He's probably done all his sneaking around for the night. Good work, Spry." He smirked at his assistant. "Incidentally, remember when he told us that Mr. Bellington's nephew left town a week ago to tend his sick mother? Well, Mrs. Hooper told me that Sam Bellington's mother died a few months ago."

Spry's jaw dropped. "Mr. Hickory lied to us, sir!"

"Hmm. Mrs. Hooper also said that she saw the nephew at Market yesterday with the slave, Uno."

"Sir, it sounds as though we need to chat with Sam Bellington."

"Agreed. I'd welcome any ideas on where to find him." Spry shrugged, so Michael filled him in on Sam's description as related by Anne Hooper, as well as her label of Bellington as neutral and Lavinia's suspicious knowledge. "And that's all I have to contribute right now on the Bellington investigation. Anything else to report before we move on?"

"Sir." Spry grinned. "Recall that portfolio that Mr. Hickory claimed mustn't leave his office?"

"Ah, yes. Don't tell me—he took it home with him or gave it to his host in the tannery."

"Neither, sir. Mr. Fairfax left the office with it."

Michael barked a laugh. "Clearly I was too pleasant to Mr. Hickory earlier. But this could work in our favor. Mr. Fairfax will be leaving at dawn with a patrol, their destination the Bellington estate."

Spry's grin opened up with his big horsy teeth. "That means he'll be gone most of the day. All we have to do is wait for his departure. Sir."

"And make sure we leave everything in the study exactly as we find it."

* * *

Michael made note of the new investigation details, then he and Spry mapped out multiple routes to and from the designated meeting place on Thursday to minimize the likelihood that they'd be ambushed while riding with the white flag. They drew up a list of three-dozen men they recommended for the special assignment of guarding William Hooper while he was in transit, at his house, walking around town, and at the Friday night supper party. As Michael was unsure how long the signer would remain in Wilmington, they scheduled duty rotations for five days.

The Wilmington ladies hadn't provided them with a venue for the supper party, so Michael chose the Anglican church building. Every pew had been removed in the spring and put to use as fence posts, leaving a hall that was rectangular, empty, and easily monitored, even if it wasn't as large as the taproom of a tavern. Prior to the arrival of tables and chairs for the party, the Eighty-Second would remove the church's portable furniture and ensure that the building was clear of hidden weapons. And before any civilians entered the building Friday night, they'd be searched for weapons larger than a personal knife.

Michael rubbed his hands together. "Let's set up a special screened-off area where matrons search the ladies. They'll find it adventurous and exotic. They'll gossip about the experience for days."

"They'll gossip about it for far longer, sir, if it's a soldier doing the searching."

They guffawed. Michael pushed up from his desk and stretched, then checked the time. "Ten-twenty." He walked over and shut his window. "Let's get some fresh air. It'll help us realize if we've forgotten anything." He shrugged his way into his coat. Spry covered a yawn and opened the door.

Michael donned his hat, scooped up the pile of letters on his desk, and shuffled those from Lord Faisleigh and Miriam to the bottom. Three of the remaining missives were from officers with whom he'd been corresponding. Those could wait until the morrow. The final letter was addressed in a masculine script that he couldn't place. Curious, he broke the seal and read: *S, I've a Message from Claude and the Team. Meet me alone at the back Door of the Grocer on Front St., ten-thirty to-night. Yrs in Service, N.*

Michael's eyebrows hiked up his forehead. The date on the note was 24 July. That meant he and Spry had ten minutes to get into place.

He passed the note to his assistant, who scanned it, looked up at him, and mouthed, "Neville?"

Michael nodded, sleepiness vanquished. Spry handed the note back to him. He burned it without another word, allowing the ash to fall into a small tin plate beside the candle, then transferred the remaining letters, investigation notes, and draft of his plans for Hooper's protection to his trunk. Candle in hand, he led the way downstairs to their meeting with Adam Neville: ranger, scout, and double-spy.

Chapter Seven

MICHAEL AND SPRY slipped out the front door and headed for Market Street. In the spring, their meeting with the ranger and scout hadn't ended with civility. Fed up with Neville's disaffected stance and murky allegiances, Michael had punched him. Then Neville gleefully drew his dagger on the two of them. Because Neville was a fellow officer—a lieutenant with Colonel Thomas Brown's loyalists—and he'd had a few beers that night, Michael defused the situation. But he'd made it clear that he'd arrest him and throw him in the outdoor pen for rebel prisoners if Neville ever drew a weapon on him again.

Neville had left town. In the weeks following the incident, Michael decided he'd been too lenient with the ranger. There'd been a maniacal element to Neville's glee that spring night.

If the scout were a different sort of man, Michael could see a peace offering in his act of couriering news from Claude Devereaux, a French assassin, about the special project they shared. But Neville didn't trust Michael, and the feeling was mutual. The next time Neville menaced him or Spry in any way, Michael would make good on his threat to arrest him.

The moon had set. Aside from an occasional torch or lantern, their only source of light came from the stars. Spry's tone was low, taut. "Been thinking about what happened the last time we met Mr. Neville, sir. His temper sparks faster than—" Spry caught himself and swallowed the rest of his sentence.

Tension yawned between them. Spry was censoring himself. Annoyance buzzed in Michael's head. His assistant's judgment was generally excellent. He snapped, "Speak your mind, Spry."

"Well, sir, I know he's a fellow officer, but—" The private tapped his temple. "I question the reliability of his judgment. Sir."

In a dry tone, Michael said, "It's as reliable as any double spy's judgment can be. But I hear your concern, and I shall arrest him at his first provocation."

"Yes, sir. A question. He specified that you meet him alone tonight. When you and he have talked before, just the two of you, has he ever drawn a weapon on you?"

"No."

"Perhaps seeing both of us back in the spring felt like a threat to him. Two against one."

Michael hadn't considered that explanation. They reached Market Street. He held up his hand to halt the private, then faced him. "You've made a good point. Very well, I shall met him alone tonight."

"Sir? I know he requested it that way, but he drew a weapon on you last time. I don't trust him."

"That makes two of us." Michael crossed his arms and drummed the fingers of one hand on his other arm. "You will arrive ahead of me and conceal yourself in the back yard next door." He scratched beneath his hat and unfolded a map of Wilmington in his head. "That business is—"

"Mr. Bellington's office, sir."

"Yes, it is. Use caution. Sneak into position. Crouch near the back steps. Mr. Neville and I will chat. If he becomes pugnacious again, step out of concealment and help me arrest him."

"Sir. Won't he grow suspicious at my absence and suspect I'm lurking in wait of him?"

"I expect him to inquire about you. I shall inform him that you're on assignment at Herons Bridge. Any other questions?" When Spry shook his head, Michael sent him on his way.

After his assistant turned the corner and headed for Front Street, Michael climbed onto the nearest porch to wait a moment, give Spry time to sneak into position. At so late an hour, he spotted few people in the street. Most civilians who weren't in a tavern were home abed.

A soldier strolled past in the humid night with a young brunette on his arm. Michael squinted at him, then smiled with recognition. Private Jackson had recovered his mettle after his close scrape earlier and was taking Clayton's advice to heart.

After a minute, Michael left the porch and continued on for the grocer's shop. He made his gait loose and easy as he passed through the side yard. In the sand and wiregrass behind the grocer's, he turned a slow circle and made a survey of surrounding lots. He didn't let his gaze linger on the steps behind Bellington's office and made sure he was standing between the two yards.

By then, Spry should be in position. Michael said softly, "Neville, are you here?"

Sand and grass rustled no louder than the breeze. He spotted a lanky pillar of darkness dislodge from the back wall of the grocer's shop inches from where he'd passed seconds earlier. Michael grimaced at missing Neville's concealment. The ranger was part Catawba Indian and derived amusement from creeping up on people.

"Thank you for meeting me." Neville glanced over the yard. "Where's that man of yours?"

"Posted to Herons Bridge."

"Herons Bridge. Bah. That place is a waste of the regiment's time and resources. Sooner or later, you'll lose the outpost to the patriots." The scout halted several feet away.

His left arm was in a sling. Michael cocked an eyebrow at him. "Well. You've looked better." Even by starlight, he could see that Neville's black hair was unkempt, and he'd received a swollen left eye and cheekbone at least a day ago. Someone had thrashed him well. Michael wrinkled his nose. "And you've certainly smelled better. Don't try to tell me you fell off your horse."

"No. I barely escaped a welcoming committee from the Reverend Greene near Brunswick yesterday. What the hell has the Eighty-Second done to rile the patriots in these parts since I left in the spring? Everyone's ready to cut each others' throats."

"Apparently you didn't hear of Major Craig's proclamation a few weeks ago. All civilians must swear allegiance to the Crown, and men must enter the loyalist militia by the first of August."

Neville gaped. "What foolishness! The patriots almost killed me over that proclamation!"

Michael chuckled. "I thought you enjoyed their company every now and then."

"Not when they want to torch or shoot everything in sight."

"Yes, there is that." Eager for the scout's news, Michael drummed his fingertips briefly on his thighs. "Now that we've exchanged greetings, let's proceed to the business indicated in your note. You wrote that Claude and the Team have a message for me. What message might that be?"

A glint appeared in Neville's dark eyes. "They won't arrive in the area until at least next January, possibly later."

Michael allowed his disappointment to vent in a stream of breath out his nostrils. "What a pity."

Neville studied him, his face in part-shadow. "Yes. It means you'll have to act without them."

"Act? And why is that?"

"Why? You've a monster in your midst." The other man stepped in closer to tower over Michael, and his voice became a growl. "Today I heard of the local financier's murder. Are you going to let Fairfax get away with it?"

Michael's heart hammered at the threat in Neville's proximity, and he forced himself to stand his ground, not back away from the ranger. "What makes you think that Fairfax killed the fellow?"

"Indeed!" Neville's right forefinger thumped Michael's chest. "You're Major Craig's investigator. Did you not ride out there and see the corpse?"

"I did."

"Well, then, you must have seen that he'd—he'd been flayed!"

Michael hardly breathed for several seconds. From the direction of Bellington's back steps, he detected a scraping noise. He willed Spry to settle down and keep quiet, not disclose his location. Fortunately Neville leaned toward him, a sign that he was keen on hearing Michael's response and not paying attention to the sounds that Spry was making. Michael blasted the ranger with a glare. "Where did you hear that the financier had been flayed?"

The taller man waved his right hand about. "I got it from a regimental private, who said he got it from a slave man who was running around town and blabbing the details."

That slave again—the same one Lavinia had mentioned? Who was this slave? And he really hoped a man from his patrol hadn't violated his order for silence. "Which soldier gave you the news?"

"I don't know." Neville rolled his eyes. "You're the one who knows every man of the Eighty-Second by name. Bah, never mind where I got this information. Can you not see what's happening? You know what a monster Fairfax is. You know his pattern." Neville bounced on his toes and gesticulated with his right hand. "After he's been quiet for a while, the urge comes over him to kill. He gets a taste of blood, then he has to kill again quickly, more times than a heathen god. He's started torturing people to death here in Wilmington—"

"I'm familiar with his pattern, Neville. Cease your babble. Let me think."

"What's there to think about? Claude and the Team won't be available to help you until next year. You have to do something now. For God's sake, arrest Fairfax before he takes another life!"

Michael did back away then, an abrupt motion. "Lower your voice. You're raving like a lunatic." He hoped that Spry was positioned to pounce. The ranger was shaking all over.

Neville hung his head, inhaled deeply, and took a moment to compose himself. "My apologies."

Michael studied the other man for several seconds, then made his tone firm yet considerate. "You know what happened to me last summer in Georgia, with that Spaniard who was tortured to death. I think it's time you told me how Fairfax has wronged you."

The ranger lifted his head, eyes gleaming. "Last August, he murdered two members of my family near Camden, South Carolina."

Michael's attention on the ranger sharpened. In the same area, at the same time, Fairfax had tortured to death at least four people and hidden his acts in the chaos of battle. All of Fairfax's victims had belonged to the Ambrose ring, an international group of spies who supported the rebel cause and created havoc for Crown forces in South Carolina. Neville had been an Ambrose leader—perhaps he still was—and Michael wagered that his dead kinfolk had been members. If they'd been Indians, it would have been a double strike against them. Fairfax hated Indians.

"My horse had thrown a shoe about four miles from their cabin, so I walked him the rest of the way." Caught up in memory, Neville stared over Michael's shoulder. "Arrived an hour late. Noticed another horse picketed out front and brought mine around to the stable to pull off his tackle. Then I heard the front door of the cabin crash open." He stiffened. "I peered out the stable and watched Fairfax ride away on the other horse, his breeches spattered with gore. Soon as he was gone, I ran to the cabin and found—" Neville's expression rippled with revulsion. "Like the Spaniard in Georgia."

The thought must have gone through Neville's head dozens of times since then that if his horse hadn't gone lame, if he'd arrived at the cabin on time instead of late, he'd have shared the fate of those kinfolk. From a corner of his soul, Michael scrounged up some compassion for the ranger. Did Fairfax know that Neville was a fourth living witness to his depredations?

The ranger shook off his memories and fixed his gaze on Michael. "Good for you, getting Mrs. Chiswell out of Wilmington before the monster arrived in April. I've no doubt that he'd have killed her if she hadn't escaped him."

Neville was correct about that—and how fortunate that Helen Chiswell was now hiding in China, rather than in Wiltshire, England, where Fairfax presumed she'd fled. Fairfax's desire to kill her wasn't due solely to the fact that she'd witnessed his "sport" in South Carolina. She'd confided her knowledge to Michael that a few days before Fairfax left Wiltshire to join his first regiment, he'd murdered his stepfather, Henry Clancy Lord Ratchingham, and made it look like the nobleman's suicide. How Fairfax had escaped both suspicion for murder and the stigma associated with a family member's suicide was a true mystery.

Fairfax's superiors might overlook his wickedness with the King's enemies, but the murder of a peer demanded action from the Courts. Having initiated his own quiet inquiry into the matter, Michael awaited corroboration from several people referenced by Mrs. Chiswell. The process was slow, and he reminded himself daily to be patient.

Neville's voice darkened again. At his side, his right hand clenched and unclenched, over and over. "Don't say I didn't warn you when he kills again. The pattern will show itself."

Michael took in Neville's fidgeting while trying to steady his own pulse. The ranger's endorsement of Fairfax as Bellington's murderer supported everything Michael understood and detested about his adversary. Neville knew that. How annoying that the ranger was trying to push him into an action before he was ready to take it.

Neville sighed, hard. "It doesn't sound as though you're ready to arrest Fairfax. What a shame. But at the very least, surely you realize that you need to find the slave and stop him from blabbing about what he's seen. He'll start a panic among the civilians."

Michael narrowed his gaze on Neville. Odd that a panic hadn't already started as a result of the slave's blather. Whoever he was, he must have seen Bellington's body to be able to report on the condition of it. And the odds were that he was one of Bellington's slaves. "Did you see this slave?"

"No." Neville swept a glance in the opposite direction of Bellington's office. "I told you, I heard about it from the regimental private."

Michael must question the men of his patrol, find out who had spilled details of the afternoon's mission. He'd also stop by Hooper's house and speak with Lavinia. She'd had contact with the slave. If he was one of Bellington's, he probably hadn't been at the house when his master was murdered. Otherwise he'd have been killed, too. Where were the slaves? And where was Sam Bellington?

"If you want to find the slave, my skills are at your service." Neville's chuckle was bone dry. "I'll even discount my rate, just for you."

"How considerate." Michael didn't bother to hide his sarcasm. Neville did know how to track, but Michael didn't want to farm out any piece of the investigation to him. He didn't trust him that far.

Neville had delivered his message from Claude; now Michael wanted him gone from Wilmington. He didn't need Neville underfoot, even though he was being helpful. Previous encounters with the ranger had taught Michael to play his hand close. "When I'm ready to use your help, where may I find you?"

Starlight turned Neville's smile frosty. "Oh, I'm here and there, so it'll be easier if I find you." He withdrew one step, then another, graceful as a cat despite his injuries. "Now, I've another appointment tonight, but I'm very glad we had this chat, Stoddard." He snickered. "And I cannot tell you how much I appreciate your honoring my request to come to the meeting alone." He cocked his head to one side and wiggled his eyebrows for emphasis.

Michael couldn't help but glance in the direction Neville's head jabbed: Bellington's back yard, where Spry was supposed to be hiding. Dread shot through his blood and bones and ripped a snarl from him. Fists balled, he advanced on Neville while the ranger retreated before him. "Damn you, what did—"

"Better check your man's breathing!" Neville pivoted and bounded off like a gazelle. "That's for punching me last spring. Pleasant dreams, Stoddard!"

His mocking laugh followed Michael's sprint for the back steps of Bellington's office. On the other side, Spry lay hog-tied in the sand, his mouth stuffed with a wadded handkerchief. As soon as Michael pried the sodden fabric from Spry's mouth, his assistant coughed and cursed. Thank God Spry hadn't swallowed the gag and choked.

Michael whipped out his dagger and sawed through Spry's bonds, silently lambasting himself for letting his guard down. This nasty prank of Neville's was typical of him. Spry ranted about how the ranger had sneaked up on him from behind. The private stood, spat off to the side, slapped sand from his uniform, then spat again. "Damn him, sir! I wager he wiped his arse with that handkerchief."

"Spry, you're strong enough to wrestle him down." Michael sheathed his dagger and planted his fists on his hips. "How did he overpower you with one arm in a sling?"

Spry rolled his head and stretched his shoulders. "He didn't have a sling, sir. He used both arms on me." He spat one more time.

Sweat on Michael froze. Then he ground his teeth. Neville had hoodwinked him with the sling. If he'd provoked the ranger during their conversation, Neville would have been able to clobber him without warning. How fortunate that he'd given the ranger the impression that he was open to working with him.

But he was damned if he'd work with that snake, even to take Fairfax out of the picture. "Assault on a King's man, threatening an officer of the King—that dog has earned himself an arrest warrant."

Spry squared his shoulders. "I'm delighted to hear it, sir."

Chapter Eight

AFTER HE'D POSTED Neville's arrest warrant all over town, Michael returned to his room in the house on Second Street. He tossed and turned abed, his mind grinding over the investigation's largest puzzles: the identity of the mysterious slave, and why shooting the first dog hadn't brought the other dogs around. Even after he unwound, he wasn't asleep long before he dreamt of chasing a shadow that ridiculed him from behind trees and stayed just beyond his reach. Typical.

A storm blew up and pelted leaves and limbs with hail. Rattle, rattle, rattle.

Michael shot upright in bed fully awake, his pulse thrashing about. What in blazes had awakened him? Something small like pebbles rattled against the exterior wall beside his open window. The devil!

He rolled out of bed in his shirt and pawed aside the curtains. On the ground below was a dark figure, pitching arm cocked back. "Ho! What are you doing?" He waved out the window to halt the next spatter of dirt, which might have caught him instead of the wall.

The pitching arm lowered. A woman's soft voice reached out to him. "Mistuh Stoddard, you got to help us!"

"Lavinia?"

"Yessuh. Please help!"

"I shall get dressed. Stay right there." He shoved the window closed and dressed by sense of touch, knowing where he'd set out a fresh shirt, clean pair of stockings, and every other article of clothing a few hours earlier. Shoes in one hand, the other hand on the banister, he padded down the stairs in stocking feet, avoiding the creakier parts of the steps. At the back door, he buckled on his shoes, eased the bar off, and let himself out.

William Hooper's slave hustled to him. "So sorry to wake you, suh, but you the only one I know who could help."

"You said *us*, Lavinia." He saw that she was wringing her hands. "I'm going to make a guess. Is this about one of Mr. Bellington's slaves?"

"Yessuh." Her voice trembled on the edge of tears. "Uno's hurt bad, lost blood. He says Mistuh Bellington's killer shot him in the arm last night. Now he's barely conscious."

Uh oh. A possible witness to Bellington's murder was in shock. Of course, Uno could be other than a witness. He could have murdered his master, then shot himself in the arm to look like a victim. And there was one other slave unaccounted for. "Where is Uno?"

"With his cousin. Hiding."

"Who's his cousin?" Michael spread his hands. "Where are they hiding?"

Her teeth flashed, then she bit her lip. "Promise me you won't hurt him none, Mistuh Stoddard. He says a redcoat shot him, then killed his mastuh. God bless Mistuh Bellington."

God damn Fairfax! He must have put that ball in Uno's arm. This moment he could be out hunting the slave to finish the job—

Michael sucked in a deep breath and forced calm into his pulse. He reminded himself to take everything slowly and not jump to the conclusion he desired. The soldiers of the regiment had no reason to shoot Bellington.

Except if there was a personal grudge involved.

Depending on the court and judge, testimony from a mere slave in solving the murder of a white man might be worthless—

No. A man's life was at stake. "I've no reason to hurt Uno, Lavinia, and I promise you that I shall do my best to bring the murderer to justice."

"Thank you, suh. Uno got hid about an hour ago by his cousin, Eli, and me."

"Eli—Mrs. Duncan's cook?" She nodded. Michael estimated the distance out to Bellington's estate. "How did Uno make it to town wounded? Surely he didn't walk all that way?"

"Nosuh. He rode one of Mistuh Bellington's horses."

Ah. That explained the missing horse. "Where's the horse now?"

"In Miz Duncan's stable behind her house. Except she don't know about it yet. See, Eli took care of the horse. And him and Uno are now hiding in the grain shed out back the tavern."

Ah, that grain shed. Neither a safe place for Michael's heart nor for a man who needed medical attention. As for where they might move a possible witness to murder so he could recuperate, it wouldn't be to the barracks—not if a soldier had shot him.

For as long as he'd been in Wilmington, he hadn't known Kate to rent the three rooms on the second floor of her tavern. If she had a bed up there, they wouldn't have to carry Uno far, and the second floor could be secured. From the snippet of conversation he remembered between Eli and Kate in the kitchen earlier that evening, he wondered if Kate was already in on this situation to some extent. "Let me fetch my man. We'll need his help."

Spry slept near the kitchen in the small building that had once housed the Chiswell servants. Less than five minutes after Michael tapped on the door to wake him, the private was fully dressed, briefed on the situation, and striding with Michael and Lavinia to Front Street. They arrived at White's Tavern and proceeded around back. In passing, Michael glimpsed the glow of a lamp or candle in the tavern. Kate hadn't yet left for the night. Good.

Faint light also showed through cracks in the paneling of the grain shed. Lavinia tapped on the door to the shed. "Eli, it's me. I brung help. Let us in."

The cook for White's Tavern opened the door about six inches and recoiled at the sight of Michael and Spry. "Vinnie, they're redcoats. You heard what Uno said."

"Yeah, but Mistuh Stoddard and his man didn't kill Mistuh Bellington."

The cook's gaze hopped between the soldiers. "I don't know. I think I saw somebody following us tonight when we moved Uno from the cellar. Could be the killer trying to get him."

"Eli, I wasn't following you. Ask Lavinia. I was asleep in bed when she woke me to help you." Michael stepped to Lavinia's side. That was when he noticed that the cook was holding a large butcher knife. He firmed his jaw. "If the murderer was following you, perhaps it was because your cousin can identify him. He could break in this flimsy shed easily and kill Uno. We must move him to a location that we can guard, then treat his wound." His gaze bounced from Eli's face to the knife. "Lower the knife. Let me look at him, see how badly he's injured." The cook bowed his head, opened the door, and stepped out of the way, knife at his side.

Lavinia scooted in first. Michael entered, followed by Spry, who shut the door. In the warmth of the shed, the metallic stench of blood and the rankness of old sweat overwhelmed the clean scents of barley and rice.

Lavinia sat on a blanket near the head of a supine Negro about forty years old. By the light of a lantern hanging from a hook on the ceiling, the man's face and throat were shiny with sweat. The material of his left upper arm sleeve and a handkerchief wrapping it was soaked through and stiff with dried blood.

Tension gripped his body at the sight of Michael and Spry. His expression screwed up. "No redcoat, no redcoat." His voice was hoarse. For a moment, he lifted himself up on his uninjured elbow and tried to scoot away. Then he collapsed to the blanket, his right arm flung up as if to block a blow.

Eli set down his knife, then squatted and grasped the man's unhurt shoulder. "Lay still, Uno. He's come to help."

"No no no." Uno squeezed his eyes shut and shivered. "Come to kill me. Shot me, then chased after Mistuh Jasper. I saw it."

The slave was in terrible shape. If he'd murdered his master and shot himself the previous night, his act as victim was seamless. However, Michael's gut told him that Uno wasn't the murderer. Few men, cognizant that their life was so imperiled, could maintain such a lie. No, Uno was a witness, not a killer.

How had he possessed the strength to walk around earlier that day describing what he'd seen—and after riding the horse to town? Surely he knew that in doing so he'd make himself visible to the murderer. And surely his injury would have become the source of sensational gossip. Something was wrong with Lavinia's story. Furthermore Michael must find the soldier who'd spoken with Neville about Uno, because that story wasn't adding up either—unless there was a second slave involved.

"Eli, cut his sleeve open." Michael stripped off his uniform coat and handed it to Spry so the sight of his uniform up close wouldn't agitate the slave more.

Eli switched sides and rent the bloody handkerchief and sleeve with the big knife, then moved over near Lavinia. Michael knelt, took Uno's left hand in his, and found it warm with fever. Not good. "Uno, squeeze my hand."

Fortunately the slave still had a good grip. Likely his humerus was unbroken. Uno's grip relaxed. "C-cold." He shuddered.

"Uno, who hurt Mr. Bellington?"

"R-redcoat. Tried to kill me, too. C-Crazy man. Evil. D-Demon." A shudder raked through him. "I seen him following me everywhere. Looked over my shoulder tonight and saw him in the shadows. He standing in the doorway looking at me now."

No one was looking at them, as Michael confirmed with a glance over his shoulder at the door. The slave was delirious. Nevertheless a shiver of precaution inched down Michael's back.

He resisted the urge to ask Uno for a better description of his attacker. The Negro wasn't coherent enough for it. Nor could he point out Mr. Bellington's killer from the regiment's two hundred soldiers. "Don't worry, my good fellow. We'll find him and bring him to justice." He set Uno's hand on the blanket and glanced over the inflamed mess the ball had made of his upper arm. Because the light was poor, he couldn't tell if the ball was stuck in the man's large bicep or had passed all the way through—not without causing him a great deal of pain. If the ball hadn't passed through, it had been lodged in his arm for a day.

He rose, returned to Spry, and retrieved his coat. Lavinia stroked the side of Uno's face once. She and Eli turned large and frightened eyes to the two soldiers. Michael said, "I shall speak with Mrs. Duncan immediately, arrange to lodge Uno in a room on the second floor of the tavern. Then I shall fetch a surgeon. Expect my return with him in a quarter hour. Make sure that Uno remains quiet and still during that time. And figure out a way to reinforce a blanket so we can carry him up the stairs. I doubt he can walk. Eli, hand Spry that knife."

When the cook had done so, Michael turned his back to the slaves and donned his coat. The sight of the knife in his assistant's hand trickled relief through him. Nick Spry came from a seafaring family of smugglers and pirates—a background that he and Michael kept to themselves and well out of regimental records. Michael knew what Spry could do with a sword and wagered that he'd be as adept with a large knife. He leaned close to him. "Keep them safe."

Spry's lips flattened. "Sir."

Michael let himself out of the shed and stood still to listen. He studied the pockets of blackness formed by the corners of buildings. Had someone followed the three slaves earlier?

Crickets chirped in the cool of night. The smell of the ocean came to him on a quick breeze. The night seemed as it should. Nevertheless, as he marched across the yard for the tavern, the spot between his shoulder blades prickled the way it did when he was being watched. He was glad he'd left Spry with the knife.

Through a shut window beside the rear door, he spotted Kate carrying a tray of tankards across the room, her shoulders round with fatigue. He knocked on the door and heard her call out that the tavern was closed. Next he moved before the window and waved both arms. She deposited the tray on a table, snatched a lamp, and trudged to the door with it.

Her brows rose when she recognized him. After setting down the lamp, she unbarred the door. "Michael, what are you doing here so late? Oh, my. Something must be wrong. What's happened?"

He entered the tavern, shoved the door closed, and scanned the dim interior of the first floor. As far as he could tell, he and Kate were alone with the lingering smells of beer blended with men's body odor. "Anyone else here?"

"No. The servers are gone, and Aunt's at home." She stifled a yawn. "I was headed home myself in a minute. You just caught me."

"Have you heard the news that Mr. Bellington was murdered?"

She nodded. With a little grunt, she massaged her lower back with her fist. "He'll be missed by many. He helped both loyalists and patriots in need."

"You mean financially."

Her gaze fell to the floor then veered away. "There were other ways, too."

Oh ho. The financier had become a very interesting dead man. Were those "other ways" significant to the investigation? He might question her later about it. "We haven't caught the killer yet, but Mr. Bellington's slave Uno witnessed the murder and is hiding in your grain shed, injured."

"Oh, my God!" She straightened. "He's not safe out there!"

"Precisely. And before I forget to tell you, the horse he rode to town is currently lodged in your stable. First thing in the morning, I shall have Spry move him to the regiment's stable." He pointed upward. "For now, have you a bed for Uno in one of those rooms upstairs?"

"In all three, but—"

"Then I'm going to hide him upstairs."

"Why? Won't he be safer with the garrison?"

Michael shook his head. "He says a redcoat shot him and killed his master." Her eyes widened. "I dare not place an injured witness where a murderer might have access to him. I shall return shortly with him and a surgeon."

She plucked at his sleeve. "Wait. I need time."

"Time? Time for what? See here, Uno's almost unconscious. He won't mind if the room's a bit dusty."

"That's not it." She rolled her lips inward. "I-I need to move some—some furniture upstairs."

He scowled. "Furniture?" Jove's arse. She had whiskey stored up there, not furniture.

"Chairs. Extra chairs. And benches." She smiled. "I've so much business that I needed more."

She lied so easily. He made his tone droll. "Does a quarter hour give you enough time to move all those benches and chairs?"

"Yes. I shall make it work. Just for you." She stroked his arm once. "Take Uno to the room that's farthest from the top of the stairs."

He swiveled for the door. "Thank you."

Her lips full and soft, she stepped over by the window. "I'd like to apologize. I said some cruel things to you earlier."

Kate's contrition always came at the most damnable moments. This moment, a man's life depended on him. Michael inhaled a deep breath of resolve. "We can discuss it later." He fumbled with the handle, yanked the door open, and barreled out.

* * *

"A slave says a soldier shot him and killed Mr. Bellington?" Surgical bag in hand, Clayton matched Michael's stride through the yard behind White's and slanted him a look. "Quite a story. Of course I shall keep quiet about it while you investigate—but how do you know I'm not the guilty party?"

Michael sighed at the starry night. "I don't know that. But I wager you have more alibis for the past thirty-six hours than anyone else in the regiment has for an entire year."

Clayton's teeth gleamed. "That I do."

"Not to mention the lack of an apparent motive." They halted before the shed, and Michael tapped the door. "Spry, it's me."

The door inched open, then the private allowed them to enter and closed them in. Clayton removed his coat and knelt beside Uno, who was muttering and shivering with his eyes closed. The surgeon pointed to the lantern. "More light down here, please." Eli unhooked the lantern and passed it to Lavinia, who held it steady near Uno's shoulder.

No sooner did Clayton lift the injured arm than Uno writhed in pain, tried to roll away, and cried out. "Ah! Watch out, Tucker!"

Clayton set his arm down. Panting, Uno sagged to the blanket, new beads of sweat on his forehead. Lavinia bit her lip. Eli pressed a hand to his cousin's mouth. The panting quieted. "Shh! You got to be silent, Uno!"

"He won't be silent." Clayton pushed up to his feet. "Even with laudanum." He turned to Michael, who was standing beside Spry. "The ball may be lodged in his arm. If you want me to save his life, I shall have to operate quickly. He may lose his arm. And he may die anyway."

Michael unclenched his jaw. "Give him laudanum."

"You realize the price of laudanum has tripled, along with the price of everything else in town."

"If need be, I shall pay for it. Give the man laudanum while he can still swallow it."

"Yes, sir." The surgeon fished a phial from his bag on the ground, then eyed the two other slaves. "I must put a few drops of this in a bit of liquor." With a nod, Eli stretched over to a tote sack near him, pulled out a small leather flask, and handed it to Clayton, who uncorked it, sniffed, and took a sip. He coughed. "Oh, yes. That's some fine whiskey, my man." He cocked an eyebrow at Michael. "Mr. Stoddard, if you wish this business to remain between the six of us only, find a more secure location than this shed for the surgery. The patient may complain while I prospect around in his arm, and I'd rather not jostle him about after the procedure is over."

Michael nodded. "I shall return shortly." Uno would be feeling better by the time he did. "Be sure to latch this door behind me." He signaled for Spry to join him, and after Spry returned the knife to Eli, they let themselves out of the shed to stride for the tavern. "Did you find a way to carry him?"

"Yes, sir. Eli grabbed a couple poles from another shed. We'll need a second blanket. Don't you want me back there guarding the slaves?"

"When I spoke with Mrs. Duncan about a quarter hour ago, she indicated that she'd have to move some—er—furniture out of one room into another to make space for Uno. If she hasn't finished, you and I will expedite the job."

"Furniture?" Spry laughed, low.

Michael grinned, heartened that his assistant had caught on and remembered their whiskey adventure in late March. They arrived at the back door of the tavern. This time when he peered in, there was no sign of Kate, and the tavern interior was dark. He rapped on the door. When there was no response, he tugged at the door, but it was barred from within. He muttered an oath.

The nearest window wasn't secured. He pushed it open, and he and Spry crawled in. After shoving the window closed and latching it, Michael walked over and peered up the staircase. Faint light came from the second floor. He said, "Hullo! Anyone here?"

"Michael?" Shoes clomped across the upstairs flooring, and with a swish of petticoat, Kate appeared at the top of the stairs in the yellow glow of a lit lantern. "How did you get in?"

"Window."

She sighed. "I've almost got things moved about. Give me another five minutes."

"We don't have five minutes. Uno's life is at stake." He waved his assistant to follow him and took the stairs two at a time. "Spry and I will finish moving your furniture."

Kate's eyes bulged. "No!"

Michael gained the landing, grabbed the lantern from her, and headed for the open doorway of the room farthest from the top of the stairs, Spry one pace behind. In the room, lantern light illuminated a small and curtained window, clean sheets on a bed with a straw tick, a washstand, a chamberpot, one chair—and ten wooden crates. The aromatics coming from the crates were unmistakable. And from scuff marks on the floor, the ten crates had recently been more.

With a toothy grin, Spry lifted the loosened lid off the nearest crate, slid one of six unlabeled bottles of amber whiskey out, and cradled it to his breast. "Oh, sir, I've died and gone to heaven." He inhaled deeply, leaned against the wall with the bottle, and blinked at the ceiling.

Michael rotated his head to Kate, who'd stormed after them. "No tax on whiskey in heaven."

A scowl screwed up her face. "Do you want my help or not?" She hunched her shoulders.

Michael raised his eyebrows at his assistant. "I think she's blackmailing us, Spry."

"Yes, sir." Spry replaced the bottle with mock reluctance and patted the lid closed on the crate. "Where would you like the furniture moved, Mrs. Duncan?"

She jabbed her forefinger once past her shoulder. "The middle room."

In less than two minutes' time, the ten crates of whiskey were stacked neatly against a wall in the next room along with the two-dozen others that Kate had moved there. Michael told her to fetch hot water and clean rags, grabbed the blanket off the bed in the second room, and raced downstairs with Spry.

Back at the shed, Uno had relaxed to the point of dozing and whispering. On the ground beside him, they assembled the second blanket and poles. On the count of three, Eli and Spry transferred the injured man over. Lavinia in the lead with the lantern, they carried him from the shed to the tavern and upstairs to the prepared bed. Kate had left several lit lanterns in the room.

While Clayton was cutting away a docile Uno's shirt, assisted by Eli, Kate puffed in lugging a covered bucket. She swapped it for the empty bucket below the washstand. "Lavinia, fill this bucket with water from the kitchen cauldron. On a shelf to the right of the hearth, there's a canvas bag of clean rags. Bring those, too."

"Yes, Miz Duncan." The slave woman grabbed the empty bucket from Kate and rushed out.

Clayton pitched the final piece of shirt into the pile he'd been making in the corner. The surgeon swept his scrutiny over Eli, who stood beside him, and Michael and Spry, at the foot of the bed. "I'll begin as soon as Lavinia returns. I might need you three fellows to hold him steady for a few minutes."

Spry and Eli gave decisive nods. "We'll be here," said Michael.

Kate waited to one side of the bedroom door—shoulders straight, and expression calm. Michael walked over to her. "I want a brief word with you, madam." Without waiting to see if she complied, he strode for the second room, opened the door, and entered the whiskeyed darkness.

Chapter Nine

"AS SOON AS Uno is cared for, you intend to arrest me, don't you?" Her back to the closed door, Kate ran her forefinger over the lid of a whiskey crate and kept her voice low. "And you'll arrest Kevin, too, when he returns." The lantern she'd brought with her sat atop a taller stack of crates, spilling its yellow over her expression and carving valleys of bleakness there.

Michael faced her from several feet away. "We had this discussion on the final day of March." The corner of his mouth pinched. "Aptly the eve of Fool's Holy Day, as I recall. Nothing about my position has changed from that night."

"Well, then, if you aren't going to arrest us, why make the whiskey your business?"

"Because I—" He swallowed in a throat that felt too small. "Because I care." He spread his hands. "After all that's happened, I care about the three of you. Isn't that obvious?"

Her neck lengthened, and her eyes widened—as if he'd changed shape. Then she laughed a little. "No. I've hardly seen you in three months. Surely if you cared you'd make more time to stop by, at least wish us a pleasant evening every now and then. Even with your busy schedule."

A flush shot up his neck. All those weeks, he'd been convincing himself that he was protecting his career, his professional credibility. The truth was that the woman standing four feet from him scared his guts into a knot.

He yanked his gaze off her and slapped a crate with the flat of his hand. "You're making a huge mistake. This whiskey is evidence against you. It's beyond foolish to store it here. You must move every bit of it out before mid-morning."

After several seconds, she exhaled noisily. "I don't have a way to move it that quickly. If Captain Fairfax does visit, I'll make sure he doesn't come upstairs and find the whiskey."

Fairfax. Michael took several deep breaths and counted to ten before returning his gaze to her. His voice emerged even and quiet. "When we chatted in the shed Tuesday evening, I omitted a few details. Circumstantial evidence points to Captain Fairfax as the main suspect in Mr. Bellington's murder. If he's the killer, he's covering his trail very well, as usual, and that means he's looking long and hard for Uno, who can identify him."

With a trembling hand, she covered her mouth. He knew what she was thinking. "Yes, Kate, that's correct. Uno said a redcoat shot him. Thus I doubt you'll be able to control a bloody thing if your charming, courteous Captain Fairfax finds Uno and all this whiskey under the same roof. He's a master at twisting details and creating false stories to suit his purpose."

"What sorts of false stories?"

He massaged his temple for a few seconds while he put himself in the head of Fairfax. "He might claim that Uno had been sneaking out for months to consort with Lavinia, performing poorly on his chores as a result of all that wooing. Mr. Bellington, having tried increasingly harsh disciplinary means to dissuade him without success, threatens Uno, then accidentally shoots him in the arm." Michael repressed a shudder at how truly Fairfaxian his fabrication sounded. "An enraged Uno then murders his master gruesomely and flees. Giving him sanctuary here in White's Tavern makes you guilty of harboring a fugitive. The fact that you've been storing whiskey here for which you've never paid taxes casts more blight upon your character. In jail you go—"

"Why, that's horrendous! Even if I were thrown in jail, surely I'd be let out shortly—"

"In case you haven't noticed, no courts have been held in New Hanover County in half a year, not since before the Eighty-Second occupied Wilmington. Justice for everyone in jail and in that outdoor pen is long delayed. You could be stuck in jail for weeks—months. Move the whiskey. Today."

She bowed her head and twisted her fingers together. "With Kevin gone, I don't have enough people to move it so quickly. Help me, Michael. You and Spry. Please."

The rapiers gouged his heart again. He winced and was glad her gaze was lowered, so she didn't see it. "Unfortunately I've been removed from the murder investigation and placed in charge of another project which will demand all my attention, starting in a few hours. Mr. Fairfax is now the lead investigator of Mr. Bellington's murder."

She gaped at him. "You're joking!"

"Not at all. The same conflict of interests occurred in Georgia last summer. Mr. Fairfax revels in the environment of investigating murders he's committed. Thus it's critical that you hasten to find someone who can help you move the whiskey." He shook his head. "And as I'm certain that you've been keeping much of this from your aunt, you must confide in her." The two women had a history of withholding information out of a mistaken desire to protect each other.

"I-I cannot. It would crush her."

An image of the formidable Aunt Rachel, almost his height and the past owner of her own tavern in Hillsborough, flashed through his mind. "I doubt that very much."

"She moved here expecting that she'd have an easier life than what she'd had in Hillsborough."

"Unfortunately life doesn't always deliver on our expectations. And Kate, after you've moved this cache, you must shut down production, once and for all."

"No!"

"Why the hell not? This tavern is the most prosperous business in the Cape Fear! You don't need the extra whiskey!"

Her gaze flicked over the crates. "This is little more than a one-month supply. Yes, the tavern's wildly prosperous this moment, but it won't last. I've seen how business ebbs and flows, and besides—" Her words came faster, tighter. "—Most of our business is due to the Eighty-Second. After the regiment leaves, Aunt, Kevin, and I will—and then—" She threw up her hands. "Oh, very well, I'll tell you." Tears sparkled in her eyes. She blinked them away. "My uncle who transferred ownership of the tavern to me years ago had a gambling debt that we didn't learn about until after he died. The only way Kevin and I have been able to make payments without my brother selling his house is with untaxed whiskey production."

"Let me be certain I understand. You own the tavern, and your brother owns the house?"

She nodded. "And he isn't in New Berne buying another tavern. He's ten miles north operating the still. He took what little savings we had to hire some help and purchase supplies."

This wasn't the moment for Michael to let Kate know what he'd seen on Bellington's account summary. She had enough to worry about, figuring out how to move the whiskey. But damnation, what a fool Kevin was! He knew about the family's debt and had still taken out the massive loan, effectively putting himself, his sister, and his aunt in danger of losing their home.

If Kevin wasn't buying a second tavern in New Berne, had he borrowed such a huge amount of money to hire help and purchase supplies for whiskey production—perhaps to set up another still? Obviously someone needed to talk to him about his imprudent move. Michael doubted the women in his family would make a suitable impression on him. "I'd like a word with him. When will he return?"

She spread her hands. "By Friday. I'll give him your message."

"Very good." Beyond the closed door, he heard Lavinia's tread up the stairs. Kate tilted her head toward the door when the young woman clomped past. He said, "Let's go. Uno needs us."

"Wait!" She seized his arm as he walked past and steered him to face her. "Michael, I'm sorry for being such a shrew and insulting you yesterday evening. I don't know what got into me. I called you provincial and tame and—"

"It doesn't matter. I've heard far worse from rebels."

"But you're angry with me about something. If not that, then what?"

Spry tapped on the door. "Mr. Stoddard, sir. Clayton is ready to begin. I shall make sure everything's locked up downstairs."

"Yes, thank you, Spry, and especially the windows." Michael squeezed his eyes shut for an instant while his assistant moved on toward the stairs. Then he grasped Kate's upper arms and poured his gaze into hers. "You lied to me, Kate," he whispered. "Many times." Her face looked waxen, her eyes enormous. He shook her once. "Stop lying to me!" Heart pulverized, he released her and pivoted. After yanking the door open, he strode out, pain buried in brisk business. "And make sure you bring that lantern with you, madam. Clayton will need it."

* * *

The surgeon straightened, having finished bandaging Uno's upper arm. As he rolled his shoulders back with a sigh, a lone, ambitious mockingbird chirped a few times outside. Clayton stepped around Eli, who snored softly on a blanket on the floor near the foot of the bed, and ambled over to Michael, who'd propped himself against the doorjamb standing up to keep from snoozing.

Washbasin in one hand, Lavinia took Clayton's place bedside and wiped down Uno's naked torso with a damp cloth. Exhaustion and the poppy kept the injured slave's sleep still and deep. The surgeon looked from the two of them to Michael. "Well, that's it, sir. Uno's in the hands of Providence now—and his own innate ability to heal."

"Thank you for everything." Michael matched the other man's low tone.

"You're welcome. I shall arrange to stop by and check on him this evening. Clear broth until his fever breaks. Of course, if it doesn't in the next day, my skill will have been for naught."

Come on, Uno, Michael thought. *Stay with us.* "Lavinia appears committed to tending him."

"Indeed, and if you can arrange to keep her here for another day, it would benefit him."

Local slave owners had grown accustomed to the Eighty-Second tapping their slaves for short-term special projects, sometimes without advance notice. Michael could make up an excuse to hang onto Lavinia for a day. Anne Hooper wouldn't like it, but too bad. "I shall think of something." When he rolled his head around, he felt every taut, sleep-deprived muscle in his neck.

The surgeon glanced about. "Where are Spry and Mrs. Duncan?"

"I sent Spry downstairs for guard detail." He hoped his assistant wasn't asleep on a bench. "And I sent Mrs. Duncan into the next room to sleep—told her I'd wake her if we needed anything."

"That's good. Got a bit crowded in here." Clayton plucked a small chunk of metal from his pocket and passed it to him. "This is what came from Uno's arm."

Michael turned it this way and that in the lantern light. It was smaller than the balls issued by the British Army for musket and pistol. And he'd seen this before. "From a civilian pistol." Fairfax had a brace of them, a matched set. In Georgia the previous summer, he'd shot the Spaniard in the knee with one.

"Yes, most likely." Clayton yawned. "Some of our lads have civilian pistols."

Perhaps it was time for a routine weapons inspection. Michael handed the ball to the surgeon. "The patrol heads out to Mr. Bellington's estate in about two hours. You still want to go?"

Clayton frowned. "Of course. No surgeon's worth his salt if he cannot do without sleep every now and then." He pocketed the pistol ball. "And as the financier's other slave hasn't turned up, I've a bad feeling that he became acquainted with the civilian pistol."

Michael grimaced. "I admit the thought has crossed my mind, too. Well, Major Craig has placed me on another assignment today. Captain Fairfax will be leading the patrol."

Clayton's shoulders sagged, and he looked down. "Yes, sir."

Bad enough that the men would be dealing with Bellington's incinerated body and possibly the summer-ripened corpse of the third slave, but Michael couldn't think of anyone in the regiment who was overjoyed to work with Fairfax. At least he had an idea of how to sweeten Clayton's stinky deal a bit. "Wait here a moment."

He tiptoed to the middle bedroom, eased the door open, and listened. When he heard Kate's even breathing, he slipped into the room and groped to his right. The crate of whiskey with the lid that Spry had loosened earlier was exactly where he'd left it.

As he withdrew one of the six bottles, it clinked against its neighbor, and he froze with the bottle halfway out. Kate murmured, but in the gloom, her stocking feet and the hem of her petticoat didn't move. For an instant, he envied her slumber. The way events were playing out, and with dawn little more than an hour and a half away, he wasn't likely to grab more sleep that night unless he crawled into bed beside her—whoa, no, that was a bad idea for more reasons than his fogged brain could tally.

Exerting more caution, he extricated the whiskey bottle the rest of the way in silence, then replaced the crate lid. Loot in hand, he tiptoed out and closed the door behind him. In Uno's room, he extended the bottle to the surgeon.

"For me?" Clayton's expression brightened. "Is this the same stuff in Eli's flask? Bribery, how I do love it. Thank you, sir."

"Let me know what you find at Mr. Bellington's estate. And if you're finished in here, I shall walk you to the infirmary." Right around the corner, in the barracks, Michael would recruit the first shift of guard duty at White's Tavern, two soldiers who had alibis for Monday night.

"Excellent. I shall grab my bag."

* * *

"How do you like that, sir? He's taken your bait." Spry allowed his side of the drape in Mrs. Chiswell's parlor to ease into place over the front window.

"Bait? Now, now. I merely reminded him of his duty." In the diffuse light of dawn, Michael continued to peer out from behind his side of the curtains and monitor the chaise driven by Fairfax. It turned north onto Market Street. Toward the barracks—excellent.

Then he realized that Spry had made for the closed doors with the lantern he carried. Michael twisted his shoulders and frowned at him. "Where are you going?"

The private waved the lantern at the doors. "Don't you want a look at the portfolio, sir?"

"I do very much." Michael extracted his watch. "But we shall wait at least a quarter hour before we step into the study."

"You mean in case Mr. Fairfax forgets something and returns for it, sir?"

Fairfax never forgot anything. Michael motioned his assistant to the window. "Bring that lantern over here so I can check the time."

Nine minutes later, Fairfax drove back around, halted before the house, and helped himself out of the chaise with the aid of his cane. Lips pinched with anticipation, he swaggered into the house through the front entrance. On the other side of the closed parlor doors, Michael and Spry listened while he opened the study and confronted a room empty of intruders. He spent another minute in the study before leaving. Michael wiggled his eyebrows at Spry, and they returned to the window to watch the chaise clatter off for the second time.

"Sir, I recommend waiting another quarter hour before we proceed."

"My assistant is a wise man."

By the time the two soldiers sneaked across the foyer and entered the study, pedestrian and vehicle traffic had picked up on Second Street. Muggy daylight had spread over town and seeped in the study windows. Shadowy, empty shelves lined the walls, the only other furnishings a cot, chair, small table, and trunk. The trunk's padlock sat atop a folded blanket on the cot.

Spry brought the lantern down beside the padlock. "Look at this, sir. Surely Mr. Fairfax didn't forget to lock his trunk. How do we know he hasn't set up a trap?"

Michael opened the trunk. The portfolio rested in plain view atop a pile of folded shirts so immaculate that they seemed to glow in the dusk. "Of course it's a trap, lad. There's the prize in plain sight. He wants me to steal it so he can find it among my belongings later and discredit me. But I shall examine the summaries here and leave them here, thus disappointing him." He retrieved the portfolio and eyed the window. "Not enough daylight yet. Bring the lantern over there."

The table, which Michael moved beneath the window, wasn't large enough for him to spread out all the summary pages, as he'd done in Bellington's office. While Spry held the lantern, Michael arranged the six pages in chronological order and examined each one, taking his time. Even though he knew it was coming, he couldn't help but gawp at the loan to Kevin Marsh earlier that month. It was a hundred times larger than the other thirteen loans on the page. What the hell was Kevin buying with all that money—and with so much at stake? Yes, Kate and her aunt would be devastated when they found out what he'd done.

The peculiar long and narrow shape of the ink smudge that partially smeared the notation about Kevin's collateral caught his eye. He studied it a moment before switching to the June summary page. Low on the right side of the paper was another ink smudge, not as dark as that on the July page, but the same basic shape. He shuffled to the May page, and there was the smudge again, very faint. February through April were clean of ink smudges.

He spread the May, June, and July pages out as much as possible on the table, then tapped the smudges on each with his forefinger. "What do you make of these, Spry?"

The private leaned in for an examination, then straightened. "Sir. Perhaps the side of Mr. Hickory's hand got ink on it, and he tracked it onto these pages."

Michael straightened, too. "He had an ink stain on his right hand when we arrived yesterday. Did you see it?"

"No, sir. I was watching out the front window."

"Of course. The ink on Mr. Hickory's hand must have been fresh, because while he and I first chatted, he managed to rub most of it off with his handkerchief."

"Well, then, sir, I suppose that before we arrived, he was copying over—" Spry caught Michael's gaze and frowned. "Odd. I recall him saying that he always copied the summary pages for Mr. Bellington's sake. Why would he do that if Mr. Bellington was dead, sir?"

"An excellent question. Do you also remember him telling me that he had fifteen active clients?"

"Yes, sir."

Michael handed him the July page. "Count the number of clients, please."

Spry did so and set the page on the table. "I count fourteen, sir. Either Mr. Hickory was mistaken about the number of active clients, or—"

"Or these summary pages have been created just for us, omitting one active client."

Spry blew out a breath and squinted out the window. "Eh. I don't like the way that sounds, sir, like Mr. Hickory misled us."

"Perhaps I steered you to that conclusion, Spry. Admittedly an ink stain and one number off on a list aren't much to work with."

The two men were silent a moment. The private transferred his squint to Michael. "He's already lied to you once, sir, about Sam Bellington's mother."

"Indeed. If I'm correct about this, it means that Mr. Hickory is shielding a client from the murder investigation."

"Might this be Mr. Bellington's killer, sir?"

Michael pondered the window and the growing daylight. "Possibly. But there are other reasons he might shield a client's identity from investigators."

"Yes, sir. I wonder, does Mr. Fairfax know what Mr. Hickory is doing?

I mean, could he be the missing client? How can we know for certain?"

"I suppose we must locate and examine the original financial records."

"Sir. But do you think Mr. Hickory will give us those records? Surely Mr. Fairfax informed him of the transfer of investigators."

Michael suspected that was the first piece of information that Fairfax communicated to Hickory the previous evening. He collected the summary pages, ordered them the way Fairfax had arranged them, and returned them to the portfolio. Then he placed the portfolio atop the pile of shirts and closed the trunk. His assistant had returned the table to its original spot and was awaiting his response. "Almost time for morning parade." Michael patted his stomach. "I'm hungry. Aren't you?" Spry grinned. "After parade, let's see what Mr. Hickory is having for breakfast."

"Yes, sir!"

Chapter Ten

IN THE FRONT doorway of Hickory's house, a stout woman about twenty years older than Michael made a quick survey of the two soldiers, then addressed him. "Mr. Hickory is eating breakfast. I shall be glad to give him a message from you, sir."

On the foyer floor behind her, a loaded valise informed Michael that the financier planned to take a trip. His pulse quickened. If he gave the housekeeper a message, he suspected that Hickory wouldn't respond to it before he left town. "Thank you, but I'm afraid this cannot wait. Come along, Spry." He removed his hat, breezed past the woman into the house, and heard her gasp of indignation.

His arrival in the dining room caught Hickory with a forkful of food halfway to his open mouth. The fork clinked down on a porcelain plate piled with toast, bacon, and fried eggs, and the frowning financier pushed up from a fine mahogany chair. "Mr. Stoddard, you've interrupted my breakfast! I insist that you return later."

The food smelled delectable and stimulated a growl from Michael's gut. Gods, he couldn't remember when he'd last eaten eggs and bacon for breakfast—and yes, that was a steaming cup of coffee near Hickory's plate. How refreshing to know that money still talked louder than the food shortage. He loaded teeth into his smile and moved around the table to the chair nearest Hickory. "My apologies, sir. I can see that you're headed out this morning after you dine, and I wanted to make sure we spoke before you left."

The housekeeper huffed forward with a scowl for Michael. "I'm so sorry, Mr. Hickory. He wouldn't give me a message at the door."

Michael had scanned the list of names Hickory gave him the day before.

He beamed at her. "Mrs. Bolton, Mr. Hickory and I must converse before he leaves. Be so good as to fetch me a plate of what he's eating." The financier's manservant, Tifton, rushed in and moved behind Hickory. Michael, focused on the housekeeper, ignored him and pulled out the chair. "And feed my assistant in the kitchen, too, thank you. Shall we chat, Mr. Hickory?" He seated himself and placed his hat on the table beside him.

The financier's gaze shot around the dining room to gauge the assembled company before returning to Michael. He crossed his arms high on his chest. "I won't discuss more of Jasper's murder with you. Mr. Fairfax is now the investigator. Major Craig transferred you to another assignment."

Michael waved away his words. "Never mind the murder investigation. You received quite a shock yesterday. I came to inquire after your well-being."

Hickory's frown deepened. "Are you serious?"

Michael rolled back his shoulders. Such a comfortable dining chair. He gave Hickory a pleasant smile.

After studying him several seconds, Hickory uncrossed his arms and resumed his seat. "You heard him, Mrs. Bolton. Bring him breakfast, and feed his man." She didn't move. He snapped his fingers at her and, with a jerk of his head, signaled Tifton to follow her out. When the servants and Spry were gone from the dining room, he recommended his study of Michael.

To the right of Hickory's plate was a popular magazine from Charles Town. Elbows on the table, Michael clasped his hands before him and leaned forward to glimpse what sort of world news captured Hickory's attention. "Ah. Look at that." He tapped an article with his forefinger. "Those Comuneros in New Granada are at it again. When do you think the Spaniards will quell that rebellion?"

"By the end of this year."

"Just so, and they'll manage it the same way they managed the insurrectionists in Peru. Execute the leaders."

The financier fidgeted. "Yes, of course, but—"

"Certainly those rebels have enthusiastic leaders, but a lack of resources will ultimately doom their cause."

The financier broke eye contact, blotted his forehead with a handkerchief, and spread his hands. "Mr. Stoddard, why are you here?"

Michael put on his best look of puzzlement. "As I said, sir, I'm concerned about you, thought you could use the company for breakfast." He cocked an eyebrow. "How did you pass the night?"

Hickory returned the handkerchief to his pocket, shook out his napkin, and replaced it in his lap. "I barely slept a wink, of course." When he reached for his cup, his hand quivered.

"I understand. Nightmares?" The financier grumbled and sipped coffee. "I can imagine how distressed you must be." And how ripe he was for some suggestion. Sunlight streamed into the dining room. Michael shifted his gaze to the unlit chandelier on the ceiling. "All night long, you were probably mulling over recent conversations you had with Mr. Bellington, thinking about how you'd have handled things differently if you knew those would be your final words with him." He waited a few seconds. "I wager you also wondered how much he suffered at the end."

The coffee cup clattered back to the saucer, and the financier exhaled. "Please, sir, let us not discuss such matters. It's horrendous enough to know that a criminal took his life."

"Forgive me."

Hickory's frown returned. "And now that I've had the night to toss and turn over it, I wouldn't be surprised to learn that that loathsome Captain Fairfax did murder Jasper. He probably had a motive."

Michael disciplined the little thrill in his veins and drew back his head to look surprised. "'Loathsome?' Have a care, now. He's a fellow officer. Have you recalled hearing a solid threat that Mr. Fairfax made to Mr. Bellington—something more than what you told me yesterday?"

"No, but I'm incensed that the captain is now conducting this investigation."

Disappointment weighed on Michael's spirits, even while he maintained an open expression on Hickory. Unfortunately it didn't sound as though the financier could incriminate Fairfax. He was merely grousing at Craig's choice of investigators.

Mrs. Bolton bustled in with his breakfast. After sitting back to allow her to arrange food and coffee before him, Michael smiled up at her. "Thank you." She sniffed and swept out. He inhaled lustily while he shook out his napkin. "This smells divine."

Fork in hand, he blazed a trail through the food. In his peripheral vision, Hickory picked at his meal. Perhaps he could still coax useful information from the financier. First of all, though, he applied himself to eating—not a difficult task when his belly was empty, and mere porridge had broken his fast every morning for too long.

In silence, the financier rolled his empty fork around between his fingers. His regard of the plate below him swelled into a glare. "This change of investigators is preposterous. What if it's a conflict of interests? What if being thwarted by the missing summary pages was enough to infuriate Mr. Fairfax into killing Jasper?"

Being infuriated and thwarted might be enough of a motive for some men to kill. Fairfax wasn't one to kill on impulse. He calculated each murder first. It was how he squeezed the maximum enjoyment from every aspect of his sport. Had he learned that from killing his stepfather?

Michael said, "See here, I don't wish to distress you further with details about the investigation. Heaven knows how you must be struggling, now that the weight and accountability for the business have fallen squarely on your shoulders. My father and uncle both owned businesses. While I was growing up, I saw all the responsibility placed on them, the sleepless nights." He resumed eating with enthusiasm while the financier skittered half-eaten eggs around with his fork. "By the bye, do you recall the news about the astronomer in England who announced that he'd discovered a new primary planet back in March? Herschel's the fellow, and I read that he calls the planet Georgium Sidus after the King."

"Yes, yes, what of it?" Hickory sounded bored.

Michael swallowed a chunk of buttered toast. "Well, Mrs. Farrell's astronomer brother, Mr. Carlisle, may have discovered the planet in January, two full months before Mr. Herschel. A shame he didn't publicize his findings."

"Indeed, a shame." Hickory pressed back in his chair and expelled a sigh. "Very well, get on with it, sir. I expect you to interrogate me about Jasper."

Michael touched his hand to his breast. "Not I, sir. Mr. Fairfax will be the one who does the interrogating from now on." The financier coughed and shuddered. Michael suppressed a grin. "Breakfast is excellent. My compliments to Mrs. Bolton." He forked some fried egg into his mouth. "I could tell you were shaken by the news yesterday. Any man would be. How are you going to manage all fourteen of those active clients by yourself? Won't you need help?"

"Fifteen clients." The fork clattered to the plate. Hickory covered the sides of his head with his hands, leaned his elbows on the table, and stared downward. "Fourteen. Ah, I don't remember. Fifteen."

This was going well. Michael sipped coffee and again resisted smiling. "You told me fifteen yesterday in your office, but there were only fourteen names listed on the July summary page. Who did you leave off the list?"

"No one."

"For your sake, I hope that's true." Michael shoveled bacon in his mouth—crispy, fat bacon—and savored it. "Mmm. You know, when Mr. Fairfax finds out that you omitted a name, he'll consider it incriminatory, and he'll make matters even more worrisome for you. In fact, he won't leave you alone. He'll start by questioning why, if standard procedure was that you update summary pages at the request of Mr. Bellington, you were updating those pages after Private Henshaw had informed you that your business partner was dead—"

"Not updating. Copying!" His fist pounded the dark, polished surface of the table with all three words, sending dishes and silverware chattering. He gripped his hands in his lap. "I knew you'd—you'd want to see a list of clients, and—and—I didn't want an investigator to leave the office with the originals, so I created copies." Hickory turned bloodshot eyes on him and worked his jaw. "I copied the pages. You understand?"

"Of course." Hickory had changed his story, and even for a man who'd lost his business partner and gotten little sleep the night before, he was quite nervous. There were fifteen active clients, Michael felt certain, and Hickory had omitted one of them under the pretense of copying the summary pages. The trick would be providing him with the encouragement to release that information. "But you'll have to reconcile those client numbers for Mr. Fairfax. In the notes I transferred to him, I mentioned the discrepancy. He's the sort of investigator who jumps right on discrepancies and gnaws away at them—"

"Fortunately I don't need to cater to his whims." Hickory growled. "As you've noticed, I'm leaving town today for a few days."

Michael's eyebrows rose. "Surely you'll wait for Mr. Bellington's memorial service?"

"No. I shall pay my respects when I return."

The devil—where was he going, and why? How long had he had this trip planned? Michael stopped himself from leaping in with the questions. Instead he finished eating his own food and watched how Hickory applied himself to his breakfast—rushing, not tasting a meal that was no longer hot. The financier couldn't wait to get away from Wilmington.

That was the face of guilt, if ever Michael saw it.

He finished his coffee and made his tone casual. "Well, sir, the sun is shining. It looks to be excellent weather for traveling, if a bit warm, so your trip should be pleasant. I know how tense this unfortunate business has made you. The change of scenery will do you well. And I've an idea. On your way out of town, let's stop by your office, and you can show me the original July summary sheet—"

"It isn't at the office." Hickory tilted his cup to catch the last drops of coffee.

"No? Where is it?"

"All the financial information is in a secure place." The financier dabbed his mouth with the napkin and rolled back his shoulders. "I've never trusted the office safe. Furthermore the lock on the front door there can be picked. Windows can be wedged open. The building can be set afire. So I've hidden the information as a precaution."

"I see." Michael narrowed his eyes. So much for not removing the originals from the office. Where had he stashed all that important information—that evidence?

Damnation. Hickory had slipped through his fingers. It wasn't the first time Michael had lost a witness. However, instinct hammered away at him this time that the witness sitting with him at the table was complicit in Bellington's murder, even though he could prove he wasn't present when it happened.

Wait a moment. If Fairfax had murdered Bellington, and Hickory had been his criminal associate, why was Hickory afraid of Fairfax? Were they double-crossing each other?

"Where are you headed today, Mr. Hickory?"

"Brunswick Town." Hickory tossed his napkin to the table and rose from his chair.

Michael stood, too. "Brunswick Town—where Sam Bellington's mother lives."

"Where she lived. She died a few months ago."

"Yes, I know. Why did you tell me yesterday that Sam Bellington left Wilmington a week ago to visit her when she's dead, and when he was here in town on Monday?"

Hickory's lips pressed together, then he laughed and shook his head. "Did I say that? I must have been addled from the tragic news about my business partner."

What a wretched liar. "Did you see Sam Bellington when he came to town on Monday with Uno to buy groceries?" The financier shook his head. "But he's your assistant. Didn't he stop by the office to greet you while he was here?"

"No. He's like his uncle. Both men would be hermits if they could."

Michael rested his hands on the back of his chair. "Have you notified Mr. Bellington of his uncle's death?"

Hickory gave a brusque nod. "Yesterday afternoon I posted a message to his mother's estate west of Brunswick Town. Since her death, he's spent a good deal of time there, readying the property for sale. Of course I cannot guarantee that he received my message, but at least I fulfilled my obligations."

He trusted such sensitive information to the post? What a selfish ball of slime. Anne Hooper's words about Hickory came to mind: *He hasn't the business acumen that Mr. Bellington has.* Michael was certain that Hickory wasn't the man his business partner had been, either.

The financier shifted his feet around. "Say. I heard a strange rumor circulating yesterday about Jasper's murder." He leaned toward Michael. "Have his two missing slaves been found?"

The question sent scurries of suspicion through Michael. Hickory looked far too eager for that nugget of information, like he was prospecting for it. Michael maintained a bland expression. "No."

"A pity." Hickory pulled out his watch and looked at the time.

While Michael slid his chair beneath the table and retrieved his hat, he wracked his brains for an excuse to hold the man in town. Frustration climbed in his chest that he had nothing to go on except gut feeling and vague notions. He could certainly order Hickory detained and searched, the prerogative of any soldier in the regiment, but he imagined that would be a mistake. If he found nothing incriminatory on him, he wouldn't be able to imprison him—not with the overcrowded conditions of the pen and jail. Worse, such aggression would raise Hickory's guard—and Michael didn't want to confirm for the financier how much their conversation during breakfast had elevated his suspicions.

Too bad Michael was no longer assigned to the investigation. Fairfax, who had the authority to detain Hickory for any number of reasons from the practical to the absurd, was poking around charred timbers miles away, possibly fabricating evidence there in his own defense. Michael straightened his uniform coat. "With whom are you visiting in Brunswick Town?"

"A lovely lady."

"Good for you." To Michael's knowledge, there were no lovely ladies left in Brunswick Town. The port had been reduced to a dying hamlet by the more advantageous shipping location of Wilmington. Was Hickory even going to Brunswick Town, or was that a lie, too?

Where was Sam Bellington? Would he show up for his uncle's service?

For one desperate instant, Michael toyed with the idea of asking the financier who it was that he'd met in the shut-down tannery building the previous evening, just to enjoy his struggle to stitch together another lie. But he didn't mention it. Hickory must continue to believe him ignorant of the incident. Fairfax, too. Perhaps secrets could be learned from the tannery—the next stop for Spry and himself.

"Well, I must be off before the day grows too warm." Hickory gestured for the door. "I shall walk you out to the kitchen. Thank you for joining me for breakfast, Mr. Stoddard."

"You're welcome. It was my pleasure."

Chapter Eleven

BRUNSWICK TOWN WASN'T Hickory's destination, Michael felt certain. As soon as he and Spry departed the financier's house and were out of earshot, he briefed his assistant on the conversation he'd had during breakfast, then sent him back to follow Hickory as far as the edge of town. Spry was to catch up with Michael at the abandoned tannery.

Twenty minutes later at the tannery, the locksmith, Pearson, slid his pick back into his work pouch and faced Michael. "Both merchants who own this building are now living in Boston, sir. This isn't the first criminal activity associated with it this year." He presented Michael with the lock from the front door. "Shall I put a new padlock on the door? That way you'll know that the regiment has the only keys."

"If the fellow who's sneaking in here is as handy with a pick as you are, it won't matter that we have the only keys."

The locksmith's expression grew long. "Yes, sir."

For a few seconds, Michael turned aside to cover a yawn. It was going to be a long day. Just past eight-thirty in the morning, and already his sleep deficit and the day's warmth were tugging at his alertness.

"Mr. Stoddard, has the regiment more work for me? I could use it right now."

Pearson's wife had recently birthed their first baby. Michael shook his head, wishing he could help him. Unfortunately Pearson wasn't the only civilian contractor in town who needed business. "Thank you for opening the padlock. I shall let you know as soon as I hear of work and make sure you're paid by the end of the week."

After a tug on the brim of his hat, the locksmith ambled on down the street.

He passed Spry, who trotted for the tannery yawning, and joined Michael before the door. "Your suspicions about Mr. Hickory's destination were solid, sir. Tifton loaded two valises into their chaise and drove Mr. Hickory to the wharf, whereupon he boarded a transport with both pieces of baggage."

"The wharf, eh?" And two valises. There'd been only one in the front entrance earlier. The note on the financier's office door said he'd reopen for business on July thirtieth. Did the second valise indicate that he now expected to be gone longer? "What did the harbormaster say?"

"Sir. The transport took Mr. Hickory out to the *Barbara Bea*, a brig that weighed anchor about five minutes ago. She's headed north, with several ports of call."

Unfortunate, indeed, that Major Craig had transferred authority for the investigation to Fairfax, and he was on the other side of the Cape Fear River that morning. The ease with which Fairfax could have halted the ship's departure—Michael cursed, low.

"A pity you couldn't get Mr. Hickory to tell you the name of the client he's protecting, sir. And I wonder where he's hidden the business records."

Michael studied the lock in his hand. "Likely they were in the crate you saw him carry here from the office yesterday evening."

"Yes, sir, that thought occurred to me. I suppose it's too much to hope that the crate's still here."

Hickory and his mystery ally didn't strike Michael as being dull-witted enough to leave such crucial evidence behind. He pushed the tannery door open and revealed the dance of motes in the morning sunlight. "At least they left us fresh footprints in the dust."

The private scratched his chin at the sight, not rushing in, content to observe for a few seconds. "Perhaps Mr. Hickory and his host talked there in that spot for a while, sir, before Mr. Hickory left." He pointed to an oblong area inside where shoes had cleared the wood floor of dust, then shifted his gaze deeper into the main room and its dusty floor. "Looks like a trail of one man's footprints going from the front door to the far window to the back room." With a pivot, Spry grinned at his captain. "Miscreants appear to favor the back room's character, sir."

Michael recalled what they'd discovered in that room in March. Odds were that this time it wouldn't be more property stolen from the Eighty-Second; that security breach had been closed. He swept his hand forward, palm up, in invitation. "After you."

He shut them into the musty building, set the lock on a broken bench beneath the grime-clouded front window, and dropped the bar across the door so they wouldn't be interrupted. There wasn't much to see in the main room except footprints of a man whose stride length placed him almost as tall as Spry. The rubbish bin, emptied by the Eighty-Second when they cleaned up the investigation there in the spring, was still empty. All back windows were latched. The rear door was barred.

Both soldiers headed to the second room, each footstep a hollow thunk on the wood floor. In a corner of the otherwise empty room, they found saddlebags, a partially full bottle of what looked and smelled like the whiskey that Kate and her brother produced, a powder horn, and a full canvas sack. No wooden crate. The saddlebags contained several days' supply of dried meat and fruit wrapped in oiled paper, a currycomb and brush, a picket pin, horseshoes, a few horseshoe nails, oats, a tinderbox, and shot for a rifle. Spry loosened the drawstring on the sack and, one-by-one, pulled items from within and arrayed them on the dusty floor. Three rolled shirts and handkerchiefs. Two pairs of stockings. A pair of breeches. A shaving kit and comb. A miniature of an attractive young brunette—

"Whoa, Spry." Michael squatted facing him and took the miniature for an examination. "Nicely rendered. I don't recognize her from among local civilians." He turned it toward his assistant. "Do you?"

Spry regarded it, then shook his head. "Ask Mrs. Duncan, sir."

Michael grunted his agreement. Kate's business had made her familiar with many people in the Cape Fear. "And it appears that this fellow was off to see the world." He traded the miniature for the comb on the floor, then pulled a pale hair from the teeth. "This blond fellow."

"Mr. Bellington's nephew, sir? You said Mrs. Hooper described Sam Bellington as blond."

"So she did." A moment longer, Michael examined the gold hair. Did Bellington's nephew have a brunette sweetheart? Perhaps Kate would know. Or Mrs. Hooper, since she was the financiers' client.

Both Sam Bellington and Jonas Hickory stood to gain from Jasper Bellington's death. Michael chastised himself for being so cocksure at first of Fairfax as the killer. To be sure, Uno's testimony that a redcoat killed his master had anchored that belief. But now he wondered what might have made Bellington's nephew or business partner vicious enough to torture him to death in a manner so characteristic of Fairfax's *modus operandi*.

Michael realized how much he wanted Fairfax to be the killer. His blood sang with the desire for it every time he thought of all the men Fairfax had butchered and remembered the ways Fairfax had tried to kill him—and especially when he imagined Kate in Fairfax's arms. If Fairfax had committed this murder...

With a shuddery sigh, Michael opened his hand and wiggled his fingers. The hair fell to the floor. Feeling his assistant's scrutiny, he met his gaze. "Yes?"

Spry opened his mouth, closed it, then opened it again. "If this fellow is off to see the world, sir, where are his horse, knife, and rifle?"

The point was excellent, but it wasn't what Spry had been thinking a moment ago. If Michael had to guess, he'd say the private was also questioning how much of the evidence they'd collected truly supported Michael's original assertion that Fairfax was guilty—although neither of them would admit it aloud yet. What a team they made with their stiff necks.

"Well. Maybe he hasn't left quite yet." Michael swept his hand above the array of personal belongings. "And you realize that all of this is circumstantial evidence."

"Yes, sir. Neither of us saw who brought the items here. We cannot even say for certain that there's a connection between these items and Mr. Hickory."

"Precisely. Anything else in that bag?"

"Not much, sir." Spry upended it and gave it a shake to dump out the remaining item. Wadded-up scarlet linen landed atop a shirt.

Michael pointed to it. "A waistcoat?"

Spry set down the sack, stood with the linen, shook it out, and held up the garment by the shoulders. As his gaze darted up and down, he worked his mouth. "Perhaps—perhaps a costume for a play, sir?"

Michael had risen also, shock rocketing up his neck and into his scalp. The garment was a full, red coat with black facings and cuffs. Even though it was made of linen, not wool, and daylight showed that it wasn't actually a uniform coat of a soldier in the Eighty-Second regiment, it looked similar enough to confer that impression in more muted lighting, such as in a stage production. "No play in town this year has used a soldier character, Spry."

"It could be from before the occupation, when the rebels were in charge, sir."

It might. But when the rebels were in charge, they'd banned most sources of entertainment in town, such as theater productions. Still, it was something else to ask Kate. She and Kevin were theater enthusiasts.

The private gripped the right cuff, then stretched the sleeve to Michael. "Look here, sir. Dried blood on the forearm. Down here, too. And across the front." Spry wrinkled his nose. "The dried blood is fairly new."

And some of it wasn't dry. The significance of the garment sank in, and Michael ground his teeth. "Damn him, Spry! This is the 'redcoat' who murdered Mr. Bellington and shot Uno."

"Agreed, sir." Spry clutched the linen coat in one hand and shook it once, hard. "But who is he, and why is he trying to pin the murder on our regiment?"

Michael took a deep breath to purge the outrage from his thinking. "Not necessarily on our men." The imitation was basic enough to represent the uniform of any redcoat, possibly even Fairfax's Seventeenth Light Dragoon coat. How convenient for the killer.

Spry's gaze lit. "Ah! Uno likely won't remember details about the coat of his master's murderer, will he, sir? Especially if the lighting was poor."

"Exactly. I suspect the killer was counting on that."

"Sir. Will you be wanting surveillance on this building?"

"Yes." Although now that Mr. Hickory had flown, he wondered whether his associate would return. "I shall schedule one man every two hours watching the front door through Thursday morning." Michael scooped up the miniature and tucked it into one of his pockets. After another look about the room to make sure they hadn't missed anything, he indicated the personal belongings at his feet. "Pack up all of this. I shall store it in my room for safekeeping. After I leave, maintain surveillance outside until I can send the first man over to relieve you. Then meet me in queue before Major Craig's office a few minutes before nine."

"Yes, sir." Spry rolled up the linen coat and stuffed it into the sack.

* * *

Michael dumped the saddlebags and canvas sack on the floor of his bedroom and shut his door. His trunk was full, and a quick survey reinforced his suspicion that if he wanted to keep the items out of sight, he'd no option that moment except to shove them under his bed. Under the bed was the first location that Fairfax or another criminal would search. It also saw action from the hired woman's broom. Hoping that he could find a more secure location for the evidence soon, he pushed saddlebags and sack beneath the bed, then made sure that nothing of what they'd found in the tannery was visible.

Brushing off his hands, he turned on his heel to spot a new letter on his desk. The postmaster must have missed it at morning parade and sent it to the housekeeper. The sender, using handwriting that Michael didn't recognize, had addressed him as "Lieut. Stoddard"—likely someone who wasn't local and hadn't yet heard of Michael's promotion. He broke the seal and looked at the date—June the second—then the salutation. *Mon ami Michel.*

His jaw dropped. This letter, signed "Affectionately C," was from the French spy and assassin, Claude Devereaux, of "Claude and the Team" fame. Why had Claude mailed him the letter and sent Adam Neville to deliver a message? Shock and suspicion shot through Michael. His gaze darted over the content, and his confusion deepened. And why in God's name had Claude written him a full page of drivel about his cousin's wedding in Provence?

He dropped the letter on his desk, walked away from it, swung his arms, and rubbed eyes grainy from lack of sleep. When he returned and reread the missive, nothing popped out at him from the extravagant detail of Cousin Gilbert's nuptials with a damsel named Simone. But instinct nagged him that something covert was going on in the letter.

Was it a cipher? If so, where was the key? He wasted several minutes traipsing among the flowery detail, looking for a pattern. "Damn you, Claude," he muttered.

He stalked away from the desk with more savage arm swinging this time. He didn't have the leisure for the Frenchman's game. No doubt Claude was sipping a glass of red wine in some tavern and laughing at him. *Stupid Englishman, stumped by a Frenchman, a friend to rebels.*

Rebels. Michael halted facing a bare wall, relaxed his arms, and let them hang at his sides. Rebels wrote in invisible ink, didn't they? Invisible ink between the lines of innocuous sounding letters. Obnoxious, florid letters about weddings and such.

An instant later, he was at the desk, tinderbox in hand. He lit the candle and hovered Claude's letter about a foot above the flame. Nothing. Maybe he had to bring it closer, almost burn the paper to reveal a hidden message. He lowered the letter, inch by inch. And yes, something appeared in the spaces between lines in the first paragraph. Two sentences only:

> *I do not trust Neville and have therefore fed him false Information.*
> *Expect the Team in October.*

Michael set the letter on the desk, exhaled hard, and rolled his shoulders back. Maybe the ranger had drawn a knife on Claude. Maybe he'd snuck up on him and hog-tied him, as he'd done to Spry. From what little Michael knew of Claude, he couldn't imagine Neville's twisted sense of humor forming a favorable impression on the Frenchman. Spry would be pleased with this latest development.

October, Claude had written. Well, now, that wasn't so far away. On the fingers of his hands, Michael could count the weeks until the Frenchman's arrival. He set Claude's letter afire, and while he watched it become acrid ash, his lips peeled back from his teeth. He hoped Claude was bringing Mathias Hale and his Indian cousins from Georgia. Those Indians had unfinished business with Fairfax.

He extinguished the candle, retrieved his proposal for ensuring William Hooper's safety, and left for the barracks to schedule surveillance on the tannery. After sending the first man over to relieve Spry, he headed for Craig's office via the Hooper house. As usual, one of the beefy fellows answered the door. For a change, he insisted that Michael wait for Mrs. Hooper on the front porch step.

When she arrived in the doorway, she was frowning. Strands of hair escaped her mobcap, which adorned her head at a crooked angle, and dust dotted her nose. In Lavinia's unexplained absence, Mrs. Hooper must have had to pitch in and help clean in preparation for her husband's arrival. He swept off his hat and bowed. "Good morning, madam." When he straightened, he spied the fellow who'd answered the door, now standing several feet behind Mrs. Hooper, his height giving Michael a clear view of his disdain for him in the curl of his lip.

She clasped her hands before her. "Good morning, Mr. Stoddard. Do forgive me for not inviting you in, but we're tidying the house, and that slave of mine, Lavinia, is nowhere to be found."

"Yes, of course, and actually that's what I came to speak with you about. The Eighty-Second has borrowed Lavinia and some other slaves for a few days." The disdain on Beefy's face changed to a smirk at Michael's announcement, as if he'd figured out the true reason why soldiers needed a young slave woman for a few days. Michael ignored him. "Mrs. Duncan and several other ladies need the slaves' assistance in preparation for—"

"—for the Wilmington ladies' dinner, of course." She clapped a hand to her forehead, then sighed. "Yes, yes, that's very important, but how I wish you'd taken her on the morrow instead. We're trying to get this cleaning done today, before my husband comes to town."

"I understand. With luck, she'll be returned to you early on the morrow."

"Well. Thank you for telling me." She propped her hands on her hips. "She's been attracted to Mr. Bellington's slave, Uno, and I admit I thought the worst of her—that she'd run off with him. That wasn't very charitable of me, was it?"

Michael smiled at how close she'd come to the truth. "Don't worry. I know exactly where she is. And speaking of the Bellingtons, do you know whether Sam Bellington is sweet on a young brunette?"

Mrs. Hooper nodded. "Her name is Deborah Flanders."

Triumph shot through Michael's veins. There was a Flanders family in town. He worked the miniature free of his pocket and turned it toward her. "Is this Miss Flanders?"

The eyes of Anne Hooper and her bodyguard bulged with recognition. Then both of them recovered a neutral expression. Mrs. Hooper cleared her throat. "No. No, that isn't Miss Flanders." She looked past his shoulder into the street.

"Who is she? I've a question for her."

"I thought I recognized her for an instant, but no. She's someone I don't know." Behind her, Beefy smiled and shrugged.

Without a doubt, they'd both recognized the brunette and were protecting her. To Michael, that meant she was probably associated with the rebel cause. He didn't feel like browbeating Mrs. Hooper or her bodyguard over the young woman that moment. Besides, there were other ways to learn her identity. He returned the miniature to his pocket.

Anne Hooper shifted from one foot to the other, her gaze having followed the path the miniature took to his pocket. "It's a lovely portrait, though. Where did you find it?"

Very well, they'd dance that gavotte. With a grin for her ill-concealed curiosity, he lowered his hat to his head. "Thank you for your time, madam. Enjoy your house-tidying. I shall send Lavinia back to you as soon as possible."

Chapter Twelve

GODS, CRAIG'S OFFICE was stuffy that morning. Michael took his customary stance opposite the table from his commander, who was engrossed in reading a letter, and suppressed the urge to fan his face with his hat. Splayed out on the floor beside the major, a bulldog named Trouble snoozed, oblivious to the heat.

Craig set the letter aside. That was when Michael noticed his pursed lips and the tautness immobilizing his face. He stiffened.

"Mr. Stoddard. Punctual, as usual."

"Sir." Michael glanced at the letter. "Ill news?"

"From Colonel Balfour. Rebels have captured another of our supply trains in the South Carolina backcountry, thanks to a spy or two in our midst, possibly from that bloody Ambrose ring. I'd give my eye teeth to know the source of the information leak."

"Sir." Michael understood that the major's distress wasn't about only lost wagons of supplies. Too few men had guarded the train because the King's might was stretched thin in South Carolina. And that meant Colonel Balfour's letter also contained another "no" in response to Major Craig's plea to send him troops from South Carolina.

Thank God for trained militia leaders like Colonel Fanning. But even Fanning and his loyalist fighters were no substitute for the rock-solid dependability of the King's regulars.

Craig tried to straighten his sweat-wrinkled waistcoat. "Your proposal to ensure Mr. Hooper's safety?"

Michael handed it to him. He and Spry, who stood nearby, remained silent and still while Craig opened the folded report and perused it. The dreaming bulldog's forepaws twitched a few times, and he snored.

With one fist on the proposal, Craig looked up. "The rebels have switched the meeting site for Mr. Hooper again. Here's the new location." He passed a slip of paper scripted with directions to Michael. With his handkerchief he blotted a bead of sweat rolling down the side of his face. "They also changed the time to seven o'clock in the morning, so you and your men will have to skip parade. They're afraid that loyalists have learned about the venture and will sabotage the site or assassinate Mr. Hooper *en route*." His brows bunched like battling caterpillars. "With whom have you discussed this assignment?"

Michael nodded his head toward his assistant. "Just Spry, sir. And Mr. Fairfax, of course."

"Not with any men you've selected for the assignment?"

"No, sir. I shall apprise them of the necessary details after we've set out on the morrow."

"Excellent." Craig again struggled with his waistcoat. "It doesn't sound as though we've an information leak on our side. Apparently the rebels are just being excessively cautious and suspicious, as if we've no moral fiber whatsoever." He skimmed over Michael's proposal one final time.

Information leak. Which of Michael's men from yesterday's patrol had wagged his tongue with details of the murder scene?

In a brisk motion, the major scooped the pages together in a stack and tapped them on end to align them. "This all looks good, Mr. Stoddard. Do you have any questions?"

"No, sir."

"Best of luck to you, then." Tension in his expression subsided, and a faint smile moved over his lips. "I look forward to meeting Mr. Hooper first thing on the morrow when you return to town. You and Spry are dismissed."

Spry was so quiet while he and Michael trotted downstairs that Michael glanced at him when they reached the street. "What's on your mind, lad?"

"Sir, Major Craig seems a bit impressed with Mr. Hooper. The fellow's a criminal."

"True, but he's a high-ranking criminal with a great deal of influence."

"Yes, sir." Spry sighed. "I admit that when I joined the Army last year, I wasn't expecting to have to guard the life of a Signer. Not in a hundred years would I have believed it." He grinned. "Digging latrines, yes. Chopping firewood, of course. Marching all day, absolutely." He paused. "Of course, I do enjoy criminal investigation."

"And as soon as we return Mr. Hooper to his cohorts all safe and sound, we'll go back to it."

While the major had examined his proposal, the gravity of the situation had finally settled on Michael. Guarding Hooper would require a great deal of concentration and vigilance. The remainder of that day must be spent notifying each soldier involved of his special duty rotation and gathering supplies and horses needed for the trip. It was a tremendous amount of busy work to complete in one Wednesday. The subsequent days promised to be even more hectic.

If Fairfax wasn't Bellington's murderer, what were the odds that he'd correctly identify the killer—?

No. No. Michael forced the tangle of thoughts and frustration out to arms' length. Until Hooper was gone again from Wilmington, he mustn't concentrate on finding the financier's killer. Before supper he'd check in on Uno; he owed the slave a visit. He'd also ask Kate if she knew the woman pictured in the miniature. And he had soldiers watching the tannery. But he must let the remainder of the investigation—such as following up with his patrol about leaking information—go for a few days, as much as he detested having to do so.

* * *

A thunderstorm pounded Wilmington mid-afternoon. Civilians and soldiers who could do so sought shelter. The streets became muddy streams. Half an hour later, the sun returned. Steam from the mud mingled with wood smoke from cook fires. Flies swarmed over manure in the streets and harassed people and animals.

Pondering how to swap shifts for three soldiers on Thursday, Michael stumped up Market Street through the humid stenches of fish, smoke, and tar. Several geese honked at him. He ignored them. He'd posted the special assignment duty rotation in the barracks. Now he hoped a loyalist on Third Street could loan them his mount, as Thursday's white-flag party was still one horse short. The sleep deficit from the previous night weighed on his shoulders. He straightened his back with a groan and fanned away a fly that had followed him out of the barracks.

Two seconds before the chaise creaked up beside him, he smelled fire and death. With a jerk of his head to the right, he found himself staring at the soot-streaked sneer of Fairfax. His shoulders tensed. He kept walking.

Fairfax paced the horse at the speed of Michael's stride and pitched his voice low, so the people they passed on the street couldn't hear them. "Well, well, well. You've finally seen the sense of restricting that rapscallion's comings and goings."

"What are you talking about?" Michael kept his voice low, too.

"Lieutenant Neville, of course. So he's in the area? It's been months since I've seen him." The rattlesnake chuckled. "How I'd appreciate the opportunity to chat with him again. There's so much he could tell me."

"No." Michael glowered at him. "Neville's going to the provost marshal when I get my hands on him." Maybe Fairfax did know that the ranger had witnessed his depravities.

"A pity. He won't receive the justice he deserves from a court martial." The angelic light burned in Fairfax's eyes. "And the Ambrose ring will continue to plague us in South Carolina. He's an active leader, I'm certain of it. If only I could learn the names of a few more leaders or agents."

Michael knew the kind of "justice" Neville could expect from Fairfax. Low and firm, he said, "Court martial." He also knew that Fairfax hadn't sought him out merely to natter about Neville. Beneath the stenches of burned timber and death on him, Michael smelled wet wool. The thunderstorm had soaked the investigation party out at Bellington's estate, too. He swatted at the fly again and scowled at Fairfax. "What the devil do you want?"

"I've finished out at the estate. I thought you'd like to know that we buried the remains of Mr. Bellington there as well as one of his slaves."

So both Otis and Tucker were dead. Michael expelled a breath and directed his gaze ahead for a few seconds, his shoulders bowed. Then he straightened. "How unfortunate another slave was murdered."

"Look at the other side of the shilling. We didn't bury the third slave."

Michael kept staring ahead so Fairfax wouldn't see what he knew. "He's probably lying dead out there, and you missed finding him."

"Oh, no. I suspect he may have walked away from the fire. Or ridden away. There's the matter of that missing horse." For several heartbeats, the chaise wheels sighed in the sandy dirt alongside Michael. Then Fairfax said, low and harsh, "Where is he, Stoddard? I consider him a murder suspect."

Just as Michael had feared would happen. He doubted that Uno was up to being interrogated and shot Fairfax a glare. "Even if I had him, I wouldn't let you near him." The fly made another annoying pass at him. His palm finally contacted it and whisked it toward Fairfax.

"Obstruction of justice?" Fairfax laughed. "Naturally, because you think I killed Mr. Bellington, don't you?" He stroked Michael's elbow with his riding crop.

Michael yanked the crop from his grasp and planted his feet. His blood boiled and his heart hammered. He fought to bring his breathing and pulse under control. "Did you?"

Fairfax laughed again, halted the chaise a few feet past him, and swiveled in the seat. "As soon as I saw Mr. Bellington's corpse, I knew exactly what went through your head yesterday afternoon." Fairfax leaned toward him. "Since then, you've been struggling to make evidence fit so you can incriminate me. You're a fool." With a languid motion, he fanned at the fly.

Fairfax was declaring his innocence of the murder. The mile-wide stubborn streak in Michael wasn't yet ready to let him relinquish his suspicions. He made his tone level. "You drove out there on Monday not long before Mr. Bellington was murdered."

"Is that what the spineless Mr. Hickory told you?"

"No." Michael jutted his chin toward him. "It's what the wheel tracks from your chaise told me."

"Ooh." Fairfax doused his smile and drew back inside the chaise. "There's a spark of intelligence in the old boy."

"What time did you make the trip?"

"That's none of your concern. I'm the investigator. I shall ask the questions."

Michael flung the crop to the side of the road, far enough away that Fairfax would have to climb out of the chaise and walk over to retrieve it, and closed the distance between them. "Well, then, make certain you track down Mr. Hickory, who took passage on the *Barbara Bea* after breakfast this morning."

Fairfax resumed sneering. "That sniveling worm of an Indian has an alibi. I questioned both his servants and two clients." The fly tried to settle on his ear, and he shook his head. "And he hasn't the stones to hire out the murder of Mr. Bellington to a common criminal."

Fairfax hadn't mentioned Sam Bellington. Maybe he was unaware of him. And that wasn't the only thing the other officer didn't seem to know about. "You're missing something—"

"No, *you* missed something!" Fairfax snarled, then lowered his voice again. "I know you glanced over the summary pages. That means you overlooked the greatest suspect of all, the man who owes the firm a tremendous amount of money. It's a good thing that Major Craig transferred the investigation to me."

Despite the heat and humidity, a wintry chill crawled through Michael. At the top of Fairfax's suspect list, even higher than Uno, was Kate's brother, Kevin. Within the day, the monster would be harassing Kate and her family in earnest. Murder in addition to tax evasion.

Damn. Had Kate moved all that whiskey? Never mind securing the extra horse for tomorrow. Michael must stop by the tavern as soon as possible today and warn Kate. He maintained his firm, even tone. "I see. You're building a case against him, just because he owes a large amount of money to Mr. Bellington. I hardly think Mr. Marsh is the sort of fellow who'd butcher a man, even over money."

"How naïve. This isn't just money. If he doesn't pay the loan, he forfeits the house in which he, his sister, and his aunt live. If the family also has debt, the tavern could be forfeited, too. Womenfolk turned out into the street—now that's incentive to kill." The fly buzzed near his hand.

If the family also has debt... Indeed, they did, the gambling debt of their uncle. But Michael still didn't swallow Fairfax's assertion. Surely debt hadn't turned Kevin into a killer. "You really suspect that Mr. Marsh and Uno teamed up to murder Mr. Bellington?"

"You really suspect that Mr. Hickory and I joined forces to murder Mr. Bellington?" Without shifting his stare from Michael, Fairfax slapped his hand downward and squashed the fly against the chaise. He shook his hand over the street. The dead fly fell into the sandy mud.

Michael, his chin still high, glanced at the fly. "When you find Mr. Hickory, make him show you where he hid the original summary pages. You sure as hell don't have them."

"How do you mean?" Fairfax lengthened his neck and wiped his palm on his handkerchief. "It appears you are withholding information from me on this investigation—obstructing the King's justice."

As soon as Fairfax could prove that, he'd sink Michael's credibility with it. Michael's pulse hopped about. "The pages you have are mere copies of the original summary pages. You overlooked something important on them. See for yourself." Michael crossed his arms high on his chest. "I'll be damned if I'll hold your hand in this investigation."

"Go rot, Stoddard." Fairfax glanced over Michael's shoulder, then narrowed his eyes. "Now fetch my crop over there."

Michael whispered, "Kiss my arse."

He continued up Market Street, then threw a glance over his shoulder to make sure Fairfax wasn't trying to run him down. Cane in hand, Fairfax had exited the chaise to recover the crop. Michael cut over one street to elude him, then headed toward White's Tavern.

Spry caught up with him halfway there and fell in beside him. "We got the final horse, sir!"

"Great news," Michael murmered. A look around showed him that Fairfax hadn't followed. He'd probably headed straight to his room to pore over the copied pages and deduce the clue to which Michael had alluded. That should buy Michael some time. He filled Spry in on the conversation with Fairfax.

They reached the tavern. No sooner had they circled around to the back when the rear door opened. Clayton exited, bag in hand, spotted them, and bustled toward them with a grin.

The surgeon's good spirits sent hope coursing through Michael's chest. Surely Clayton wouldn't look so chipper if his patient's condition had deteriorated. Michael waved him away from the din and traffic from the tavern's kitchen.

They convened in the back of the lot, in the shadow of a tool shed empty of people, where Michael resisted wrinkling his nose. Clayton also bore the stenches of fire and death, attesting to the challenges he'd encountered that day in Fairfax's party. Michael motioned for them to keep their voices low. "Good to see you."

"Likewise, Mr. Stoddard. And I'm pleased to report that although Uno still has a fever, it's reduced from what it was last night. Furthermore, his wound isn't suppurating. According to Lavinia, mid-afternoon he took some tea and broth."

"Huzzah!" Spry straightened to his full height.

"Yes, that's fine news."

"I'm certain that Lavinia's ministrations helped him, sir."

Michael nodded. "I made up a story for Mrs. Hooper, told her Lavinia would be returned first thing Thursday morning. Do you think that will be enough time?"

"Yes." Clayton nodded toward the tavern. "Lavinia's exhausted. I told her to rest. Uno's asleep, if you want to look in on him. But don't awaken him." Noting the way Michael shifted from one foot to the other, he wagged a forefinger in warning. "Sir, the next day will be crucial in his recovery. He must be allowed to have as much rest as he needs and not be troubled, and he especially mustn't be moved. That way his turn for the better will become well-established." The surgeon pursed his lips. "Whatever questions you have of him, wait until the morrow."

Michael lowered his shoulders. "All right." But Fairfax wouldn't wait until the morrow for his interrogation. He'd find a way to override Clayton's orders. How was Michael going to keep Uno hidden from Fairfax if he couldn't move him? For how long could he swear to secrecy the soldiers guarding Uno? If Fairfax called for an inquest of Michael's actions, those men would be forced to speak about guarding the witness.

His stomach gurgled. Divesting himself of the Bellington investigation was proving more difficult than he'd anticipated. And it was his own fault. The web he'd woven had grown tangled.

"In the mean time, I've a report for you from the estate of Mr. Bellington. Very interesting, sir, indeed, very interesting."

"Yes? Interesting in what way?"

"I can confidently say that Mr. Bellington didn't suffer for long and was dead before his house burned around him."

Michael frowned. "How is that?" One of Fairfax's victims who was flayed alive didn't die immediately. His prolonged agony was requisite to Fairfax's enjoyment.

"He didn't live long after being shot in the head, sir."

"In the head?" Michael recalled what he'd seen of the financier. He couldn't remember a head wound. Had he not noticed it because of the greater wound on Bellington's chest? No, surely a head wound would have showed up on that man's wig—

"I'm guessing that his wig wasn't on his head when he was shot in the temple. The killer replaced it afterwards, perhaps to hide the injury from initial observation." Clayton fished around in his pocket, withdrew two dented pistol balls, and handed them to Michael. "One of those I pulled from Uno's arm last night. The other I pulled from Mr. Bellington's knee."

Knee. Ah, that was more like Fairfax's style. Shoot the victim in the knee first to incapacitate him.

"My guess is that his knee was shot first. The fire obscured signs such as bruising, which would confirm that he struggled with his killer before he was overcome. The mutilation to his chest definitely occurred after he was unconscious and moribund. Probably after he'd been hoisted up, too."

Michael's gaze met that of his assistant, and he saw his own suspicions reflected there. It didn't sound like Fairfax had killed the financier. Fairfax's victims were conscious when he tortured them. Michael swallowed the rank taste of frustration.

Yet why had the murderer shot Bellington in the knee and carved up his chest—so like Fairfax? Why make sure Bellington was unconscious before starting the mutilation? Michael clicked the two pistol balls together in his palm. "I wager these came from the same weapon." He handed them to Spry, who examined them.

"Yes, sir." With a pleasant smile, Clayton extended his hand to Spry, and the private returned the balls to him.

"Tell me about the dead slave your patrol found, Clayton."

"Oh, you heard about that, eh? Multiple stab wounds and a slit throat."

"Hmm. Like the slave my patrol found yesterday."

"Indeed? From what I saw, sir, I suspect that the killer stalked this fellow and stabbed at him until blood loss weakened him enough to be caught. Rather like the way wolves attack prey."

What a horrible way to die. Michael studied the surgeon for a moment. "From what you saw out there today, speculate for me. Construct the sequence of events at Mr. Bellington's estate late Monday."

"Certainly. The murderer killed the dogs first to prevent their warning the men." Clayton stared into the middle distance and pondered a moment.

Of course the dogs had been killed first. But Michael still wasn't sure how the criminal had done it without warning Bellington and his slaves.

"Then, sir, I'd say that he stalked and killed Tucker and Otis outside, likely one at a time. The slave I examined was bruised, so he'd put up a struggle." Clayton's voice took on an almost dreamy quality. "The killer then gained entrance to the house. Uno must have startled him inside. Rather than drawing his knife, he shot the slave, but Uno escaped. Perhaps the killer broke off a chase for Uno when he encountered Mr. Bellington. He barricaded the two of them in the library so Uno couldn't render assistance. They struggled, and the wig was knocked off. The murderer had more than one loaded pistol, and Mr. Bellington's knee was shot to keep him from escaping. Then he was shot through the head." Clayton nodded to himself. "The killer would have made a good search in the house for Uno at that point. Not finding him, though, he returned to the library, hoisted up Mr. Bellington, replaced the wig, carved up his chest, then set the house afire. Perhaps another, longer search for Uno outside, but—" The surgeon shrugged. "By then, I suspect the evening was advanced."

Michael said, "Why do you think the killer didn't take the horses?"

"Horses weren't what he was after, sir. And perhaps he was still searching for Uno."

"Any idea why the murderer mutilated Mr. Bellington's chest?"

"Not really, except that it must have been a very angry man who did it, Mr. Stoddard. And it troubles me that Uno stated his attacker was one of us—"

"Not one of us. Someone disguised as one of us. We know that now."

"Ah. Good. I'd hate to think that the regiment harbors a lunatic. So perhaps the chest was a statement of the murderer's fury."

"Thank you. This was all very helpful, Clayton."

The surgeon's eyes sparkled. "Perhaps I could be a criminal investigator."

"You wouldn't like it. Most of the time, it's boring."

"That's too bad."

"Have you time early on the morrow to look in on the patient once more?"

Clayton puffed out his chest. "I shall make the time. And if that's all for now, sir, I'll be heading back to rid myself of the smell of dead men."

"That's a very good idea."

The surgeon gave a nod to the tavern. "By all means, do look in on Uno, sir. I know you'd like to see for yourself how he's improved. But remember, don't wake him up."

Chapter Thirteen

THE USUAL CLAMOR of conversation, laughter, and fiddle music spilled from the tavern's open windows and back door. Michael and Spry jumped aside for a serving wench who bustled out carrying a tray heaped with empty tankards. As soon as the way was clear, Michael darted in, followed by the private.

About fifteen feet away, Kate and Kevin's aunt was immersed in conversation with a server. Michael prodded Spry toward the stairs, before Aunt Rachel spotted them. She loved to gossip with him.

On the second floor, the noise of jollification wasn't as loud. Stationed down at Uno's sickroom, the soldier on duty came alert. Michael and Spry arrived at the closed door of the middle room, and Michael pushed the door open far enough for the two of them to get a look at the interior. Both men exhaled with relief. All crates of whiskey were gone, and the floor had been swept clean, showing no sign of what had been stored there. Good for Kate.

He closed the door, and he and Spry continued to Uno's room. Michael returned the guard's salute. "Report, Henshaw."

"Sir." In a voice just loud enough for them to hear, the guard said, "Jackson and I came on duty a few minutes ago. He and the two slaves are inside. You just missed the surgeon."

"I chatted with him in the yard." Michael removed his hat. "I shall have a peek inside." The private stepped out of his way.

The stuffy room, dimmed by curtains over the window, smelled of soap, saddle leather, and a chamberpot that needed emptying. Michael shuffled one pace to the side of the doorway, gaze sweeping past saddles and tackle that he'd sent up via Spry to sequester away for the Hooper assignment, and over the slave asleep on the bed. Jackson, still wearing his head bandage, made to stand, and Michael motioned him down in his chair. From where he stood, he could see the easy rise and fall of Uno's chest. He leaned toward Jackson. "How's the head?" he murmured.

"Well enough, sir." The short soldier kept his voice down. "Aches a bit, that's all."

Michael patted his shoulder. "There's the good lad. Today you've the perils of light duty."

"As well as on the morrow, sir. I've the final surveillance shift at the tannery."

Behind Michael, Spry had entered the room and set the chamberpot outside. As he closed them all in, Michael said, "That's in the wee hours of the morning. No falling asleep for that duty, Jackson."

The private grinned. "No, sir. Er, do you suppose you could have some food sent up for us?"

"Let me see what I can do." Motion in the corner drew Michael's attention to Lavinia, who'd risen on one elbow from a pallet of blankets on the floor and blinked at them with sleepy eyes. He crouched before her and kept his voice low. "I appreciate all you've done for Uno. You may have saved his life."

She hung her head. "Must go back to Miz Hooper now." Her voice was thick with fatigue.

"You rest." He held out a hand to stop her from rising. "I told Mrs. Hooper that we borrowed you to help in preparation for the supper party. She doesn't expect you back until dawn on the morrow."

Lavinia sighed. "Thank you, suh." She relaxed back onto the blankets and closed her eyes.

Michael rose, tiptoed to Uno's side, and set his hat atop the empty washbasin. A little sweat beaded above the slave's upper lip and on his brow, but he was no longer covered in it, as he'd been twelve hours earlier. Clayton had changed the bandage. What Michael could see of the wounded arm looked healthy, not swollen. His shoulders felt lighter.

Uno's eyelids fluttered, and he looked at Michael, sleep tugging on his lids. This time there was no fear in his expression. "You—you helped me last night," he whispered.

"I did." Michael bent closer. "Captain Stoddard, at your service, Uno."

"The investigator?"

"Yes. You're safe in here. How does your arm feel?"

"Aches. Surgeon poked it, changed bandage." Uno blinked to stay awake.

Michael nodded in sympathy. Uno was no longer delirious, an excellent sign. "Well, your job for at least the next day is to rest here and heal."

"Yessuh."

"I'm pleased to see you looking much better." Michael made his tone casual. "And Captain Fairfax is also concerned for you and may stop in to see you later today." He kept a keen eye on Uno's reaction.

"Yessuh." The slave yawned, calm. "He visited at the house, talked with Mistuh Jasper. I served them coffee in the parlor."

Uno had to be referring to Monday. Significantly, mention of Fairfax didn't distress the slave. Michael kept his expression neutral while imagining Fairfax in a cordial visit with the financier. Maybe he'd decided to approach Bellington with a carrot and not a stick. As Kate had observed, Fairfax could be quite charming when the need presented itself. "How long did he stay?"

"Not long. When Mistuh Sam and me rode to Market, the captain drove back to town with us."

It didn't sound as though Fairfax had alarmed Uno or either of the Bellingtons. "After you returned from Market, did Mister Sam stay for supper?"

"Nosuh." The slave yawned again. "He headed home to New Berne."

New Berne? That was four days north of Wilmington. According to Jonas Hickory, Bellington's nephew had ridden one day south to take care of his mother's estate near Brunswick. Damn. Hickory had done more lying. Michael wagered that the financier hadn't sent any messages, either, and Sam Bellington didn't yet know of the murders.

On the bed, Uno stiffened, and his eyes widened. "Mistuh Jasper! I remember now!"

Michael pressed his palm to the slave's shoulder on his uninjured arm. "I'm sorry—"

"Dead, ain't he?" Uno panted. "Otis and Tucker, too. I recollect!" Sweat popped out all over the slave's face, and he gripped Michael's forearm. "It was a redcoat, suh—"

"Was it Captain Fairfax?"

"Oh, nosuh, not him! You got to arrest the killer!"

Michael shot a glance at his assistant, whose curt nod was acknowledgement that he'd heard Uno exonerate Fairfax. The slave pawed at his arm. Michael turned back to him, his pulse jumpy. "Give me a description, then. His hair color. His build." He felt the coil of tension in the slave.

Uno's gaze darted about. "Tall. Lean. Hair—not like yours." He trembled.

His skin had grown hot in the few seconds they'd spoken. In no way was he up to an interrogation. Clayton was prudent to advise against agitating the patient. Michael pulled out of Uno's grasp and straightened.

Hair—not like yours. In the tannery, he'd pulled a strand of golden hair from the teeth of the comb. Was their fugitive blond?

Uno's head lolled to the side so he was facing the wall. "C-Crazy man. Demon."

"Don't worry, my good fellow. Go back to sleep and heal." Michael took a step from the bedside. Silent sobs quivered the slave's chest. Michael glanced at Lavinia, wondering if she were awake to comfort Uno, but the Hoopers' slave was sound asleep. "Thank you, Uno." How lame his gratitude sounded. The man had lost his home and his people.

Private Jackson's eyes were wide over Uno's testimony. Was he the member of Michael's patrol who'd blabbed information about Bellington? This wasn't the moment to question him—not while Uno could hear. Michael frowned at the soldier. "You will keep everything you heard to yourself, Jackson."

"Oh, yes, sir!"

At the door, Spry said, low, "Sam Bellington lives in New Berne, sir?"

"It appears that way." And it was one of several conflicting pieces of information in this investigation. Had Sam Bellington escaped the carnage? Was his uncle's killer after him, too, or had Sam been a co-conspirator in the murders? Perhaps they should be looking for a tall, lean blond fellow who was enraged enough by Jasper Bellington to murder him and his slaves brutally— and who wore that bloodstained linen coat well enough to masquerade as one of the King's finest. Somehow Michael must follow up with this information, even though the Hooper assignment was taking up so much of his time and attention.

If he apprised Fairfax of all he'd learned, the other officer would insist upon interrogating Uno and likely incarcerate him as a murder suspect. Or Fairfax, who suspected Kevin Marsh, might arrive at the tavern in the mood for a thorough search, having realized how Hickory had deceived him, and find Uno. The slave wasn't yet strong enough to hold up to interrogation. Until he was a day further along in his recovery, Michael must continue sliding along the slippery path of insubordination and obstruction of justice that he'd brought upon himself.

His gut felt like it was loaded with jagged rocks. Swallowing a bitter taste, he pointed his assistant to the door.

Henshaw had a clean, empty chamberpot waiting for them as well as a bucket of water for the room's washbasin. While Spry toted the items in, an idea came to Michael about how to keep Fairfax from entering Uno's room. Outside, the door to the sickroom closed, Michael addressed Henshaw. "I suspect that Captain Fairfax will stop by during your shift. When he orders you to stand aside so he can enter, you must say the following. 'You'll have to clear that with Mr. Stoddard first, sir. He's stored gear and supplies for his special assignment in here and ordered me to refuse entry to anyone without his express permission.' Repeat that, Henshaw."

"Sir." The soldier stared past Michael and Spry, cleared his throat, and repeated it verbatim.

After Lord Cornwallis's army refurbished in Wilmington in April, the Eighty-Second no longer had a surplus of equipment. Fairfax, who'd arrived in one of Cornwallis's wagons of the wounded, knew that. The veracity of Michael's story was bolstered by the fact that he'd actually sent those saddles and tackle to Uno's room earlier, where they wouldn't be appropriated by the rest of the regiment.

The ruse might work, buy Uno time to heal so he could hold up to Fairfax's interrogation. "Very good, Henshaw."

Kate awaited them before the closed door to the middle room, hands clasped atop her apron, back straight. As Michael and Spry walked to her, he spotted the full chamberpot near the top of the stairs. Kate, too, had been taking care of Uno. "Thank you for all you've done, Kate."

"You're welcome." Her face was drawn with exhaustion. "Soon as I empty that pot over there, I'll bring up some food."

Michael bowed with gratitude. "You know a great number of people in the Cape Fear. I've a few odd questions for you. Have you a moment?"

"Very well." They followed her into the second room. She walked past the foot of the bed to open the curtains and window. Spry shut the door and took up position before it. At the window, Kate faced them and gestured to the empty spot on the floor where the crates had been stacked. "No doubt you're wondering where I put the whiskey."

Hair that escaped her mobcap picked up light from the window and became strands of gold. Gold like the hair in the comb, like her brother's hair. Uneasiness stirred in Michael's breast. Surely Fairfax was stumping for the first explanation that crossed his mind, not giving a damn to look past the debt on that summary page. Michael knew Kevin; he didn't have the temperament of a murderous man—especially not one who would kill with such rage. He gave Kate his best disarming smile. "Shall I guess where you put it?"

"No. Mr. Smedes has it. All of it."

The wainwright, Smedes, had been part of their smuggling operation back in the spring, hauling whiskey for them in his wagon in the dead of night every two weeks or so. Michael wasn't surprised that he was still involved. "Good."

She rubbed one eye. "I told Aunt what was happening with Uno so she can help me."

He nodded. "Does she also know about the whiskey?" At the press of Kate's lips, he scowled. "Kate, for God's sake, you're exhausted. You want sleep? Get her help with everything."

"All right, all right. I shall tell her."

"You may receive a visit from Mr. Fairfax today."

Her eyes narrowed on him. "Why?"

Reluctant to tell her that Kevin was Fairfax's top suspect, he rolled his eyes. "Oh, some piece of circumstantial evidence that he's uncovered. He also thinks that Uno played a role in Mr. Bellington's murder. If he finds him here, he'll haul him out of that sickroom and throw him in irons, likely injuring his arm again."

Kate pointed in the direction of the sickroom. "He'll see your man down there guarding the door. If that doesn't look suspicious, I don't know what does."

"My man's guarding supplies hoarded for my special mission on the morrow."

"Supplies? Special mission?" Kate's nose wrinkled, as if she smelled the half-truth.

"It's why I was removed from the Bellington investigation. My new mission has priority over the murder investigation. If Mr. Fairfax asks Major Craig for permission to enter that room, he won't get it."

Color rose to her cheeks, and her eyes flashed. "So you and Captain Fairfax are using my tavern for a battleground?"

"Well, no, I didn't say—"

"I won't have it! You men go squabble somewhere else and leave me out of it."

Although Michael's instincts warned him to drop the subject and move on to his questions about the linen coat and the miniature, he pitched his tone to soothe. "If he wants to perform a brief search while he's here in the tavern, just cooperate with him."

"A search? Great heavens, if he does that at the most popular time for my customers, I'll lose business! Losing money isn't an option for me. I no longer have the whiskey as a buffer."

Michael felt his ears grow hot. Gods, what an inept oaf he was. Knowing that Kate was in a financial corner, he shouldn't have said anything at all about Fairfax.

She tapped her palm with the forefinger of her other hand. "See here. No one interrupts my business. I shall file a complaint with Major Craig about this."

Jove's arse. He needed a complaint filed against him like he needed a hole in his head. And unless he calmed her down, he'd never get her cooperation for his questions. "Please don't do that, Kate. It isn't certain that Captain Fairfax will stop by. In fact, I shouldn't have mentioned him at all."

She blasted him with a scowl. "He'll certainly get a piece of my mind if he walks in that door with any intention other than to be a paying customer."

He practiced more of that soothing tone. "I do apologize for upsetting you." Her scowl didn't budge, and his ears stayed hot. Women seemed to appreciate it when men discussed feelings. He swallowed in a throat that felt too tight, then squirmed. "It was insensitive of me."

Her shoulders relaxed, and her expression softened. She shifted her gaze to the furniture. "I accept your apology. You said you have some questions for me?"

A sigh of relief left him. "Yes." And what was the smoothest way to segue into those questions? He thought about how Spry had wondered whether the coat was a costume in a play and took a deep breath. "Regarding Friday night's supper party, is it true that there's a short theater production planned?"

She shook her head. "No. I'm aware of all the activities we've planned. There won't be a play."

"But you and I are supposed to be king and queen for the night or some rubbish like that. What if the other ladies wanted to sneak in an activity to surprise us?"

She opened her mouth then shut it and frowned at him. "What sort of production?"

"Something with redcoats in it." He smirked at Spry. "Er, Spry, do you recall what we heard? Those coats, remember?"

Spry, bless him, rose to the fluff. "I believe it was dancing redcoats, sir."

Michael snapped his fingers. "That's it. Dancing redcoats, a single-file line of them across the floor. Funny, eh?"

She rubbed her temples. "Ye gods, the Eighty-Second is going to dance for us."

"Not soldiers from the Eighty-Second. Civilian men from Wilmington dressed as soldiers." He chuckled. "Where are you getting the uniforms, though? We aren't loaning you ours. You want my men to march naked to their posts? Think of your poor aunt's heart."

Her eyes widened in response to what was clearly a realization triggered by his words. "Of course! Alice Farrell must be in on this."

"Ah." Michael nodded, following her lead. "Mrs. Farrell again. I should have suspected."

Kate beamed. "There were some old costume uniforms from a play the men performed back in seventy-four for Governor Martin. Mrs. Farrell's husband and brother were in the play. So was Kevin."

Yes, costumes for a play. Then he gaped at her news. Mrs. Farrell's brother. "That bookish astronomer was in a play?"

"Mr. Carlisle is quite talented." She batted her eyelashes. "He composes music, too."

The way she spoke of Carlisle sent a twinge of jealousy through Michael. Had the astronomer courted her? Behind him, Spry said in a sunny tone, "Sir, it sounds as though they still have those costumes from the play seven years ago stored somewhere, and that's what might be used Friday night. Are they made of wool, Mrs. Duncan?"

"No, linen. And to my knowledge, Mrs. Farrell was the last person in possession of them, so she must be the culprit here."

The bloodstained coat in the tannery must have come from Mrs. Farrell's collection. Michael wondered whether he and Spry had time to visit her that afternoon before her husband's tobacco shop closed, find out where she stored those costumes and who was in the play, and perhaps learn how the killer had accessed them. He disciplined the excitement in his blood so he could finish out the thread of conversation. "Then we must wait and see whether Mrs. Farrell springs a surprise upon us Friday."

She gave a breathy little chuckle. "You fellows should be forewarned. The sight of naked redcoats won't bother my aunt at all."

Michael and Spry laughed. When Kate joined them, Michael thought how pleasant it was to see merriment ease the strain from her lovely face. Spry mouthing the word "miniature" to him brought him back to business. "Oh, one more thing, Kate." He fished around in his pockets for the little portrait, having removed the silk ribbon that originally suspended it. "Right before we threw a rebel spy in the pen yesterday, we—er—removed this miniature from his possession. He refused to tell us who the lady in the picture was, so I showed it to Mrs. Hooper. She knows but isn't telling." He shifted the picture toward Kate. "A rebel, no doubt. Who is she?"

Kate's eyes widened with recognition, then her nose wrinkled. "Naomi Levy. A rebel indeed. And that fellow you threw in the pen yesterday is likely also a Jew."

A Jew? Michael's eyebrows rose. Every Jew he'd met in America was a rebel. Not surprising, considering the persecution they endured across the Atlantic—persecution the American "patriots" didn't extend to them. Not yet, at least. Had a Jew borrowed money from Bellington, then killed him—a blond Jew? "How do you know Mrs. Levy?"

Kate stared at the miniature a moment longer before turning her back on them at the window. "It's *Miss* Levy. Her father's a wealthy silversmith in Charles Town. Last year, she was betrothed to an attorney near Boston. Something went wrong with the arrangement, and the betrothal was called off." Kate fluttered her hand, as if to dismiss events. "We'd had some stormy weather, and her ship put in here for a few days to wait for calmer seas. That was when the news caught up with her. She returned to Charles Town straightaway."

Still trying to fit the pieces of evidence together in his head, Michael returned the miniature to his pocket and grinned. "Perhaps her fiancé turned out to be a blond-haired Gentile."

"No, I'm sure he was a dark-haired Jew. Jews marry Jews. And I lost track of how many times I reminded Kevin of that."

Michael's head yanked back, as if he'd been slapped. "Kevin?" Behind him, he heard Spry suck in a soft breath of shock.

"Yes, Kevin." Kate ran her forefinger along the windowsill, examined it for dust, and wiped the sill with her apron corner. "That silly goose brother of mine fell in love with Miss Levy while she was here."

Michael's gaze slid to Spry. In his assistant's expression, he saw his own disbelief and suspicion reflected. He swiveled and studied the back of Kate's head, now bowed, and thought of the blond hair in the comb, and the clothing neatly folded for a long trip. A trip to Charles Town?

"He wrote her twice. She wrote him back once and sent him a miniature like the one you just showed me." She sighed. "What money she must have to favor so many men with portraits."

Michael's stomach felt as if someone had punched it. Ye gods. What else could he possibly say to Kate?

Those must be Kevin's belongings they'd found in the tannery. Clearly Kate's little brother wasn't ten miles north distilling whiskey. But surely he wouldn't have left Wilmington without all his traveling gear. Where the devil was he? Michael resisted the urge to ask Kate whether Kevin had a key to the tannery or knew how to pick locks.

She braced one hand on the window frame. "I lost track of how many conversations I had with him on the topic this past year. 'Kevin, Jews don't marry Gentiles unless maybe a Gentile man shows himself to be quite wealthy and promises to raise the children as Jews. Kevin, you're just a manager of a tavern in Wilmington. You don't have any money.'"

Oh, damn. Yes, Kevin did have money. The revelation of how he'd acquired his money would devastate Kate. Unless she was in on the entire horrific mess.

Had Kevin murdered his creditor? Had he made a deal with Jonas Hickory to kill his business partner in exchange for having the debt written off the books? If so, why had Hickory erased another name from the books and left Kevin's name in? Had he double-crossed Kevin?

How much of this did Kate know?

Her head still bowed, Kate pleated her apron and gave a weak laugh. "Thank goodness he finally came to his senses this spring. It was after I had a long talk with him. 'Kevin, I know you dream of a life with her, but we don't have the wealth to make dreams come true. We were born in Wilmington, and we'll die in Wilmington. We own a tavern and a house—nothing more.'" She wiped her cheek with the back of her hand. "'Dream all you like. But at the end of the day, don't forget to pick up the empty tankards.'"

Instinct told Michael that the correspondence between Kevin and Naomi Levy was far more extensive than three letters. He suspected that Kevin, understanding his sister's disapproval, had continued wooing the woman in secret. Perhaps he had a discreet arrangement with someone in town to help him conceal Miss Levy's letters from his sister and aunt. As there'd been no letters among his belongings in the tannery, either he'd burned all of hers, or he had a pile of them hidden somewhere.

And with his beloved a member of the rebel ranks, it meant that Kevin was probably no longer neutral in the war.

In his head, Michael knew his duty. However, his heart was quite the laggard and pinched him for having a difference of opinion. His gaze tracked to his assistant. Spry nodded. "Uh, sir, I'd best take that chamberpot downstairs and empty it before someone trips on it."

An officer couldn't have a more perceptive assistant than Nick Spry. "Thank you. And shut the door behind you."

Chapter Fourteen

THE DOOR LATCHED shut on Spry's departure. Michael made his way to Kate's side and gazed out the window with her. "Ah. Dreams. It's astounding how rebel leaders talk of this land as a world of golden opportunity for the common man, even the poorest of men, and only the King's oppression stands in the way of everyone and their dreams."

"Yes." Kate gave a soft snort. "What's truly astounding is how many people believe them. I did ten years ago, when I inherited the tavern and married Daniel. Those dreams didn't last long." She glanced at him, then resumed her stare out the window. "But you've done well for yourself in the Army. It's obviously one of the few routes a worthy man can still take to make his dreams come true."

He laughed easily. "One of the final things I told my parents before I left to sail to America was that I'd be a general in ten years. Here I was a lieutenant for almost a third of my life."

She faced him, one eyebrow lifted. "But you've just been promoted to captain. I can imagine you rising to general and commanding the respect of all your officers and men."

"From captain it's three giant steps to general." He met her gaze. "The truth is that the Army has the quaint custom of ripping a recruit's dreams from his head and heart, pressing a hot iron to them to reshape them in an image suitable to the Army, then thrusting them back inside the soldier. 'There, lad, now you're a man. Thank us for it.'"

The insides of her eyebrows tilted upward. "How sad. I'd no idea it was that way."

"One of the many secrets that recruiters don't share." The urge pressured him to warn her that Fairfax considered Kevin his top murder suspect. He held his tongue; he'd learned from that scene a few minutes earlier.

She took his hand, gave it a gentle squeeze, and didn't let go. "When Kevin was a youth, he thought military life might be his way out of Wilmington's mediocrity." Kate gave a half-hearted laugh. "He spent time with Governor Martin's militia. After those 'patriots' ran the governor out, he drilled with their militia."

Michael made himself relax while his mind raced. Had Kevin been with the militia long enough to confer upon himself the semblance of military bearing when he donned a linen costume? In the dark on Monday night, had the illusion been complete enough to convince a terrified, wounded Uno that his attacker was a King's man? He turned to Kate and took her other hand. "And how long did that dream last for him?"

"No more than a year. Of course, the militia put pressure on him, like they did with every able-bodied man." She closed the distance between them. "About three years ago, he sprained his ankle. He sprained it several more times until they ceased regarding him as able-bodied."

How clever of Kevin.

He held her gaze. Background noise from the tavern faded. For a moment, the world held only the two of them—not the first time that tranquility had overtaken him in her presence. He murmured, "You miss your brother."

"Mm-hmm. But he'll be back soon enough."

The openness of her expression and posture spoke to Michael in a way her words could never have done, convinced him that if Kevin had killed Bellington and his slaves and planned to ride off for Charles Town, Kate didn't have an inkling of it. Nor did she know about that huge loan. No, she believed he'd be returning to Wilmington by Friday with more whiskey.

Where the devil were Kevin, his horse, and all the money he'd borrowed? Conflict tensed Michael's stomach. Again he considered blurting to her what Fairfax thought of Kevin; again he stopped himself. Fairfax had the uncanny ability to sniff out when someone was lying, especially to protect another person. If he confronted Kate, accused her brother of the murders, and sprang the ugly surprise of the loan on her, her shock and confusion might exonerate her.

She blinked, as if shaking off an enchantment. "All right. I'm not going to put this off any longer. There's something I need to discuss with you."

Oh, no. He must have misjudged her a moment earlier. Here it came, her admission of her brother's guilt. He steadied himself.

Her expression grew resolute. "It's fairly clear that you and I—that we— you know, we fancy each other."

It took him a few seconds to wrap his mind around the unexpected direction she'd taken. "'Fancy.' That sounds like a word for dreamers. Moments ago, you and I didn't sound much like dreamers."

"You're right. We aren't dreamers." She dropped her gaze to their clasped hands, then opened her mouth to speak.

Footsteps in the hallway outside preceded a rapid knock on the door. Spry said, "Mr. Stoddard, are you still in there?"

A beastly time for an interruption. Then Michael registered the way anxiety had yanked up the pitch of his assistant's voice. He and Kate would have to finish the conversation later. He released her hands and walked to the door. Head and shoulders stiff, Spry stood just outside. "Yes? What is it, Spry?"

The private glanced past him to Kate, then lowered his voice. "Apologies for interrupting, sir. We've a visitor." He stepped to one side and left the doorway open.

Only one person roused that level of tension in Spry. Cold made a rush up Michael's back. He eyed Kate. "Stay in here. I shall handle this." He exited, closed the bedroom door, and strode for the stairs with Spry.

Fairfax was already halfway up, making good time with his cane. After rolling back his shoulders, Michael descended to intercept him. Three steps down, he saw Fairfax's head lift.

"As you were." Eyes like green frost, Fairfax continued his ascent. "Let's chat up there. Not quite so noisy."

He wore a clean shirt and had scrubbed off the day's grime. What a pity that Spry had removed that full chamberpot at the top of the stairs. Michael returned to the second floor and, with his assistant, stood across the hallway past the first door. Above the noise of merriment below, Fairfax's thumping progress continued. Again, Michael steadied himself.

At the top of the stairs, Fairfax ignored Spry and nodded at Michael. "I see what you mean now. It appears that the summary sheets I received from Mr. Hickory were hastily copied prior to his giving them to me. As I've no access to the original records, I cannot help but wonder how many client names he might have intentionally omitted. At least one, it appears..."

Michael clapped softly. "Bravo."

"...and whose names you saw on those original records."

"Like you, I never saw the original records."

The right side of Fairfax's lip curled, and his left eyebrow hiked, creating a diagonal slash of disbelief across his face. He slithered his gaze between Michael and Spry to the sickroom door. Then he entered the first guestroom and nosed about.

Michael made his tone as bored as possible. "For what are you looking?"

"Hmm. It might be what Henshaw's guarding down there."

"I sincerely hope not." Michael let contempt drip into his voice.

The door to the second guestroom squeaked open. A pillow tucked beneath one arm, Kate exited wearing her business face, pushed past Michael and Spry, and huffed to the doorway of the first room. "Excuse me, Captain, I will thank you to leave the room immediately." No longer smiling, Fairfax withdrew to the head of the stairs and observed Kate when she breezed in. Her voice, somewhat muffled, continued. "All three rooms are rented for tonight. It's ungentlemanly of you to invade the privacy of my paying customers." *Sans* pillow, she emerged, shut the door behind her, and stepped forward.

Fairfax shoved his cane out to block the stairs. "Where is your brother, Mrs. Duncan?" He leaned toward her and trapped her gaze in his. Kate's face and shoulders went rigid—locked in the frost of Fairfax's glare, Michael knew. "I've a matter to discuss with Mr. Marsh. It concerns Mr. Bellington."

If even Michael could recognize the flicker of suspicion and calculation that moved in Kate's eyes, he knew Fairfax had picked up the scent of a lie in the making. In his peripheral vision, he saw Spry tense. A primal urge in the back of his head encouraged him to bolt forward and shove Fairfax down the stairs. He clenched his fists to stop himself from acting on it.

Kate hiked her chin. "My brother is headed for New Berne."

Fairfax's voice lashed her. "I think not. He's headed south instead, hasn't he?"

"No, he's gone to New Berne!"

"When did he leave Wilmington?"

"Monday."

"What's his business in New Berne?"

"He's opening up a new tavern there."

"You're lying. Where did he get the money for such a venture?"

Kate stamped her foot. "How dare you call me a liar? And how is our money your business?"

"It's my business because you've evaded paying taxes on whiskey production for over a decade. And it's my business because your brother is a rebel spy, and I believe he murdered Mr. Bellington Monday night."

Michael's gut burned. What made Fairfax believe Kevin was a rebel spy— or was he bluffing? No, Fairfax believed it. He'd found solid evidence against Kevin when all Michael had was conjecture.

And what made Fairfax think that Kevin had ridden south? South toward— where? Michael's eyes bulged. Toward Charles Town?

Jaw gaped, eyes wide, Kate backed a step from the cane and Fairfax. "*Murder?*" She gasped, then shook her head with vehemence. "No. You have the wrong man!"

"I don't think so, madam. It's all about the money."

"Why so? Why would Kevin murder Mr. Bellington when—when Sam Bellington is one of his business partners in New Berne? That would be like cutting off his nose to spite his face!"

Oh, no. That lie would rebound on her for sure. Michael held his breath.

Fairfax pulled away from her slightly. Michael had a view of the back of his head and imagined shrewdness eating away at his expression. Fairfax's shoulders straightened, and he said, low, "So your brother and Samuel Bellington are in an alliance. Excellent. Just as I'd suspected."

Christ Jesus. Before arriving at White's, Fairfax had deduced that Sam Bellington and Kevin Marsh had teamed up to kill Jasper Bellington, possibly with the help of Uno. Kate's lie had fed that deduction. She'd blundered straight into Fairfax's trap.

From Uno's brief statement, Michael suspected that Sam Bellington had been on his way to New Berne while his uncle was being murdered. Of course, he couldn't tell Fairfax that without revealing Uno's location. And that meant he couldn't rescue Kate.

She was trembling all over. Jabbing her nose in the air, she managed to make her fear look like righteous indignation. "How dare you accuse my brother of murder?" She clenched one side of her petticoat. "Get out of my way!" She kicked his cane aside and stomped down the stairs.

Fairfax recovered his balance and monitored her descent, calculation carving his expression in profile, a panther watching prey. After a moment, he pivoted and advanced toward Michael, the angelic sparkle in his eyes. "How I wish I had the time today to dismantle her lies. I doubt I'd find her brother here, but I'd certainly learn where she's hiding her untaxed whiskey and whether she's sheltering the surviving slave." His glare seared Michael. "But interrogation isn't a process to be rushed, and I'll be leaving for New Berne shortly."

New Berne?

At the bloom of curiosity in Michael's expression, a noise that was half-cough and full-scoff issued from Fairfax's throat. "Yes, New Berne, where Samuel Bellington, nephew and business partner of Jasper Bellington, resides. Those servants of Mr. Hickory's are worthless at helping me locate the original financial records, but at least they knew about Mr. Bellington's nephew." He passed between Michael and Spry. "With Mr. Hickory and the records inaccessible, the nephew's memory for detail on those summaries is my best chance of learning what Mr. Hickory has intentionally concealed. And why."

Even though it didn't sound as though Fairfax was going to interrogate Kate and her aunt just yet, tension refused to leave Michael's stomach. "What makes you think Mr. Marsh is a rebel?"

Fairfax yanked open the door to the second room. After a look around inside, he shut the door. Without a backward glance at them, he strutted for Henshaw.

The private guarding the sickroom eyed Michael. Michael shook his head in a decisive, sharp motion. Only God knew how he'd straighten out all the subterfuge.

Fairfax spoke to Henshaw, who recited his earlier litany. His eyes green glaciers, Fairfax spun about and returned to Michael. As he drew breath to speak, Michael cut in, his voice soft. "I spent all day rounding up enough saddles and tackle for my mission on the morrow. Got rained on twice." He crossed his arms and sneered at Fairfax. "I'll be damned if I'll let you put your paws on it. Not that you legitimately need any of it with that chaise of yours."

Fairfax showed his teeth and whispered, "You're lying, too. Very well, you and I will dance."

"No, we won't dance. The murderer has moved at liberty for two days." Michael jabbed his forefinger at him. "Go to New Berne. You may be able to save Sam Bellington's life."

"You sound certain that he's innocent of his uncle's murder. Why is that?

And you never mentioned him in your report. Really, Stoddard, the amount of information that you've withheld—"

"Stop shoving your words in my mouth! And why is it you think Mr. Marsh is a rebel?"

Fairfax whipped a folded paper from his pocket and handed it to him. It was a letter, Michael realized as soon as he'd unfolded it—a letter scented of gardenia blossoms and addressed to Kevin Marsh. In flowery script, it had been dated 14 July 1781 from Charles Town, South Carolina.

> *My darling Kevin, your Bank Draft arrived today. How grateful I am. Seldom has our Cause been so generously gifted. Together we shall rid this Land of the Enemy. Hasten, Beloved. I shall greet you with open Arms and Kisses. Your most devoted Love, Naomi Levy*

Bloody hell. Kevin, what a fool, Kevin. At least now Michael knew why Kate's brother had transacted that loan. He passed the evidence to Spry.

"I've posted arrest warrants for Mr. Marsh and Mr. Hickory. How I'd love to get my hands on Mr. Marsh." Smirking, Fairfax pressed toward Michael. "Consorting with those infamous Levys. According to the letter, he's donated a large sum of money to those Jews in the Charles Town synagogue. Likely the money he borrowed from Mr. Bellington. That qualifies him as a rebel. Yes?"

"Yes. Where did you find the letter?"

"For a year, he's had an arrangement with the town stationer to hold all incoming letters from Miss Levy, to be released only to him. As soon as the stationer understood that this was about a murder investigation, he surrendered the one letter he'd been holding since Monday to me."

"And now you'll inform his sister and aunt that he's a rebel."

Fairfax frowned. "Were I not headed to New Berne, yes, and I'd conduct a proper search this very moment of his house and this tavern for more seditious letters, then interrogate and possibly imprison his relatives. Fortunately you have a special relationship with the simple folk in this rustic establishment. You may conduct the search and interrogations." He flicked his hand toward Spry without looking at him. "And you'll need that letter. Otherwise the shrew downstairs will continue to deny her guilt."

Guilt? Search? Interrogations? Panic crashed over Michael. He didn't want to be cast in the role of the villain. "You heard Major Craig. My assignment has priority over yours." He snatched the letter from Spry and thrust it at Fairfax, who kept his hands at his sides. "This is your investigation. Conduct the search and question witnesses yourself."

"When I return, then." Fairfax placed his hat on his head and swept past Michael and Spry. "Good evening." He thumped his way downstairs.

* * *

By the time Michael and Spry descended to the taproom, Fairfax had exited through the front door and climbed into his chaise, parked in the street and visible through the windows. Kate was nowhere in sight. Michael didn't know how he could bear to tell her of her brother's betrayal.

And search? Interrogations? No, that was so wrong. Kate and Aunt Rachel couldn't be guilty of abetting rebels in South Carolina.

Outside, Front Street radiated with the day's heat. He blotted his sweaty face with his handkerchief and stomped toward Market Street. "Come along, Spry."

With his longer legs, Spry was at ease keeping pace with him. "There is a bright side to this, sir. Mr. Fairfax won't be underfoot for several days. Imagine all you can accomplish in that time."

All he'd have no choice but to accomplish—Michael growled. "Mostly what I'm imagining is that Mr. Fairfax finds Sam Bellington alive."

"Yes, of course, sir."

The letter that had damned Kevin rustled in his pocket. Blast Kevin for not listening to his sister's advice last year. "It's clear from Miss Levy's letter that she's been writing Mr. Marsh for quite a while."

"Yes, sir. Do you suppose he had the sense to burn her previous letters?"

"Sense" no longer applied to Kevin. He was a fool for the woman in South Carolina. "No."

If he hadn't burned the letters or packed them in his traveling gear, where might he have stored a year's worth of letters to prevent his sister and aunt from finding them easily? Not in the house. Likely not in the tavern, either. But that wouldn't stop Fairfax from turning both inside out in a malicious search.

Michael had too many things to think about that shouldn't be his concern. "We've two more stops today. Then I'm done with this black, bloody mess."

"Really, sir? If you say so. Stop number one is the tobacconist shop and Mrs. Farrell, yes?"

"Correct."

"But stop number two, sir? I confess that you have me stumped."

"The items we found in the tannery must be the property of Mr. Marsh. What's the largest item missing from his belongings?"

"His rifle—no, his horse!"

Michael nodded. "Charlie is a sorrel gelding with a white blaze. I got a good look at him when I was in Hillsborough. And I'm concerned that neither Mr. Marsh nor Charlie has turned up in the two days since the murder."

Spry's tone sobered. "Sir, after what Mrs. Duncan told us about Miss Levy, and especially after what I read in Miss Levy's letter to Mr. Marsh, he could be hanged for treason if we catch him."

"Yes, he could. But the letter doesn't tie him to Mr. Bellington's murder."

"Agreed, sir. Been thinking about how he's disappeared. Suppose he did kill those men at the estate but was wounded, crawled off somewhere?" His voice dropped to a whisper. "Somewhere to die."

Leave it to Spry to voice the suspicion that had gnawed at Michael. "If that's the case, why didn't Mr. Fairfax find him today? I guarantee you he performed a thorough search of the estate." Spry didn't respond, so Michael continued. "After we've finished at the tobacconist's shop, I shall post a description of the horse, say he's been stolen."

"That will get back to Mrs. Duncan, sir."

And precipitate their chat of extraordinarily bad news—No, he must focus on tying up as much of the Bellington investigation as possible today so he could provide a safe escort for William Hooper on the morrow and Fairfax could solve the murders. And Michael had no doubt that as soon as Fairfax returned from New Berne, he'd embark upon a flurry of letter writing to acquaint all regiments and loyalists in Charles Town with the traitor Kevin Marsh.

Dismayed over Kevin, Michael passed the remainder of the walk to the tobacconist shop without further comment. As he and Spry arrived, Mrs. Farrell drove out from behind the store in her gig, a fashionable straw hat with yellow ribbons on her head. Spry waved her down. She halted her vehicle and beamed as Michael walked over. "Oh, Captain Stoddard, have we ever a wonderful night planned for you and Mrs. Duncan!"

Michael forced a polite upturn to his lips. "Thank you, madam."

"And you'll be escorting her to the fête. How divine."

He'd be escorting Kate? He wished someone had given him access to the protocol manual for fêtes. "What time should I arrive at her house?"

Mrs. Farrell flashed him a cross look. "No one told you? She'll expect you at seven-thirty sharp. Don't be late." She sat back and preened. "It will be a night you'll never forget."

He couldn't take any more and launched straight into business. "Madam, I've heard you might be storing some soldier costumes from a play created for Governor Martin."

Her eyes widened. "Why, yes! They're in a Front Street warehouse."

"May we have a quick look at the costumes?"

"Of course you may. I even have the key to the padlock with me. Come along."

Chapter Fifteen

ALICE FARRELL TWITCHED the reins and got the horse moving, and as soon as Michael and Spry fell in beside her, said, "I haven't thought of that production for years—it was in seventy-four, if memory serves me correctly—and my, how fun it was, and how Governor Martin laughed at—"

"How many actors were in the play?" Michael tried not to sound impatient.

"Five. My husband, Richard. My brother, Godfrey. Mr. Jonas Hickory. Dr. Edgar Tillman—he's since passed away. And young Kevin Marsh. Of course, his coat was baggy on him, as he was only about fifteen years old at the time, but that just made everything vastly amusing, because he looked like a scarecrow." She laughed with delight. "A redcoat scarecrow. Imagine it!"

Instead, Michael was trying to envision Jonas Hickory, of all people, acting with any sort of conviction or pleasure upon a stage in the costume from the tannery. There his imagination failed him. He couldn't see the financier enjoying himself at anything—except, perhaps, counting money.

"Godfrey penned all the play's music in between discoveries of two sets of binary stars. My brother is so talented."

Her brother roused Michael's ire when he realized what an excellent suitor the astronomer made for Kate. No doubt he'd have let her touch his telescope and showed her the stars. Would Kate have refused such a refined courtship? The tobacconist's wife prattled on with memories of the play, and for the first time in his life, Michael wished he'd been cut from more polished stone.

At the warehouse, he helped Mrs. Farrell from the gig. Then he and Spry followed her in past the fellow on duty. From the padlock in his hand and sour expression on his face, he must have been ready to lock the warehouse for the night.

Ribbons on Mrs. Farrell's hat fluttered like banners on a flagship. Michael and Spry trailed her in a maze of narrow, dim corridors formed from racks of lumber and stacked barrels of naval stores interspersed with occasional shelves of personal items. Turpentine aromatics bore down on them until Michael wondered if his head was growing light and his lungs were becoming coated in the smell.

The tobacconist's wife turned a corner and halted before a chest on the floor, shoved beneath shelves of full baskets, buckets, and sacks. "Here we are! Might you charming fellows be kind enough to pull the chest out so I may reach it better?" After the soldiers had done so, she produced a ring of keys from her pocket and the correct one for the padlock. The chest opened with a puff of stuffiness.

Aside from books, it was filled with the sort of odds and ends of life that people never got around to trading away, perhaps due to sentimental value: a faded world globe, several well-used pipes, a rolled rug, three ceramic vases, a much smaller version of the wooden Indian statue in the front of the tobacconist shop. Through the clutter, Michael spotted the folded costumes. With Mrs. Farrell's permission, he pulled the top one out, held it up by the shoulders, and turned away to study it. She poked around in the trunk behind him.

Although made for a man with some girth on him, the costume's design was a match for the one they'd found in the tannery, all the way down to the black facings. The murderer of Bellington and his slaves—or perhaps a cohort of his—had made a stop in the warehouse before he'd gone a-hunting. Who knew the costumes were stored in the chest? As Michael already suspected the killer could pick locks, he might have come by anytime before Monday night, even on Sunday, when no one was around, to fetch his disguise. Still, it was worth inquiring of the man at the front whether Jonas Hickory or Kevin Marsh had been by earlier in the week.

Mrs. Farrell cleared her throat. "That was Dr. Tillman's coat. And here is his hair."

His hair? Michael pivoted, the linen coat still in his hand, to see Spry, his mouth set with forbearance, modeling a messy wig made of bleached, white horsehair. "Good God."

Then memory whispered Uno's words to Michael: *Hair—not like yours.* He stopped the realization from tightening his expression. To hide his hair, the killer must have worn a wig like the one that adorned Spry. That meant no one knew the true color of his hair, not even the only living witness.

Mrs. Farrell whisked the wig off Spry's head, stuffed it into a canvas sack, and dropped the sack into the chest. "All right, my good fellows. I've been patient so far, but you must know that I'm ready to burst with curiosity." Her dark eyes glittered. "Why are you interested in these old costumes?"

Michael folded the coat he'd removed and, while replacing it, counted the total there, four. Yes, the fifth coat was missing. He wagered the sack held only four wigs, too. "Oh, we heard there was going to be a play at the supper party." He straightened and winked at his assistant, who was smoothing his hair back into place. "Right, Spry?"

"Yes, sir. Dancing redcoats, a line of them."

"Dressed in those costumes?" Mrs. Farrell clapped once. "Oh, my, that would be an amusing sight, indeed! But to my knowledge, there's no such production planned."

"I'm sure you're correct. Five doesn't make much of a line. And I suppose all five of those actors knew where you'd stored their costumes?"

"Goodness, the whole town knows it."

That meant anyone with lock-picking ability could have helped himself to a costume and wig. Michael forced a smile. "Thank you for showing us in here, Mrs. Farrell."

"You're most welcome." She closed and locked the chest. They shoved it into place beneath the shelves and followed her out into fresher air and the angled sunshine of early evening.

Michael motioned for Spry to help her into the gig and, while the dockworker was closing the doors, nodded to him. "Thank you for remaining open a few minutes longer for us, sir."

"Of course, Captain." The padlock clicked shut, and he pointed to it. "And seeing as how you're Major Craig's investigator, I figured you might want to know that those scratches on the padlock were new on Monday morning, like a burglar tried to break it when no one was here."

Michael bent over to study the damage. Sunday night, had Bellington's killer scratched the lock in the process of picking it so he could get inside and steal a costume and wig? Michael stood taller and chose his words with care. "What's missing from the warehouse?"

"I inventoried the naval stores. Looked like everything was still there." The dockworker shrugged. "A number of people in town rent space here. To be sure, nothing looked out of place when I walked through, but I've no idea whether something personal might have gone missing."

Michael threw a glance over his shoulder in time to see Mrs. Farrell wave goodbye to him and Spry amble his way. He signed for Spry to hurry. "Who other than yourself has a key?"

"The dock manager, Ned Peabody. But he and I discussed it, and he didn't come by the warehouse on Sunday. I told him we should change the lock, just to be safe."

"That's a good idea. The locksmith Roger Pearson has done excellent work for the regiment." At Michael's side, Spry took up position.

"Thank you for the recommendation, Captain."

"Certainly. Another question for you. At the beginning of this week, did either Mr. Hickory or Mr. Marsh stop in here?"

The dockworker nodded. "Mr. Marsh did. First thing on Monday morning, he was here waiting, patient and polite, for me to open the warehouse. But he's no thief. One look at him, and you know he's a decent fellow."

If anyone, particularly Kevin, had tried to pick the lock at night and failed, he doubted that person would be waiting "patient and polite" to be let inside on Monday morning. He'd be fidgety, with a short temper, especially if he plotted murder. Still, Michael coaxed his expression into what he hoped was blandness while the fifty-pound weight of disappointment sank through his gut. "What did he carry out?" A costume and wig stuffed into a sack, perhaps?

The man shook his head. "Nothing. He went in with nothing, and he came out with nothing. Quickly, too."

It occurred to Michael that that was exactly the way it would have appeared if Kevin had carried one of Miss Levy's letters in his waistcoat and stored it in the warehouse. He eyed the padlock, then returned his attention to the dockworker. "Have you seen Mr. Marsh since Monday morning?"

"No, sir."

"Show me his storage area." The man frowned and opened his mouth. "Yes, I know, you were headed home for the night. But this concerns a murder investigation."

"Murder? Mr. Marsh didn't murder nobody. He's a good fellow."

"Unlock the door, sir, and show me to his storage area."

The sullen drag to the fellow's lips returned. He swiveled to the padlock with the key, and the doors swung open. Back Michael and Spry walked through the narrow, dim corridors, this time with the dockworker their guide. A quarter minute in, they stopped, and the man pointed to a top shelf. "He rents that little space up there."

As far as Michael could see, the shelf held only a canvas bag. He eyed his assistant and nodded upward. Spry stretched tall, got a grip on the bag, and dragged it down. It landed on the floor with a cloud of dust. The private positioned it upright, and Michael loosened the drawstring enough so that only he could peer inside. Letters, dozens of them. And the scent of gardenia.

A blend of victory and misery wound through him. He straightened and faced the dockworker. "We're confiscating Mr. Marsh's property as evidence in the murder investigation."

Gaze downcast, the man shook his head. "I don't see how he murdered nobody. He's a good fellow."

"When Mr. Marsh returns, have him see me immediately. Do you understand?" That was in case Kevin didn't get arrested and thrown in the pen first.

"Yes, sir."

"His Majesty thanks you for your cooperation. Lock up behind us."

Spry hefted the bag to his shoulder, and Michael led their exit from the warehouse. All the way to the house on Second Street, neither man spoke. Crushed shells beneath their shoes crunched with their passage, the sound like brittle bones snapping.

The hired woman had another stew cooking in the kitchen—chicken that night, from the smell of it—and the aroma followed the men upstairs. Michael shut the two of them into his bedroom and, as Spry loosened the drawstring on the bag, pointed to the floor. "Not on my bed. Dump them out on the floor."

Spry did so, then pinched his nose shut and fanned the air. "Christ! Must be a hundred letters here, sir, and she perfumed every one of them."

They made Michael's room smell like he'd entertained several gardenia-scented doxies. Even after he shoved open his window, gardenia edged out the aroma of chicken stew. "Let's see whether we can order them chronologically." And, he hoped, observe the story between Kevin and Miss Levy as it unfolded.

By half an hour later, dusk swallowing the room, Michael had tasted the disappointment of watching Miss Levy disassemble Kevin's objections to the rebel cause. Slowly, appealing to his fancy, she brought him around to the point where he agreed to yank his house from beneath his sister and aunt, donate the money to the rebels, and join her in South Carolina. Although she mentioned rebel military leaders—Thomas Sumter, Nathanael Greene, and Francis Marion—not once did she reveal any information that would compromise them.

Spry dropped a letter on the pile, his expression downcast. "Mr. Marsh is such a likeable fellow. This is rather difficult to take, sir."

"I'm having difficulty with it, too, Spry."

"I don't see any sign that he gave information about the Eighty-Second to her, sir. Surely that's in his favor, isn't it?"

Michael shook his head. "Miss Levy is too good at this game to incriminate a source. Mr. Marsh may have been reporting all manner of information about us to her."

"While serving us beer and smiling." Spry's tone stung with bitterness.

Michael waved the final letter from a randomly selected group close to the flame of a candle on his desk. As far as he could tell, the woman from South Carolina hadn't used invisible ink. He blew out the candle, scooped up the letters he'd tested, and dropped them onto the larger pile beside his assistant.

At the window, he propped his hands on the sill and stared out, thinking of his conversation with Kate about dreams. A stoic American woman, she carried on when her dreams weren't realized and adjusted her expectations. But her brother didn't have that maturity or resilience. He'd buckled beneath the crush of six years of war, lacking the ability within himself to transform his dreams, clinging to transformation from an external source.

Would Kevin have murdered Bellington and his slaves? If so, why? A disagreement in the terms of the loan? No, from what Miss Levy had written, he seemed to have accepted that Bellington now owned his house, and there was no turning back.

Spry, shoveling letters back into the bag, said in a subdued tone, "Well, Mr. Marsh certainly was mad with love for the woman, sir. Odd that he would leave without her letters, though."

"That bag is heavy and isn't essential traveling gear."

"He also left without his essential traveling gear, sir. Which is why I think he hasn't left."

Where was Kevin? Was he lying dead somewhere in the brush after attacking Bellington and his slaves, as Spry had opined? Michael wasn't sure which type of news would be more upsetting to his womenfolk: learning of his betrayal, learning that he'd died, learning that he was a murderer.

Spry cinched the drawstring, stood, and stretched his back. Bitterness returned to his voice. "I know this is evidence in Mr. Fairfax's investigation, sir, but must we let him have it?"

Uno had exonerated Fairfax. Fairfax had declared his own innocence. Michael no longer saw a conflict of interests in giving his adversary the evidence, and it would be further obstruction of the King's justice if they didn't do so—even if doing so felt horribly wrong, and he wasn't quite certain why. Personal reasons again? "The thought gives me no pleasure, either." In fact, he detested the idea.

"Sir, regardless of whether Mrs. Duncan and Mrs. White are innocent of Miss Levy's schemes, Mr. Fairfax will torment them with this information."

Yes, he would. But the mission with William Hooper loomed. Michael's platter was full. He squirmed. "Don't remind me. Let's just get it done. I shall walk down there with you and post notice of the missing gelding."

"Of course, I could leave the bag open down there, sir. What with Mr. Fairfax gone for several days and his window shut and the summer heat, it ought to smell quite floral in there when he returns."

Michael felt an unpleasant smile stretch his lips. "Do it."

* * *

When Michael posted notice of Charlie, he spotted the arrest warrants for Jonas Hickory and Kevin Marsh. How comforting to know that Fairfax could be depended upon to carry out his duty. *Those servants of Mr. Hickory's are worthless at helping me locate the original financial records...* Michael grimaced. Fairfax must have questioned Tifton and Mrs. Bolton just before he'd come to White's. He couldn't have spent more than five minutes at it; he didn't linger where he wasn't making headway.

Michael returned to his room and shuffled through the unanswered letters on his desk. Lord Faisleigh's note resurfaced in the stack: *My dear Mr. Stoddard, we've a certain Matter to discuss. Please see me at your earliest Convenience. Discretion and Hour as usual. Faisleigh.* Yes, that did look auspicious. Michael's shoulders relaxed, and he fancied pressure from the barb in his soul decreased. Good news from his benefactors would be welcome after the day's many disappointments and vexations. He slid the letter to the bottom of the stack.

After supper, after dark, he'd walk over to the house that Faisleigh had been renting since March and knock softly at the back door as he'd done so many times. Faisleigh would admit him, but instead of directing him to the second floor, he'd show him to the study. Perhaps he'd offer brandy. Then the happy tidings. In a day or so, the household would resume its journey to Charles Town or wherever it was that Faisleigh had been headed to escape the trouble his brother had stirred up in Yorkshire. Michael would be free of them at last. Within the year would come his promotion to the rank of major.

For a few seconds, he allowed himself to think of Faisleigh's heir, ten-year-old Geoffrey, Lord Wynndon, whom they'd been keeping out of sight—and for good reason. With his dark hair and dark eyes, he looked too much like Michael as well as Michael's father, Abraham. Michael swallowed the taste of bittersweet. Some day, Wynndon would control a vast fortune and sit in the House of Lords. It was far more than an impecunious baron in the Scottish Highlands could offer him.

But that barony in the Highlands wouldn't be his unless he petitioned King George for it and got his formal request in the post. He uncorked the inkbottle, took out a sheet of paper, and composed his thoughts. Then, after he dated the letter, he began with the salutation: *Your Majesty.*

Chapter Sixteen

AT TEN MINUTES to nine, escorted by the enchanting twinkle of fireflies, Michael walked up to the rear door of Lord Faisleigh's dwelling and tapped on it. His benefactor admitted him straightaway, barred the back door behind him, and escorted him through a darkened house to the stuffy study lit by a few candles. After motioning Michael to sit at one end of the couch, Faisleigh closed the two of them into the room. With a pang of disappointment, Michael watched the other man bypass the brandy.

For an instant, his mind again circled the possibility of withholding Miss Levy's letters from Fairfax. That it would be an obstruction of justice was clear to him, yet some moral aspect of the situation was at work fueling his ambivalence. Then his benefactor seated himself on the opposite end of the couch, and Michael gave him his full attention.

"As always, I appreciate your visit, Mr. Stoddard."

Michael inclined his head. There was more silver in the hair at Faisleigh's temples than there'd been when he first arrived in Wilmington in the spring. He also looked thinner. Not unexpected, considering that his brother, John, had once schemed to kidnap Wynndon. But to Michael, he looked like a man who still had all those worries. "How is Lord Wynndon?"

"Wynndon is well, thank you."

Michael no longer asked to see his son. Faisleigh would only refuse his request. He shoved away the memory from early April of a rescued Wynndon in the saddle before him. "And your brother?"

Faisleigh made a dismissive motion with his hand and dabbed at his brow with a perfumed handkerchief. "My brother has been subdued." He worked an indigo phial from the waistcoat pocket of his fine wool suit and passed it over.

Michael was skeptical that John had truly given up the fight. There was too much at stake. As Faisleigh's cunning black-eyed gaze was on him, he rotated the phial in his fingers, then uncorked it long enough to sniff an herbal concoction in alcohol.

"Don't taste it." Faisleigh tucked away the handkerchief and extended his hand, a smile warping his lips.

Michael had yet to see a pleasant smile on the face of his benefactor. "I hadn't intended to do so." He corked the phial and returned it to him. "What is it?"

"My dear wife became distracted by matters of the household the other day and accidentally left it out. As I'd never seen it before, naturally I appropriated it and investigated." The phial vanished into his waistcoat. He relaxed against some pillows, stretched his arm along the back of the couch, and drummed his fingers several seconds. "According to a local midwife, it's a tincture containing several herbs that have been traditionally used to discourage conception."

Michael's eyes bulged, and his jaw dangled. "What?" Damn Lydia!

"I'd wondered what was taking you two so long. Even considered stepping in and supervising."

Michael glared at him and received a smirk in response. Without a doubt, Lydia had used the tincture to buy herself time to sport with her falcon boy. "I had nothing to do with that phial."

"Oh, I know it. When confronted, my sweetheart admitted that you were completely innocent." He chuckled. "Well, now she's had her fun. Let us commence with business."

Michael scowled at him. "I've done what 'business' I can, Lord Faisleigh—"

"Now, now, for you, it's Faisleigh, as I told you in the spring."

Faisleigh omitted adding the sentence about how they were almost family, as he'd done in the spring. He knew he wasn't fooling anyone. Michael was nothing but a stud to them. He allowed himself a slow, even breath to recover reason in his tone. "You said you have your brother under control at last. North Carolina is finally in the hands of the King's Friends again, and His Majesty is in command of Charles Town, South Carolina. The time has never been better for you and your household to continue your journey south."

"I disagree and must ask you to stay the course, sir."

"Why? Don't you see? Your wife has been using that phial for years. It explains your inability to get her with child. If you'd recognized that sooner, you'd never have recruited me."

Faisleigh rolled his gaze to the ceiling. "Alas, you're the one who doesn't understand. Both she and the midwife admitted that she contracted the production of it here, in Wilmington, for the first time."

With a hard sigh, Michael sank against the couch and stared at the shadowy fireplace. He was sick to death of the arrangement. Within seconds, he made up his mind that being promoted to major wasn't important enough to him personally to continue the gavotte with these devils. If the farthest he advanced in rank was captain, so be it, even if it made reversal of the attainder more difficult. He pushed himself up to his feet and jutted his jaw at Faisleigh. "I appreciate the way you've helped me, but I'm done with this. Good night, my lord."

The nobleman's jaw tightened, and the command in his voice whipped out. "I've more to discuss with you, Mr. Stoddard. Do resume your seat."

The switch from apology to anger was smooth, well-practiced. With little work, his "benefactor" might be able to get him demoted—or even cashiered out of the Army. Steaming, Michael sat.

"That's better." Faisleigh steepled his fingers. "Now, then. I've finally found you a major's commission. Those senior officer commissions are few and far between, and it turns out that another officer has expressed interest in it." He smiled. "Coincidentally, he's stationed here in Wilmington."

Although he held Faisleigh's stare, Michael felt the color drain from his face. No. It couldn't be.

"I invited Captain Fairfax for tea Monday afternoon. Quite an intelligent fellow and deserving of promotion." The older man stood, ambled to the brandy service, and poured some in two glasses. When he returned to the couch, he gave Michael a glass and resumed his seat. "Shall I outbid Mr. Fairfax? If I don't, it may take me a while to find another commission."

What a busy little bee Fairfax had been Monday. Coffee with Bellington, followed by tea with Faisleigh. Michael studied the seductive swirl of amber liquor in the glass. If it were any man other than Fairfax going after that commission, he'd have had the luxury of debating his decision. But Fairfax would use the vantage of a senior officer as the gateway to committing more elaborate and heinous abuses. There was simply no way that Michael could allow him to have the commission.

His lips pressed together. A spike of cold, iron misery rammed through him and splintered off a chunk of his soul. The stinger it left behind supplied more of the dank, gnawing ache that had plagued him for months. "Outbid Mr. Fairfax," he said, low.

"Consider it done." Faisleigh saluted him with his glass. "Here's to your continued robust health, sir."

While Faisleigh sipped, Michael brooded into his glass. The bouquet told him that the nobleman had acquired brandy far better than what sat off to the side on Major Craig's table. Lately, it seemed he was always being offered a glass of quality brandy under the wrong conditions to enjoy it. For the sake of Geoffrey, Lord Wynndon, he hoped his benefactor hadn't been imprudent and spilled the wrong information during his teatime conversation on Monday.

Faisleigh rose, returned his empty glass to the tray beside the decanter, and grabbed a candle. "I do hate to rush a man with his brandy, but my dear wife can be so impatient sometimes." Shielding the candle's flame, he walked to the doors. There he awaited Michael with his warped smile.

Michael belted down the brandy and, resisting the urge to cough, made his way to the service and deposited the glass beside Faisleigh's. Three cheers for brandy. By the time he was transferred off to Lydia upstairs, the bleeding edges on the new hole in his soul would be cauterized, and the Michael Stoddard she'd seduced repeatedly a decade earlier would be silent.

Outside the second-floor bedroom door, the nobleman planted himself in a chair, as usual, and set the candle on a small table to wait out the session with a copy of Defoe's *Robinson Crusoe*. The shipwrecked adventurer had sat on the table since early May, and Faisleigh's bookmark hadn't budged much. As the novel wasn't tedious reading, clearly his benefactor was entertaining himself in another manner. Teeth clenched, Michael entered the bedroom and closed the door behind him.

By candlelight, Lydia had been pacing back and forth dressed only in her lacy shift, a scarlet ribbon catching most of her curly blonde hair up off her neck. At his entrance, she rushed forward to grab his hand and halt his advance into the room. Her smile showed off her even, white teeth. "Did you and Faisleigh have a good chat downstairs?" She spoke low. Aside from Michael, only her husband with his ear to the door outside could hear.

Michael opened the folded note she'd palmed him and read: *Don't believe what he told you about his brother. John has now hired professional assassins to hunt down and kill Wynndon.* Damn it all. Assassins coming to Wilmington. His son needed to be gone from the area. Michael kept his voice down. "As I explained to your husband in the parlor, it's time for all of you to leave Wilmington."

Lydia snatched the note from him and chuckled. "Did Faisleigh tell you what I did?" Without waiting for his response, she pranced to her writing desk, set the note afire, and dropped it in a metal dish full of the blackened bits of nobility's schemes.

Still at the door, Michael shook his head. "You were using that phial on him back in Yorkshire, weren't you?"

Pouting, she returned to him. "No, dear. I've told you before. My husband has no seed." She drew him over near the bed, where the sheets had been turned down and perfumed with her scent, roses. "I'm afraid our time for fun is over. We must now apply ourselves to business." She walked her fingers up and down his chest. "A brother or sister for Wynndon."

The brandy coursed molten gold enthusiasm into his veins. Lydia was a beautiful woman. And this was going to be quick. Michael shrugged out of his coat and draped it over a bedpost. "I've been applying myself to business." He unbuckled his shoes and pulled them off. "Since April."

Her pout was still there. "But it sounds like you weren't enjoying yourself." With one tug at her shift's drawstring, she loosened it. The neck of it gaped open, exposing the tops of her large breasts. A roll of her shoulders and flick of her arms slid the shift down below her navel. She freed her arms and yanked the hair ribbon loose. Curls tumbled down her back. She wound the ribbon around one breast in a spiral. "Oh, wonderful Michael."

Oh, wonderful brandy. Even the watch in his waistcoat ticked faster. Working fingers at his trouser buttons, he shuffled forward.

With a hip shimmy, she dropped the shift to her ankles and stepped out of it. "I want you to enjoy yourself." She reclined on the bed and sighed deeply, the sweat on her breasts glistening. "I'd hate to think this was torture for you."

No, she'd love to think it was torture for him. He'd seen how much she enjoyed tormenting her son's first tutor last spring. But with the full boost of brandy heating his blood, he didn't give as much of a damn as he probably should have. He released the final button and dropped his trousers.

Duty. For King and Country. Huzzah.

* * *

The problem with a shot of brandy, even superb brandy, was that it wore off—and for Michael, it was wearing off by the time that Faisleigh saw him out the back door, then barred the door behind him. The fireflies were gone for the night. He stepped out into the yard, gazed up at the starry sky and a slender crescent moon in the west, and took a deep breath. Gods, how he reeked of roses and rutting. At least he could remedy that problem straight away. He ambled toward his quarters.

In his pocket crackled Faisleigh's parting gift, a note describing the favorable qualities and addresses of six marriageable young gentlewomen from the south of England. Each had dowries large enough to buy back that Highlands estate from the Crown. That would prevent him and his family from having to sell everything but the clothing they wore to reclaim the property and title. Duty.

At the servants' quarters in the back yard, Spry didn't answer his knock. The private was probably with his darling, Molly. As Michael lugged a bucket of water upstairs, he imagined the gentle winters of Hampshire, Surrey, and Kent. In those southern counties, the first breath of springtime often came in late March or early April. He shut himself into his room, lit a candle, closed the curtain, and stripped down. At the washbasin, he scrubbed Lydia off his skin and thought of six young ladies, their windows open to April, their dainty, white hands upon harpsichords, their feet snug in satin slippers.

According to his sister's letter, the Crown had invested its requisite minimum to maintain their great-grandfather's estate for three generations. That meant at least a year of work awaited his Yorkshire family before the place could be made presentable, let alone profitable. The Stoddards would welcome the toil, and the rough-hewn Highlanders would accept them for it. But a gentlewoman from the soft lands of southern England would resent him for transporting her into a world where snow lay upon the ground in May, peat fires lit the home, and glittering, perfumed dances were few and far between. To her face, the Scots would be polite. However, they would always see her as a symbol of their English oppressors at Culloden, where in 1746 the Duke of Cumberland ended Jacobite dreams of seeing Charles Stuart on the throne.

Wide-awake after ten o'clock—clean teeth, clean shirt—Michael rose from bed, lit a candle, and pulled his infantry hanger from its scabbard. As he'd done numerous times before when Spry wasn't available to spar with him or teach him a new twist in swordplay, he made certain he had room behind and before him. The keen focus required for sword work, even for practice, cleared his head, helped him find solutions to issues that plagued him. He assumed a front *en garde* stance.

His benefactor had championed pedigreed ladies who could smooth the edges off of him. Yet how could Michael possibly prepare any of those young ladies for the reality of what life would be like in the Highlands? Rough, cold, isolated. And on an estate that the Crown had held in attainder for decades.

He stepped back with weight on his right foot and drew the sword pommel in to his waist for a parry right. Swordplay, as Spry had first taught him in April, was as much about the legs as it was about the arms. Michael returned to *en garde* and parried right again, following it with a thrust. Next he parried left, his footwork even, balanced, silken steps in the dance of defense. Four months of instruction from a swordsman who'd honed his technique on the wrong side of the law had made Michael's motions fluid. And when he and Spry had seen Fairfax observing the unorthodox moves in their sparring three weeks earlier, they'd adopted even more caution and privacy with their practice.

Certainly, he could write all six ladies, advise them of what lay ahead, see if an interest was there. But in his heart as well as his head, he suspected his future wife wasn't among those tender damsels. What he needed was a partner who, like his family members, was pragmatic, undaunted by the prospect of working side-by-side with him. A woman content enough with herself that she wouldn't be crushed by any coarse manners or standoffish personalities.

He followed another parry left with a horizontal slice across the space where his opponent's belly would be. Block. Dodge. Advance. Sweat rolled down the sides of his face. Bash his opponent in the head with the sword's pommel. Slice for his Achilles tendon. Sand in his face. All moves the Army never taught.

In his memory, Kate Duncan's face tilted up to his, her mouth unsmiling. *You're right. We aren't dreamers.* He halted the practice to catch his breath and blotted sweat with his sleeve. His head cleared.

She must be told the bad news about her brother. If he conveyed the information to her, he questioned whether there'd be anything left of the friendship they'd managed to cultivate in half a year. On the other hand, if he left the task to Fairfax, the friendship would surely be destroyed. Fairfax would go to work on Kate and Aunt Rachel over all those letters, that staggering mountain of undeniable evidence, and—

Evidence.

Frowning, Michael slid the hanger into its scabbard and set it on his desk. At the window, he pushed the curtain aside enough to peer out. His breathing and pulse slowed, and he gazed past the fishy darkness to the conversation he'd had with Spry earlier about whether they should give Fairfax the bag of Miss Levy's letters. *Must we let him have it? Mr. Fairfax will torment them with this information.* He and Spry had followed the official course of action with the evidence. But in doing so, what had troubled Michael—and likely Spry—was that they abetted a moral wrong.

Evidence.

Even without all the correspondence they'd found in the warehouse, Kevin wasn't escaping the pit he'd dug for himself. The single letter Fairfax had taken from the stationer provided enough evidence against Kate's brother to throw him in the pen, possibly to hang him. No court needed the entire bag of letters for a verdict when the rebel activities of the Levys were so well known.

A grim press to his lips, Michael dressed, stood before his desk a moment, and steadied his nerves for the moral right. When he left his room with a lit candle, the officers in the house were quiet, asleep. Downstairs in stocking feet to aid his stealth, he opened the door to the study. His nose wrinkled at the smell of gardenia; if necessary, he'd air out the room early on the morrow, before he left town.

The bag of Miss Levy's letters was right where Spry had left it. From the top of the pile, he pocketed the single letter that Fairfax knew about and resealed the bag. After buckling on his shoes, he blew out the candle and hefted the bag to his shoulder.

Only he, the dockworker, and Spry had seen the bag. Only he and Spry knew that the bag contained letters and the content of those letters. Only he would know that he'd taken the bag from Fairfax's room. Spry might suspect the fate of the bag, but he'd keep quiet about it.

If Michael weren't careful, and this act was traced to him, he could be arrested for treason. If convicted, he'd be executed. All the way to the house where Kate and her family lived, he took a route which ensured that no one saw him.

He thought long and hard about his motivations for handing powerful evidence against Kevin to his sister and aunt, thus informing them of the sedition. After reading the letters, Kate and Aunt Rachel would destroy the evidence. Michael felt no remorse over that. If Fairfax got his paws on the letters, he'd make dozens of charges against Kevin public, and he'd harass the women. The negative and gratuitous publicity would ostracize Kate and Aunt Rachel.

Michael cared enough about both stoic, proud women to give them the news of Kevin's betrayal in private. That way, the community wouldn't see the worst of their grief. And Fairfax couldn't turn it into an exhibition with himself as the celebrity.

What Michael hoped was that he could let himself into the house through an unlatched window. Then he'd deposit the letters in a visible spot and clear out. Maybe Kate and Aunt Rachel would conclude that Kevin, unable to face them with the truth, had returned long enough to drop off the letters—the coward's way of confessing that he'd betrayed his own family.

* * *

The house was dark when he arrived. Through the windows, he saw no one inside. At this hour, both women had their hands full at the tavern, although he'd have to hurry to avoid running into Aunt Rachel. There was a padlock on the front door, and the back door of the house was barred from within. He went around the house and pushed at windows until, with a sigh of relief, he found one that Kate had forgotten to latch.

He heaved the bag inside. Under his breath as he crawled in after it, he tsk-tsked her for her forgetfulness. She'd left a window open at the tavern last night, too.

Back in his bedroom at eleven-fifteen, he shoved the empty bag under his bed with the rest of Kevin's possessions. After undressing, he blew out the candle and settled down for the night. An image came to his groggy mind of the letters where he'd mounded them on the floor and on a dining chair in the entranceway of Kate's house. In the dark, even if Aunt Rachel didn't see the gardenia-scented gift, she'd smell it first and thus not trip over it.

As Clayton would say, it was all in the hands of Providence now. Michael relaxed, his conscience divested of the weight of all that paper. After exhaling a deep breath, he rolled on his side and slept.

Chapter Seventeen

BY FIVE O'CLOCK Thursday morning the twenty-sixth, the town farrier's roosters had been trying to outdo each other for at least half an hour. Two blocks away, Michael heard the crowing cacophony while tiptoeing downstairs. When his knock on the study door yielded no response, he poked his head in. The profound silence he encountered told him that the preternaturally quiet Fairfax wasn't inside.

He took a long, deep sniff. His nose detected no trace of gardenia. Relieved that he wouldn't have to air out the room, he set the bag containing all items found in the tannery on the floor where the bag of letters had been the night before, shut the door, and retreated to his bedroom.

With the curtain open to daylight, he used the remaining water in the bucket to clean his teeth and shave. Sleep the night before hadn't been long enough, but it had been solid, conferring upon him the perspective that it was Major Craig, and Major Craig alone, with whom he must speak about withholding evidence from Fairfax. His commanding officer would make note of the insubordination in Michael's service record. Rightly so. Michael had been arrogant, and the incident had provided him with a tough lesson on why criminal investigation should never be about him.

He finished dressing, left the house, and grabbed some stale bread from the kitchen. At White's Tavern, he brushed breadcrumbs off the front of his uniform and tapped at a rear window to get the attention of Private Ferguson, who, with Private Stone, had gone on duty there at four in the morning. Ferguson, standing at the base of the stairs, let him in. "Good morning, sir. Spry and Wigglesworth are upstairs fetching gear for the horses."

"Good. Anything unusual to report?"

"Yes, sir. Right after Stone and I came on duty, around a quarter after four, someone tried to break in."

Michael recoiled. "Here?"

"Yes, sir. Stone and I were on the second floor. We heard the burglar rattling back windows downstairs, trying to find one that was unlatched. We went down with lamps. Soon as he saw us coming for the door, he fled."

"He?"

"Well, neither of us got more than a glimpse of him, sir, it being night, and he was dressed all in dark clothing. But the outline was definitely that of a lean man."

Michael's instincts pealed the alarm that the mysterious visitor had been neither a burglar nor a drunk. He'd been Bellington's murderer. "Fine work, chasing him off, Ferguson."

He revisited his memory of the sensation of being watched after he'd left the grain shed, and he recalled the suspicions voiced by Eli and Uno that someone had followed them to the shed. Maybe the killer had picked up the slaves' trail in the wee hours of Wednesday morning—somehow seen them move Uno to the shed—and later monitored their transfer of Uno to the tavern. Early Thursday morning, he'd come to kill Uno.

A lean man. Uno said that the afternoon before. Was it Kevin Marsh? What was certain was that the tavern was no longer safe for the slave—especially if the killer was Kevin, who might know ways to get in that didn't involve doors or first-floor windows.

He heard a creak of descent on the stairs and looked up to see a yawning Lavinia. When she reached the ground floor, she smiled, anticipating his question. "Uno's snoring, sleeping right through the noise of them men fetching the saddles. He's gonna make it just fine, Mistuh Stoddard." She rubbed sleep from one eye. She and Uno had probably snoozed through the "burglar" alarm at four-fifteen.

"Excellent news." He studied her a few seconds, prodded in the back of his mind with the sense that he needed to ask her something concerning the Bellington investigation. But with William Hooper's escort and safety his top priority, he had too much else to think about. "Again, thank you for your help, Lavinia." He opened the rear door and let her out to return to the Hoopers' house.

Again he considered Uno's safety. Fortunately, he now knew that Bellington's murderer wasn't a soldier from the regiment. If Clayton agreed with Lavinia's assessment, he'd release Uno to the surgeon's supervision, get him out of the tavern. Uno would be safe in the barracks. By the time Fairfax returned, Michael hoped to substantiate the slave's role as witness *versus* criminal.

Laden with gear, Spry and Wigglesworth descended, the stairs groaning and popping beneath their boots, and huffed out the door that Michael had left open. He said to Ferguson, "Clayton will stop by shortly to evaluate the patient. If he agrees to move him to the barracks, the duty rotations here are done." He squinted the length of the tavern. Three youths were standing at the front door.

"Yes, sir. There's one more thing you should know."

Michael held up his hand to silence the private. At the front door, one of the youths appeared to be picking the padlock. The devil! Michael started forward, then halted when the front door swung open, and the three entered, one twirling a key on a strip of leather, the other two with buckets, brooms, and mops. Ah. The early morning cleaning crew had arrived.

They spotted the soldiers and froze. "Is—is everything all right?" said the fellow with the key.

Michael waved to them. "Yes. Carry on." He returned to the open rear door. "Ferguson, you said there was another item."

"Yes, sir. Jackson came by looking for you a few minutes before you arrived. Said he had a report about something from his surveillance of the tannery early this morning."

Really? Fascinating. Michael would definitely follow up with Jackson today. He thanked Ferguson, reminded him to bar the door after him, and headed out to the stables, where grooms readied the ten horses for the white-flag party.

In the infirmary, he waited while Clayton finished bandaging a soldier's thumb. Then he accepted the surgeon's offer of lukewarm coffee from a pot. After he related the incident with the "burglar" at the tavern, Clayton agreed to transfer Uno to the barracks. The injured slave wouldn't get as much rest there, but at least he'd be safe.

Outside, Michael inspected the men selected for the mission and found them set to go. A soldier strode up and handed him a note from Major Craig, an update that the rebels had again changed their meeting location. At least the new location was closer to Wilmington.

As the horses were brought around, Spry sidled up to Michael and said in a voice just above a whisper, "Has Mr. Fairfax returned to town, sir?"

"If so, I'm unaware of it. Why do you ask?"

The private's gaze skittered away for an instant, then returned to him. "I looked in on the—" He straightened his spine. "The bag of letters is gone, sir."

Michael felt muscles in his face relax and held his assistant's gaze. "Don't concern yourself over it, Spry." His assistant's shoulders lowered, and the corner of his mouth curved in a faint smile, and for a few seconds, Michael allowed himself to mirror Spry's stance. At some point late last night, his like-minded assistant had sneaked to the study driven by the same ideals. What a team they made. "Paper's heavy. I could have used your help."

Spry diverted his gaze with a furtiveness unusual for him. "Oh, uh, my apologies, sir—"

"Never mind." Perhaps Spry was being reserved about his relationship with Molly. "Incidentally, Ferguson tells me that someone attempted to break into the tavern around four this morning."

Spry's eyes widened. "To kill Uno, sir?"

"I believe so. Clayton will move him into the barracks before noon." His assistant nodded.

The soldiers mounted horses. Muskets across their laps, they trotted northeast out of Wilmington at six-thirty, Spry bearing the unfurled white flag. They passed the sentries, and a warm, briny breeze whipped at the flag. As soon as the patrol splashed across a stream, Michael called a halt and gathered the men around. "Lads, about five miles ahead, we'll meet a group of rebels. We'll then bring their delegate, William Hooper, back to Wilmington to speak with Major Craig about a prisoner exchange."

Wigglesworth sat tall in his saddle. "William Hooper—one of the signers of the Declaration of Independence, sir?"

Michael gave him a sharp nod, glanced over his men, and pointed to the white flag. "Whatever our personal opinions of the signers, on this mission we honor truce. We will transport Mr. Hooper safely to town, guard him while he's there, and return him safely to his cohorts when negotiations are over. Understood?"

Nine voices said in crisp unison, "Sir!"

"Duty rotations for all men selected for this special mission were posted in the barracks yesterday." Not a man spoke. He knew every soldier in the regiment had seen the schedule—titled simply, "Special assignment with Capt. Stoddard"—and wondered about it.

"Be aware that the rebels have changed our meeting location at least three times. They believe we will dishonor the truce by capturing or assassinating Mr. Hooper. Thus at the meeting ground, the rebels will be anxious. They may outnumber us to compensate for their apprehension. More of them equates to more firearms aimed at us. Is there any man here who hasn't experience keeping his composure in the midst of nervous rebels?"

He also knew the experience of every man in the patrol. It pleased him that all nine continued to sit still in their saddles, chins lifted.

"Any questions?" He made eye contact with each soldier and saw no hesitation, no fidgety hands. The patrol was ready. Gods, how he hoped the transfer would proceed smoothly. "Let's be off."

For a few minutes, dawn's deep, cool shadow clung to much of the arid landscape. Then the sun boiled higher in the white-hot sky, and the occasional live oaks the men passed no longer provided adequate shade. Sweat rolled into Michael's neck stock.

The patrol encountered a dairyman and three produce farmers, all bound for Wilmington with their creaky wagons. Hawks whistled and stooped, and crows cawed. Rabbits sprang across the sand-and-shell road, back and forth from patches of wiregrass and cacti.

Around seven o'clock, where a narrow cart track split off to the west from the main road, a lone rider wearing a hunting shirt awaited them in the road, face partially shaded by a much-trampled hat, a rifle in his hand, a long piece of straw dangling from one corner of his mouth. Michael ordered his party to halt twenty-five feet away. Farther north on the road, tucked in brush, he saw sunlight glint off rifle barrels of the man's reinforcements.

He advanced his mare ten feet beyond his patrol. "Good morning, sir. We're to convey Mr. Hooper to Wilmington for negotiations with Major Craig." The man tongued the straw to the other side of his mouth and pointed down the track with his rifle. "Thank you." Michael signaled his men down the track, single-file.

After about two hundred feet, overgrowth alongside the track thinned, opened up to a sandy field that someone had tried to cultivate, but wiregrass had reclaimed it too fast. Michael and his men spread out along the edge of the field and waited. In the distance, he spied the northeast branch of the Cape Fear River. On the other side of the field from them and much closer than the river, at least thirty riders were clustered. Sunlight reflected off their rifles.

Straw-Chewer and his three reinforcements had brought up the rear of Michael's party on the track. They headed across the field toward the larger group, motioning for the soldiers to follow. When the patrol had traversed the field, the larger group loosely surrounded them, and all riders came to a halt. A glance over his patrol told Michael that each man appeared calm in the face of being so outnumbered.

No one was in a hurry to identify himself as the leader of the rebel party. Michael had played that game before. He made a quick assessment of all the rifle-toting rebels in hunting shirts, noting the cockades in their hats. These were militia Colonel Young's men, perhaps some of the same scoundrels who'd turned tail and run from the battle at Herons Bridge in January. Now that they outnumbered the redcoats three-to-one and had them surrounded, they'd finally found their courage—

Wait. Among them were two riders wearing suits. Michael's attention fixed on one of the men. He had intelligent blue eyes and full lips. His face had begun to soften, his hairline to recede, signifying that he was in his late-thirties or early forties. The hands holding the reins were slender and pale, without calluses. Delicacy clung to him.

An attorney if ever Michael had seen one. He held his gaze and made his tone flat. "Mr. Hooper." Unsmiling, the man inclined his head. "Captain Stoddard at your service, sir. My men and I have the honor of conveying you to Wilmington for negotiations with Major Craig. While you're in town, we'll also be responsible for your security."

"Thank you, Mr. Stoddard." Hooper dabbed at his brow with a handkerchief and settled a cocked hat on his head.

Michael quieted his voice. "And your lady asks me to ensure that you've brought additional funding for your family."

Hooper's lips tightened. "I have done so." He glanced at the sky. "The day grows warm. Let us be off." He sent his mount toward Michael.

The darker fellow in a suit followed. Michael held up his hand to halt him and frowned. "Wait a moment. Who are you, and where are you going?"

Hooper halted also. His orator's persuasive voice reached out to Michael. "This is my associate, Mr. Maclaine. He's accompanying me to Wilmington."

Alexander Maclaine's family was also held hostage in town. Michael disciplined a hiss of annoyance and made another scan of the group. No more suits among them, no more rebels trying to take advantage of the escort to grab a visit with their kinfolk. He stared down Maclaine. "My orders are to escort only Mr. Hooper to Wilmington. If it's your intention to join us, Mr. Maclaine, I cannot guarantee that we'll be responsible for you. And you'd best not lag behind."

Maclaine's lips pinched with irritation, then rolled inward. He nodded. "I understand."

The rebels backed off, allowed the patrol to reform with Hooper and Maclaine in their midst, then followed as the soldiers rode for the track. Michael spared one more glance at his charges when they weren't looking at him and shook his head. Surely Major Craig would throw the non-essential Maclaine in the pen. And he wondered how Hooper, a slave owner, could have signed a document proclaiming that "all men are created equal."

After the patrol headed southwest on the road, the band of militiamen trailed them. Without needing to look over his shoulder, Michael was aware of them. Within a few minutes, the rebels scattered.

During the trip, Hooper and Maclaine kept to themselves. Their silence allowed Michael time to review in his head the measures that he and Spry had set up to provide for Hooper's safety and draft an adjustment to the duty roster to add surveillance on Maclaine—in case Craig didn't throw him in the pen.

What he couldn't prepare for was the speed with which news of Hooper's arrival spread through town after the patrol rode in—and the crowd of civilians that swelled around them in welcome. He had no idea that Hooper's fellow Wilmingtonians appreciated him so much. The signer's face brightened. It was all Michael and his men could do to stay ahead of the waving hands and expressions of adoration.

At Craig's headquarters, the crowd hung back in the street but didn't leave. Michael sent Henshaw and Wigglesworth for reinforcements to help disperse the civilians. The provost marshal's guard waved him up to the porch. Michael and the rest of his men hustled their charges up the front steps.

As they reached the porch, Major Craig opened the front door, advanced past the guard, and wrung Hooper's hand. "A pleasure to meet you, Mr. Hooper. How excellent of you to come. Step right this way." His hand on the signer's shoulder, Craig steered him through the doorway. "May I offer you a cup of tea this morning? Or do you prefer something stronger?" They disappeared into Craig's study.

Completely ignored by Craig, Maclaine moved to follow. The guard blocked him from entering the house and scowled at him. "You. Wait here on the porch." Maclaine backed away frowning.

In six months of occupation, Michael had never seen Craig greet anyone at the door. From a brief look of bafflement he exchanged with the guard, neither had he. With a jerk of his head toward the house interior, the guard gestured for him to follow Craig and Hooper. Michael left his fusil on the porch and entered the house.

Major Craig's adjutant sidestepped to avoid colliding with him while leaving the study. In the dim, stuffy room, Hooper and Craig stood facing each other near the curtained west window, Craig listening, Hooper enumerating the titles of books he'd read that year. Standing at attention out of the way of the adjutant's return, Michael waited for Craig to notice him and saluted when he did.

Craig offered Hooper a gracious smile. "Excuse me a moment." He walked over to Michael. "Everything went well?"

Michael dropped his voice so Hooper couldn't hear. "Mr. Hooper insisted upon bringing Alexander Maclaine with him, sir."

Craig's eyebrows shot up, but he kept his voice low. "Why?"

Michael shrugged. "His family, perhaps."

"Mr. Maclaine is spying."

"They're both spying, sir."

"Of course they are. And that was Mr. Maclaine on the porch?"

"Yes, sir. What are your orders for him?"

Craig studied the open double doors and rubbed his chin a few seconds. "Assign surveillance. Let him go on to his family and know that he's being watched twenty-four hours a day."

Michael nodded, glad that he'd used the trip to work out assignment details. "Sir." He glanced over Craig's shoulder at Hooper. "I will need a few minutes to set up surveillance for Mr. Maclaine and also to disperse the crowd outside before we can safely escort Mr. Hooper home."

The adjutant breezed in with a steaming teapot and cups on a tray. Craig twisted about to watch him place the tray on a table between two chairs near the west window. As the adjutant returned to his writing table, Craig gave his attention to Michael. "Will half an hour do?"

Tea's fragrance lingered in the air. Michael didn't blame Hooper for his choice of refreshment. "Yes, thank you, sir."

Out on the front porch again, Michael looked over the throng waiting in the street. "Mr. Maclaine." He faced the rebel, who'd stood tall at Michael's exit from the house. "Rather than imprison you, Major Craig permits you to visit your family."

Maclaine exhaled with relief. "Thank you, Captain." He stepped toward the stairs.

Michael grabbed his arm and hauled him back around. Two soldiers from his patrol and Spry blocked access to the stairs. "I wasn't finished, Mr. Maclaine." He released the man's arm. "While you're in town, soldiers will accompany you. If you attempt to go anywhere without your escort, you will be arrested and conducted to the pen." Maclaine clenched his jaw. "You will wait here on the porch until your escort arrives. Do you understand me?"

"Yes," Maclaine muttered, gaze downcast.

"Remember, it was your choice to come here, Mr. Maclaine." Michael shifted his gaze to his assistant at the stairs. "Spry, you're with me." He signaled the remaining members of his patrol. "You have the first shift as Mr. Hooper's escort." He gestured to Maclaine. "Watch him. I shall send his escort promptly." The provost's guard returned his fusil to him, then he and Spry headed down to the street.

Civilian voices reached Michael. "Captain Stoddard, we want to see Mr. Hooper!" "Is Mr. Hooper a prisoner?" "What's Mr. Hooper doing in there?"

Michael and Spry walked out beyond the yard's fence and faced the crowd. Michael passed his fusil to Spry and raised his arms high, fingers spread. "Attention, everyone! Mr. Hooper is visiting for a few days on a diplomatic mission. He's enjoying a cup of tea with Major Craig this moment." Civilians squinted at him in disbelief, no doubt remembering the regiment's foul treatment of Cornelius Harnett and John Ashe. "I order you to disperse. Return to your homes and businesses immediately!"

No one budged. He heard the approaching clank-stomp of soldiers and lowered his arms. People twisted around to view ten redcoats trotting around the corner, muskets in hand, Wigglesworth and Henshaw in the lead. Before the soldiers arrived, every civilian was gone from the street.

Michael assigned Maclaine's first-shift escort of three from among the newly arrived men. Back at the barracks, he posted a duty schedule for Maclaine's escort alongside the schedule for Hooper's guard. Men gathered round to inspect the updated schedules.

When he stepped away to give them room, he spotted Jackson's head with its scabbed patch. He waved the private over, and Spry joined them. "Ferguson said you'd some information for me."

"Yes, sir. Around four this morning, I watched a man pick the lock on the front door of the tannery and let himself in."

"I'll be damned," muttered Spry.

Michael cocked an eyebrow. "What did he look like?"

"Well, sir, it was full night, and your orders were to not follow anyone who came to the tannery, so all I can tell you is that he was tall and slender, and dressed in dark clothing. Wore a hat to cover his hair." Jackson frowned, consulting his memory. "And he wasn't old, sir. He moved with—with agility."

Agility. That was an interesting word. Did it describe Kevin? "How long was he there, Jackson?"

"Not a minute, sir, before he left the same way he'd gone in."

"And empty-handed."

"Empty-handed, yes, sir." Jackson studied him with respect. "How'd you know?"

This had to be the same rogue that Ferguson and Stone had chased away from White's Tavern. Michael recalled seeing Kevin grab from midair an empty tankard that a drunk had thrown and prevent it from hitting another patron in the head. That had looked like agility to him. "I know because I have what he was looking for."

How much longer would Kevin search for his traveling gear—and hunt for Uno, the witness who could identify him?

More importantly, what would happen if William Hooper accidentally got in his way?

By then, Fairfax was well on his way to New Berne. That meant Michael had no choice but to keep his nose to the ground on the Bellington investigation there in Wilmington. Major Craig must be notified of the development.

Michael glanced over the short private, head to toe. He needed as many men as possible. "How are you feeling, lad?"

"Much better, sir. Clayton says I can go back to full duty today."

Michael flicked his gaze to the schedules. "That's good news, indeed."

Chapter Eighteen

MAJOR CRAIG'S HEARTY laughter spilled from the study. Michael slipped from the foyer between the parted doors. Craig's source of pleasure was his conversation with the signer, and while Michael had been busy in the barracks, it appeared that both men had consumed all tea in the pot.

Maclaine had been escorted to his house. The rest of Michael's patrol waited out on the porch to take Hooper to his family. Michael slipped a note to the adjutant to request a private audience with Craig on Friday morning. Then he stood at attention and softly cleared his throat.

Craig glanced in his direction, leaned over the little table toward his guest—for Hooper was clearly not a prisoner—and said, "Pardon me again, sir," before walking over to Michael and acknowledging his salute. "Has half an hour gone by already, Mr. Stoddard?"

Michael looked from the smiling Hooper to the high color on Craig's cheeks. Why was Craig so fascinated with Hooper? Then he recalled that Hooper had two brothers, merchants who spent a good amount of time in Charles Town and didn't support the rebel cause. Perhaps Craig was attempting to reconcile Hooper with the King. What a feather in his cap that would be. "Yes, sir. Half an hour."

"How time does fly."

Michael kept his voice down. "Sir, there's a matter I must discuss with you before we escort Mr. Hooper to his home. I believe that Mr. Bellington's murderer is here in town to kill an injured witness."

"Injured witness?" Craig scowled. "Why isn't Mr. Fairfax managing this situation?" He snapped his fingers. "Ah, that's right. He's gone to New Berne to find Mr. Bellington's nephew. But why did he leave town with a killer still on the loose?"

Michael said nothing and kept his expression neutral. He wasn't one hundred percent certain that Sam Bellington was innocent of the crime. However, Uno's "tall and lean" description of the murderer was at odds with Mrs. Hooper's description of a plump nephew, and if he'd shared that information with Fairfax, perhaps he wouldn't be juggling both high-profile assignments that moment—something that Fairfax had expressed a desire to do on Tuesday afternoon, there in the study. Oh, the irony.

The major sniffed. "It's too late to transfer this investigation to yet another officer. I must ask you to handle it. Yes, I realize that this puts extra work upon you."

"Not to worry, sir. I've arranged for the witness to be lodged in the barracks to protect his life. I've also increased security around town to make sure that none of this affects Mr. Hooper's visit." And—shoving concern for Kate and Aunt Rachel from his head—he'd set up surveillance on White's Tavern through six o'clock Friday morning. If the murderer returned in search of Uno, this time he'd be caught.

Craig nodded. "Excellent work, as usual." His appraisal of Michael sharpened. "Do you know the killer's identity?"

"Not with certainty, sir, but I suspect it's one of Mr. Bellington's clients."

"I appreciate your diligence and attention to duty. Keep me informed." Craig swiveled back to his guest and made his tone bright. "Mr. Hooper, my officer has reminded me that I'm keeping you from your family. Do take advantage now of the escort to your home that he's provided. Let's resume our conversation at three this afternoon."

Hooper stood and bowed his head. "Thank you, Major."

* * *

At the house on Third Street, the front door closed Hooper inside before the tears sparkling in his wife's eyes could spill over. Michael saw the patrol of six soldiers guarding the house settled into their routine, then moved on to Maclaine's house, where the three soldiers there were already settled. His next stop was the church building, where Spry supervised a team of soldiers who removed all chairs and portable benches that had replaced pews torn out for fence posts back in March and set the makeshift furniture outside on the lawn. After they'd emptied out the furniture, they'd check over the interior for objects that could be used as weapons and transfer those to the shed out back. Michael didn't have to observe longer than a minute to confirm that his assistant had matters well in hand.

He made a quick pass to the kitchen building behind the house where he was billeted. The hired woman was scraping into a bowl the porridge crusted at the bottom of the pot. Those stale bread slices hadn't gone far at five o'clock that morning. Michael claimed the crunchy, scorched bits of porridge—ever so much better than what oozed from the pot in the mess and passed for corn mush.

In the barracks he found Uno sitting at the table near the entrance, his expression downcast. Someone had provided the slave with a clean shirt. A mug of coffee waited on the table near his right hand, and his left arm was in a sling, a bandage bulky beneath the sleeve. The fever-gleam was gone from his eyes. His constitution looked good.

Michael slid onto a bench across from him and set his hat on the table. "Uno, it's good to see you up and about. How do you feel?"

"Surgeon changed my bandage again. Every time he change it, my arm hurt."

Not many soldiers were in the barracks that time of day. Nevertheless, Michael scooted his bench closer to the slave. "At least your arm is healing."

Uno's gaze on him was steady. "You must know that I didn't want to come here at first, Mr. Stoddard. Then the surgeon told me you figured out it wasn't a redcoat who killed Mistuh Jasper. A crazy man in a costume, he said."

"That's correct." Michael held his gaze and kept his voice down. "You'll need to stay close to the barracks with the soldiers for a few days."

"That crazy man is coming for me, ain't he?"

"No. We shall nab him first. And the more you can tell me about Monday night, the better our chances of catching him."

Uno's eyes narrowed. "How you gonna use information I tell you, suh? I'm a slave. Ain't nobody gonna accept what I say."

"Fortunately this investigation can be approached from several angles. Spry and I have uncovered relevant evidence independent of your ordeal. In addition, Clayton the surgeon has made some interesting predictions of the sequence of events Monday night, based upon what he saw at the estate yesterday. I expect that all of it will support the story you have to tell." He leaned toward the slave. "Now. Was the killer Mr. Bellington's nephew, Sam?"

"Nosuh!" Eyes wide, Uno sat tall. "Mistuh Sam ain't got no reason to kill his uncle. And he's a plump man, medium height. The killer was tall and lean."

"So you've said. Had you seen this man before?"

Uno licked his lips and shifted his gaze away. "Hard to say, it being dark, and him wearing that wig, suh." He stared at the wall. "But he mighta been one of Mistuh Jasper's customers."

There it was, Uno's confirmation of what Michael suspected. He thought of Kevin's name on the July summary page and held in a sigh. "How recent a customer?"

Uno's stare became unfocused, and he sat still. The seconds passed, and Michael waited without fidgeting in his chair. Then the slave stirred. "Beginning of this year, suh, maybe."

Beginning of this year? Michael revisited his earlier theory, Kevin agreeing to murder Bellington in exchange for Hickory expunging his information from the ledgers. Had Hickory omitted Kevin's name for previous months, then forgotten to remove the entry for July?

But no, that theory couldn't be right if the firm had fifteen clients in July. Hiding Kevin's record would have brought the number down to thirteen clients on the false summary page. Hickory must have removed information for another client.

"What was the customer's name?" Uno shook his head. Michael scratched his temple. "Tell me what happened this past Monday night. Where did you first see the killer?"

The slave blinked and looked at him. "In the house, suh. It was twilight. I'd been in the library when I thought I heard Tucker yell outside, so I left, turned around to close the doors. Then that demon come out of the shadows with eyes as black as the devil's soul." Uno shuddered but held Michael's gaze. "I startled him. In the next second, he pointed a pistol at me and would have shot me in the face right there, but Mistuh Jasper showed up, caught his eye. I punched the pistol out of the killer's hand, ran toward Mistuh Jasper, and hollered for him to get out, run for his life."

His words came faster. "Mistuh Jasper yelled at the man, 'How dare you invade my home? Leave here!' I grabbed the Mastuh, pulled him toward the door. Then I saw the killer had the pistol again, pointing it toward Mistuh Jasper, and I—I—" Uno's eyes glistened. He dropped his gaze.

"You jumped in front of Mr. Bellington and took the ball in your arm," said Michael softly.

"Yessuh," Uno whispered. He coughed. "Mistuh Jasper tried to grab one of the loaded pistols we keep around the house, but the drawer jammed, so he ran for the study. More pistols in the study." A tear tracked down his brown cheek. He sniffed and lifted his chin. "I was bleeding, Mistuh Stoddard, couldn't move my arm well, couldn't help the Mastuh. I ran outside yelling for Otis and Tucker. Them brothers weren't nowhere I could see." He hung his head and grew still again.

A minute or so passed before Uno found Michael's gaze. "I heard shots fired in the house. I wandered in the almost-dark calling for the brothers. Then I tripped over Otis. He was covered in blood, still warm, his pulse gone. Farther out, a few minutes later, I found Tucker's body. Then two of the dogs, dead.

"The killer hunted me. He had a lantern. I got a good distance away from Tucker and watched him plunge a knife into his chest, out of anger. That devil picked up my trail in the dark. See, I was leaving drops of blood behind and stepping on plants, and he was finding my trail with the lantern. It was all I could do to stay ahead of him and be quiet about it." Uno's voice was raspy.

Hair stood out on Michael's arms and the back of his neck. He pushed up from the bench and paced before the table, tasting Uno's fear, experiencing the killer through the slave's eyes. Clayton had done an eerie, accurate job of envisioning the nightmare, based upon the dead men he'd examined. "How did you escape him?"

"I stopped the blood with my handkerchief. I was dizzy and had me a swoon near a fallen log. When I come to, I lay real still and watched the killer sniff around fifteen feet away. He finally left, lost my trail. Soon I smelled the house set afire. I think he came back again looking for me, but I don't remember some of the night." The slave sank back in his chair. "I did me some hiding, yessuh. And soon as I could, I got out of there."

Michael studied him. "You rode one of the horses."

"Yessuh. Couldn't lift the saddle or stirrups none with my hurt arm, but I helped Otis often enough with the bridle, bit, and reins that I could get it done in the dark." One of his eyes twitched. "Tried to get help from the Davises. Neb Davis shot at me with his rifle, thinking I was a bandit that late at night, and his dogs run me off." Uno sipped his coffee. His jaw quivered.

Michael considered the half-truth Lavinia had told him Tuesday evening in the Hoopers' house to protect the injured Uno. She must have encountered him Tuesday morning. "How did Lavinia find you?"

"I rode for town, made my way to our meeting tree about dawn. She spotted me soon enough."

Meeting tree? Michael had no idea where that was, but it did sound as though Uno was courting Lavinia, as Mrs. Hooper believed. "Aside from Lavinia, did you tell your story to anyone?"

"I remember telling some to Eli Tuesday night. See, Vinnie hid me in a cellar during the day, brought me food and water. I was so weak that I mostly lay in a daze. That night, her and my cousin come and moved me out back the tavern."

Lavinia had shielded Uno by telling Mrs. Hooper she'd heard of Bellington's demise from a plantation slave. There hadn't been a second slave spreading word of the incident. A soldier from his patrol on Tuesday afternoon had gossiped about it, then tried to cover up his blunder by claiming he'd heard the story from a slave.

Michael must talk with each of the six men to find out who'd leaked the story, then dispense disciplinary action. How disappointing to think that a man he'd handpicked possessed such indiscretion. If that man couldn't be relied upon to keep his mouth shut, he couldn't be trusted to guard William Hooper.

"Uno, how well would you recognize the killer if you saw him again?"

"Don't know, suh. I only got a glance at his face. We was in the shadows. He did look like a redcoat. Held himself like a soldier." The slave darted a nervous look at the closest soldiers. "You sure he ain't from the regiment?"

Kate's words about Kevin's stint in the militia returned to Michael's memory. He stopped pacing and held Uno's gaze. "Remember I told you that we have evidence of our own. We found the costume he used. It had fresh blood on it." Uno's shoulders sagged, and he let out a pent-up breath. "Before early Wednesday morning, when was the last time that you were in White's Tavern?"

The slave shook his head. "Ain't never been in White's Tavern before then, suh."

It had been worth trying that angle to see if Uno could recall Kevin's face. Kevin was well-known by the people of Wilmington. Even many infrequent patrons recognized the tavern's manager.

For the time, it looked as though Michael had gotten as far as he could with the slave's testimony. "Very well, I must take my leave of you for now. If I can, I shall stop by this evening. What did Clayton say about your injury?"

"Rest up. Get my strength back."

"Then do so. Should you recall more details about Monday night, send for me or Spry." He clasped the slave's right shoulder briefly. "You're a brave man, Uno."

* * *

"Look here, sir." With a grin, Spry plopped a bucket on the wooden floor at Michael's feet. The clatter of it echoed through the empty nave of the church. A hatchet, mallet, scissors, and four rusted nails rattled together in the bucket. "You ask for weapons, and we find you weapons."

"My men are the King's finest." Michael toed the bucket closer. "Someone was woodworking."

"Perhaps in the spring, on those makeshift benches." Spry caught his gaze and presented a sober expression. "We've searched the entire church, sir. Even looked beneath the rugs in the chancel and behind the altar." His mouth twisted. "Plenty swept beneath those rugs. No weapons, though."

Michael tilted back his head and scanned the tops of the windowsills. "I don't imagine the vicar likes you very much right now."

"No, sir."

He spied a long, flat object atop the north windowsill. Buchanan, one of the men who'd ridden in his patrol out to Bellington's estate on Tuesday afternoon, passed in front of the window brushing a pile of dirt before him with a broom. Michael said, "Buchanan, reach atop that windowsill."

"Sir." The soldier propped the broom against the wall and stretched his fingers up. He brought a metal file over to Michael, who then waved the file at Spry and dropped it into the bucket with a clang.

Spry sighed. "Yes, sir. I shall check the tops of all windowsills and door frames." He meandered over to the south window.

Hands clasped behind him, Michael directed his attention to Buchanan and kept his voice low. "A question for you. After our patrol returned to Wilmington on Tuesday afternoon, with whom did you discuss the details of Mr. Bellington's murder?"

The private's eyebrows dipped. "Why, no one, sir."

"Not with Lindsey? You two wind up in a number of assignments together." The soldier shook his head. "Not even a quick comment on the fire damage?"

Buchanan maintained eye contact with Michael. "No, sir. Before we left the estate, you ordered us all to keep silent about it. I've done so."

Michael took in Buchanan's relaxed facial and shoulder muscles, the composure of an honest man. "Very good." He nodded at the broom. "Carry on."

"Yes, sir."

Buchanan hadn't been the gossip. One man down, five to go.

Chapter Nineteen

JUST AFTER NOON, William Hooper hopped in the family gig and enjoyed a leisurely drive around town. He smiled at friends and acquaintances and soaked up their benevolent wishes for his health and the success of his diplomatic mission. His guard of six soldiers strode alongside the gig in the hot sun.

As soon as Michael heard of Hooper's ride, he located the signer and halted his progress. A hand on the horse's bridle, Michael scanned the sweaty faces of his men, who were panting from having dashed about. Civilians gathered around and waved at Hooper, who waved back.

"Mr. Hooper." Michael elevated the volume of his voice above the buzz of good wishes. "Excuse me—Mr. Hooper!" The signer focused on him. "I must ask you to return to your house immediately, sir."

The civilians quieted, and Hooper frowned at him. "Why? Has something happened to my family, Mr. Stoddard?"

"No, sir. Any time you wish to take the air in a manner other than on your own two feet, you must first schedule the excursion with me."

"Major Craig gave me full access to Wilmington."

"Indeed, he did, but you must access it in a manner that allows us to easily protect you. If you drive your gig, the soldiers with you must be on horseback." Michael released the bridle and stepped back. Civilians made room. A droop to his shoulders, Hooper guided the horse around the way he'd come and headed home. Michael and his men accompanied him.

For the remainder of Thursday, Hooper stayed home except to attend his three o'clock meeting with Major Craig. Alexander Maclaine didn't venture forth from his home at all. Perhaps he'd realized that being non-essential could get him in trouble too easily.

Mid-afternoon, Michael interviewed Private Lindsey from his patrol. Lindsey was even more tight-lipped about the events Tuesday afternoon than Buchanan had been. With four more men to question, his thoughts began circling around Private Jackson as the source of the information leak. At Bellington's estate, Jackson had received the fright of his life and been wounded. If memory served Michael correctly, the private would be on duty at the supper party Friday night. A little chat with him was in order.

A messenger found Michael with an update from Spry. Benches, chairs, trestles, and planks for the party had been delivered to the church, and the soldiers there set them up. The building was now secured and locked to prevent anyone from sneaking in to plant a weapon. The vicar had registered a complaint with Major Craig.

Clayton reported that Uno's condition continued to improve. He was eating solid food again, regaining his strength. Michael stopped by the barracks long enough to see the slave absorbed in watching a game of checkers between two soldiers. Uno's sling had been removed.

Outside the barracks, he ran into Wigglesworth, another member of his patrol. The private had kept silent about the events Tuesday afternoon. That left Henshaw, Ferguson, and Jackson for questioning. Michael had seen Jackson strolling with a local girl on his arm Tuesday night—seeking solace for the day's turmoil? Yes, he'd definitely chat with the private soon.

As anxious as he was to find out what had happened with Kate, Aunt Rachel, and Kevin's correspondence, Michael made himself avoid White's Tavern—in spare moments diverting the energy of his concern for the women to the conquering of his pile of overdue correspondence. That morning, he'd wondered whether Kate and Aunt Rachel would close the tavern to give them time to adjust to their misfortune. They didn't do so, probably because White's would be closed the following night due to the supper party. Their ability to persevere in the face of such shocking news seemed astounding to him.

Shortly before he retired Thursday night, he received a confirmation note from Major Craig's adjutant. His request for a private audience with Craig had been approved for nine o'clock the next morning. Craig would give him a quarter hour of his time.

After that quarter hour, Michael's military record would no longer be spotless. In the sultry dark, he lay abed, his mind grinding over how to confess insubordination to his commander. Sleep was a long time coming.

* * *

Friday morning, July the twenty-seventh, he left the house at a quarter to six to make his rounds. Uno, up and about in the barracks, chafed against Clayton's insistence that he continue to rest. All was quiet at the Hooper and Maclaine homes. All had also been quiet since closing time at White's Tavern. Whoever had tried to break in early Thursday morning hadn't revealed himself with an attempt Thursday night. Michael saw no point in posting guards around the tavern Friday night.

New aromas—predominantly roast beef for the supper party that night—rose above Wilmington's stink and awakened his appetite. In the dining room of the house on Second Street, Spry brought him coffee and porridge from the kitchen, and Michael devoured breakfast. When the two officers sharing the table with him left, he brought his assistant up to date on the investigation, including Uno's testimony.

During his brief walk alone to Craig's headquarters, Michael's nose detected peach tart with cinnamon mingling with the roast beef. Since Hillsborough, peaches had reminded him of Kate. He was supposed to be at her house at seven-thirty that night. He winced. No, he wouldn't think about it until seven.

The guard signaled him up to the porch. The adjutant wasn't in the study, and Major Craig hummed as he draped a nice swatch of rose-colored linen over the little table between two chairs where he and Hooper had enjoyed tea the previous morning. Apparently Hooper was invited for tea again.

Michael closed both doors and saluted. With a smile, the major waved off his salute. "Good morning, Mr. Stoddard. How are you?" Craig placed teacups on the table.

"Well enough, sir." Michael petted the bulldog, Trouble, who'd made the effort to amble over to him. The obligatory chitchat grated on him. He was ready to commence with the abasement. "And how are negotiations for prisoner exchange progressing?"

Craig straightened and chuckled. "Negotiations aren't progressing at all." At Michael's puzzled look, he strutted behind his table and sat. "That pompous rebel 'governor' never sent me a signed agreement for concessions. Thus I've nothing to work from." He leaned back in his chair, still smiling, high color returned to his cheeks. Trouble settled at his feet.

Michael swiped sweaty palms on his trousers and took a step toward Craig's table. "Shall I return Mr. Hooper and Mr. Maclaine to the rebels today, sir?" Not that he wanted to put off his own business any longer.

"No. Let them visit their families for a few days. Monday the thirtieth will be soon enough. And we've that supper party tonight to entertain Mr. Hooper." Craig's eyes twinkled. "I'm finding it quite a pleasure to converse with him. Such an intelligent and erudite fellow. He's knowledgeable about so many topics." He motioned for Michael to sit in the chair across from his table. "Enough of my business. What may I do for you, Mr. Stoddard?"

Craig was in the most agreeable mood that Michael had ever seen. Maybe it would last, and the blistering would be minimal. He perched on the edge of his seat, resisted the urge to wipe his palms again, and made eye contact with his commander. "Sir." He cleared his throat. "I have withheld evidence from Captain Fairfax in the Bellington murder investigation."

The twinkle faded from Craig's eyes. His smile drained away. "Why?"

So much for that agreeable mood. Michael swallowed. "Mr. Fairfax was my first suspect for the murder, sir. A few days before the murder, a witness reported him arguing vociferously with Mr. Bellington in the office. Shortly before Mr. Bellington was killed, Mr. Fairfax drove out to the estate."

"Mr. Bellington was one of the King's Friends, Mr. Stoddard!" Craig slammed his fist to the tabletop, rattling the inkbottle, a coffee cup, and several other items. "Mr. Fairfax had no reason to harm him."

"To the contrary, sir, Mr. Bellington was a neutral, as reported by several residents. I know from my acquaintance with Mr. Fairfax that he considers all neutrals to be covert rebels, and he has dealt harshly with them in the past. Thus until I was confident that he hadn't committed the murder, I deemed that giving him access to certain pieces of evidence would be a conflict of interests."

With a growl, Craig pushed back in his chair. "Conflict of—what conflict of interests? What evidence?"

Michael's pulse hammered in his ears, and he spoke slowly so he didn't stammer. "The injured witness of whom I spoke yesterday, the man I've been hiding and protecting, is Mr. Bellington's sole surviving slave, Uno. The killer shot him with a pistol Monday night. Uno said the man was a redcoat."

Craig's scowl deepened. "Redcoat—bah! Testimony from a slave, Mr. Stoddard—what did you expect? Uno probably killed Mr. Bellington himself."

"I've had the chance to question him extensively, sir. I don't believe he was complicit in the murder. While Mr. Fairfax was still a suspect, he was searching aggressively for Uno. I couldn't be certain that if he found him, he wouldn't finish the business of killing him, so he couldn't identify him."

The major pursed his lips and drummed the tabletop with the fingers of both hands. "If I assigned your fellow officer to this investigation while you suspected him of the murder, why did you not come to me afterward and question my assignment?"

Yes, that would have been the logical, responsible thing for a junior officer to do. But Michael had relished keeping information from Fairfax. Now he'd have to gloss over the exact timing, hope that Craig didn't notice any discrepancies. "Sir, I questioned the assignment only while Mr. Fairfax was a strong suspect. During that time, I was also immersed in the business of making certain that Mr. Hooper is safe in Wilmington. You emphasized that that assignment had priority over the murder investigation."

Craig rubbed his hand over his face and expelled a hard breath. "Yes, I did tell you that." He flung up his hands. "What about New Berne, eh? Has your withholding of evidence resulted in Mr. Fairfax being sent on a wild goose chase?"

"Not at all, sir. Before he left town, Mr. Bellington's business partner, Mr. Hickory, falsified copies of the financial records he gave Mr. Fairfax and me so he could conceal the identity of the killer. He also hid the main books." Michael released his grip on his knees. "It's critical that Mr. Fairfax find Mr. Bellington's nephew, Samuel, who is another business partner. This nephew lives in New Berne. He may be able to reconstruct from memory the missing information and thus verify the murderer's identity."

"You said yesterday that the murderer is in town."

"Looking for Uno, yes, sir. Also looking for a bag of supplies he left behind."

The major sat forward, balled his fists on the tabletop, and bunched up his shoulders. "Where are those supplies now?"

"In Mr. Fairfax's room, sir." Michael was relieved to tell a whole truth for a change.

Craig's shoulders and fists relaxed. "That's refreshing to hear. At least you didn't hide the bag of supplies from Mr. Fairfax."

Of course he'd hidden Kevin's travel gear from Fairfax. And he'd given all but one of Kevin's letters to Kevin's sister and aunt. No point in correcting the misconceptions. By then there were too many of them. Truly, he was damned. Why had he compromised himself so deeply?

"Let me see if I understand. The evidence you withheld from Mr. Fairfax was the injured slave?"

"Yes, sir." Hiking his chin did three things for Michael that moment. It sealed in his lies. It made him look more honest than he felt. And it kept him from squirming.

"And in concealing the slave from Mr. Fairfax, you've involved a number of the men."

"Yes, sir. Note that those men also kept the witness safe from the true killer."

"Duly noted."

"I accept full responsibility for the deployment of regiment resources in this act, sir."

"As you should." Craig studied his expression a long moment. "Who murdered Mr. Bellington?"

"A client who borrowed a large amount of money from the firm, sir."

Craig nodded. "That sounds logical. Well, then, leaving that bag of supplies in Mr. Fairfax's room while he's in New Berne is risky. Take responsibility for it. Make certain the killer doesn't get his hands on it."

"Yes, sir."

When Craig pushed up to his feet in a lithe movement, Michael rose, too. Relief trickled through his insides. Was that it? No punishment? Surely it was too good to be true. If so, why hadn't his commander dismissed him? He made fists of his hands to still their trembling.

The major paced for half a minute before the tea table. Then he said, low, "I shall document your insubordination in your military record. Everyone makes mistakes, Mr. Stoddard. I sincerely hope that this will be your last mistake while you serve His Majesty."

"Sir." Even though Michael had expected the mark on his record, it still stung. But that wasn't the worst facet of this incident. Because Fairfax now looked like the injured party in Craig's eyes, it would be an uphill battle convincing the major of Fairfax's brutal history, should he need to do so.

"I believe I understand your rationale, though, and will add my comments to your record as explanation." Craig veered off from the pacing and came to stand before him. "You're a fine officer with an excellent career ahead of you.

From this moment onward, I expect better judgment from you."

Michael kept his chin up. He must tread very carefully to make certain he didn't get tangled in the web woven by Claude Devereaux and the Team. "Yes, sir."

"You're dismissed."

* * *

At the edge of the front porch, Michael gazed over the front lawn and sucked in a deep breath of cinnamon-scented tar to steady his jitters so he didn't stumble down the stairs. How little he'd revealed to Craig. The details he didn't confess to his commander hovered like hornets. Quite a devilish dilemma.

He'd left himself vulnerable to Fairfax's discovery of and reporting that Michael had committed additional insubordination. Most importantly, if Michael had misjudged Kate and Aunt Rachel, if they'd decided to keep Kevin's letters out of sentiment, and Fairfax found them, Fairfax wouldn't stop until Michael was, at the least, kicked out of the Army; or, preferably, hanged for treason. Thus a business conversation with Kate must be had tonight, regardless of how upset she might be and grieving over her brother's betrayal.

He had a long day ahead of him. It hadn't started well, and he doubted it would end better, and in between, some of it must be spent covering his own arse. In the yard below, William Hooper was making his way toward the stairs. Michael trotted down and wished him a good morning in passing. Then he headed for his quarters on Second Street and his next order of business, transferring Kevin's bag of gear from Fairfax's room to the barracks for safekeeping.

Chapter Twenty

THE KNOCK ON Michael's bedroom door yanked him thousands of miles: from a cool, misty summer at his sister's Yorkshire farm to the muggy heat of July in Wilmington. His gaze traveled from the letter he'd just finished writing to the closed door to the faded daylight in the window. What time was it?

From the other side of the door came his assistant's voice. "Sir, are you in there?"

In the distance, he heard the grumble of thunder. "Uh, come in, Spry." He signed his name to Miriam's letter.

The door creaked open a few inches. Spry pushed his way in, a glass of what looked like claret in one hand, a bucket of water in the other, and a swatch of white fabric draped over one shoulder. He set the bucket on the floor below the washbasin, then placed the goblet on Michael's desk with all the aplomb of a good valet. "Courtesy of the Wilmington ladies, sir." He walked back over, shut the door, and smiled. "Seven o'clock, as you requested. I'm here to brush out your better uniform and see that you arrive at the church in a timely manner."

Michael grimaced and pushed back from his desk. "What's that draped over your shoulder? Looks like a shirt."

"Indeed, sir. I took the liberty of borrowing it on your behalf and hope you don't mind." He opened the shirt fully and held it up by the shoulders.

Michael stared at it, hard, a few seconds. "Lace?" He barked a laugh and dismissed the shirt with a wave. "No, no, that's not me. I'll look like a peacock."

"Beg your pardon, sir, but I heard a rumor that a certain lady in town appreciates seeing gentlemen who wear lace well."

As Michael had never worn lace at all, he wasn't sure he could wear it well, but the longer he eyed the shirt, the more his sense of derring-do stirred up. "Very well, I shall try it." He gestured to the wine. "Now, come on. The Wilmington ladies didn't send that."

Spry's smile never faltered. "Yes, they did, sir. Especially Mrs. Farrell. They know you're working hard, and they want to make sure you have a good time tonight." He winked at the glass. "So drink up." The private spread the shirt out on the bed and moved back over to the washbasin to ready towel and soap.

Not for several weeks had Michael been able to afford wine. Who was he to look a gift horse in the mouth? Likely there was more where that came from anyway. Huzzah.

As he savored the first sip, thunder rumbled closer. Spry shoved the window closed. The heavens were going to open up and delay his arrival at Kate's house. How prudent of him to insist that supper be held inside a building. He'd enjoy his claret and not worry about it. The night was in good hands.

By forty minutes later, the thunderstorm had done its worst and moved on, leaving behind a cloudy sky and soaked town. Every button and buckle on him shining, a froth of lace at his wrists and throat, Michael presented himself at Kate's front door and knocked. Curtains in front windows jiggled. Above the intermittent drip and plunk of moisture off eaves, he heard muffled feminine laughter from within and a scurrying around.

The door eased open far enough to reveal Alice Farrell, all wide smile and bosomy in her burgundy red gown. She curtsied, and he bowed, and her gaze stropped him from hat to shoe. "My, oh my, don't you look delicious." Her perfume fondled him. She pushed the door open wide. "Come in."

Hat in hand, he stepped over the threshold into lamplight, then moved past the stairs. Nearly a dozen hens of Wilmington, beribboned and be-feathered in their finest, spilled from the parlor to ooh and ahh over him, and he bowed left and right to please them. "Good evening, ladies. Did I thank you for the claret earlier? You're all so generous."

Mrs. Farrell traded his hat for a second glass of claret. "Have a seat in the parlor. Your lady won't be but a moment longer." She whispered, "It's good that the rain delayed you."

His lady. Well, a fellow could dream, couldn't he? He gulped claret. The bevy of women cleared from the parlor doorway to let him enter.

From the second floor, Aunt Rachel's voice halted him, sent his gaze high up the stairs. "No, no, your lady is coming down now. Just a minor problem with her wardrobe." As she descended ahead of her niece, she worked a large, painted fan at her flushed face. "How fortunate that the rain cooled everything off." Emeralds to match her gown glistened at her earlobes, and lace trimmed her mobcap.

Aunt Rachel was a handsome woman still. He abandoned the claret on a small table beside the door, and when she reached the ground floor, he gave her a proper bow. When she rose from her curtsy, he didn't miss the puffiness around her eyes, the redness that told of grief. In his heart, he felt a pang of guilt; dumping letters on their dining room floor had been such an impersonal way of telling them what Kevin had done. Yet the warm smile Aunt Rachel gave him provided reassurance that neither she nor her niece had figured out his role in it.

The stairs squeaked. "It didn't cool off enough, Aunt." Kate descended, her fan a blur. Her hair, coiled atop her head, was woven with ribbons and lace, exposing the elegant curves of nape and throat. A pearl choker dangled a garnet before the hollow of her throat, matching the garnets at her earlobes. By lamplight, the creamy expanse of naked skin above her bodice glowed no less than the gold of her hair and the brocade of her polonaise gown.

Michael rooted where he stood, his gaze transfixed. Dimly aware of another round of oohs and ahhs from the ladies, he realized his jaw dangled open, and he shut it. Kate arrived at the bottom of the stairs. Her gaze on him swelled, roved up and down. Color dusted her cheeks.

Oh, yes, she liked the lace. How about that Spry, helping him out? Michael swaggered out the best leg he could. As soon as Kate curtsied, he stepped forward, hand extended, and brought her fingers to his lips. All the ladies applauded. And even though Kate's eyes also showed signs of weeping, she favored him with a soft smile.

"Oh, that was enchanting!" Mrs. Farrell clasped her hands over her heart.

Kate's smile on him wouldn't be so beguiling if she'd figured out that he'd been the one to leave those letters. No, it had been as he'd anticipated. The two women had concluded that Kevin dropped them off. Michael eased out a slow breath. How grateful he was that he and Kate still had a friendship and could enjoy themselves that night.

While the tobacconist's wife herded women out the front door for the church, Kate gripped his hand and leaned in close to him. "Let's talk later," she whispered.

Her gown sighed like oak leaves on a balmy, breezy summer night. Her cinnamon-honey scent caressed him. He tried to speak, but his throat hung onto his words—at least the intelligent words—so he kept quiet and nodded. It sounded like she wanted to talk to him about what Kevin had done. That was well. He knew how to listen to a woman's grief.

Aunt Rachel extinguished the lamps behind their exit and locked the front door, and Mrs. Farrell plopped Michael's hat on his head. More thunder muttered, accompaniment to the group's procession. On their approach, it looked to Michael as though every window had been thrown open in the church building. That would make security more difficult to—no, he mustn't think about it. Security that night was in the hands of the capable Nick Spry. A soldier was stationed every fifteen feet around the outside of the building. Soldiers were in place around a tent where civilian attendees were being inspected for weapons. And Michael knew that soldiers were posted inside, too.

After Kate cleared inspection in the tent, he escorted her up the stairs to the front doors, thrown open wide. The din of conversation, audible all the way over at her house, almost drowned out three fiddlers' sluggish offering on site. Michael had been a guest at enough officers' parties to suspect that the tune was a mutilation of "The Arrival of the Queen of Sheba." The instant he and Kate entered the candlelit nave, the musicians picked up the tempo and volume. A roar of approval went up from everyone crammed into the makeshift dining hall. Wine glasses and tankards lifted to Michael and Kate. Holding hands, the two of them bowed. The rafters resounded with three Huzzahs. Let the feast begin.

Buffeted by the noise and smell of two hundred summer-warm bodies—how in the world had they packed so many in there, and wasn't that hazardous?— Michael pasted on his best fake smile, saw Kate do the same, then glanced around, nervous because two hundred people couldn't possibly exit quickly if they had to. Damn. He and Spry should have created a plan for that. Then Spry waved at him from the back of the room, a bastion of confidence, and a reminder for him to relax and enjoy himself. He exhaled his anxiety.

Mrs. Farrell prodded and guided them to their reserved spot, generous enough for one and a half persons, and set his half-finished glass of claret on the table before him. "We're crammed tightly in here tonight." She grinned. "Fortunately you two are friendly!"

When they'd squirmed into place, Kate's pannier smashed against his hip, and her leg tangled with his leg. "Sorry," they both said at the same time, then looked at each other and laughed. His gaze traveled from the blue of her eyes to her golden hair, and his laughter relaxed into a smile.

She leaned toward his ear, offering a wonderful view of her lace-bordered cleavage. "Oh, my goodness. Look at Ned Peabody over on the right. Don't stare. Be casual about it."

Michael's gaze roved around and latched onto the dock manager. His eyes bulged as he took in Peabody's coat. He muttered to Kate, "He's—he's certainly green tonight."

Kate tittered. "He looks like a caterpillar!"

They laughed again together. He patted her hand. "Now, now, don't be cruel. You know that's probably his best coat." And when else would a lowly dock manager get the chance to rub elbows with Wilmington's top merchants, professionals, and artisans?

A server brought Kate's glass of wine, and Mrs. Farrell, who sat on the other side of her, asked her a question. It gave Michael the chance to make a visual inspection of the soldiers stationed around the interior, those lavishly-garbed civilians who'd been able to afford tickets, and the vicar and Craig's senior officers. At the back of the room sat the major himself—Spry and three soldiers standing behind him, and the Hoopers sitting on one side of him with expressions ironed out into cordiality. On Craig's other side were Lord and Lady Faisleigh.

Christ Jesus—Lydia. Michael snatched his gaze away, but not before Lydia had angled her fan to flirt and blown him a sultry kiss.

He expelled a slow breath. What a relief to be sitting beside Kate instead. He'd never relaxed fully around Lydia. Around most women, come to think of it. He savored the sensation of feeling comfortable, feeling settled, in Kate's company and favored her with another smile, which she returned.

The first course arrived with the second thunderstorm. Guests squealed and shrieked with delight when a wind gust spattered rain in and blew out a quarter of the candles. Between soldiers and servers, windows were shut and candles relit before any guests had finished the *hors d'oeuvres*. The musicians didn't even miss a beat of what bore some resemblance to "Dance of the Blessed Spirits."

Michael's appetite, forced into submission for so many weeks, roared to life. His serving of beef broth vanished about the same time as the remainder of his second glass of claret. While he and Kate chatted about the doings of local merchants, he managed to pace himself and not gobble the *poisson*, a sliver of tasty ocean fish. His stomach finally quit growling during the *entrée*. And how clever he was to tuck in all the lace at his wrists so he didn't drag it through his food. He hoped he didn't spy Kate concealing her amusement at him for that.

Every ten minutes or so, someone called for a toast or made a speech to praise the regiment. Midway into his third glass of claret, Michael's tongue loosened up. Kate was so easy to talk to. Plus Mrs. Farrell leaned past her to chat with him several times and with her tobacconist husband, Richard Farrell, sitting on the other side of Michael. And on the other side of Mrs. Farrell sat her owlish astronomer brother, Mr. Carlisle, who must have forgone his stargazing that night to drive into town for the fête. They all kept Michael plenty occupied. For long stretches of time, he even forgot that Lydia was in the same room.

The windows, open again to full night, brought in a breeze made cool and fragrant by rain. Michael finished his fourth glass of wine and a course of baked summer squash, shook out his lacy wrists, and extricated himself from his seat to find the vault. Moths swirled round candle flames. The musicians had taken a break. If the grass outside wasn't too soggy, there'd be dancing later; how late the fiddle music would continue depended upon the sobriety of the dancers.

While he waited outside in a short queue, only mildly inebriated thanks to the excellent meal, torchlight enabled him to spot Private Jackson on duty outside the building. Jackson. Ah, yes. That afternoon, he'd been able to question both Ferguson and Henshaw on leaking information about what they'd seen at Bellington's estate. Both soldiers had insisted that they'd kept their lips sealed. Jackson must be his man.

He finished his business in the vault and ambled over to him. "Evening, Jackson."

"Sir!" The private stood at attention.

"Stand at ease. How's everything out here tonight?"

"Very well, sir." Jackson smiled. "Except for the rain, of course."

"I understand. How does your head feel, lad?"

"So much better, sir. It hardly bothers me at all."

"Splendid." Michael flashed him a knowing smile. "Say, who's the young lady I noticed on your arm Tuesday night?"

The private grinned, and his head bobbed. "Ah. That's Esther McCall, sir."

Michael waited until the private met his gaze again and kept his tone casual. "How long have you been seeing her?"

"Two months, sir." Another grin split Jackson's face, and he danced from one foot to the other.

"Ooh. That sounds serious. She must have been concerned and curious about the bandage on your head."

"Yes, sir, that she was."

"And I'm sure that after all you went through that day, you needed some consolation. What did you tell her happened to your head?"

Jackson laughed, short and easy. "Oh, sir, forgive me. I lied to her. I told her I'd been working near a cannon. There was an explosion, some hot metal hit the top of my head, and it ripped off a piece of my scalp."

Michael squinted at him. "You—you didn't tell her about being—" He made a spiraling-up motion with his forefinger to simulate the act of Jackson getting caught in the snare.

"No, sir."

"Did you tell anyone about it?"

Jackson shook his head. "Sir, you ordered us not to talk about it, so I've obeyed your order. But it wasn't very heroic of me to get caught in that snare and hang upside down like a bat, needing my mates to help me out of it. If I'd told Esther the truth, why, I'd have looked like an idiot for bringing it on myself."

Michael felt his smile sag into oblivion. "I see your point." What the hell— he had the impression that the soldier was telling the truth.

"You said I needed some consolation, sir. You're right, I did. And she gave it to me." He chuckled. "She sure does know how to console a man. Yes, she does."

Despite his bafflement, Michael found himself drawn into the private's good spirits. He knew it well, the escape of death followed by the affirmation of life. "All right, Jackson, I shan't tell anyone about your little lie." Gods, no. His own deceptions were massive in comparison.

"Thank you, sir." The private's chuckles subsided, but he wore a giddy grin. "I'm in love with her. Have you ever been in love, sir?"

The question caught Michael by surprise, made him gape. "Uh—er—"

"I see you have." The private's smile went lopsided. "I think I want to marry Esther, sir."

Michael's head snapped back. "Whoa." Esther must have given him some serious consolation. "Slow down, lad. Now this is a conversation that you and I need to have in broad daylight."

The private rolled back his shoulders and sobered. "Yes, sir."

"You know, marriage is a big step in a man's life. I want you to think about it, long and hard." Spoken as if he knew what he was talking about and was guaranteed to follow his own advice. Michael massaged his neck in annoyance. The lace flopped against his cheek. Damned lace. "Lad, don't go off marrying a girl, just because she's capable at—at one particular thing. Spend some time thinking about this. Be sure you talk to me if you need help figuring it out."

Jackson drew a deep, measured breath. "Yes, sir. Thank you."

Hands crossed behind his back, Michael strolled away, past other soldiers on duty to the front of the church and tried to make sense of what Jackson had told him. Not the love and marriage part, although he would have to research Miss Esther McCall and make sure she and her family weren't rebels. What puzzled him was that the private, who'd been rattled by the incident with justification, had denied blabbing to anyone what he'd seen of Bellington's body.

Michael knew a soldier who'd witnessed battlefield horrors and jabbered about them, only to forget later that he'd ever spoken to anyone about them. That soldier's head had been grazed by a ball, as Jackson's head had been. The mind was certainly a peculiar thing; could Jackson have spilled what he'd seen at the Bellington estate, then forgotten he'd told anyone, courtesy of his head injury? It sounded like a question for Clayton on the morrow.

The good news in all this was that the leak about the condition of Bellington's corpse hadn't expanded very far. Otherwise, the sensational horror of it would have traveled through town like a lightning strike. People loved to gossip. The more appalling the incident, the farther word spread of it.

Raucous laughter spilled from windows. A great many partygoers would have hell to pay on the morrow from drinking too much. Four glasses of claret had done it for Michael. He'd best get back to his post inside and at least look the part for a while longer. Plus he didn't want to miss the peach tart.

Lydia's voice sought him from the gloom behind. "Mr. Stoddard, may I have a word with you?"

Blast. Michael turned to face her and her maid, Dorinda, and made his carriage and tone as formal as possible. "My lady." He bowed, his shoulders taut. "A brief word, as I must assume my duties inside."

She sashayed past him. "Come along."

Chapter Twenty-One

HE CAUGHT UP with Lydia, and they walked past the tent where civilians were inspected for weapons. Dorinda held back far enough that she wouldn't overhear a low-voiced conversation between them. He wondered how many times she'd trailed along after Lydia's schemes.

Her gaze straight ahead, Lydia fanned herself with an agitated wrist flick. "My husband has ruined everything. He's now trying to kill you."

For a second, rage, despair, and fear blasted through Michael. Then he barked a quick, dark laugh. "I warned you this would happen in the spring, when you first presented your business proposal."

"Yes, I remember. I just didn't believe Faisleigh would stoop to murdering you."

"My lady, you've been naïve. He's a man. More importantly, he's your husband." He shook off the glow of wine, rammed alertness into his brain, and glanced around for shifty, loitering ne'er-do-wells to emerge from night with their daggers. "So. What will it be? Poison in my coffee? A knife between my ribs? A rattlesnake in my bed?"

She rolled her eyes. "My husband wouldn't hire a local criminal for such an act. He'll never resort to crude methods. Your assassin will be a fellow officer. Captain Fairfax."

The world held still for an instant, tilted crazily, then righted itself. Michael shot a hard stare at Lydia. "Explain." He redirected his gaze forward and made himself breathe at a normal rate.

"Monday afternoon, my husband had Mr. Fairfax for tea in the parlor. There's a thin spot in the wall of the dining room, so I sat in there with my ear pressed to the wall and listened to them. Apparently this wasn't the first time the two had spoken." The breeze from her fan fluffed escaped tendrils of hair at her ears and neck. "Mr. Fairfax had learned that my husband outbid him for a major's commission that he intended for you weeks ago. And by the end of their conversation, Faisleigh told Mr. Fairfax that he'd sponsor him for that major's commission, should anything—*anything*—happen to you."

No assassin would jump at Michael from the shadows. And Faisleigh's request that Fairfax murder him hadn't been explicit. Nevertheless, horror dragged its jagged claws through his entrails. "Damnation," he whispered. Monday over tea, Faisleigh had signed a verbal contract for his own doom—and the doom of Michael's son.

Lydia's voice trembled. "I regret to inform you of such news. I do like you, Michael, and hope Mr. Fairfax doesn't use the heat of some battle to disguise murdering you. Please watch your back around him. He must hate you very much now and has an incentive to kill you."

They were still walking. He gritted his teeth in silence for several steps, then relaxed his jaw. "And I regret to inform you that Mr. Fairfax needed no encouragement to kill me before Monday. He's already attempted to do so several times. That means the real problem here isn't that your husband gave him incentive to kill me. The problem is that your husband aroused Mr. Fairfax's curiosity—and that's something you never want to do."

She squinted at him. "What are you talking about?"

"Mr. Fairfax is also a criminal investigator. The conversation with your husband will have made him curious why my benefactor wants me dead. I'm certain that by Tuesday noon, his preliminary queries about the matter were already in the post to his contacts back home. He'll research Faisleigh's history and family background, and he'll dig until he can piece together the truth about Lord Wynndon. Then, threatening to tell your brother-in-law the truth of the boy's paternity, he'll blackmail you, over and over. Within a decade, he could own Ridleygate Hall, making that wrangled-over major's commission irrelevant."

"Oh, my God." Lydia pressed her hand to her mouth.

Michael couldn't stop bitterness from tainting his tone. "I expect he'll let me live, just so I can watch the implosion of Lord Wynndon's future. How much better it would have been for us all had Faisleigh merely hired a local criminal and been done with it."

They circled the church together in silence. It allowed Michael time to reflect, to process the fact that on Tuesday night, while he'd undergone a struggle of morals to give his "benefactor" permission to outbid Fairfax, the outbidding had been done well in the past. That night, Faisleigh had staged the scene to control him like a dog and been entertained when Michael jumped on command. What scum.

Michael knew the secret that would ruin Faisleigh, so yes, Faisleigh wanted him dead. Regardless of the fact that he'd bid for the commission, Faisleigh wouldn't allow Michael to achieve the rank of major beneath his "patronage." Obviously their business arrangement was void, finished. Pretense at furthering it was pointless.

Torches were being lit around the designated dance ground, and the fiddle players were setting up to one side. The feast would be over soon. The stroll brought him and Lydia behind the building, where the line to visit the vault was three times longer than it had been earlier. They kept walking, and when they again arrived at the side of the church, Lydia spoke, a tough edge to her voice. "Thank you for apprising me of the ramifications of my husband's poor decision. It enables me to plan ahead. If Faisleigh does end up being dragged down by his mistakes, I've the means to make certain that Wynndon and I don't suffer his fate."

That dish of burned letter fragments on Lydia's writing table attested to her many connections. Michael nodded. "It would be wise of you to do so, my lady. I hope it's apparent by now that I wish the best for Lord Wynndon and would never compromise his inheritance."

She smiled. "I knew that back in the spring, when you rescued him." The party inside was still ripping along. They arrived at the front of the church and faced each other. Dorinda halted to keep her distance. Lydia sighed. "And I must continue to protect Wynndon from my brother-in-law's assassins."

"There's no benefit to your remaining in Wilmington. I counsel you to ride with Lord Wynndon to Charles Town as soon as possible. You'll be well protected there."

She pressed her lips together. "No benefit—?"

"See here. Our business arrangement is over." Sensing opposition building in her, he spoke quickly and low. "Let's officially terminate the agreement. Your husband has in his possession a signed copy of the contract. Give it to me—"

"But Wynndon would benefit from having you in his life. He's never forgotten the way you saved him. You're his hero."

Another rapier drove through his heart. Gods. His own flesh and blood. Now Lydia was manipulating him with that charge of emotion. He squared his shoulders and brought the conversation back on topic, his tone firm. "Lord Wynndon would benefit far more from safety. Now, you give me that copy of the contract, and I shall destroy it, along with my copy." And damn this game. He'd find his own, honorable way to major. Or not.

Her lips pursed. She collapsed her fan with a snap and tapped his chest once with it. "As my husband clearly has no intentions of promoting you to the rank of major, what if I gave you my word that I shall sponsor you for the rank?" She smiled at the widening of his eyes. "Faisleigh has more connections than I, thus it will take me a bit longer. But I can see it done. Perhaps I can even prevent his bid from being withdrawn."

He found his voice. "Thank you, my lady. But—"

"Yes. You want to know the cost of my sponsorship." She chuckled. "My expectation is that you take an active role in Wynndon's upbringing after we leave Wilmington. At the very least, you shall correspond regularly with him. Whenever you are in town together, you shall make reasonable effort to call upon him."

That wasn't bad. In fact, he looked forward to staying in touch with his son in such ways. He felt his shoulders relax. "Of course, my lady." He studied her a moment. "I'm surprised that you didn't resist ending the contract."

She jabbed her nose in the air and looked past his shoulder. "Why should I do so? As you've pointed out, my husband's recent actions have rendered the agreement void. However, I also question whether the fruition of those terms is possible."

He expelled exasperation through his nostrils. "Then you should never have used the phial."

"The phial. Hah. The midwife and I lied about it to Faisleigh." Slyness curved her lips, and she eyed him full on. "Late June, he began nagging me daily for results. I'd grown weary of our endeavor. Not weary of you, but of my husband's incessant monitoring. So I instructed the midwife to combine a few harmless herbs in a tincture and left the phial where Faisleigh would be certain to find it."

Michael could find no words to express the depth of his distaste over her duplicity. He thanked his lucky stars that his circle of friends and family contained no one so manipulative. "I see." What he wanted more than anything that moment was to be free of Lydia's company. "Well, my presence is expected inside. I must return to the table."

"Here's my counsel, then. Faisleigh provided you with a list of suitable ladies." She pointed her fan in the direction of the party. "Don't make the mistake of marrying that American minx in there. Oh, yes, I've seen you ogling her, and she does carry herself well. But let's be practical. A woman of her class hasn't a dowry large enough to help you with your estate. And as she hasn't a drop of nobility in her veins, she'll never be able to respond to challenges with politesse. As a result, the Scots won't respect her."

Michael's understanding of what Highlanders respected differed from Lydia's and stemmed from conversations he'd had with Scottish officers over the years. However, it wouldn't do to offend his patroness by telling her to mind her own business. He gave her a cordial bow. "Thank you, and good night, my lady." After turning on his heel, he strode back into the revelry.

* * *

The peach tart, complemented with sweet cream and served with coffee, was every bit as enchanting as the rest of the feast had been. Alas, Michael couldn't give it his full attention. Regardless of which angle he used to analyze his dilemmas, it seemed that sooner or later, Fairfax was going to own him. He saw no way he could prevent the monster from delving into Faisleigh's background and blackmailing the family when he learned the secret. No way, either, that he could stop Fairfax from unearthing all the ways he'd withheld evidence in the Bellington investigation, then reporting them to Major Craig. And no way to halt Fairfax from persecuting Kate and Aunt Rachel over their delinquent taxes and relationship to Kevin the traitor.

Through it all, he must keep his own counsel. He'd no confidant, no "ear" to help him figure things out. What a fool he was.

And what a relief when the dance was announced and everyone filed out of the overheated church building. With Kate again on his arm, Michael followed the masses next door to the dance ground rimmed with straw bales and torches. Straw had also been strewn on the ground itself and wicked away most of the moisture from the rainstorm. A soldier was stationed about every twenty feet.

When people insisted, he guided Kate to the head of one of the lines for the first dance. Across the line from him, she flashed him a quick smile. In another time and place, the night might have been magical for both of them. But her eyelids looked heavy, her face drawn. She and Aunt Rachel had suffered a wrenching several days. Fortunately the dozens of dancers there didn't expect them to stay all night. He'd check with Kate after a few tunes and offer to escort her home when she became weary.

They changed partners for the following dances but smiled at each other every time a moving line brought them together for a few measures. Michael lost track of Major Craig, the Hoopers, and the nobles; perhaps all had retired for the night. The musicians were fiddling the folk tunes they were born to play, and no more struggling with composers' scores. The fifth dance, Michael wasn't quick enough to snag a partner, so he walked around the sidelines to cool off and chat with townsfolk. Several women complimented him on the lace.

As the dance was winding down, Mr. Smedes, town wainwright and Kate's occasional business partner for whiskey transportation, caught up to him with a grin. "How you do move around, Mr. Stoddard." He slid his gaze back and forth in a furtive motion and lowered his voice. "Say, I've some information for you that may be connected with your investigation."

Michael's eyes widened on him, then he glanced around a redcoat-rimmed dance ground full of inebriated, happy Wilmingtonians. Aunt Rachel was bearing down on him to make good on his promise to dance the sixth tune with her. How urgent was the wainwright's information? He leaned in close to Smedes. "Is this information that we can discuss early in the morning, say, eight o'clock? Or do I need to hear it now?"

"Eight o'clock in the morning should be fine, sir."

"Very good. I shall come to your shop."

Smedes nodded once, then slipped into the crowd. Aunt Rachel gripped Michael's upper arm and towed him off the sidelines to one of the four lines of dancers. "Thought you could get away from me, did you?" She wagged her forefinger at him. "It's about time that you and I danced."

The wainwright had vanished, but he was an intelligent enough fellow to recognize when a piece of information was time-sensitive. Michael relaxed his shoulders and gave Aunt Rachel his full attention. "Indeed, madam. There's no escaping you."

"And don't you forget it. Kate says you're a superb dancer. I'm looking forward to it after two fellows from your regiment stepped all over my feet."

A quarter hour later, he spotted Godfrey Carlisle leading Kate from the dance ground. He swept in and, arm circling her waist, stole her away with a cheery thank-you to the astronomer. Michael noticed she was limping slightly and continued on to the sidelines with her. "Who's the oaf who stomped on your feet—Mr. Carlisle? I'll throw him in the pen for such poor manners."

A gust of laughter escaped her. "No one stomped on my feet. I wore the wrong shoes."

Hair had escaped the coil atop her head, and her face was shiny with sweat. She looked exhausted. He released her and stepped back. "Shall I escort you home now?"

She didn't respond straight away, listening to the languid, mournful melody in three-quarters time that the fiddlers were producing. Rather than lines of partners, it was couples promenading together on the ground, a step-step-close pattern to their feet. "Do you know how to dance to that? I think they call it a 'waltz.'"

He studied the way the dancers placed a slight accent on the first beat of each measure. "Would you like to try it?" She nodded, and he led her out. It took several measures to synchronize their feet, then they sank into the rolling rhythm and moved around the ground with the circle of dancers. "I wonder who invented this dance?"

"I believe it's Prussian."

Memory provided him with the image of drunken, singing, swaying Hessians. "Oh, that explains everything," he muttered. Across the ground, he spotted a man twirling his partner. That move looked interesting. "How do your feet feel?"

"I'll live."

"Good. Now, don't panic. I'm going to try something. Follow where I lead you. If it doesn't work, just keep walking."

Their first twirl, a little rough, was still successful. "Oh, my goodness, that was different. Fun!" Kate's expression brightened. "Let's do it again!"

He twirled her again, rested a measure, then twirled himself. They laughed, danced a quarter circle that way, then stepped up the challenge by leaving out the resting measure for another quarter circle. When they settled back into the straight waltz, grinning at each other and breathless, applause broke out from the sidelines.

Michael looked around the ground. All other couples had exited to the perimeter. When had that happened? Most of the partygoers as well as the soldiers in attendance had been watching them twirl and wore huge smiles.

He steered Kate for a straw bale, and none too soon, for she was hobbling. She sat and fanned herself while he fielded a stream of praise for several minutes. Aunt Rachel handed them mugs of the refreshing, minty summer drink that Kate had invented for her patrons back in March and patted Kate's shoulder. "That was magnificent!"

"And it was enjoyable." Kate's gaze on Michael softened.

Someone had set up a punchbowl on a table nearby, where civilians and off-duty soldiers queued up to purchase more refreshments. The fiddlers had quit playing and were taking another break. Aunt Rachel prodded Michael's arm. "Soon as those musicians come back, you two must dance for us again."

"Not in these shoes, Aunt." Kate took a long drink.

"You've a more comfortable pair at the tavern."

Kate lowered the mug with a frown. "I do?"

"I put them upstairs. Second bedroom. Why don't you pop over and fetch them, dear." Aunt Rachel regarded Michael, and tenderness crept into her eyes. "I'm sure Michael won't mind escorting you."

Kate drained her drink, and they handed their mugs to Aunt Rachel. After standing, she took Michael's arm. As he led her from the dance ground, he glanced over his shoulder. Aunt Rachel, her arms crossed, watched them. Torchlight picked out a glistening in her eyes before she blinked and turned away.

Chapter Twenty-Two

KATE UNLOCKED THE front door at White's, invited Michael to follow her into the yeasty darkness, and lowered the bar across the door. He heard her drop the padlock on a table, and she said, "I've a candle somewhere. Odd. I don't remember leaving my shoes here, but if Aunt says they're in the second bedroom, they must be there." With a knock and scrape of steel on flint, she brought a spark to life and lit the candle. From the flame, she also lit a lamp, and she handed him the candle in a holder.

He made sure the front and back doors were barred, then followed several steps behind her when she headed upstairs. Midway, he plucked up his courage. "Is Mr. Carlisle courting you, Kate?"

She yawned. "When I was newly widowed, his sister tried to interest us in each other romantically. But you see one binary star, you've seen them all."

It didn't sound as though Carlisle was competition. A tightness in Michael's chest relaxed.

Kate reached the next floor. He heard her open the door to the second bedroom and say, "Oh, my. Aunt was right."

"About what?" He stepped off the stairs and, by lamplight, saw her comfortable work shoes waiting just inside the door of the second bedroom. She picked up the shoes and proceeded inside. He walked to the doorway, where he waited with the candle.

She placed the lamp on the bedside table and, with a groan, sat on the bed, her panniers spreading out around her hips, to pull off her shoes. Feet and ankles flexed in silk stockings. Toe joints popped. "Ooh, that feels so much better. Serves me right for being vain and trying to wear new shoes to the fête." She made an attempt to shove her feet into the work shoes but gave it up and frowned at him. "I think my feet have done all the dancing tonight that they're going to do. I'm sorry, Michael."

He shrugged, not displeased. If they returned, people would expect an encore performance of those twirls, and he wasn't quite ready for all that attention. More importantly, he'd never talked with a woman for so long and about so many topics. In Kate's company, suppertime sped by. They could probably converse the rest of the night. What a treat that would be.

But she was tired. "I shall walk you home. Put on your old shoes."

"Actually—" She patted the seat of a chair on the other side of the little table. "—we may as well chat here first, where Aunt cannot interrupt us."

She was ready to confide in him about Kevin. Good. He entered the room, closed the door behind him, and set the candle on the table. The bedroom was a little stuffy. He pushed aside the curtains and opened the window and was rewarded with a cool breeze on his face.

As he lowered himself into the chair, he realized with a flick of annoyance that sometime that night, he'd misplaced his hat. One more expense that he didn't need. Maybe Spry would recover it.

Kate clasped her hands in her lap and studied her fingers. "When I came home early Thursday morning, I was astonished to find several lamps lit and Aunt still awake. She was in the dining room, dozens of letters spread out on the table before her." Kate grimaced. "Foul smelling letters. And she was weeping. Almost never does she weep. She told me that Kevin had come home long enough to drop off all those letters. Then he'd left again."

Michael kept his expression mild and open and met her gaze when she searched his face. Perhaps it was the way her stare probed him that prompted his instinct's whisper. The two women hadn't accepted the theory that Kevin was the one to leave them the letters. On what explanation had they settled, then? Puzzled, he made himself sit without restlessness.

"Ninety-eight letters stinking as if each one had been soaked in a vat of gardenia blossoms. I'll never forget that perfume. It was as if Naomi Levy was standing right there in the dining room with us. Laughing at us." Kate's eyes flashed, and her thumb rubbed her palm, over and over. "Ninety-eight letters telling us the story of how she bewitched my brother into joining her group of rebels." Her lower lip trembled. "He sold the house from beneath us and donated the money to those rebels in Charles Town." Tears sparkled in her eyes. "Kevin isn't operating the whiskey still. He's on his way to South Carolina to be with her. He took our only horse and all our savings, about forty pounds."

Somehow she hadn't yet learned that Michael reported Charlie as stolen. Maybe that was for the best. "I'm sorry to hear that, Kate. How frightened and hurt you must feel."

Her eyes flinched shut for an instant. "In ways you cannot imagine. The whiskey business was our buffer income." She shook her head. "It's no longer available to us. I paid Mr. Smedes to drive out there today with his wagon and tidy up. He brought me the equipment, which I've hidden."

He wondered whether in the morning, Smedes would relate to him something he'd seen while breaking down the still. He regarded Kate a moment. "Had you any idea before you saw those letters that your brother was going to Charles Town to be with Miss Levy—any warning of his intentions?"

"None."

"How unfortunate. Did you know that the two were corresponding?"

"No." A tear rolled down her cheek. "Maybe I should have realized something was amiss." With the back of her hand, she dashed away the tear. "In retrospect, he acquiesced too easily last year, when I thought I'd talked him out of his infatuation."

"Where are the ninety-eight letters?"

"Aunt and I burned every noxious, stinking one of them in the kitchen early Thursday morning, before Eli arrived."

Michael relaxed back in the chair and exhaled a breath he hadn't realized he'd held. "Good."

Her lashes wet, Kate studied his reaction. Then her shoulders lowered. "Yes. Good. When I questioned Aunt, though, she told me she hadn't actually seen Kevin. She'd assumed that he'd sneaked back to drop off the letters while we were at work because he couldn't face us with the truth. And perhaps he'd picked up some spare shirts and stockings while he was home. So I went upstairs to his room to see for myself." She chewed her lower lip. "There was no sign that he'd been back. The room was unchanged from when I last saw him on Monday.

"Downstairs, the foul smell from those letters was so thick that I felt I couldn't breathe. I told Aunt to bundle them up in a sack, while I went around unlatching and opening windows to air out the room." She leaned toward him, her eyes piercing as sunlight. "I found one window that I'd left unlatched. Just like the window I'd left unlatched early Wednesday morning here. The window that let you climb in. And that was when I realized who'd brought the letters, and I told Aunt."

Michael's heart hammered. Ye gods. She thought like a criminal investigator. Yet she didn't seem angry with him. Why wasn't she railing at him? His gut flipped around. "Kate," he said low, "I-I'm sorry. I had to find a way to tell you and Aunt Rachel about what your brother had done. I'm not polished at discussing matters like this." He rubbed sweaty palms on the knees of his trousers. "And—and I know I didn't handle it with any sort of grace. Forgive me."

"Forgive you?" She covered one of his hands with hers. At her touch, both his hands stilled their rambling. "Oh, dear God, Michael, you're the last person who needs my forgiveness." She blinked again at tears. "Who else knows about those letters?"

"Only Spry. He won't say a thing about them."

"Not that horrid Captain Fairfax?"

At least Fairfax had depreciated from "charming" to "horrid." "He knows only of the very latest letter. It wasn't included with those I gave you." He took her hand in both of his. "The content of that letter leaves no doubt that your brother has cast his lot with the rebels."

Two more tears rolled down her cheeks, and she bowed her head. "So it's too late for Kevin. If the Crown catches him, he'll be hanged for aiding and abetting that synagogue in South Carolina."

Michael's heart felt squeezed. He shifted over to sit beside her on the bed and wrapped an arm around her shoulders. "I'm afraid it's much worse than that," he murmured. "We've found evidence to implicate Kevin as a suspect in the murder of Mr. Bellington, his creditor."

With a moan, Kate folded against his shoulder. He'd learned that it was best to say nothing when a woman's heart was broken, and so he held her without speaking while she sobbed for several minutes. When her weeping lost force, he worked loose his handkerchief—clean, thanks to Spry—from his waistcoat pocket and handed it to her.

She blotted her face between sniffs and hiccups. Spent, she balled the handkerchief in her fist. He slid his arm from around her shoulders. She straightened, shoved hair from her eyes, and stared at the wall. "Kevin's a fool. What he's done has made life so much more difficult for Aunt and me. I don't suppose we shall ever see him again." She bit her lip, let down her hair, and tossed pins, ribbons, and lace to the table with the lamp and candle. "Yet perhaps I'm a fool, too. How I wish to see him once more and know that he's safe."

"That isn't a foolish wish. He's your brother, no matter his choices or actions."

After another silence, she swiveled to him, face blotched and hair disheveled, and rested one of her hands atop his, her gaze steady on him. "I've a question for you, Michael. If you'd been caught giving those letters to us, you'd have received court martial, wouldn't you?"

He slanted his gaze down. "Let's not discuss such matters—"

"Yes, I knew it. You didn't want Captain Fairfax to get his hands on the letters because of—because of what he'd do to Aunt and me with all that information. You risked court martial and gave them to us instead." She gripped his hand. "Look at me. Am I correct?"

He met her gaze again and nodded, mute. Her eyes were swollen, and her hair was tangled, yet she'd never looked more beautiful. And it wasn't the claret talking.

Fresh tears hovered in her eyes. "You put our welfare before your own career and life." She tossed the handkerchief to the bed and stroked the side of his face once with her fingertips. "You risked everything for us. I've never known a man like you. You're kind, and considerate, and noble. I've heard you even treat William Hooper with respect."

He squirmed. "Kate—"

"Thank you, Michael." She leaned forward and brushed the corner of his mouth with her lips.

He lingered in the kiss, stupefied when she caressed his face again. Then the realization hit him. Grateful she might be, but she was also grieving. What fine use he'd make of her sorrow-fueled appreciation if he didn't take the high road soon—get up off the bed and deliver her home. With Herculean effort, he pushed to his feet and straightened his coat. She gazed up at him with moist, pink lips, her brows pushed inward with perplexity.

He cleared his throat. "See here, you're upset over your brother and need a good night's sleep. I shall take you back to the house." He gestured to her old shoes. "Put those on." He pointed over his shoulder. "And—and I shall wait for you."

He made for the door, yanked it open partway, and stood just outside. There he sucked in deep breaths and realized after a moment that he'd neglected to bring a source of light with him. Without it, the tavern yawned around him, dark as Carolina tar.

Dark as a shadow that lately he'd found abiding in his own soul, in that place where he'd judged himself so smug and clever at withholding evidence.

He imagined that somewhere out in the night, Fairfax was resonating with his shadow. Fairfax had lured him there, then trapped him in the sticky, tarry web of his own arrogance. Claude and the Team wouldn't arrive until October. Well before then, Fairfax could bring Michael down, along with everyone close to him.

Kate thought him kind, considerate, and noble. She'd never seen the side of him that communed with Fairfax. Indeed, it was best that he took her back to the house.

But the bedroom was silent. The woman waiting in there hadn't put on her shoes. She wasn't taking orders from his darkness.

A number of deep breaths had slowed his pulse but failed to tame the tiger in his trousers. The tiger wasn't taking orders from his darkness, either. It obeyed a different master—thirst. Each encounter with Lydia had intensified his thirst. After four months of her, his soul was a withered, gnarled shade. What a terrible way to die, thirst. And he'd seen it in Kate's eyes.

Even without checking his watch, he knew he'd been out there several minutes, long enough to look like a buffoon. After expelling a breath, he walked back into the bedroom, closed and barred the door, and faced Kate, who still sat on the edge of the bed. She'd made a hasty braid of her hair over one shoulder and shoved both pairs of shoes aside, out of the way. While he watched, she peeled the stocking slowly off her left leg and dropped it to the floor, atop a pile made by her garters and right stocking.

His gaze devoured the curves of calf and ankle, and his soul shuddered with thirst. He shrugged out of his uniform coat, rolled it up, tossed it onto the seat of the chair. The bed squeaked a little from his weight when he settled beside her.

Earlier that evening, the first sight of her descending the stairs had taken his breath away. The garnets at her ears, the graceful slope of her neck—oh, yes, she could glitter among the stars when she put her mind to it. But in her soul, Kate was of the earth, as he was. He caught her hand in his, traced the journey of each of her fingers with his thumb, up and down, up and down, until he found what he sought: a callus here, a hangnail there. Earth. His breathing and pulse steadied. The knot between his shoulder blades released.

She took his hand, rested it on her thigh, and guided it along the shape of her leg beneath her gown. Her eyes were vast and midnight blue, like the empyrean. "In Hillsborough, in February, you promised to massage my feet."

"Yes, I did." He cupped her face with his palm and leaned forward to taste the softness of her lips. Their foreheads pressed together. There was no rush. There was only the sacredness of night and its pledge on the cool breeze. He murmured, "I don't know how I could have forgotten such a promise to you, sweet Kate."

Chapter Twenty-Three

UNO WHISPERED IN his ear, "Do you see him, suh? That demon come out of the shadows with eyes as black as the devil's soul. And now he's at your door."

Michael jerked awake and bolted into a sitting position, the bed unfamiliar, his shoulders tense and fists balled. His gaze darted around a room rendered almost featureless by the cloak of night. Where the hell was he?

Soft breathing and the scents of cinnamon and slippery passion to his right—now he remembered. He exhaled dream-triggered vigilance from his mind and blood. Even though he barely discerned Kate's pale shape, he smiled, his memory full of what he'd seen before the two of them had outlasted both light sources and, sated and sweaty, sought sleep.

Too bad she was asleep. He eased down on his right elbow beside her, where the night surrendered more detail of her features. She lay facing away from him, her naked buttocks perfect little hemispheres. He stretched out his left hand to brush the hair from her brow and hoped she wouldn't resent for long an interruption of her sleep.

His hand froze in midair. He cocked his ear toward the door, toward a sound he'd heard just beyond it, like the scuff of a shoe sole on the flooring. Hair standing up on his neck, he rolled as gently as possible away from Kate to sit on the edge of the bed.

On the tabletop, his sheathed dagger was where he'd placed it a few hours earlier, his watch ticking beside it. He freed the dagger, slunk to the barred door with it, and pressed his ear to the wood, blood pounding. Naked man with a weapon in his right hand, ready to battle an enemy, the ferocity of his ancestors pumping in his veins. All he lacked to complete the picture was woad.

Both doors downstairs were barred. Kate must have again left a window unlatched, and now someone was prowling around the tavern. Could it be Bellington's murderer, still looking for Uno? How Michael wished he'd set guards around the tavern that night, too.

From farther away came another sound, like the groan of a stair beneath someone's foot. Did he have time to throw on his shirt and shoes and apprehend the scoundrel? Could he even do it in the dark without tripping down the stairs and breaking his neck?

Kate's breathing changed. She murmured, "Michael?"

"Shh."

"Where are you?"

"Shhhh!"

The bed creaked a little. In a few seconds Kate was at his side and pressing herself against him to listen at the door. "What did you hear?" She sounded sleepy and a bit bored.

Her skin was soft and warm and smelled of feminine salt. Nothing like facing danger with a delectable woman. His voice was thick. "I think you left a window unlatched again downstairs."

"Not possible. Aunt came through after I locked up and checked every window and the back door. Then I checked it all behind her. Tavern's locked tight."

"It certainly sounds like someone's walking around." And whoever it was could hear them prattling away in the second guest room.

"Ah. Like a shoe on the floorboards? Footsteps on the stairs? A door latching shut?"

"Yes." How did she know?

She chuckled. "Oh, Michael, don't worry. It's just Uncle Alfred. Kevin first told me of his late-night visits about two years ago. I didn't believe it until I was here late a few times myself."

Michael squinted at her. "Who is Uncle Alfred? Not the uncle with the gambling debt?"

"Yes, Alfred White, my mother's brother. He left me the tavern in his will."

He gawped. "Wait a moment. That uncle is dead."

"Gone for ten years. He stops by to check on us every now and then, though."

Michael worked his dangling jaw. "A spirit? Oh, come on, Kate!"

The fingers of her left hand tickled over his right forearm, and she gave his wrist a squeeze. "'Is this a dagger which I see before me, the handle toward my hand? Come, let me clutch thee.'" Her fingers followed the trail of hair down his belly, then closed, prompting Michael's quick inhalation of pleasure. "Ooh, a second dagger. Let's not stand here any longer."

Who was he to complain about Kate's interpretation of Shakespeare? He allowed her to tow him back to the bed, depositing the dagger with a thump on the nightstand. They crawled in and squirmed around, his hand caressing the soft swell of her breast. Then he paused, remembering a riveting ghost story his grandfather had told Miriam and him one winter night. "Surely you're teasing me about this uncle of yours."

"No. He's probably watching us right now. But don't pay him any mind. He won't hurt us."

Frowning, Michael snatched his hand off her and sat back. "I refuse to believe that we made love for the first time in a haunted building."

"For the second time, too." She pushed him onto his back and stroked his belly. "Or did you forget the second time?" Her fingers wandered lower.

He moaned, his thoughts diverted. Gods, yes, he hoped Uncle Alfred had an eyeful of them. That moment, his niece seemed well pleased. "Sweet lady, I remember it all."

"Good." She straddled him and pinned his shoulders down with the heels of her hands. "I appreciate your sharp memory."

"Mercy." He smiled at her, even though she probably couldn't see it in the dark.

"No mercy. Now that you've awakened me, I've another reminder for you."

* * *

From the dark sky out the window, the tentative crow of a rooster, and cricket song, he estimated he'd awakened at half past four. On his back, he closed his eyes and surrendered to the luxurious sensation of Kate asleep on her stomach, her head on his right shoulder, her right arm and leg sprawled over him, and the gossamer breeze of a new summer morning cooling their nakedness. He lay so relaxed that he knew when their hearts beat every so often together, then apart, then together again.

The next time he opened his eyes, it was to dawn and birdsong. Kate had shifted onto her side, and her fingertips made lazy trails across his chest. In the wake of her fingers, his skin prickled and shivered into tiny bumps, but he held still, enthralled by the erotic vulnerability quivering between them.

They drew a deep breath together, and she pushed up onto her left elbow. In silence their gazes met. He half-expected the openness between them to collapse. But it didn't. In the quiet, his mind called out the contrast: the brute lust that had dominated and powered each moment with Lydia, and the expansive, steadfast tenderness of his consummation with Kate. What a wealthy man he'd be if he could wake up to that tenderness every morning.

Some early riser down on the street whistled a few bars of a happy song. Michael smiled, reached up, and caressed a strand of hair off Kate's brow. "A good morning to you, madam."

"And a very good morning to you, sir. I enjoyed myself last night, and I fancy you did, too."

"I'm still enjoying myself." He pushed up to a sitting position, delighting in the way she wriggled up also and didn't cover her body. "The best part is that it's now light enough for me to see the fine details."

Her gaze inspected him boldly. "The looking goes both ways. And you appear ready to make more memories."

He snorted. "Pay no attention to that unruly fellow down there. He wants only for me to dawdle here with you for hours, caring not the slightest for the negative impact it would have on my professional career."

She shifted up onto all fours and stretched her back. Michael sucked in a breath at the sight of her dangling breasts. She grinned. "Then bring that unruly fellow back here tonight after closing time. Half past one."

His heart gave a leap of pure joy. "Yes, madam." Sleep? Who needed sleep?

They scooted to the edge of the bed and sat side-by-side a moment longer. Michael reached for his wadded up handkerchief, sodden with seed, but Kate scooped it up and dropped it on the floor near a covered basket about two feet tall. "I'm sure there's a clean handkerchief around here somewhere that I can give you." She giggled. "Or maybe a dozen handkerchiefs. I spy a full bucket of water, enough for both of us to use. Aunt must have brought it up yesterday." She stood.

His gaze wandered from the bucket, to Kate's legs, to the washstand, to two towels. How convenient to be able to wash before heading out, but he wasn't looking forward to buttoning himself back into the lacy shirt that Spry had inflicted upon him. By then it was light enough that he couldn't skulk back to his room and change shirts without someone seeing him still dressed the dandy from last night. Too bad he didn't leave the tavern earlier. He pointed to the basket. "What's in there?"

"I don't know. Looks like one of Aunt's baskets. I didn't notice it here yesterday afternoon." She removed the lid. "Well, my goodness." She held up a clean shift, petticoat, short gown, apron, and stockings.

He'd seen her wear the petticoat and gown before. "You're set for the day." Clearly Aunt Rachel had anticipated the outcome of her niece's sojourn to the tavern to find comfortable shoes.

Kate dumped her clothing on the bed beside him, reached into the basket, and withdrew a clean shirt. Not just any man's shirt. It was one of his shirts. She passed it to him, along with a clean handkerchief and pair of stockings.

When she saw him run his tongue over his teeth, she handed him a small jar full of salt and wood ash, with a hint of clove. Yes, he'd even be able to clean his teeth. "Well, the evidence is clear. Your aunt and Spry have been conspiring."

"Indeed." She gave him a mock pout. "'What's done cannot be undone.'"

He pointed to the washstand. "Ladies first. It troubles me that you've twice quoted from *Macbeth*, my sweet. Significantly after you've shared a bed with me."

She laughed as she curtsied. "'Thou know'st the mask of night is on my face, else would a maiden blush bepaint my cheek.'"

Maiden blush, hah. "And thou know'st that tragedy ends even worse than *Macbeth*. No more Shakespeare this morning, please." He dropped his clothing on the bed, rose, and stroked her hip on his way to wind his watch and sheath his dagger.

Twenty minutes later, they exited the bedroom fully dressed. Michael tucked the bundled lacy shirt and previous night's stockings beneath one arm, his other hand wrapped around the handle of the covered chamberpot. Kate carried her party gown, petticoat, and uncomfortable shoes. He closed the door behind them.

At the top of the stairs, he could see the first floor. The morning's early sunbeams danced on windows. Outside the tavern, cicada-song swelled in the warmth. Rejuvenation was in the air. He swaggered a bit. "So. Do you still think I'm provincial?" His lips twisted over the word.

She cocked her chin to him. "A bit, yes." At his scowl, her eyes sparkled. "Stubborn, too, but definitely not tame. I was quite wrong about that. And don't change anything about yourself, especially not to please me." Her gaze on him didn't waver. Her tone gentled. "I like you well enough as you are. I know I've never said so before, but it's true."

His bluster subsided. He recalled Private Jackson's giddiness and wondered whether Esther McCall had treated him to such words. Michael didn't feel giddy that moment. He felt awed. To have someone appreciate you for who you were, why, that must be the greatest gift one person could give another.

He set down his bundle and the chamberpot, took Kate's gown from her, and draped it over the banister. When he caught her waist between his hands, she slid her arms around his neck. They enfolded each other. She lifted her lips to his.

At length, he set her out from him and took a deep breath. The clove-flavored kiss would have to hold them both another eighteen hours or so. Smiling, they retrieved their items and headed downstairs, she following several steps behind him.

Near the back door, he dropped his clothing on a table and placed the chamberpot on the floor. He reached for the door and froze. The door was unbarred. Kate arrived on the first floor, followed his gaze, and gasped.

Michael pulled the handle. The door swung wide. He closed it, his skin crawling, and spotted the bar propped against a wall off to the side. His gaze traveling between the door and bar, but not to Kate, he scratched his head a few seconds. "I can say with certainty that this door was barred when you and I went upstairs last night. Either your uncle the spirit has a corporeal side to him, or an intruder got in somehow and left this way. Check to see if anything's been stolen."

He pivoted away from her, went to the closest window, and tugged on the sash. Latched tight. On to the next window, also latched, and the next, and the next, until he'd tested all first-floor windows and found them latched. He took the stairs two at a time and pushed at windows in the other bedrooms. Then he returned downstairs.

A white-faced Kate met him at the unbarred back door. "I went through the tavern. At least on the surface, nothing's been stolen that I can see. There's even a small amount of coin that's been left untouched."

"Coin wasn't what he was after."

"Uno?"

Michael nodded. "The door to that far bedroom where Uno stayed was ajar."

Kate hugged herself and looked away from him. "Gods."

"That wasn't your uncle's spirit last night, Kate. It was Jasper Bellington's murderer." He pried her arms open and held one of her hands. "You and I were bloody fortunate that our bedroom door was barred. Otherwise he might have killed us, too." He tilted her face to him. "He didn't walk through a wall. He got in some way that was difficult for him, because he judged it easier to exit out the back door, rather than retrace the way he'd first entered the building. How did he get in?"

She licked her lips. "There's an entrance to a shallow, unfinished space beneath the building on the north side. After you're down there, you crawl straight ahead and come to a wooden door about three feet high. Uncle Alfred installed a lock on the door, but..." Holding his hand, she took him into the room where officers socialized and pointed out a little door, which gaped open.

"I'm guessing that you have a key to this door, and so does your brother."

"Yes, but the intruder wasn't Kevin."

"How do you know?"

"Because there are spiders down there, and Kevin hates spiders."

Michael released her hand and rubbed his forehead. A man desperate to kill a witness who could identify him as a murderer might take on spiders, snakes, scorpions, even hell itself to get to that witness. "Show me the entrance on the north side. And make sure you lock this door as soon as you're able."

Birds chortled and soared in the humid blue sky. The air and ground were still damp from yesterday's thunderstorms, especially on the north side of the building, where the rising sun had yet to reach. Their shoes sank in the sandy dirt as they walked. Kate pointed ahead about fifteen feet. "There."

Where the exterior wall met a layer of brick, Michael spotted the small wooden door. Like the door in the officers' room, it was just wide enough to accommodate the spread of a man's shoulders, and it, too, gaped open. He halted and caught Kate's upper arm. "Wait here."

"You're looking for footprints, aren't you?"

His nod was curt. The thunderstorms had been a boon. On the second sweep of his gaze over the weedy, sandy ground, he found the tracks of their unwelcome visitor. He studied the approach and the stride length, then knelt and examined the depth. The man was taller than he was, and lean. Like Kevin.

He bent closer and eased fingertips along the hollow made by the nearest print, the left foot. There was no distinct depression for the heel of the shoe. Had the visitor lost his left heel? He scooted forward for an examination of the print left by the right foot. No heel print there, either. How odd. No heels, yet from the shape of the prints, the man clearly hadn't been barefoot.

Still kneeling, he glanced over his shoulder at Kate. "Tell me about the shoes that your brother took with him."

"He took the ones with the brass buckles. And his riding boots, of course."

Michael at last recognized what he was seeing in the footprints. "Did he take his moccasins?"

"No, he left those on the floor near his bed. He hadn't patched them in a while and wasn't wearing them much. After Aunt and I did that bit of burning in the kitchen early Thursday morning, I returned to his room and put them in his trunk." Her voice lowered and wavered. "Out of sight, so I wouldn't have to see them and be reminded. Of him."

"What other shoes did he have?"

"None."

A chill swept over Michael. Understanding buffeted him, sent a queasy feeling into his gut. He stood and faced Kate. "Our visitor last night wasn't your brother." Likely the man hunting Uno wasn't Kevin Marsh, either. No, he was the client whose name had been omitted on those copied records, which meant that on the original, untouched master, his name and Kevin's appeared as two separate entries.

Her shoulders relaxed, and with a fleeting smile, she expelled a breath. "There, you see. I told you so. Kevin wouldn't do something like that."

"I believe you." He walked to her, holding her gaze. "Help me understand, then, why your brother would tell Mr. Bellington's murderer about this little-known entrance to the tavern and give him the key to let himself in."

She stamped her foot. "See here. Kevin's obviously a fool for that woman in South Carolina, and he made the wrong decision to aid the rebels there. But if a man casts his lot with insurrectionists because he's foolishly smitten over a woman, that doesn't make him a conspirator in murder or give him reason to traffic with a murderer here or anywhere!"

Her point was valid. Up until then, Michael realized that he'd been willing to cast Kevin in the role of a murderer, simply because he'd hopped the fence into the rebel camp. "You're correct. In my thinking, I've been unfair to your brother. But it doesn't change the fact that he told someone, likely Bellington's murderer, the secret entrance to the tavern and gave him the key to get in."

Kate stamped her other foot and exhaled through her nose. "I know my brother, Michael. He wouldn't do it. He has no reason to do it. As it appears that he was in quite a hurry to take himself to South Carolina and collect his kisses from Miss Levy, why would he even stop to do it?"

That time, her point was excellent. Indeed, why would Kevin, anxious to evade Crown forces and reach the safety of his sweetheart in South Carolina, stop to give all that to Bellington's murderer?

Dread raked up Michael's back as he realized the obvious answer. Without responding to Kate, he strode back into the tavern, where he awaited her. A number of people were about on the streets already. He and Kate needed to finish this conversation inside, where she could have privacy.

She entered after him, shut the door, and faced him, eyes wide and face ashen. "Oh, dear God." Her eyes glistened with tears. "You believe that—that Mr. Bellington's murderer forced Kevin to tell him about the entrance and give him the key."

"Considering your points, it's a logical explanation."

She looked to the ceiling, blinked hard several times, then swiped away a rolling tear with the back of her hand. "Where is my brother, then? On his way to South Carolina? Or—or—"

"I don't know."

Her eyes widened. "That miniature of Miss Levy that you showed me on Wednesday—it's Kevin's, isn't it?"

"Yes."

"You must have found some of his belongings—but not Kevin. Is that what you're trying to tell me?"

"Yes." He stepped within reach of her and paused, arms at his sides and aching. "Kate, I shall do my best today to find him."

She sniffed. "So the regiment can execute him for treason." More tears streaked her cheeks.

He hung his head, unable to bear the sight of her sorrow. She wouldn't accept an answer that was coated in syrup. It was a characteristic he appreciated about her.

Her misery made him feel as though organs had been ripped from his body. He retrieved his bundled clothing from the table and, at the back door, rested his fingers on the handle. "There isn't a thing in the world I can do to make this easier for you."

She made no sound. He imagined tears rolling down her face while she stifled her sobs.

Instinct alerted him that the day's events weren't going to improve and that at one-thirty Sunday morning, he wouldn't be holding her in his arms. He continued to face the door so she wouldn't see his melancholy. He stopped himself from jabbering that when he found Kevin, he'd use his authority as an officer to give her and Aunt Rachel time with him. Time with a condemned man wasn't time.

Instead, he said, "I shall send word to you as soon as I can."

Even that sounded lame. Damnation, he wasn't any good at this. Who was? Best to stop flogging himself and get out. "Remember to lock that access in the officers' room." He yanked the door open and sought the summer sunshine, which wasn't half as bright as it had been ten minutes earlier.

Chapter Twenty-Four

AT HALF PAST six, Michael climbed the stairs to his bedroom and spotted his hat on the desk. He lobbed the bundle of clothing to the bed and donned his hat. No criminal investigator could have a better assistant than Nick Spry. He spun on his heel for the door.

And there stood the man himself taking up the entire doorway with his sheer size and horsy-toothed grin. The instant Spry registered Michael's expression, he sobered. Michael said, "Breakfast."

"Sir. I've eaten. A pot of porridge just came off the stove for the officers."

"Good. One way or the other, you and I are finding Mr. Bellington's killer and Mr. Marsh today."

"Yes, sir!"

By seven, they were on their way to ensure that all was well with their two rebel guests, the private updating Michael on the night's activities as they walked. Lord and Lady Faisleigh had retired immediately after supper, followed soon by Major Craig and the Hoopers. The dance ended about one-fifteen. Soldiers broke up two fistfights, nabbed one cutpurse in action, and dumped five drunks on the front steps of their houses. All in all, an easy night for the Eighty-Second.

Spry then listened without interruption while Michael related the gist of his conversation with Private Jackson. "Esther McCall, eh?" Spry frowned. "Sir, you think Jackson was lying about blabbing information to her?"

Michael shook his head. "Perhaps Clayton can shed some light upon the situation."

"I heard her family are rebel sympathizers, sir."

"I was afraid of that. I shall check the register." In Major Craig's office was a record book detailing known facts of local miscreants. It wasn't entirely up-to-date, but it would give Michael a start should he need to order Jackson to cease courting the young lady.

At the Hooper house, all was calm. Soldiers on duty reported no suspicious activity and related that the previous set of bodyguards had likewise enjoyed an uneventful shift. The tranquility extended to Alexander Maclaine's house.

En route to the barracks and infirmary, Michael told his assistant about the invader gaining access to the tavern in the wee hours of the morning using Kevin's key and the hidden entrance. He was pleased at how quick Spry was to draw the conclusion that Kevin hadn't willingly handed over the key. They arrived at the infirmary to find Clayton and Uno in conversation in the anteroom.

"I feel good, suh! You don't understand. A man who feels good got to be doing things, working hard, or his mind gets loose." Uno twirled his left forefinger near his temple for emphasis, then caught sight of Michael. Radiant with health, he bounded over. "Mistuh Stoddard, suh, good morning! Please tell this man to let me out of the barracks today." He flung his arms wide with good mobility in the injured left arm, despite stitches the surgeon had put there three days earlier. "I'm glad to work outside in the sunlight for the regiment. Fetch firewood. Clean pots in the kitchen. Cook. Anything, suh."

Michael looked past him to Clayton. The surgeon nodded and folded his arms across his chest. "His arm is healing soundly, sir. I recommend light physical work today."

"Well done, Uno." Michael flashed him a smile. "I'd be delighted to grant your request, but here's my dilemma. Last night, Mr. Bellington's killer was looking for you again at the tavern. We're going to catch the scoundrel today. Until we do so, I cannot afford to assign men to guard you." Uno's smile deflated. "That means you remain in the barracks until I've ensured your safety." He shifted his attention to the surgeon. "What can he help you with today?"

Clayton pondered a moment. "Let's see. Uno, I've several men down with malaria in the sick room. It hasn't been swept in a while and could use the attentions of a broom." He grabbed a broom propped in the corner and extended it to Uno. "After you finish with that, help my orderlies change the bedding. When you're done, I shall find more tasks for you."

"Thank you, suh." Shoulders thrown back, the slave strode for the sick room.

Clayton rolled his eyes at Michael. "Thank *you*, sir. There's almost nothing worse than having to coop up a healed patient past the hour of his release."

"Do you think he could be scrubbing pots in the kitchen on the morrow?"

"If he doesn't overtax his arm today, absolutely. So do us all a tremendous favor and apprehend the criminal today, sir."

Still holding the broom, Uno returned to the antechamber and bowed, expression sober. "Pardon me for interrupting, Mistuh Stoddard. You been busy since I told you what I remember of Monday night. But there was something else happened—" The slave frowned. "—at least I think I remember it happened Monday night. It mighta been a dream. Maybe you want to know about it?"

Michael's interest fixed on the slave. He sensed quiet and alertness from Clayton and Spry. "Certainly. Tell me."

Uno swallowed. "After I was shot, I told you I run from the house to find Tucker and Otis to help Mistuh Jasper. But they were dead in the woods. And then that demon hunted me, so I lay still to hide from him, suh."

"Yes, you told me all that on Thursday, Uno."

"Suh. But one time when I revived, I heard the sounds of two men in a fistfight not far from me, out by the road. First I thought it was wild hogs crashing through brush. Then a man yelled, 'Let me go! I saw nothing! Let me go!'"

Ice crawled up Michael's backbone. "Was this before or after the house was set afire?"

"I don't remember, suh. I'm not even sure whether it was a dream. That night's all mixed up in my head. Specially after I got on the horse. But I figured you'd want to know. I hope it wasn't the killer robbing some poor traveler."

"It's very good of you to speak up about it, Uno. Thank you."

"You welcome, suh." The slave bowed again and headed off for the sick room.

Michael's gaze swept from Uno's retreating figure to Spry to the surgeon. Clayton cocked an eyebrow at him. "What do you make of it, sir? Was that of value in the murder investigation?"

"I'm not sure." Uno himself had doubts that the incident had really occurred. However, if the event hadn't been a dream, an innocent bystander may have been swept up in the killer's net.

One of Bellington's neighbors, perhaps? The Davis family had several homesteads near Bellington, and it had been one of the Davises who'd reported the fire. He must find time to ride out there today or on the morrow to interview them.

Clayton said, "And how may I help you this morning, sir?"

It took Michael a second to remember. He blinked at the surgeon. "Ah. I've a question about Private Jackson. Is it possible that his ordeal and head injury Tuesday afternoon could cause him to forget things he talked about later, after he'd returned to garrison?"

Clayton's brows rose. "You know, sir, I've heard stories of men with similar head injuries who later lost patches of their memories. The brain is a strange and remarkable thing, but if you push it too far, pffft."

Michael sighed. "I figured as much. Poor lad."

"But no, sir, not Jackson."

"Why not Jackson?"

"The man never lost consciousness. That seems to be the deciding factor with a head injury. As far as I could tell, Jackson's memory is fine."

Michael frowned at him. According to the surgeon, the private had all his memory, so had he lied to him last night? It certainly seemed that Jackson had spoken what he knew as truth. "Why do you say that he didn't lose consciousness?"

"While I was treating his wound, I asked him to describe his ordeal. He did so in meticulous detail, one second to the next, from when he felt the snare grab his ankle, to the ball burning his scalp, to the upside down dangle, leaves and twigs raining down on him through blackpowder smoke, to seeing you take cover behind a potted tree." Clayton shrugged. "To be sure, the fellow was terrified. But he didn't hit his head, and he didn't get a concussion. And frankly, if the ball had struck him hard enough to cause unconsciousness, he'd be dead."

"Thank you, Clayton."

Outside, Michael found some shade and pondered a moment, Spry at his side. So Private Jackson had no memory loss. Instinct nudged him to believe Jackson's testimony the previous night. Despite his harrowing brush with death, he hadn't leaked to anyone the grisly details he'd seen of Bellington's body. Neither had Lindsey, Buchanan, Wigglesworth, Henshaw, or Ferguson. All six soldiers of the King who'd accompanied Michael Tuesday afternoon had kept silent, as he'd ordered.

His mind circled the facts slowly. A tall, lean man who wore a red linen coat with enough military bearing to convince Uno that he saw a regimental soldier invade Bellington's house. A financier murdered and his body mutilated in a fashion that resembled the work of Fairfax. A snare set up with cruel mockery and deliberation to kill the first soldier who saw those horrific details. The lock on the tannery door picked by that tall, lean man dressed in black, who then tried to break into the tavern. Footprints made in rain-softened ground by a tall, lean man wearing moccasins.

Spry stirred. "Pardon my interrupting your thoughts, sir. With all this busy work around Mr. Hooper and Mr. Maclaine, I cannot seem to recall why it is that you believe one of the six men from your patrol on Tuesday gossiped about what he saw out there at the estate."

Staring without seeing up the street, Michael followed Spry's prompt, and a trail in memory. It funneled him to late Tuesday night, in the sand-and-wiregrass yard behind the grocer's shop, with Adam Neville looming over him—tall, lean, dressed in black—and answering his question of where he'd heard that Bellington had been flayed. *I got it from a regimental private, who said he got it from a slave man who was running around town and blabbing the details.*

"Damnation," whispered Michael.

How chillingly eager Neville had been to help track down Uno: *If you want to find the slave, my skills are at your service. I'll even discount my rate, just for you.*

"God damn, him, Spry. Damn that whoreson!" Michael looked his assistant straight in the eye. "I don't yet know his motive, but it was Adam Neville who murdered Mr. Bellington!"

"Aaah!" Eyes wide, Spry took a half-step back. "God help us, sir. We're lucky he didn't slit both our throats Tuesday night."

Michael hissed out an agreement. Early on, Jonas Hickory had incriminated Fairfax by describing an argument he'd had with Bellington. Had Fairfax and the financier truly argued, or had Hickory lied about that, too? In Michael's memory, Neville pinned the murder on Fairfax: *Today I heard about the local financier's murder. Are you going to let Fairfax get away with it?* Hickory and Neville had collaborated, with Neville knowing how to wield Fairfax's history to steer Michael's conclusions. "Mr. Neville mutilated Mr. Bellington's corpse with the intention of framing Mr. Fairfax."

Spry's mouth tensed. "As if Mr. Fairfax needs help being framed for gruesomeness. Sir."

Neville, a ranger, knew how to set snares. Neville, part-Catawba, had a bow and quiver; he'd quietly killed the dogs, one by one, with his arrows to avoid alerting Bellington and his slaves, then removed each arrow to cover his trail. Michael punched a fist into his palm. "Mr. Neville must be the client that Mr. Hickory concealed by omitting his entry from the monthly statement. How are those two men connected, I wonder?"

"Well, Mr. Hickory has Indian in him, too, sir. Maybe he's Catawba, like Mr. Neville is."

"If so, perhaps Mr. Hickory's a member of the Ambrose spy ring, as Mr. Neville is. The costume uniform we found must be Mr. Hickory's." Michael delivered another punch to his palm. "Damn. Mr. Marsh is caught up in this evil business somehow. How did his bag of gear wind up in the tannery? Did he even set foot in the tannery?"

The sick feeling in Michael's gut that had grown since he'd seen the hidden entrance to the tavern throttled more words. Silence between him and Spry built. Finally Spry said, "Maybe Uno's 'dream' was real, sir, and what he overheard was Mr. Neville attacking Mr. Marsh on the road."

"No, the timing isn't right, Spry. Mr. Marsh's family says he left town Monday afternoon. That means he should have been in Brunswick well before dark that night, nowhere near Mr. Bellington's estate when Mr. Neville set fire to the house."

"But suppose Mr. Marsh was delayed after leaving town, sir. Suppose he wound up traveling that stretch of road at night and spotted the fire. He thought he could be of assistance, but he blundered into Mr. Neville." Spry's mouth tightened. "Is he still alive, then? Or did Mr. Neville kill him that night?"

Spry's theory made sense. Michael's gut felt like lead. "I've no idea whether Mr. Marsh is still alive. But I doubt he was killed Monday night. Mr. Neville knew that the slave he shot in the arm had escaped. He was desperate to track him down. And Mr. Marsh was a valuable resource."

The private's eyes widened. "Yes, Mr. Neville's been in White's Tavern before, sir. He'd have recognized Mr. Marsh when he accosted him on the road. Perhaps he then demanded his help."

"And maybe he's since imprisoned Mr. Marsh. Remember he was in Wilmington Tuesday night trying to pump information out of me. At some point late that night, he saw Eli and Lavinia moving Uno to the shed, and he watched all of us transport Uno into the tavern. Early Thursday morning, he tried to break into the tavern. But he didn't yet have the key and knowledge of the hidden entrance."

Spry grimaced. "So he went back and forced the information from Mr. Marsh."

Michael punched his palm yet again. "Gah! I've no idea how to find Mr. Marsh or Mr. Neville." Kevin wouldn't have made it easy for Neville to restrain him or hang onto him. Odds were that Kevin was imprisoned somewhere on Bellington's property—or perhaps on the Davis land. Did he have time to ride out there for a search or send a patrol out? He whipped out his watch and checked. No, he'd an appointment with Mr. Smedes at eight o'clock.

A glint came to Spry's eye. "Do you suppose Mr. Hickory's servants might be of assistance, sir?"

Hmm. There was an idea. Fairfax had labeled the smug Tifton and Mrs. Bolton "worthless" at locating the original financial records. Maybe they were unable to put their hands on those records, but Michael wasn't convinced that they knew nothing. "Come along, Spry."

* * *

Michael hammered Hickory's door four times with his fist. When no one responded, he pounded again. "Open in the name of His Majesty King George!" He heard the patter of running footsteps inside, and the bar slid back.

The door opened inward to the glower of Tifton, reinforced by Mrs. Bolton's imperious scowl. The servants' eyes bugged as they counted Spry and six other soldiers backing Michael up on the front walkway. They both gasped.

Michael gestured, sharp, for his men to follow him inside. With their entrance, the servants retreated deeper into the foyer. One soldier wrapped his hand around Mrs. Bolton's upper arm. She shrieked and tried without success to pull away. Tifton attempted bluster. "What is the meaning of this?" Spry and another soldier grabbed his arms. "Let go of me, you beasts! I've done nothing wrong!"

"Spry, Scott, Matheson—bring them." Michael made for the dining room. "The rest of you men, search the property for the crate Spry described." The remaining four soldiers dispersed.

In Hickory's dining room, Michael yanked two chairs away from the table. He planted them a couple feet apart and facing the sun. "Be seated." When the servants had done so and were blinking in the light, he stood before them, feet shoulder-width apart, hands on his hips. "Cooperation in my investigation of Mr. Bellington's murder will go a long way toward deferring undesirable consequences. As of this moment, I consider both of you complicit in the murder of Jasper Bellington—"

"Have a care, sir!" Tifton leapt out of his chair. Spry forced him back down.

"Oh, my God!" Tears filled Mrs. Bolton's eyes, and she groped for her handkerchief.

Michael focused on the manservant. "Mr. Tifton, I insist that you remain seated until I'm finished. And don't interrupt me again."

He growled at Michael. "I shall have you know that I have an alibi for that night."

"Indeed, both of you have alibis. Easy enough to cover for each other." Michael paced slowly before them. "Let's see if you can redeem yourselves from that precarious accessories-to-murder position, shall we? I shall start with the obvious question. Wednesday morning, Mr. Hickory set sail on the *Barbara Bea*. Where was he going?"

The servants eyed each other. Mrs. Bolton blotted her eyes and flinched at Michael. "He didn't tell us."

"This is the shortest conversation ever," said Michael. "Very well, I shall arrest—"

"Williamsburg!" both servants shouted at once.

"Williamsburg, Virginia?" The servants bobbed their heads in affirmation, and Michael stifled a sigh of disappointment. Hickory had found a way to at least temporarily evade justice by putting some distance between them. "When will he return?"

"Three weeks!" said Mrs. Bolton.

"Middle of August," said Tifton, nodding.

"What is his business in Williamsburg?"

"Visiting an attorney friend of his, I believe." Tifton chewed his lower lip and again nodded.

"And the attorney's name, Mr. Tifton?"

"A Mr. Gladwell, I believe he said."

Michael crossed his arms and drummed the fingers of one hand on his other arm as he paced. Hickory had hidden the firm's business records. The senior business partner was dead. Hickory might be consulting with Mr. Gladwell as a way to solidify his claim on the business as the new senior partner.

He stopped pacing and regarded the man and woman before him. "When and where was the last time you saw Lieutenant Adam Neville?" Although the servants kept their faces turned to Michael, they eyed each other in peripheral vision. At a jerk of Michael's head, Spry and the two soldiers closed in.

"Tuesday evening, here!" shouted Mrs. Bolton.

"No, it was in the wee hours on Wednesday morning. You were abed and didn't hear the knock on the door." Tifton scratched an insect bite on the back of his hand. "Mr. Neville brought a crate full of papers to the door. Mr. Hickory argued with him for doing that. Mr. Neville told him that something had come up, and he hadn't had time to transfer the crate to the warehouse. They took the crate to Mr. Hickory's bedroom."

Ah, those missing financial records. Michael imagined Neville's pre-dawn appearance with them placing Hickory in a huge bind, as he'd expected the crate to already be stored in the warehouse by then. Hickory must have been spooked by Michael and Spry's appearance on his doorstep a few hours later—

On cue, one of the soldiers searching the house entered the dining room with a wooden crate. "Found this in the bedroom, sir."

Spry said, "That's it, Mr. Stoddard, the crate I saw Mr. Hickory carry to the tannery."

The records! Michael signed for the soldier to set the crate down. How in the world had Fairfax missed this? Sloppy investigating wasn't Fairfax's style. Michael stepped over and pried the lid off. The crate was empty. Maybe Fairfax had found the same empty crate.

Fists balled, he whipped around and got in Tifton's face. "Where are the records?"

Mrs. Bolton responded. "A-After you left Wednesday morning, sir, Mr. Hickory ordered me to pack all the p-papers from the crate into a second valise. He t-took that with him."

So the second valise that Spry reported hadn't contained clothing. Damnation. Hickory had absconded with the firm's records. That was risky. He must have been desperate. The regiment must fetch him and the records back to Wilmington as quickly as possible.

Michael straightened and ordered the fourth soldier to recall the others. For a moment, he pondered the morning outside the window before again regarding the servants. Mrs. Bolton looked deflated, nothing like the huffy woman she'd been on Wednesday morning. He addressed her. "Mr. Hickory wasn't born in North Carolina, was he?"

"No, sir." The spunk was gone from her voice. "South Carolina."

"Are he and Mr. Neville related?"

She averted her gaze. "They're distant relatives, sir. I-I don't know more than that."

Perhaps Hickory *was* in the Ambrose ring, their eyes and ears in Wilmington, reporting on the Eighty-Second's movements. And as blood was thicker than water, maybe Hickory had removed Neville's name from the records in exchange for Neville murdering his business partner. How much money had Neville borrowed, and why? "Was Mr. Neville a client of the firm?"

Gazes on the floor, shoulders hunched, the servants shook their heads. "Don't know, sir," mumbled Tifton.

Michael couldn't think of a good reason why Hickory would confide in his servants the names of his firm's clientele, thus he didn't see the merit of continuing down that track. For a moment, he massaged the bridge of his nose and considered the Tuesday evening scene described by Spry, when Hickory handed over his records to someone in the tannery. As Neville had delivered the crate to Hickory less than twelve hours later, the logical assumption was that it had been Neville who accepted the crate from Hickory in the tannery Tuesday.

He regarded the servants. "When and where was the last time you saw Mr. Kevin Marsh?"

Again, Mrs. Bolton shook her head. "Perhaps at Market two weeks ago?"

Tifton rubbed his jaw. "In White's Tavern last Saturday evening."

From what he could tell, Hickory's servants had contributed everything they knew of value to the investigation. What a disappointment that the chat with them hadn't given him immediate access to Hickory, Neville, or Kevin. And now, Michael must be on his way so he could chat with Smedes.

"I may have additional questions, but at this time, I don't think it will be necessary to arrest either of you. Note that should you leave town before the investigation is concluded, I shall reverse my decision about your arrests." He pasted his faux-pleasant smile on his face. "On behalf of His Majesty the King, I thank you for your cooperation."

Chapter Twenty-Five

THE JINGLE OF the bell over the door to the wainwright's shop didn't sound half as merry as the bell for the infirmary—an indication either of Clayton's bizarre sense of humor and Smedes's paucity thereof, or of Michael's lack of sleep throughout the week. He propped an elbow on the front counter and gave full attention to Smedes, who approached from the large back room, where his apprentices were working with an axle. Spry stood out of the way, to one side of the door.

"Good morning, Mr. Stoddard, Spry." The wainwright gave them both a nod, then leaned back into the work area. "Lads, I shall be chatting with Captain Stoddard at the counter for a few minutes."

Michael straightened. From what he could see, the apprentices had their hands full with the axle for at least those few minutes. Smedes had timed his tasks well.

The wainwright stood opposite the counter from Michael. "Thank you for being punctual, sir. We've a good bit of work today to stay on schedule. I was out most of the day yesterday at a job more than fifteen miles to the north, and—" He squinted at Michael. "Why the smile?"

Michael ceased smiling and lowered his voice. "Thank you for your diligence at removing the rest of the equipment. It's best that the operation be shut down, once and for all."

Smedes fiddled with an assortment of nails on the counter. They clicked and clacked together. "I shall miss the income but not the danger of that enterprise." He returned his gaze to Michael, his expression somber. "And I encountered danger yesterday, on my way back to Wilmington. A horse thief. About one o'clock, I stopped for a pint at a tavern off the northeast road near

Topsail Inlet. Parked my covered wagon, hitched my mare at the post, looked beside us, and there was Charlie."

For a moment, Michael's brain went blank. He didn't know any horse thieves named Charlie. Then his pulse did a jig. "Charlie—you mean the gelding belonging to Mrs. Duncan and Mr. Marsh?"

Smedes gave one quick nod. "He still had his white blaze, but his coat, mane, and tail had been darkened to an ugly gray."

"Then how can you be sure it was Charlie?"

Smedes chewed the inside of his lip a few seconds, but his gaze on Michael didn't waver. "I've worked with him before. Had to borrow him once to pick up a load of whiskey when my mare threw a shoe late one evening." He snorted. "I bloody well couldn't rouse the blacksmith out of bed to help me with a midnight whiskey run, could I?"

"I suppose not."

"Charlie recognized me, too. I'd read the notice in town that he was suspected of being stolen. Got that feeling on the back of my neck that someone was watching me. I didn't want a horse thief sticking a dagger between my ribs, so I gave Charlie some pieces of dried apple, pretended like he'd sniffed it out in my haversack. Gave some to the horse beside him, too, and my mare. Patted them all, so as to not seem partial."

"Did you meet the horse thief?"

"Oh, aye, when I went inside for my pint. Tall, lean, dark fellow. Looked like he might have Indian in him."

Michael slanted forward. "Had you ever seen him in town before?"

"No, sir. Around town, I mostly keep to myself and my family. And I make it a point to not visit White's Tavern, seeing as how they and I have had that little side business going for so long."

Smedes had been cautious for years. That was good. "Did this fellow recognize you?"

The wainwright shook his head. "I saw no sign of it. After I was into my pint, he walked over and joined me at my table. That's when I saw his black eye."

Ah, yes, Neville's black eye. He surely hadn't received it during a welcome to North Carolina from the Reverend Greene. More likely Bellington, Otis, or Tucker had given it to him in a final struggle—

Or Kevin, fighting with the ranger on the road Monday night while protesting that he'd seen nothing. Something clenched in Michael's heart, a swift spike of pain that was gone in the next second. Neville had Charlie and the key to the tavern's hidden door. The traveler whom Uno had heard fighting with Neville had been Kevin. And it was Neville who'd brought Kevin's traveling gear to the tannery. Whatever his motive for doing so, the action was imprudent—uncharacteristic of the man that Michael had known the previous year.

"The thief said his name was Mr. Adams. He'd noticed that the gelding and I seemed to have a rapport, whereas the gelding didn't particularly care for him. And he pointed out his bruised eye for proof." Smedes thumped fingers on the countertop a few seconds. "He offered to sell Charlie to me."

Michael disciplined rising agitation from showing in his expression. Neville had stolen and was trying to sell a local horse. He was desperate for money. God Almighty, what manner of debt hole had he fallen into? And since he'd accosted Kevin and stolen his horse, he would also have robbed him. According to Kate, the money her brother was carrying was their savings.

Thus far in the story, Smedes had conducted himself with remarkable calmness. How had he lived to tell the tale of his encounter with such a desperate man? How did he avoid being robbed by Neville? "Did you strike a deal with Mr. Adams?"

Smedes coughed into his hand and glanced at Spry. "Well, sir, naturally I didn't have the funding with me to buy Charlie, and even if I did, I wouldn't have said so. Adams is a horse thief. After I finished my pint, he and I walked out together. I pretended to show an interest in Charlie, looked him over closely as if I were considering his suggestion, mentioned that I was expanding my business in the autumn and would need a second horse for it." He rolled back his shoulders, set his jaw, and flicked his attention between the soldiers. "The scoundrel had the stones to stalk over to my wagon, whip back the canvas, and look in it to see exactly what sort of business I was in."

Spry snorted. Michael said, "Mr. Smedes, your story grows ever more intriguing. Did he recognize the equipment parts?"

"Oh, yah." Smedes closed his eyes to wag his head a few times. "What's the old saying? 'Honor among thieves.' Mr. Adams laughed at what he saw and slapped my back with approval. Then he made me a low, low offer to take Charlie off his hands." The wainwright expelled a deep breath. "We went back in the tavern, where he bought me a pint. I agreed to meet him today at three o'clock, in an abandoned barn up there, where I'd pay him for Charlie. All the time, I was hoping to God that I could find you before then and explain what happened, and that this was something truly worth your while pursuing."

Worth their while? Michael eyed his assistant and grinned while Smedes watched them and fidgeted. "Good God, Mr. Smedes, we've been looking for that rascal since Tuesday. What a great service you've done for the Crown, letting us know where to find him."

The wainwright's attention jumped back and forth between them. "So, is that it?" He hiked a thumb over his shoulder at the back room. "I go back to my work—"

"Well, actually—"

"Aw, I knew it." Smedes slapped the counter. "You want me to ride out there and lead you to this bugger."

"No. Recall your erstwhile second business. I want you to drive your covered wagon out there."

Smedes's gaze narrowed on Michael. "With the two of you in the bed again, I suppose."

Michael smirked, remembering when he and Spry had performed that maneuver back in the spring. "It worked in March." And the wagon could provide cover for all of them if Neville lost control.

"But this time it's dangerous for me, Mr. Stoddard. That sneaky devil Adams or whatever his name is might blow my head off. I've a family and a legitimate business to consider."

"I'm well aware of it. Fortunately, a meeting at three o'clock this afternoon gives me plenty of time to set some men in place."

"An ambush, then. You'll make sure I'm good and covered?" When Michael nodded, Smedes sighed. "You'd better give me some money, too, to make the transaction look authentic at the beginning."

"Small coin. He'll be forced to take time to count it, giving us time to aim. Have you a map of the area?" Smedes rummaged around beneath the counter for a moment. Then, to Michael's satisfaction, he straightened with a paper cylinder and unrolled it on the countertop. Michael waved Spry over. "Show us where this barn is located, and describe the surrounding terrain."

* * *

Despite the strategy of planting a team of soldiers in the area in advance of the confrontation, Michael knew they'd need a sizeable amount of luck to succeed in the capture that afternoon. Neville was wily and an expert tracker— and now more frantic than ever. The only reason he and Spry were alive after their encounter with him on Tuesday was that Neville had had no reason to kill them that night.

Michael tapped the regiment's six most proficient marksmen, detailed the assignment for them, and requisitioned horses and gear—including six medium-brown blankets, each with a slit in the middle for a man's head to pass through. A soldier who wore one of those blankets could hide most of the scarlet of his coat. At their destination, each man would don a blanket to help him blend in with shade provided by pine, oak, and mulberry trees in the area around the barn.

Michael wagered that since Monday night, Neville had gotten even less sleep than he'd had. He'd be looking for them, but his attention to detail would be diminished. He'd probably show up early so he could check for a trap. Thus Michael included a couple of loyalist scouts in the party to ensure that his men had time to pick their posts. At a quarter to twelve, he saw them all off. Barring interference from rebels in transit, they'd arrive on site around one o'clock, giving them plenty of time to conceal themselves.

He sent his assistant to check on their rebel guests once more and also to confirm with the wainwright their departure time of one o'clock. At the house on Second Street, he helped himself to bread, cheese, and dried fruit, then penned an update to Major Craig. From the armory, he selected firearms and ammunition for himself and Spry and, with the assistance of Uno, brought them to the table in the front of the barracks so he could ensure that they were ready to fire.

Uno, his back to the door, had just replaced a worn flint on a musket when the doorway darkened. A large-boned, well-dressed civilian in his early twenties rapped on the frame. Michael raised his eyebrows. "May I help you, sir?"

The man carried a portfolio beneath his left arm, and his shoulders sagged with weariness. "I'm looking for Captain Stoddard."

As soon as he spoke, Uno bounded to his feet and faced him. "Mistuh Sam!"

The man's blue eyes widened and his jaw gaped. Then he grinned. "Uno! Thank God you're alive and safe!"

The men embraced and indulged in a hearty round of back thumping. Michael, feeling as if twenty pounds of weight had come off his shoulders, ambled over and steered them out of the doorway. Uno moved closer to the table but kept grinning.

"Mr. Samuel Bellington, I presume?" Michael extended his hand to the visitor. "Captain Stoddard at your service."

Bellington returned a firm handshake. "I'm pleased to meet you, sir, although I wish the circumstances could be more pleasant." He removed his hat, revealing straw-colored hair.

Michael took note of his reddened eyes. "My condolences on your loss, Mr. Bellington."

"Thank you. This is difficult to believe."

"I understand." Had he heard the bad news from Fairfax? If so, Michael didn't see how Fairfax could have reached New Berne so quickly, even if he'd run his poor horse to death chasing Bellington down. "From whom did you hear the news?"

"Captain Fairfax. Ah. This is a roundabout story." Bellington tossed his hat to the table. "I left my uncle's estate across the river early Monday evening to take advantage of a few hours of daylight driving while the sun wasn't overhead. Just before the road to Exeter on Tuesday evening, I stopped at the home of a cousin, intending to visit her and her family a few days and resume my trip to New Berne on Friday morning. But Captain Fairfax found me Thursday evening at my cousin's house and gave me the dreadful—" His voice caught. He hung his head.

As there was no sign of Fairfax, he must have become convinced that Bellington wasn't complicit in the horrific events of Monday night. Otherwise, he wouldn't have allowed the nephew free rein. "Would you care to sit, Mr. Bellington?" Michael gestured to the nearest bench at the table.

Bellington placed his portfolio beside his hat. Then, sitting, he took a moment to compose himself, Uno standing at his side. Michael sat across from them and waited. Bellington cleared his throat. "I've so many questions before I head out to the estate this afternoon and pay my respects. First of all, have you caught the villain who killed my uncle?"

"Not yet, sir. Possibly today. Until I can do so and assure your safety, I insist that you remain in Wilmington."

Bellington nodded. "That's reasonable. Mr. Fairfax also informed me that my uncle's business partner, Mr. Hickory, has left town. Is that true?"

"It is. On Wednesday morning, he absconded to Williamsburg, Virginia with the business records. We will, of course, bring him back here for justice."

"What are the charges, Mr. Stoddard?" Bellington made two fists on the table.

"Conspiracy to murder. Withholding evidence in a criminal investigation. Perjury." Michael studied him. "Would you care to hear additional charges against him?"

Bellington's fists relaxed. "No." He rolled his shoulders back. "For almost a year, my uncle and I have suspected Mr. Hickory of scheming against us. One of the precautions we took appears to have saved the business." He opened the portfolio, withdrew a sheet of paper, and turned it to Michael.

"Ah." Michael nodded at the July record. "You've a copy of the master records. Excellent." He studied the nephew. Given how long Fairfax held onto suspicions of people, he found it incredible to believe that he'd let Bellington go. "I'm curious, sir. Did Mr. Fairfax question you as being potentially complicit in your uncle's demise?"

"Oh, yes. In particular, he wanted to know if I were in a business arrangement with this fellow." The tip of Bellington's forefinger landed to the left of Kevin Marsh's name and that huge amount of money, now lost to rebels in South Carolina. "Mr. Fairfax was of a mind that this fellow was the man who took my uncle's life and those of his slaves. I know that Mr. Marsh works in one of the taverns here in town, but I'd no business dealings with him before the beginning of this month, when my uncle transacted this large loan for him. He's put a house up for collateral on the loan." His mouth hardened. "Typical. Probably another of those houses abandoned by rebels when the Eighty-Second arrived—and now neglected."

"Not this house, sir." Michael caught his gaze. "It's occupied by two widows, Mr. Marsh's only kin, and is in excellent condition." The edge came off Bellington's expression. "For what it's worth, I don't think Mr. Marsh is the criminal." He tugged on the paper. "May I see this?" Bellington released it.

The top entry was Adam Neville's name beside the amount for another large loan, albeit not quite as big as Kevin's. Michael quickly added the number of entries on the page. Fifteen clients, not fourteen. He turned the page back to Bellington and placed his forefinger to the left of the ranger's name. "Mr. Hickory omitted this entry from the monthly statements that he gave us."

"I know. Mr. Fairfax showed me those statements, and I was able to make a comparison with my copies."

Perhaps that had convinced Fairfax of Bellington's innocence. "What can you tell me about Mr. Neville's loan?"

"He transacted it in January, wrote from the interior of North Carolina in March with an attempt to renegotiate the terms—but my uncle refused—and has yet to make a payment, so the interest on it grows. My uncle was hesitant to loan him money at all, but Mr. Hickory is apparently a relative and spoke well of Mr. Neville."

The ranger's collateral was some land in South Carolina about an hour's ride from Camden. Had he put the family homestead on the block for that loan? Why wasn't he paying it off? And why had he needed it in the first place?

He mused, comparing the Adam Neville he knew last year, even in early February of this year, with the man who'd pulled a knife on him and Spry in late March, and the man who'd toyed with the two of them in such a fey manner Tuesday night. They weren't remotely the same men. Even Claude Devereaux had expressed his disapproval of the ranger in invisible ink: *I do not trust Neville.* For whatever reason he'd needed the money, Michael suspected that something had gone wrong, leaving him in the lurch—the ramifications of which were devastating enough to unhinge his mind.

Sam Bellington said, low, "Mr. Fairfax was quite interested in that entry, too."

"Mm-hmm."

"Is Mr. Neville the criminal, then?" Bellington glowered.

Michael handed the July report back to him. "Where is Mr. Fairfax?" Although Michael hated to admit it, he could use the other officer's help bringing Neville in. Fairfax was an excellent marksman.

After a second or two, Bellington slid the report back into his portfolio, sat back, and crossed his arms—annoyed, perhaps, at having his query dismissed. "Thursday night, my cousin provided hospitality to him and the two soldiers riding with him. He and I parted company yesterday morning. He headed north to pick up the more westerly road to Exeter. I drove on south for Wilmington. As my uncle's killer is still at large, Mr. Fairfax was concerned for my safety. Thus he gave me the escort of his two soldiers and suggested that I seek you out when I reached town."

Michael frowned. What the devil was Fairfax up to, driving alone to Exeter? How typical of him, thumbing his nose at safety precautions, probably being sneaky about something. Well, there were plenty of sneaky rebels in those parts. That little side trip could get Fairfax killed, which would be a blessing, even if it meant he couldn't depend upon him in the capture of Neville—bah, Michael and his men would bring down that son of a mongrel themselves.

Bellington's gaze took in all the weaponry spread out on the table, then shifted to Michael. "So who is Mr. Neville, that both you and Mr. Fairfax seem so interested in him?"

Out of a desire to hold his hand close in the inquiry and also to not alarm Sam Bellington, Michael played down the ranger's importance. "He's a person of interest in the investigation." He checked his watch. In thirty minutes, he'd need to meet Spry over at the wainwright's shop. He stood, followed by Bellington. "I shall be occupied with regiment business through late afternoon. Have you a place to stay in town? Your fiancée, Miss Deborah Flanders, and her family live here."

A little color seeped into Bellington's cheeks. "Yes. They'll make room for me."

Michael noticed Uno's big smile and the way he shifted from one foot to the other. "Incidentally, Uno is a brave man, Mr. Bellington. He was injured

Monday night trying to defend your uncle and is the sole survivor. Because he may recognize the killer, we've kept him in the barracks under guard." His resolve to capture Neville doubled, and he transferred his attention to the nephew. "I'm certain that Uno would feel more at ease in the quiet of a house than among the comings and goings of soldiers. And he has quite a tale to tell you. If you agree to not let him out of your sight for the next day and keep him inside, I shall release him to you."

Bellington tucked his portfolio back beneath his arm and reached for his hat. "Agreed, Mr. Stoddard. And thank you for everything."

* * *

After they left, Michael signaled a private in the barracks to help him carry the weaponry over to the bed of Smedes's wagon, emptied of distilling equipment and swept out. He dismissed the private, and after he covered the weapons with the canvas, Spry hallooed him. "Glad I found you, sir!" Spry trotted over from the street. "Clayton needs to see you immediately at the infirmary."

Michael's attention snapped to him. "Did something happen to Uno?"

"No, sir." Spry caught his breath. The insides of his eyebrows lifted, and his forehead furrowed. He quieted his voice. "This morning, one of the Davis brothers who lives south of the northwest road found Mr. Marsh's body behind his woodpile and waved down a patrol. The soldiers knew there was a warrant for Mr. Marsh's arrest. They borrowed the man's wagon and brought back the body."

Kevin's body. In an abrupt motion, Michael turned and strode for the infirmary. A few seconds later, his assistant caught up and matched his pace, but Michael only looked straight ahead. It wasn't as if this was a surprise, no—not after seeing Kevin's traveling gear in the tannery and the open secret entrance to the tavern, and knowing that Charlie had been stolen. And after Uno had told him the new information that morning, a part of him had been expecting it. Nevertheless, his gut felt kicked by despair while his head floated in a cottony numbness.

In the infirmary's antechamber, the surgeon was waiting for him, his lips flattened and tight. So was the town cabinetmaker, who undertook construction of coffins as needed and had brought a roll of shroud material with him. Clayton led Michael back to a stall where a blanket covered a solitary body on the floor and said, "He was wearing only his breeches when he was found, sir. Nothing else on him. No shoes, no money, nothing."

While Spry stood at the entrance to the stall, Michael proceeded in and knelt on one side of the body, and Clayton knelt opposite him. Michael fanned a few curious flies away and tugged the blanket down far enough to see that Kevin had died of a shot to the temple—and recently, perhaps that morning, as the odor of death wasn't yet pronounced. But even death's pallor didn't conceal bruising on Kevin's jaw and cheekbone, or his nose crusted with old blood and crooked from a blow. Michael lowered the blanket over his head and stared at the shape his corpse made beneath it.

Monday night, riding alone on his way out of North Carolina, Kevin had blundered into Adam Neville's web of horror. Thinking of Uno's "wild hogs" description of the fight between the two men, Michael knew that Neville's black eye had come from Kevin. Neville's trip into the tavern through the hidden door hadn't yielded Uno; thus Kevin's usefulness had ended, and Neville murdered him.

That meant Neville had imprisoned Kevin for at least four days. The Davises had several houses near Bellington's estate. There was a good deal of coming and going in the area. Neville must have kept Kevin bound and gagged a good portion of those four days.

"Have a look at this, sir." Clayton flicked aside the blanket covering the arm and hand closest to Michael.

There was more bruising on his arm and a number of what looked like puffy, scorched stab wounds running up and down the arm. And swollen, bruised, abraded skin on the wrist. Michael let out a long breath. "He was tied up and struggled to free himself. He was beaten and tortured." Damn Neville. Fury stirred in Michael's gut, edging out the despair.

"Yes, sir." Clayton twitched the blanket over the arm, exposed the head again, and pointed out Kevin's cracked lips and the sunken skin beneath his eyes. "I doubt this man had any water to drink for the final two days of his life. Even in January, that would be torment."

God Almighty. Michael pushed up to his feet and shook his head to clear it. His stomach tightened around the fury.

Clayton also stood. "Sir, if this is the work of the same man who murdered Mr. Bellington and his slaves—"

"It is."

"Then this is a man consumed with rage. He's now murdered four men brutally. I suggest that you find him and lock him away as soon as possible."

Michael squeezed his eyes shut and massaged his temple for a few seconds. Then he blinked at the surgeon. "Have you sent word to Mr. Marsh's sister or aunt?"

Clayton glanced at Spry, then returned his attention to Michael. "No, sir."

He'd left that onerous task to Michael. "I shall inform them. Have the cabinetmaker prepare the shroud." He turned for the entrance. "Come along, Spry." As it wasn't yet one o'clock, perhaps he could catch both Kate and Aunt Rachel at the house, before they left for the tavern.

Chapter Twenty-Six

EACH OF MICHAEL'S footsteps stomped the earth. Beside him, Spry sounded winded. "I know just what you're thinking, sir."

"Do you?"

"Yes, sir. With every step you take toward Mrs. Duncan's house, you're grinding your shoe into Mr. Neville's face."

Actually he'd been imagining himself strangling Neville with his bare hands, watching the ranger's eyeballs and veins bulge. But Spry's idea was close enough. "My assistant reads minds."

"No, sir. I feel for you. If ever a man needed to be killed, it's Mr. Neville." He paused for several shoe stomps. "But you mustn't kill him. At least not in the way you're thinking this moment."

"Why the hell not?"

"Mr. Marsh wasn't an innocent, sir. He was working with the rebels. If we'd caught him, we'd have had to hang him. Everyone in town would have known. Suspicion and maybe persecution and censure would have fallen on his sister and aunt." Spry gulped. "Sad to say, he goes out in a better light being murdered by an outlaw, and townsfolk expect that outlaw to meet a more official sort of justice."

"I don't need a bloody sermon from you!"

"Sir, I've never seen you so furious. If you don't have your wits about you, you won't be able to capture him this afternoon." He flung up his hands. "Don't you think I know how clever he is after he hog-tied me Tuesday night? And you definitely cannot knock on her door angry like this to deliver the foul news. You won't be helping her at all that way. Sir."

The solid sense of Spry's words sank home. Killing Neville with his bare hands like a barbarian wouldn't right any wrongs. It especially wouldn't bring Kevin Marsh back to life. All it would do was satisfy Michael's selfishness for a moment in time.

The ferocity of his footfalls faded. Fury ceased hammering his veins. Beside him, he heard his assistant's breathing—labored as he'd sought to keep pace with his demon-driven captain.

How in the name of heaven was Michael going to break the news to Kevin's sister and aunt?

They'd almost reached the house. Up ahead, he saw Kate walking for the tavern, pace brisk, straw hat bobbing. He broke into a trot and reached her side before she turned the corner, Spry right behind him. "I'm glad I caught you. We must talk in private. Let's go back to the house."

Her gaze skittered back and forth between the two soldiers, then searched his face. "Why? What's happened?"

Michael opened his mouth, but his voice failed him. His jaw quivered before he clamped it shut. He watched her register the torment he knew was in his expression and the compassion on Spry's face. Without a word, she spun about and rushed for her house, as if trying to outdistance the news.

She flung the front door open and entered, leaving the door gaping. "Aunt Rachel!"

Michael strode up the front walkway with Spry. When he reached the threshold, both women awaited him in the foyer, faces pale. Kate had unpinned and removed her hat. He stepped in and aside. Spry entered after him and pushed the door shut.

Now that the fire of fury was gone from Michael's blood, something automatic took over, the remembered way of communicating loss to murder victims' loved ones. He straightened his shoulders and let his gaze move between the women. "I regret to inform you that Kevin has met with foul play and been killed."

The women shuffled into each others' arms. Kate sobbed once and hid the agony in her face against Aunt Rachel's shoulder. The older woman's face drained of color, and her voice sounded hollow. "Will you need one of us to confirm identification of his body?"

"No. I have done so. He's in the regiment's infirmary with the cabinetmaker."

"We appreciate your letting us know, Michael." She turned to Kate.

"Apologies that this is a short visit. Spry and I are on regiment business and must leave Wilmington." Although he doubted that they were paying attention to him anymore, he added quickly, "I'm sorry," reached for the door handle, and let himself out.

As soon as his assistant caught up, Michael said, "Thank you." What would he do without Spry?

"Sir. Not an enviable task back there. You handled it well. Short and respectful."

Michael glanced at his watch. They'd two minutes to reach Smedes's wagon. He tucked the watch back in his waistcoat pocket. "Let's see justice served."

* * *

A bottle or three of whiskey had broken in the wagon bed during Smedes's career on the shady side of the law. Although the glass shards and dampness were long gone, the aroma remained. By five minutes into the trip, with the summer sun beating upon the canvas above their heads, Spry commented, "So this is what it's like being pickled, sir."

His dry humor drew Michael from thoughts of Kevin, Kate, and Aunt Rachel. "Quiet, you." He grunted when the wagon hit another rut—maybe the wainwright was hitting every rut he could to punish them—and patted his brace of pistols. No, they weren't being pickled. More like pummeled.

The trip took almost two hours, the final leg of it slower after Smedes left the road and cut onto the quarter-mile long grassy drive that would take them to the vicinity of the barn. Cicada-song swelled around the wagon. Brush swished against the sides.

A crow cawed, followed by the whistle of a hawk, then another crow. Spry said, low, "The signal, sir?"

"Yes." The six marksmen from the regiment and two scouts were in position.

He'd wondered how much more he could sweat and was thus overjoyed when the wagon rolled to a stop in the shade of a tree. The wagon shivered a little as Smedes exited. "Halloo! Anyone here?" Wind sighed in leaves overhead. "Mr. Adams? Halloo!"

Michael heard a metallic squeal like the protest of rusty hinges. He made himself relax and flexed his grip on the pistol in his right hand. He heard another man's murmur and strained his ears. Was that Neville?

Smedes dumped a little irritation in his tone. "What do you mean, why am I carrying a rifle? You saw the equipment I haul back there. I don't want anybody stealing that. And a good afternoon to you, too. Christ Almighty."

"Where's the money?"

That was definitely spoken by Adam Neville. Excellent. Michael's lips flexed with a grin.

Smedes countered, ornery. "Where's the horse? You bring him out here, I give you the money."

The wainwright was playing this well, even though he must be on-edge. All those years of hauling contraband had taught him how to browbeat troublemakers. Michael held his breath and listened, wondering how close they'd parked to the barn. Because Uno might not be able to positively identify Neville, and neither Michael nor Spry had actually seen the ranger in possession of Kevin's traveling gear, Michael had explained to his men that he was waiting for Neville to at least accept money from Smedes in exchange for the horse. A technicality, but that way, they could peg him for horse thievery.

After about half a minute, he heard the thud of hooves approach the wagon at a walk. Smedes said, "When was the last time you fed him?"

Neville grumbled. "This morning."

"He looks hungry."

"You can remedy that later. Take his reins, and give me the money."

Michael's purse of coins and fake coins that Smedes had stuffed inside his waistcoat in Wilmington jingled. "There you are, Mr. Adams." Transfer complete.

After a brief pause, the ranger yelled, "What the hell is this—pennies? For a horse?"

"Be glad I didn't give you paper. Pennies have value."

"Don't you tie that horse to your wagon yet. I'm going to count all of this first."

"Be my guest. And I shall tie the horse to my wagon because I have to strap down some equipment back there that jolted loose during the trip." Smedes' voice drew nearer. Michael sucked in a deep breath, muscles ready, grip closing on a pistol, and heard Spry's even breathing. The wainwright released the canvas ties at the foot of the bed, lifted the edge, and peered in at Michael, his expression a warning to get ready. He dropped the canvas and raised his voice for Neville to hear. "Yah, I've a loose part back here. It'll get damaged if I don't strap it down. Finish counting while I do it."

Neville groused again about the currency, not yet finding the wooden coins, and Smedes made his way quickly around the bed releasing the rest of the ties. Then, in one smooth motion, he whipped off the canvas. In the next second, he dove behind the wagon.

Michael glimpsed live oak branches above him before he sprang up and out of the wagon, taking aim on the ranger from behind it while Spry did the same. "Hands in the air, Neville!"

The ranger, eyes hollowed from lack of sleep and face grimy, gawped at them, rifle cradled awkwardly across his chest while he held the purse in one hand and coins in the other. Then he hurled coins and purse at Michael and took off for the open half of the barn door, about ten yards away. Michael flung up a forearm to deflect the spray, then took aim on Neville again and fired at the same time as Spry and several hidden marksmen.

Sandy dirt exploded around Neville's feet, and he yelped, but his momentum carried him inside the barn. Another marksman's shot splintered wood on the doorframe right behind his passage in. The ranger pulled the side of the door shut as far as it would go on its rusty hinges. Pieces of worm-eaten wood shook off and hit the ground. The air grew quiet.

Smedes had halted the wagon with the broad side of it facing the barn, providing excellent cover. The three men were crouched behind it that moment, as the tree under which the wagon was parked had a trunk too slender to conceal all of them. But the horses, nervous in the shooting, shifted around. If Neville had enough ammunition to waste, he could scatter the horses and expose the men.

From inside the barn, the ranger said, "I've two flesh wounds only off that barrage, Stoddard. I've also spotted all four of your soldiers wearing those ridiculous blankets, but none of you can see me. Come in and fetch me, if you can. Or show some wisdom. Tell everyone to stand down, and leave the area immediately."

Michael didn't respond. Seconds passed. The ranger fired his rifle. Wood above Michael's head exploded in chips. Two marksmen returned fire, probably aiming for where they saw smoke, and Michael heard wood on the barn siding crack. The horses danced. The wagon creaked.

Then came Neville's mockery. "Missed me, missed me! Oh, please come in and fetch me! Please."

Smedes cursed. "That scoundrel's far more than a horse thief." Pennies clinked together in one hand.

"Yeahhh." Michael rubbed his chin. "I knew there was something I forgot to tell you."

"If that lunatic destroys my wagon or shoots my horse, the Eighty-Second is paying for it!"

Of course, Smedes was welcome to submit an invoice in the event of either outcome. But Michael didn't want it to come to that. He must figure out how to disarm Neville and place him in custody with as little injury or property damage as possible.

The ranger wanted them to go in after him. Michael couldn't quite put his finger on why. Perhaps he preferred to end his life in a spray of shot, rather than being hanged.

Spry cleared his throat and said, low, "Sir, possibly we could wait until twilight, when he cannot see us as well, and all of us could rush in."

"You heard him. He's waiting for us to do exactly that." Michael spotted a wooden coin in the dirt and added it to the pile Smedes was amassing.

"If we all go in at once, sir, he might be able to shoot one or two of us, but the rest of us will capture or shoot him." Spry tossed a penny onto Smedes' pile.

Please, Neville had said. Memory yanked Michael back to Bellington's estate Tuesday afternoon: Jackson's scream, the shot, the spray of leaves and bark. His skin crawled.

From the barn came Neville's laughter. "I know what you're thinking, Stoddard. You're thinking like the good little redcoat you are. Wait until dark, sneak in, and grab me. Yes, why don't you do that?" He hooted again. "You'll receive a delightful confirmation of why the King will never succeed in controlling America."

"What an arrogant cur." Smedes slammed several fake pennies onto the pile. "I'd like to shoot him myself."

Michael's gaze bounced between Spry and Smedes. "He has Indian-style snares set up in that barn to kill any man who blunders into them."

Spry cursed under his breath.

Neville guffawed. "Look at you, hiding behind some civilian's wagon, Stoddard. You're a coward! I wager your bloody mother is braver than you are!"

Michael would have to set the barn afire and smoke that wretch out of hiding. Fortunately Neville didn't know about the two scouts and two other marksmen, so that meant the ranger was underestimating his opponent's force. The eight men in the brush had abundant ammunition. If he drew those men in, he could set up repeat fire for quite a while to dissuade Neville from picking off two volunteers who'd run over with torches.

There wasn't much cover between the wagon and the barn. But seared into Michael's memory were images of Jasper Bellington's shredded, crispy chest, Kevin Marsh's ruined head and tortured arm, and the damage a pistol ball had done to Uno's upper arm—not to mention the grief of Sam Bellington, Kate Duncan, and Rachel White. Without hesitation, he'd be one of those volunteers.

First, though, he'd see if Neville's arrogance would betray him, let him slip up and admit guilt. He elevated his voice. "Neville, how many snares have you set up in there for us?"

"Oh, what clever thinking, Stoddard! Let's see. One, two—er, five. That means whoever doesn't get caught in a snare will have to face me. I've plenty of weapons and ammunition."

"And how many of your snares are like the one you set at Mr. Bellington's estate?"

"Three of them."

Huzzah! Neville had confessed. "What luck for us! You don't know how to set up that particular snare correctly. My man who was caught in it is alive and on active duty." Michael grinned at Spry. "So that means you've at most only two functional traps in there, and—"

He broke off at the sound of another firearm discharge coming from inside the barn and winced. But nothing hit Smedes's wagon. And Neville screamed.

What now? Had the ranger shot himself? Neville's scream converted to a howl of agony, and his voice rose to almost a screech. "How—how the hell did you get in here without me seeing you? Stay away from me, you—you bleeding monster!"

A second man's voice came from inside the barn. "Neville is now subdued. He has only one snare set, and I shall disarm it and him. Your marksmen may stand down, and you may enter safely to secure the criminal."

Michael and Spry stared at each other. Spry mouthed, "Fairfax?" and Michael nodded, certain that his eyebrows were raised at least as high as those of his assistant.

How had Fairfax known where to find Neville this afternoon and gained access to the barn's interior without alerting him or being killed? "Spry, you're with me." Michael stood with his assistant and grabbed his fusil and ammunition from the wagon. "Mr. Smedes, I know you're bored with all this." He dropped the half-full purse at the wainwright's side. "I'd appreciate it if you stayed here and picked up the money."

Chapter Twenty-Seven

BEFORE HEADING OVER to the barn, Michael examined the two horses. Both had settled down since the shooting ceased and looked none the worse for the excitement, although their ears were still pricked and wary. He patted and soothed them. The horse Neville had given Smedes was definitely Charlie, his coat, tail, and mane stiff from a hasty dye job. Charlie came with a bridle and reins only, no saddle.

Michael and Spry pried open the more functional half of the barn door. About fifteen feet from the entrance, Neville sat in a pile of moldy straw, his left leg splayed out before him, knee a bloody, mangled mess. Michael's gaze darted to the right another fifteen feet, where Fairfax stood in profile to Neville, one of his sleek civilian pistols held upright and ready, the frostbite of his sneer searing the ranger. At his feet was a small mound of firearms and blades, atop it a bow and quiver. Diagonally back in a corner, a horse was tethered. All the ranger's, no doubt. From experience, Michael knew that Fairfax had hidden his own transportation nearby.

With Spry's musket covering him and his own fusil in hand, Michael walked over to the ranger. Neville wasn't going anywhere unassisted. Fairfax had shot out his knee. Nevertheless, precautions must be observed. "Spry, secure his arms behind his back."

"Sir." Spry handed over his musket to Michael and went to the ranger with a coil of rope he'd brought from the wagon.

After the private completed his task, Michael returned the musket to him and gazed down at Neville who, despite the tautness of pain in his face, managed a self-satisfied look. "The horse you just sold to Mr. Smedes, whom you first met yesterday at a tavern, belongs to Kevin Marsh."

"Who's Kevin Marsh?"

"Where did you get his horse?"

"That thing? Found it wandering around." Neville's smugness became a smirk. He was enjoying throwing lies in Michael's face.

Fairfax, who'd lowered his pistol, growled. "Stoddard, you're wasting your time with him."

"You stole Mr. Marsh's horse and dyed his coat, Neville."

"So send me to court martial and the gallows. It's the King's justice for horse thieves. But it looks like my leg will have to be amputated. Maybe I'll die from that first and cheat you of watching me swing, eh?" The ranger laughed.

Michael eyed his assistant. "Guard him." Then, jutting his chin in invitation to his nemesis, he strolled to the other side of the barn with his fusil, into afternoon's deepening shadow. Fairfax joined him there and wiped down his pistol with his handkerchief. Michael said, low, "I'm surprised to see you."

Fairfax transferred his sneer to him. "And I you. However, I believe I understand after seeing that wainwright in your company."

"What is your acquaintance with Mr. Smedes?"

"As little as possible." Fairfax exhaled, hard, and glared at Michael. "I'd have managed this completely by myself. No fuss for anyone else. Then you showed up and bungled Neville's capture outside. I just knew you'd try some foolish strategy like setting the barn afire, which would make him shoot at your men, so I brought him down to prevent loss of life." He shook his head. "And now, Captain By-the-Rules Stoddard takes the prisoner to Wilmington. Assuming he survives the amputation, he'll be found guilty of horse thievery, treason, and various other charges in court martial. Certainly they'll slap him around—but alas, we don't rack prisoners anymore, so he'll resist and take everything he knows about the Ambrose spy ring to his grave when he's hanged." Fairfax rumbled out another growl. "Or sooner, if he dies from the surgery. Thank you, Stoddard."

A chill scraped Michael's spine. While Fairfax set the pistol in a holster on the floor, he looked across the barn at the smirky ranger. Fairfax had seized an opportunity to ambush Neville and make him his sport. He was seething now because the appearance of Michael and his men had stymied it. Well, that was too damned bad. Fairfax could taunt him all he wanted about operating "by the rules," but justice must be served, and Neville must be properly processed—

Properly processed. A voice in his soul muttered, dragged from memory more images of Jasper Bellington, Kevin Marsh, and Uno. He shook them off and regarded Fairfax. "Early yesterday morning, you parted company with Samuel Bellington and told him you were driving to Exeter. But you didn't go to Exeter." He leaned toward Fairfax. "You doubled back and followed him because you still suspected that he was complicit in his uncle's murder, even though he'd denied any business relationship with Kevin Marsh. And as you'd informed the two soldiers you sent with him of your plans, they ignored you when they spotted you on the road behind them. What made you abandon the pursuit?"

The glint of angelic gleam flashed in Fairfax's eyes when he flicked his gaze across the barn to the ranger. Then he returned his attention to Michael. "Mr. Bellington stopped for refreshment around noon at a tavern not far from Topsail Inlet. I concealed my chaise, arrived afoot at the tavern's rear entrance, and paid the proprietor to allow me a vantage point from which to spy on him. As he left, and I hastened to my chaise, I spotted Neville's arrival at the tavern."

The pieces connected in Michael's logic. "You returned to hiding, spied on Neville, and later listened to his conversation with Mr. Smedes. They discussed this barn for a meeting place to make the transaction." Michael frowned. "How long have you been waiting in here for him to show up?"

"Since noon. When I saw marksmen and scouts move into place just after one, I realized that Neville had grown careless and let someone else know about his meeting. I almost left. But then he arrived around two, and I was amused to watch his preparations and fruitless precautions from my vantage point." He spared a glance at the loft above their heads.

Michael studied the rotted, flaky wood above him and the rickety ladder nearby. "You hid up there for more than three hours? How did you not fall through?"

"I've a certain finesse to surveillance that you'll never grasp."

Arrogant ass. Michael's gaze swept over several holstered pistols on the ground beside Fairfax's cane. That was when his brain registered other items there: a shovel, a pick, an ax, sheathed knives of varying sizes, rope, a bolt of dark cloth large enough for a shroud.

Those were the tools of Fairfax's sport.

Michael made his tone brisk to cover his revulsion. "You want Neville for personal reasons. He tried to frame you for Bellington's murder by imitating your handiwork."

Fairfax threw back his head and challenged the rafters with laughter. Face wary, Spry looked over at him. In contrast, Neville gazed at the ceiling with indifference. Fairfax resumed the low-voiced conversation they'd been having. "Imitation, my dear Stoddard, is the finest form of flattery. But in truth, no one could imitate me." His brows lowered. "Apparently you didn't listen to my words Wednesday afternoon about the Ambrose ring. Last August, the day before the battle in Camden, I had the good fortune to spy upon a meeting of the ring in the wine cellar of a brothel."

Brothel. Camden. "The Leaping Stag?" Michael remembered how he'd tried without success to evacuate the daughter of Mathias Hale from her cousin's brothel in Camden prior to the battle.

"Yes, that's the place." Fairfax's eyes grew dreamy. "There were ten men at that meeting. Neville was their leader. I've since dealt with four of the six I recognized that day, along with several others who weren't present." He refocused on Michael. "The Ambrose ring continues to disrupt our operations in South Carolina. I've reason to believe that four leaders other than Neville are still alive to perpetrate insurrection. I don't know their names, but—" He licked his lips. His voice lowered to a seductive whisper. "I can obtain that information from Neville. Then we can crush the Ambrose ring with it and recover South Carolina from the rebels."

Michael yanked his attention off Fairfax. In memory, he heard Major Craig's concern: *Rebels have captured another of our supply trains in the South Carolina backcountry, thanks to a spy or two in our midst, possibly from that damned Ambrose ring. I'd give my eye teeth to know the source of the information leak.* The dissenting voice in Michael's soul grew louder, more plaintive. Again he saw the way Neville had mutilated his victims, and his eyes flinched shut for a second.

No one deserved to be butchered the way Fairfax killed his victims.

Yet Neville had learned from Fairfax, treated his victims to a similarly gruesome end. The Ambrose ring did keep Crown forces in South Carolina chasing their own tails and prevent the transfer of additional troops to Wilmington. And Michael did suspect the ranger of knowing information about the spy ring—

He shook off the slide into rationalization and refocused his thoughts. The overall conversation with Fairfax wasn't headed in a direction he liked. He must change that. "Have you realized by now that Mr. Bellington's nephew is innocent of his uncle's murder?"

Fairfax, expression taut, blocked his view of the exit. "You changed the subject. Oh, Stoddard, let's not dither. You know I'll successfully extract useful information from Neville. Give him to me."

The men sent to drag crucial information from prisoners condemned at court martial sometimes failed at obtaining that information prior to execution. Michael shifted out of Fairfax's shadow. Across the barn, Spry squinted at him, his face long, as if he were trying to puzzle out what his commander and the monster could possibly be discussing that took so much time.

Neville flicked Michael a defiant smile loaded with confidence, despite being in pain from his destroyed knee. *Eyes as black as the devil's soul*, indeed. The ranger had accepted his fate, and if he lived past the amputation, Michael knew that son of a whore would never buckle beneath the version of justice the Crown dispensed.

From his gloat, it was clear that Adam Neville felt entitled to be served the King's justice. Very little scared him. Certainly not death itself.

Fairfax again loomed across Michael's view. "Stoddard," he murmured, his eyes now glittering with archangelic light, "it occurs to me that in the past few minutes, I've asked a rather large favor of you. Is there something I can do for you in exchange for allowing me to assume custody of the prisoner?"

Michael's thoughts leapt to that moment at the supper party when he'd struggled to enjoy the peach tart while worrying over all the ways that Fairfax was going to own him. He was vulnerable in those spots. Nothing he could do about it.

But now Fairfax had made him an offer.

His inner cynic urged him to walk away from any offer coming from Fairfax. No one could bargain with the monster. He'd find a way to invalidate terms and conditions.

And Fairfax was manipulating him.

Michael's attention again shot across the barn to Neville's smirk. Many prisoners went to the gallows mocking the Crown. But Neville seemed to look forward to receiving the King's justice. The ranger sucked honor out of the system everywhere he touched it, a special forte of the disaffected. With a start, Michael realized that that was because Neville didn't consider a court martial and the gallows justice. It meant no more to him than another phase in his life.

There was only one form of justice that Adam Neville respected. It was Michael's duty to ensure that justice was served upon him. With a deep breath, he made his decision and turned his back on him. "Before I release the prisoner to your custody, Fairfax, you must agree to my four conditions."

Instantly Fairfax was at his side, like his very own attentive and well-trained hellhound. "Four conditions? In the old myths, it's always three."

"We aren't in an old myth."

"If you say so."

"Condition number one. As we have in our custody the wretch who killed Mr. Bellington, two slaves, and Mr. Marsh, we may officially close the murder investigation. Should you come across salient information that I appear to have forgotten to pass along to you during the course of the investigation, you will drop it and discuss it with no one."

"I knew it! You withheld information from—"

"That is condition number one." Michael faced him with a harsh stare. "Do you accept it or not?"

Fairfax grinned. "Accepted."

"Condition number two. You will cease any form of persecution or defamation against Mrs. Duncan, Mrs. White, Mr. Marsh, and any of their cohorts concerning a certain side business that may or may not be associated with delinquent taxes. In other words, leave all of them alone."

Fairfax laughed, short. "You're in love with that shrew!" Michael maintained his stare without wavering, and Fairfax's humor subsided. "But that's something I cannot do. Their whiskey business is ongoing, as is their evasion of taxes."

"No more. The still has been dismantled. That was what Mr. Smedes was hauling yesterday." Fairfax pursed his lips, and Michael added, "Incidentally, I questioned Mrs. Duncan and Mrs. White about Mr. Marsh's liaison with Miss Levy, as you suggested on Wednesday. They knew nothing about it. As Mr. Marsh is now dead, the spy connection is terminated. You've no reason to publicize that liaison or even to discuss it with anyone except Major Craig."

"You aren't just in love with Mrs. Duncan. She's your whore."

"You're a waste of my time." Michael spun about to leave.

"Wait!" With a pandering chuckle, Fairfax steered him back around. "I'm trying to be reasonable about this. Suppose Miss Levy's rebel friends attempt communication with Mr. Marsh? You cannot expect me to be silent about something like that." He patted Michael's shoulder. "Can you?"

"No. If that happens, you open another investigation. But this one with

Miss Levy is closed."

The other officer studied him a moment. "Are those conditions two and three?"

"Condition number two, parts A and B."

Fairfax's lip twitched. "I think you snuck another condition into the deal. But I shall agree."

Michael nodded. "Condition number three. My former benefactor has dangled a major's commission in front of your nose with the stipulation that you kill me. You will drop immediately all private investigation you've initiated into the background of Lord and Lady Faisleigh."

One of Fairfax's eyebrows rose. The green in his eyes became malachite. "Aren't you curious why he wants you dead?"

"No. I already know why he wants me dead." Fairfax squinted at him, and Michael clenched his fists. "Drop it. Destroy any preliminary reports that you receive, and call off your investigators." He watched Fairfax's gaze swivel to Neville. Fairfax stroked his chin as if he couldn't make up his mind. Fists still balled, Michael took a step toward him. "I've no desire to spend any longer in this decrepit barn than I must. Yea or nay in five seconds, Fairfax, or the entire deal is off."

Fairfax drew in a shuddering breath, then turned back to him. "I agree to condition three. And your final condition?"

Michael relaxed his fists. "Condition number four. You and I never had this conversation." He had the bad feeling he'd forgotten an important condition, but it was too late to muse on it.

"Agreed."

The word rolled off Fairfax's tongue with such ease that Michael's hackles rose. His head drew back, and he pinned his stare to that of Fairfax. Seconds earlier, he'd witnessed Fairfax's struggle, how his longing to get his hands on Neville battled with his frustration at having to let Michael escape his schemes.

The monster had acquiesced far too easily. He'd no intention of upholding the four conditions. Thus far, nothing Michael held over him was powerful enough to chain him.

What was powerful enough to command his compliance?

Memory yanked Michael back to the spring and a conversation he'd had with Helen Chiswell, who, forced to witness Fairfax practice his "sport" on two spies that January, had managed to escape being murdered by him. Mrs. Chiswell, four years older than Fairfax, had grown up in Wiltshire on the estate of Henry Clancy, the stepfather Fairfax murdered.

Fairfax scowled. "I've agreed to your four conditions. Don't try to add a fifth."

Mrs. Chiswell's testimony of Fairfax was stamped in Michael's memory: *He's been murdering and manipulating for years...Just before he joined the Army, he murdered his stepfather, the man who'd raised him and purchased his commissions, for sport.*

Still holding the other officer's stare, Michael unclenched his jaw and said softly, "Henry Clancy." It was Fairfax's turn to draw back. He regrouped in the next second and opened his mouth, but Michael cut off whatever lie he planned to advance about his innocence. "You hanged him, your stepfather, and made it look like he committed suicide." Sudden cold in Fairfax's eyes deepened to the temperature of glaciers. Michael's fists tensed again, this time to help him stand his ground against the prey instinct for flight.

"Where did you hear such lies?" Fairfax made each word stalactite-distinct.

Michael said, low, "It's wartime, and you've gotten away with multiple murders in Georgia, South Carolina, here in North Carolina, and God only knows where else because you've killed enemies of the King. But the murder of your stepfather Henry Clancy, Lord Ratchingham, cannot be disguised as wartime action. If you violate any of the four conditions I've outlined, I shall make it known that you murdered a peer. And I assure you that killing me won't halt or slow the information from coming to light and sending you to the court martial you so richly deserve."

"Mrs. Chiswell will pay for her slander," Fairfax whispered.

The only way that Michael could see that happening was if Fairfax had extensive business connections in China, and Michael doubted he was so favored. "Let's have at this again, shall we? Do you agree to all four of my conditions?"

A muscle rippled in Fairfax's jaw. He inhaled a deep breath, let it out, and murmured, "Damn you, Stoddard. I agree to your four conditions."

This time, there was no glibness to his response. The ice in his eyes froze harder. Michael hadn't defeated the monster. He'd only chained him. He'd no idea how long those chains would hold. Long enough, he hoped, for either his own investigators or Claude and the Team to come through. "So be it, then." He rolled back his shoulders and felt the twinge of muscles held too tightly. "I'm confiscating Neville's weapons, gear, and horse, and I'm withdrawing my men. Don't move from this spot while I do so."

Fairfax's killing face glowed with anticipation. "As you wish." His tone sounded like the sweet murmur of a lover.

Michael repressed a shudder as he headed for Neville's horse. He searched gear and saddlebags in vain, not finding the savings that Kate had given to Kevin on Monday. Hoping that Neville was carrying it on his person and hadn't blown through it, he snatched a blanket, walked over to the ranger, and signaled Spry to join him. "Search him, Spry. He's stolen Mr. Marsh's savings."

Neville didn't resist. Spry found the purse in seconds, handed it to Michael, and retrieved his musket from his commander. Michael shook out the blanket and draped it over both the ranger's legs to hide the extent of his injury from the soldiers who'd come in. Ignoring Neville's request to splint his left leg, he waved for Spry to join him at the door.

There his assistant said, low, "Sir, what's going on?"

Michael held his gaze and murmured, "My orders. Fetch my money back from Mr. Smedes. Then call Elliott and Sutherland in. The three of you will impound Mr. Neville's weapons, gear, and horse."

"Yes, sir. We're taking it all back to Wilmington with us, then?"

"Correct."

Spry's gaze on him was steady. "But Mr. Neville isn't going back with us."

Michael nodded. "After removing his property, you will withdraw all six marksmen, the two scouts, and the wainwright the full quarter mile to the road. Escort Mr. Smedes yourself to ensure that he, the wagon, and both horses reach the road safely. You and only you will return and join me here while I complete my business. Everyone else is to wait at the road for our return."

Spry's jaw dropped, and he glanced from Fairfax to Neville. "Sir, I respectfully request that you reconsider. The plan you've just outlined for me leaves you alone for an extended period of time in the company of two vipers."

Yes, it did. But as soon as Neville learned that Fairfax was his caretaker, he'd become desperate. No one from Michael's party aside from Spry must hear what information the ranger was going to publicize. "Objection duty noted. I trust you to see this done." Michael patted his fusil. "Carry out your orders."

Spry left and returned with the two men. In less than a minute, they'd removed the horse, gear, and weapons. Michael took up his post by the door. From there he could keep an eye on Neville and Fairfax as well as watch while Spry evacuated everyone from the site.

The land outside quieted in an unnatural way. The ticking of his watch grew loud. Fairfax retrieved his cane and put weight on it but didn't leave the shadows. Neville griped again about needing a splint for his leg. Michael continued to ignore him, and he shut up.

It was the longest quarter hour he'd ever waited. When he spied his assistant's red uniform approaching through the brush, his shoulders relaxed. Spry entered the barn, handed him his purse—somewhat lighter than before—and took up position inside the door.

Michael rejoined Fairfax at the rear of the barn. "I shall schedule a meeting with Major Craig for the morrow at one o'clock. At that meeting, I expect you to deliver to the major and me the names of those Ambrose ringleaders whom Neville identifies to you today. Understood?"

"Understood." The unholy light in Fairfax's eyes shone.

Michael raised his voice. "Then I hereby transfer the prisoner into your custody, Mr. Fairfax."

"Thank you, Mr. Stoddard." Fairfax turned his terrible smile on Neville and limped for him, the cane thumping the earth dully.

Michael made for the door. Neville laughed. "Now, that was a stupid move, Stoddard."

"Why? We want information about the Ambrose ring. I suggest that you cooperate with him."

"I don't know anyone in the ring who's still alive. But I do know your secrets. You tried to kill Fairfax in South Carolina last December."

Fairfax halted ten feet from the ranger and yawned. "You have it wrong. He ran dispatches to the Legion in the backcountry with a schoolboy's dreams of murder. But the pustule never gave it a try. So you see, I know secrets, too."

He spread his arms wide and laughed again. "Are we not all friends here?"

Michael was two strides from the door. Neville's black eyes narrowed. "Stoddard, do tell how you've joined forces with that French assassin, Claude Devereaux, to kill Fairfax."

Damn.

"Halt!" Fairfax's voice lashed Michael's back, and Spry froze in the act of leveling his musket. "I've a loaded pistol trained at your back, Stoddard. Turn around slowly, and hold your weapon out at your side. Spry, you, too."

Michael did as he was commanded to find a civilian pistol leveled at him. He'd never seen Fairfax pick the thing up. At that proximity, should he decide to bolt, there was little chance that both he and Spry could clear the broken door without the ball from the pistol hitting one of them. He gulped and made eye contact with Fairfax.

"Very good, both of you." Fairfax bathed him in the smile he'd reserved for Neville. "Tell me about your relationship with Monsieur Devereaux."

"Early on the morning of February second, Devereaux attempted to kill me while my patrol and I were trying to capture the Reverend Elijah Spivey." Michael cleared his throat. "I'm pleased that my relationship with him isn't closer." A bead of sweat trickled over his right temple. "I suggest that you read my report for the details."

"I already have." Fairfax's stare bored into his. "Drop your weapons, both of you." When they did so, Neville hooted. Without taking his stare off Michael, Fairfax said, "Your turn, Neville. Tell me more about Stoddard's relationship with Devereaux. Where and when have they met to discuss killing me?"

"On the twelfth of June, they met in Cross Creek."

What the devil? Michael had never met Claude in Cross Creek. What lies were these?

Tiny muscles contracted in Fairfax's brow. "Tuesday June the twelfth. Are you certain of the date, Neville?"

"Yes. I eavesdropped on their conversation." Neville bared his teeth at Michael.

"On Tuesday June the twelfth at two o'clock in the afternoon, Stoddard and I were both sitting in an officers' meeting in Wilmington. It's unlikely that he was in Cross Creek on the same day."

How did Fairfax remember so much?

Neville shrugged. "Then I must have the wrong date."

"I don't think so." Fairfax tilted his pistol up, then dismissed Michael by reorienting on Neville. "Now I'm curious. Tell me about your relationship with the French assassin." He twirled his cane a second or two, then caught it without looking at it—the same way he'd squashed the fly the other day.

Heart hammering, Michael scooped up the fusil and saw Spry grab his musket. *I do not trust Neville and have therefore fed him false Information.* Good God. This was some of that false information that Claude had fed the ranger. It had just condemned Neville and saved Michael's life.

No telling how much more rubbish the Frenchman had woven through the ranger's brain. Michael suspected that Fairfax would be entertained for quite a while. He and Spry slipped out the door.

Neville's tone rose. "Where are you going, Stoddard? You cannot leave me alone with him. There won't be enough of me left for court martial!"

Spry's face was ashen. With the private at his side, Michael trotted from the barn at as fast a clip as his wobbly legs would carry him. Neither man spoke.

Neville's voice sprang from the barn, shrill with cognizance of the justice he'd been served. "Stoddard! Staaaaaaah-daaaard!"

The two soldiers made for the road. The ranger's pleas for help followed them a short distance, then cut off. Must have been the foliage getting in the way.

* * *

At the road, Michael announced that he'd transferred responsibility for the prisoner to Fairfax, who'd been hiding in the barn waiting for Neville since noon, having cleverly deduced where the horse thief would make his exchange. It was Captain Fairfax who deserved credit for the capture. Elliott, who was Michael's height, gave his commander his horse and hopped in the back of Smedes's wagon with Spry. Then the party set off for Wilmington, the late afternoon sun painting fire over their right sides.

Even with the threat about his stepfather hanging over Fairfax's head, Michael wasn't confident that Fairfax would honor the four conditions to which he'd agreed in the barn. Fairfax was adept at circumvention. Michael had seen how much of a struggle it had been for him to relinquish the investigation he'd started into Lord and Lady Faisleigh.

Over and over during the trip back to Wilmington, agitation kept his mind circling all the ways by which he'd demanded Fairfax's silence in exchange for Adam Neville's life. His own withheld evidence in the murder investigation. Kate's tax evasion on whiskey production. Kevin's collusion with rebels in South Carolina. Faisleigh's mysterious request for murder. How comprehensive was that list? What condition had Michael forgotten to cover?

Halfway to town, he realized that he'd neglected to stipulate that Fairfax cease and desist conspiring to kill him. In truth, there was only one way that Michael could get him to do that, and it was to kill him first. But acknowledging the omitted condition didn't ease Michael's anxiety. In his haste back in the barn, he sensed that he'd overlooked something else, forgotten to bar some back door.

Sooner or later, Fairfax was going to notice that vulnerability, what Michael had failed to see. Or, perhaps, what he'd ignored.

Chapter Twenty-Eight

IN WILMINGTON, MICHAEL ordered Spry to remove arrest warrants and other posts associated with the Bellington investigation. He escorted Charlie to the regiment's stables and paid the grooms one day's board in pennies to tend the poor gelding, who was, indeed, hungry and hadn't been near a currycomb in several days. Clayton caught up with him and mentioned that Kevin would be buried in the churchyard the next day at one o'clock. Just Michael's luck; he'd planned to be in the meeting with Craig and Fairfax during that time. Thus he'd have to visit Kate at home later on Sunday. After penning an update for Major Craig that Bellington's murderer was in custody as well as requesting the meeting on the morrow, he checked on his rebel charges. Thankfully they'd had an uneventful afternoon.

Having completed his official duties for the day, he presented himself at the house of Miss Deborah Flanders and informed Sam Bellington and Uno that it was safe for both to venture out. Mr. Flanders, urged by his future son-in-law, pressed Michael to stay for supper. Knowing what Spartan fare awaited him back at the house, Michael agreed. Miss Flanders entertained them after supper with arrangements of Handel on her harpsichord.

The sun had set when he found his way to one of the two other taverns in town, both teeming with customers because White's Tavern was locked and dark—and he could guess what the little sign on the front door said. He drank enough cheap whiskey to semi-numb the cored-out and brutalized places in his soul that ached from Fairfax manipulating him into providing a victim for his sport. Before he was too drunk, he paid his tab in pennies and left. In his room, he undressed and passed out in bed.

He awakened once, deep in the earth's quiet. In the distance, a dog barked.

Farther out, he imagined Neville was trying to get his attention again: *Stoddard! Staaaaaaah-daaaard!*

"Go to hell, Neville," he muttered. "I'll see you there." With a shudder, he rolled onto his side, dragged his pillow over his head, and went back to sleep.

* * *

Dawn's light revealed an unopened note smelling of roses on his desk. What new devilry was Lydia up to now? Tiptoeing around the fringes of a whiskey headache, Michael finished his morning toilette and, after easing a clean shirt over his head, broke the seal on the note.

It read simply: *Early Monday morning, household Faisleigh will depart Wilmington for Charles Town. I have the document.*

Buried beneath the avalanche of relief her note caused in him was a twinge of sadness for Wynndon. He'd stop by—not just to pick up the copy of the contract, but in attempt to see his son. He penned his request for a meeting with Lydia that afternoon.

Then he attempted to catch up on more correspondence, writing past the moment when he first heard the hired woman rattling around in the kitchen. The disagreeable effects of over-imbibing in whiskey could be vanquished with coffee, and about six-thirty, when he knew he'd find a freshly brewed pot of it, he took the stairs down. All was quiet behind the study doors. In the dining room, he found the coffee, and toast with blackberry jam plus the company of two officers with whom he shared the house.

Idle talk quickly turned to speculation about the end-of-the-month deadline on Major Craig's ultimatum that all inhabitants of the Cape Fear petition for the privilege of being considered subjects of Britain. A great many people hadn't sworn allegiance to the King. Did Craig really plan to label every one of them rebels on the first of August, seize their property, and throw them aboard prison ships? Where were the extra prison ships? How did the Eighty-Second plan to feed all those prisoners? Although he didn't say so, Michael wondered whether Craig had bitten off more than he could chew.

The two officers piled their dirty dishes on a tray and left the dining room. Michael, rid of the headache, refilled his coffee cup to fortify him for more letter writing. Then the doorway darkened, the well-groomed form of Fairfax taking up much of it.

His back stiff, Michael stood. The tautness he'd seen on Fairfax's face in the barn had smoothed. His shoulders were rolled back, his neck relaxed. An ethereal smile curved his lips.

He visualized Fairfax burying Neville's remains beneath the barn about the time that Deborah Flanders was entertaining her family and dinner guests with music. On such a schedule, Fairfax would have had time to clean off coarse evidence of his sport before returning to Wilmington. And enjoy a sound night's sleep—something Michael hadn't done.

Fairfax arrived at the table opposite him and poured coffee into a clean, empty cup. His rested, peaceful appearance and the normalcy of his movements taunted Michael, drove a geyser of anger through him. Anger and fear.

The shadow of smugness that Michael had found abiding in his soul lately stirred. He imagined it resonating with the monster. Yes, Michael had done his bidding in that barn. Was he becoming Fairfax?

Damn the fiend! That moment, Michael vowed that he'd never let Fairfax manipulate him again, no matter the circumstances. Cup and saucer in hand, he left the dining room without a word.

* * *

"Sir. Lieutenant Neville released these names in association with the Ambrose ring." Fairfax handed Major Craig a piece of paper, passed Michael a similar paper, and resumed standing at rest beside him. "Ringleaders ordered him to borrow money, the purpose to fund additional anti-Crown measures. The ring reneged on reimbursing him. Mr. Bellington refused to renegotiate terms of the contract. Mr. Neville then took matters into his own hands."

Craig grunted at the names on the paper. "Three of these men are already in custody. But Captain Jethro Doyle, bah—" The major flung the paper to the table before him and stabbed it with his forefinger. "Another rebel spy who's been posing as a loyalist for years!" He massaged his forehead.

"Yes, sir."

Michael glanced at the names on his copy. One name he expected to see wasn't there—a name Neville had managed to take to the grave with him. He slid the paper into his waistcoat pocket past Kate's savings and resumed attention on Craig and Fairfax.

Craig's fist pounded the paper once before he sat back. "And Willem Heilbron, a Dutchman. The Dutch are still at our throats in South Carolina."

"Indeed, sir."

"Well. This is fine work from you, Mr. Fairfax. I shall communicate these two new names to Colonel Balfour and inform Colonel Brown that one of his Florida rangers has betrayed the Crown. Where is the prisoner?"

"Sir. He'd concealed a small blade that our initial search of him didn't reveal. He then used the blade to cut through his bonds and free himself. When he resisted my efforts to apprehend him the second time, I shot him."

Craig gave a decisive nod. "It's just as well that he isn't parked in the pen awaiting court martial, another mouth for the regiment to feed."

The major didn't ask how Fairfax originally subdued Neville or disposed of his body. Craig looked more harried than usual. Michael guessed that he wouldn't bother to corroborate Fairfax's story with Elliott, Sutherland, and Spry, who'd been among the last to see Adam Neville alive. Fairfax was counting on that. And so long as Fairfax upheld the four conditions, Michael would parrot whatever story he concocted about Neville's final moments.

It bothered the hell out of him to collaborate with the monster, but he was in too deep and far now to expect anything better.

Craig continued, "I believe I've minimized the sensational nature of those murders and steered the interests of Mr. Hooper and Mr. Maclaine in other directions. Otherwise they'd be able to report to Mr. Burke that the Crown doesn't effectively manage crime in Wilmington."

Michael expected Hooper and Maclaine to report that anyway and concoct details to substantiate their claims. Noting that his commander presented him with a folded paper, he leaned across the table and retrieved it. *Monday 30 July, seven o'clock in the morning, Burrows farm*, it read. He met the major's gaze. "The location and time to return Mr. Hooper and Mr. Maclaine under white flag, sir?"

Craig nodded. "I want them out of town before—" He pressed his lips together and shifted his attention to Fairfax. "Have you anything further to discuss with me, Mr. Fairfax?"

For a few heartbeats, the other officer didn't respond, as if he were deliberating. In the quiet, Trouble snored beside Major Craig. What a perfect moment for Fairfax to break the pact made in the barn and discredit Michael over withheld evidence. Michael could tell that he'd hesitated on purpose in attempt to manipulate him with anxiety.

Michael eased a cramp from his shoulder muscles. Logic told him that Fairfax wouldn't waste his time picking over their agreement for holes. Instead, he'd devote himself to ferreting out and exploiting a vulnerability not covered in the pact. Besides, the blood of one mangy, disaffected double-spy appeared to have temporarily appeased the demon.

"No, sir," said Fairfax. "Nothing further to discuss."

"Then you're dismissed."

While the two exchanged salutes, Michael exhaled slowly. He stood still, facing Craig. Fairfax made for the doors.

Right about then, a funeral procession was winding through town to bury Kevin Marsh in the churchyard near the graves of his sister's babies, born too soon to live, and her husband, executed for treason against the King in '76, at Moores Creek. Michael suspected the procession would be a long one, as many people had liked the manager of White's Tavern. The Wilmington ladies would ensure that Kate and Aunt Rachel ate well for a while. And he realized that Spry had been correct the day before. How much better it was that Kevin had died a tragic figure, rather than languishing in the pen, "another mouth for the regiment to feed."

Behind him, the doors latched shut. Michael captured Craig's gaze and made his voice soft but firm. "Sir, Mr. Hickory's name wasn't on the list of spies, but he conspired with Mr. Neville to kill Mr. Bellington, and those two are relatives from the same part of South Carolina. I'd be surprised if Mr. Hickory isn't at least an agent in the Ambrose ring. I suspect that he'll also be able to confirm Mr. Neville's reason for borrowing money from Mr. Bellington—and for being unable to pay it back."

Craig's brows rose. "Thank you, Mr. Stoddard. When Mr. Hickory is returned to Wilmington, I shall see that he's properly interrogated." He stood and turned his back to Michael. After blotting sweat from his brow with his handkerchief, he parted the nearest curtain and peered out. "Well over half the civilians in the Cape Fear haven't sworn allegiance to the Crown. I intend to subdue the defiance and extract that allegiance once and for all. I want Mr. Hooper and Mr. Maclaine out of town early Monday, so they don't witness, first-hand, our preparations." He stepped around Trouble to face Michael. "Early Wednesday morning the first of August, I shall set forth with an army of two hundred and fifty men and officers and a good eighty loyalist allies and march north to New Berne. You, Mr. Stoddard, will be one of the officers who marches with the army."

"Sir."

Well, there it was, gauntlet thrown. The numbers told the Eighty-Second's plight. Fewer than fifty soldiers would remain in garrison—not enough to resist any serious rebel effort to recapture Wilmington. Furthermore, a quarter of Craig's army would consist of loyalists. Given recent events, Michael wished some of those could be proven loyalists, but they must make do with what they had. He wondered how much longer Craig could keep dancing the galliard of hanging onto Lord Cornwallis's soldiers.

"I've scheduled an officers' meeting for eleven o'clock Monday morning to discuss details of the tour. Make certain that your white flag party has returned in time for you to attend. Any questions?"

"No, sir."

"Dismissed."

* * *

Dorinda answered his knock on the front door of the house Faisleigh had occupied since March. With a quick smile, she held the door open. Michael stepped into a foyer cluttered with packing crates, for an instant disoriented at entering the house through the front door by daylight after all his nights of slinking in through the back. The ladies' maid curtsied and slipped into the parlor. Parted doors enabled him to hear Wynndon reciting Greek, his voice clear and strong, his pronunciation effortless.

The doors whispered open wider. Lydia let her perfumed self out, her gown pink and pearl-trimmed. Expression sober, she handed him a leather portfolio.

Inside it was Faisleigh's copy of the loathsome contract. A crick of tension that Michael had been carrying at the base of his neck since that spring dissolved. Amazing. Lydia had kept her word. He removed the contents and handed her the empty portfolio.

She watched him secure the papers inside his waistcoat. "And your intentions for the contract?" she said, low.

Were Kate ever to learn about this warped arrangement with Faisleigh, he questioned whether their friendship would survive. "Destruction by fire as soon as I leave here." His next stop would be his room.

Lydia gave a formal nod of approval and agreement, then extended her hand for the parlor. "Do come in for a few minutes."

It wasn't a request. Now it was his turn to keep his word. As Faisleigh had disapproved of any contact between Wynndon and Michael since April, Michael said, "What of your husband?"

Her expression softened. "Upstairs napping."

In the parlor, the clock on the mantle toned two. They entered and waited with the closed doors at their backs, Dorinda about three feet to Lydia's left. Wynndon stood three-quarters turned to the unlit fireplace, where a white-haired scholar with rheumy eyes whom Faisleigh had hired in April sat in a chair listening to the fluid recitation. The boy's dark hair was tied back. Embroidery adorned his coat, and lace flopped about at his wrists.

Michael listened half a minute. His rudimentary knowledge of Greek enabled his recognition. "*The Odyssey*?" he murmured. Lydia nodded. A smile touched his lips. What excellent work the boy was doing.

He longed for his son to have the chance to grow into a man. He'd seen signs that the rebels in the Cape Fear were becoming bolder, better organized. What a relief that Lydia had talked her husband into taking Wynndon to the safety of Charles Town.

The boy glanced over his shoulder to the door and broke off, his jaw dropping. "Mr. Stoddard! How good of you to stop by." In a blur of movement, he was at the door, hand extended like a man. "I congratulate you, sir, on your recent promotion. Well deserved."

Michael shook his hand. "Thank you, my lord."

"Wynndon," Lydia whispered.

"Wynndon. I would be pleased if you called me Wynndon, Captain." They dropped hands.

"Well, then. I can only stay for a few minutes, Wynndon, but I came to wish you a good journey on the morrow. You'll enjoy Charles Town. It's a true city, unlike Wilmington."

The boy nodded. "My dear mother tells me that I may correspond with you, if you so desire."

"I would be honored to correspond with you."

"Then it's settled." A brilliant grin lit the boy's too-serious face. For an instant, it was Michael's father's grin. "She also tells me that you're a MacKenzie, as my former tutor was. That must mean your estate is in the wilds of the Highlands. I've never seen those mountains. When I'm older, I should enjoy a visit with you, sir."

Michael chuckled. Well, that settled the matter. He'd have to get the place cleaned up now. "That's a few years off but an otherwise excellent plan. This minute, I'd like to hear more of *The Odyssey* from you."

"Right away, sir."

Moments later, Michael sneaked out into the foyer, followed by Lydia. They both eyed the ceiling when floorboards overhead creaked—Faisleigh rising from his nap—and faced each other. She nodded. "I shall be in touch."

He bowed. "A safe journey, my lady."

* * *

Flame from the candle seized the last page of the contract. Holding one corner of the paper, Michael rotated it to speed its destruction. Fire devoured and transformed Faisleigh's words. Ebony ash rained atop the charred pile in the tin plate on Michael's desk. Lips taut in satisfaction and relief, he watched the paper succumb.

With the final scrap smoldering in the plate, he strode over to open the window. A humid breeze entered. He heaved a sigh. A dark yoke had lifted off his soul—a burden he'd carried for far longer than the months since Faisleigh had been in town. For the first time in years, he saw himself clearly at the age of fifteen.

He visited in memory with that wide-eyed young man while smoke dispelled from his room. Then he shut the window and dusted off his hands. The ashes of the contract were black and cold. He shoved his hat on his head, turned his back on the tin plate, and left his room.

Chapter Twenty-Nine

WHILE MAJOR CRAIG enjoyed another late afternoon tea with William Hooper in his office, his adjutant carried the register of miscreants across the foyer to the parlor of the house and stood by as Michael paged through it. An entry for one Nehemiah McCall, rebel sympathizer, leapt out at Michael. Nothing incriminated other family members, but Spry had forewarned him about Esther McCall's kinfolk, and his suspicions were alerted.

He returned the register to the adjutant and left the house. Private Jackson would be marching with him and the regiment on the first of August, separated from Esther during the campaign. Michael would use the time to talk with him, remind him about his duty to King and country.

Except that it wasn't as simple as duty, he acknowledged as he secured Charlie in the small stable behind Kate's house. As soon as a woman found her way into a soldier's heart, she was no longer a mere civilian. From that point onward, the man walked a conflicted line—half-in and half-out of his uniform coat. Never until then had Michael fully appreciated the emotional debt his fellow soldiers bore for their ladies.

Charlie nuzzled him, pleased to be home. Some of the dye had come off when the groom brushed him, and he was looking more like himself. Michael soothed him and made sure he had fresh straw and water. All the time his mind rehashed his perplexing spectrum of emotions for Kate.

Was it love? To hear officers speak of it and read what poets wrote, love was buoyant and frilly, an uplifting experience. Someone was confused about the emotion. He didn't think it was the poets.

He trudged around to the front door of her house and knocked. As expected, a flock of Wilmington ladies roosted inside. After he was admitted, the door hen directed him to one of four empty chairs just outside the closed parlor. "Shouldn't be much longer, Mr. Stoddard. The last guests entered a full five minutes ago. Wise of you to come well after the funeral and miss the crowd. Pastry?" She thrust a tray at him and batted her eyelashes. "I made them myself."

"Thank you." He popped one of the little sweets into his mouth. It tasted like a too-small bite of that peach tart Friday night. In fact, the house smelled like peaches as well as fresh-brewed coffee, fried chicken, and bacon. A veritable repast of covered dishes weighed down the dining table, and hens busied themselves quietly cleaning and tidying up.

"You're welcome, sir. A cup of coffee for you?"

As the tray retreated from him, he snatched another pastry then shook his head. He heard shuffling around in the parlor. The previous guest was leaving. He shoved the pastry in his mouth. His molars went to work on it.

The doors opened. He stood, munching, and brushed crumbs off his mouth and chin. Mrs. Farrell exited—mistress of ceremonies—pivoted, and curtsied toward the parlor. "Thank you for visiting. How kind of you."

Smedes and his wife exited, followed by four children ranging in ages from about five to ten years old. The wainwright gave Michael a nod of chilly civility and hustled his family out as soon as the front door opened. His wagon had rifle shot holes in it, and he was behind schedule with his business. He was done having adventures with the Eighty-Second. Michael didn't blame him for helping himself to some pennies.

Curtains for windows in the parlor were drawn. Kate and Aunt Rachel sat in chairs to either side of a clutter of empty cups and plates on a small table, their shoulders sagged and gazes downcast, large handkerchiefs in their hands. Both women wore dark gray gowns with white petticoats, which set off their reddened, puffy eyes. Behind Michael, Mrs. Farrell shut the parlor doors, and her voice was quiet. "Here's Mr. Stoddard to see you."

A couch had been dragged over to face the women's chairs. He walked around before it and bowed. "My condolences on your loss, ladies."

"Thank you, Michael," said Aunt Rachel. Kate dabbed her eyes with her handkerchief and said nothing.

He sat on the couch because it was expected of him and pitched evenness into his voice for the customary, expected report. "Yesterday afternoon north of Wilmington, we tracked down the criminal who took Kevin's life as well as the lives of Mr. Bellington and his slaves. While resisting arrest, he was shot and killed." Again Aunt Rachel responded with her thanks, and Kate blotted her eyes. He focused on Kate. "I recovered your gelding, Charlie. He's in your stable. The dye that's been applied to his coat should wear off within the week."

She finally made eye contact with him. Although she threaded the handkerchief between her fingers and parted her lips, she said nothing. A tear rolled down her cheek. She dabbed it away.

His heart writhed at the misery in her pallid face. "I also recovered most of the savings you gave your brother on Monday."

Kate gasped, and her eyes lit. Aunt Rachel smiled. "Oh, Michael, what a gentleman you are."

He pulled the purse free of his waistcoat and stood with it. Mrs. Farrell bustled forward. "Here, now, let me take away some of those dishes, ladies, so you'll have room."

Aunt Rachel rose, collected dishes from the table, and handed some to Mrs. Farrell. "I'll help you, Alice. I need another cup of coffee anyway. Kate, may I fetch you anything?" When Kate shook her head, Aunt Rachel turned a firm gaze on Michael. "You may have my chair."

She and Mrs. Farrell clattered and clinked to the doors. As soon as they let themselves out, and the parlor recovered its quietude, Michael stepped forward, placed the purse on the table beside Kate, and eased into the chair vacated by Aunt Rachel. It wasn't a very comfortable seat. He squirmed his way to the edge of it, angled to Kate, and interlaced his fingers before him.

She touched the purse once without opening it. A long, empty sigh issued from her. "You've spared us through the winter. With our savings gone, I'd wondered how Aunt Rachel and I were going to get by, even in the fall." Her voice was hoarse from weeping.

"On that point, I happened to speak with Mr. Samuel Bellington yesterday about this house. Technically he owns it now. He seemed gratified to learn that two widows were living here. You might be able to strike some sort of deal with him."

She nodded. "He stopped by late morning. We exchanged condolences. He looked around the house and grounds and told us that it would take him a while to get his business straightened out—find a partner here and transfer everything in New Berne to Wilmington." She studied her hands. "He doesn't expect to be married until at least next spring. He invited us to stay here in the house, keep it occupied and maintained until he's married and is ready for it."

"That's encouraging to hear." He hadn't known whether Bellington would evict the women.

"He also spoke of manumitting Uno." She met his gaze again. "Actually we could use his help in the tavern. I'm sure his cousin, Eli, would be glad for the company."

They held each others' gazes in silence for a long moment. He said, "Kate, I'm sorry to have been the bearer of such devastating news."

"I hope you know that I don't hate you for it."

He glanced away. The previous year, a woman in South Carolina had heaped curses on him for bringing news of her murdered husband. Kate's fingers brushed his hand. He returned his attention to her.

"You spared Aunt and me from being made into a public spectacle over my brother's treason." Her eyes glistened. "How could I hate you for that?"

"Kate—"

"No, listen to me. You also put your career and your life at stake for us, risked it all without expecting anything in return from us, from me." She closed her hand on his. "I've never met a man like you. If you'd been anything less, I'd never have lain with you."

To hear her talk, he was a hero of legendary proportion. His gut felt jittery. "You don't really know me, Kate." And surely she'd be repulsed to learn of his decision in the barn the previous afternoon.

She wrapped her other hand around his hand. "Then tell me what it is that you believe I don't know about you."

Very well, let her make of it what she would. "I traded with two devils yesterday and gave one to the other to devour." He looked away and steeled himself for rejection.

Several seconds elapsed. She tugged on his hand, stood, and led him to the couch, where they sat. "Your decision plagues you. Why?"

Stoddard! Staaaaaaah-daaaard! "I forewent the King's justice."

"The King's justice." She made a scoffing noise in her throat. "We haven't had any of that in North Carolina since those patriots ran Governor Martin out in '75. It sounds as though you substituted another sort of justice, one you deemed more appropriate to the situation."

"Yes, I did." That chilling cry of Neville's would be following him around for a while.

"Perhaps—" She drew back to study him for a moment. Grief had hollowed out her eyes with shadow. "Perhaps a young man who boasted to his family that he'd be a general in ten years imagined he'd escape ever having to make such an unsettling decision."

For an instant, he again reconnected in memory to that youth who'd yet to be spattered with blood and brains from a soldier next to him on the battlefield, who'd never experienced combat-induced nightmares, who hadn't sent good soldiers to their deaths. After years of war, he'd assumed that the horrors he'd witnessed had stomped out the idealist in him. But with a start, he realized that he still possessed a sliver of it. That idealist dragged Neville behind him like a ball and chain, and it provided the means through which Fairfax manipulated him.

"I don't think you'll escape making more of those choices, Michael. At least not while you're a soldier. But so long as you've the potential of being haunted by the results of your decisions—" She nodded. "—you'll be more inclined to make the right ones."

He let out his breath slowly. Kate understood. She believed in him. Protect the idealist, she seemed to be suggesting. Without his capacity for compunction, he was the same as Fairfax.

He enfolded her in his arms, and they sat that way while the light outside changed over to evening—while, in his head, Neville's cry grew distant, less demanding of his attention. Michael stroked Kate's cheek once with the backs of his fingers. To have someone appreciate you for who you were was, indeed, the greatest gift one person could give another.

At length, his thoughts turned to the regiment's departure in a few days. Spry would remain in garrison, as would Fairfax, who'd be relearning how to ride a horse. Fairfax in Wilmington with Kate and Aunt Rachel while Michael was a hundred miles away—Michael caught himself and set that particular worry aside, more convinced than ever that Fairfax had abandoned probing conditions of the pact and was exploiting a new opportunity to manipulate and discredit him. Instinct pestered Michael that he should already know his new target, that it was right beneath his nose.

Kate lifted her head and moved back a little to look at him. He put more physical space between them as well, then cleared his throat. "Early Wednesday morning, I shall be leaving garrison for a couple weeks, out on a march." Kate needed time to grieve her brother. Perhaps the campaign would give her that space.

"Will it be dangerous work?"

He made a half-shrug. "Oh, the usual sort of mischief."

Her voice softened. "Will you write me while you're gone?"

He smiled. "I'd be honored, sweet Kate. Will you see me off?"

From the somber cast of her mouth, she knew he was headed into peril. "I'll be there," she said without hesitation.

* * *

The rebels moved the location for the Monday morning meeting another five miles out. Michael didn't receive word of it until he was assembling the white-flag party at a quarter after six. To be certain that he returned in time to attend the officers' meeting at eleven, he had to rush farewells among the Hooper and Maclaine families. Maclaine had the nerve to grouse about it. Hooper handled it with silence and dignity.

As before, Straw-Chewer was waiting for them in the road, his fellows poorly concealed in the brush. He spat the eponymous piece from his mouth to the ground and led the party to another clearing, where the redcoats transferred over their charges. As the soldiers walked their horses away, Hooper called out, "Mr. Stoddard, a word with you, please," and tapped his mount in the sides to trot it over beside Michael.

Michael halted his mare and signaled his men to continue for the road. "Mr. Hooper."

The signer lowered his voice. "My wife speaks well of you." His gaze held Michael's without wavering. "She says your treatment of my family has always been fair, just. I want you to know that I'm grateful for the courtesy you've extended to them—and to me. Thank you, Captain."

"You're most welcome, sir."

They bowed heads to each other. Hooper guided his horse away west, into the midst of three-dozen rebel militiamen and a fidgety Maclaine. Michael caught up with his soldiers, and out on the road, they proceeded south, to Wilmington.

* * *

Their shoulders straight, their buttons shiny and crimson coats brushed out, the men of Michael's company fell in behind the company directly ahead of them on Market Street. The Eighty-Second Regiment marched for the New Berne road, musicians invoking a lively pace. Wednesday morning's early sunlight gleamed on dozens of upright muskets, on the confident faces of five companies of soldiers who were fit, rested, and eager for battle after their half-year in garrison. Behind them were two companies of loyalists. Bringing up the rear were the baggage wagons, artillery, guards, and those scouts on horseback who hadn't ridden ahead with the mounted infantrymen.

Merchants, artisans, dockworkers, and slaves lined Market Street waving and cheering. Children ran hoops alongside the tramp of soldiers and militiamen, and dogs scampered merrily after them. Major Craig, in the saddle and finally taller than every man present, trotted his mount up and down the column bestowing hearty thanks upon Wilmingtonians and promises that the regiment would return soon.

Michael scanned the faces of cheering civilians. Esther McCall, the curvy brunette, waved to Private Jackson. More than a few young ladies from town had turned out dressed in their finest in attempt to spark the fancy of a soldier or two. And although Mrs. Hooper wasn't present, one of her servants monitored the regiment's departure from a shop doorway, his beefy arms crossed, his smirk ready as soon as Michael's gaze met his. He wasn't the only rebel in attendance.

At the officers' meeting late Monday morning, Craig had outlined his plan to subdue as much of southeast North Carolina as possible: destroy rebel supplies and ships, capture slaves, and evict sympathizers from their homes. Colonel Balfour's latest report had instilled the major with confidence. The Continental Army was deploying troops to Virginia and South Carolina, but not North Carolina. With the Continentals thus occupied, Craig's army could progress through the Cape Fear unopposed except for fleeting resistance offered by rebel militia. They might be on the march for longer than a couple of weeks—possibly well into September—in fulfillment of Craig's vision.

Up ahead, in front of a shop, Michael spotted the familiar gaggle of Wilmington ladies as well as the enthusiastic Alice Farrell, all bestowing their blessings upon soldiers. He crossed to the other side of the column so they could see him. Mrs. Farrell's brother, Mr. Carlisle, stood to the right of his sister.

And there were Kate and Aunt Rachel to the right of Carlisle. Both women were still in mourning, straw hats trimmed in dark gray. Carlisle murmured to Kate. She lowered her gaze. The astronomer patted her shoulder with the sort of abstract, clumsy affection a fellow eked out to his dog. No wonder binary stars hadn't appealed to Kate.

Michael was almost upon them when Aunt Rachel noticed him and tugged on Kate's arm. Kate's head snapped up, her gaze locked with his, and her face lit. The warmth of her smile leapt over all the clamor, movement, and distance between them straight into his heart. Elated, Michael threw back his shoulders.

Spry and his grin took up the front walkway of the next building. "Good luck, sir!"

On the verge of responding, Michael saw morning's shadows in the doorway behind his assistant writhe, ejecting Fairfax in a motion so silky that Spry wasn't aware of him. Fairfax, too, had a smile for Michael, a smile that sucked warmth from the summer morning. When he transferred his angelic killing gleam to Spry, Michael's gut became granite.

Nick Spry was Fairfax's next target. From the expression Michael had seen on his adversary's face several weeks earlier, when Fairfax spotted the two of them sparring, Michael knew that he'd been suspicious over how a lowly private had come by such dazzling, unconventional sword moves.

Memory played out Spry's uncharacteristic furtiveness early Thursday morning, right before the white flag party set out to fetch Hooper. The private couldn't have discovered the bag of letters missing from Fairfax's room much earlier than eleven o'clock. Where had he been Wednesday night, and what had kept him up so late? And there was one night the previous week when Spry hadn't been in his quarters late.

Was his assistant consorting with that outlaw family of his?

Fairfax vanished down a side street, his mission to sow anxiety accomplished. Michael lambasted himself for not having taken definitive action sooner with his assistant. "Spry!" With a jerk of his head, he signaled the private to march alongside him.

Spry caught up, and Michael studied his amiable face. "Where were you Wednesday night?"

Spry shrugged. "You know, sir. With Molly."

The washerwoman would cover for Spry if Michael asked her. He pitched his voice just loud enough for the private to hear. "And how's your family doing?"

Spry tripped, recovered his balance, and matched Michael's step again. His smile drained off. He looked straight ahead, lips pinched shut.

God Almighty. What information was he passing along to his pirate and smuggler kin? Michael worked on keeping his breathing even and his voice controlled. "In early April, I asked you to not let me down."

"I haven't done so, sir, I swear it." Spry blurted the words.

A thorn of doubt burrowed in Michael's heart, poisonous gift of Fairfax and an attempt to manipulate him again. But Michael was resolved to resist the manipulation. "Heed my warning, then. Your skill with a sword has caught Mr. Fairfax's interest. Assume that he or one of his agents will be following you at all times—especially if you slip out late at night again to meet—" He hesitated only long enough to stride two steps. "—to meet Molly."

Sweat shone on Spry's forehead. He said, low, "Yes, sir. Thank you."

"Whatever your late-night business, be assured that Mr. Fairfax seeks to use knowledge of it to his advantage and, if possible, see you hanged. I'm unable to help you. It's all up to you. Do you understand?"

"Sir." The private's voice was almost inaudible.

"Good. Dismissed." With a sinking heart and sick feeling in his belly, Michael turned his head north, the direction they'd march as soon as they cleared town. He wasn't surprised to see clouds gathered there, preparing a summer storm for the Eighty-Second Regiment.

Finis

Historical Afterword

HISTORY TEXTS AND fiction minimize the importance of the Southern colonies during the American War of Independence. Many scholars now believe that more Revolutionary War battles were fought in South Carolina than in any other colony, even New York. Of the wars North Americans have fought, the death toll from this war exceeds all except the Civil War in terms of percentage of the population. And yet our "revolution" was but one conflict in a ravenous world war.

From late January to mid-November 1781, Crown forces occupied the city of Wilmington, North Carolina. The daunting presence of the Eighty-Second Regiment nearly paralyzed movements of the Continental Army in North Carolina and prolonged the war in the Southern theater. Short on resources the entire occupation, Major James Henry Craig, the regiment's commander, resorted to unconventional strategies that bordered on insubordination, won the devotion of area loyalists and many neutrals (a feat Lord Cornwallis was never able to achieve), and enhanced his garrison's effectiveness.

Almost never do we hear of Craig's accomplishments. True, history is written by the victors. But also, the Eighty-Second's triumphs were bracketed and overshadowed by disasters that same year for Crown forces at Cowpens, South Carolina in January and Yorktown, Virginia in October. Had more British commanders adopted Craig's creative, fluid style of thinking, the outcome of the war might have been vastly different. And had Craig not become impatient in the summer of 1781—issued an ultimatum that all civilians of the Cape Fear must petition for the privilege of being British subjects, then marched out with most of the regiment to punish those who didn't comply—historians might consider him a more notable military strategist.

Craig had originally been ordered to strategize fortification of a supply depot in Cross Creek (now Fayetteville, North Carolina), to assist the military initiatives of Lord Cornwallis in the backcountry. Early on, Craig realized the vulnerability of a supply train to Cross Creek, and thus the unsuitability of using the location as originally planned. Fearing that Cornwallis would enact a strategy that depended on replenishing his army's supplies in Cross Creek, Craig sent three messengers to the general to warn him about lack of supplies in Cross Creek. None of the messages reached Cornwallis. Suffering severe losses amidst his "victory" at the Battle of Guilford Courthouse 15 March 1781, Cornwallis's army limped on to Cross Creek, expecting supplies. Instead, the army was forced to march several days more to the only safe haven in North Carolina: Wilmington, and the Eighty-Second. Cornwallis left his sick and wounded troops behind in Wilmington when he marched to Virginia mid-April, and Craig, perpetually short of seasoned regulars, made use of them through the summer.

During most of the Eighty-Second's occupation, Craig allowed the wife and family of William Hooper, signer of the Declaration of Independence, to reside in Hooper's law office on Third Street. For a few days in July 1781, Craig permitted Hooper and another patriot, Alexander Maclaine, to journey to Wilmington under white flag of truce. Ignoring Maclaine during the visit, Craig wined and dined Hooper. Hooper, who surely must have been on King George's "Most Wanted" list, was allowed to leave town with Maclaine under white flag of truce a few days later. Hooper was known for being politically moderate, rather than extreme. As for Craig's motivation for such lenient treatment, when he dealt harshly with other patriots like Cornelius Harnett, we can only speculate. This incident exemplifies an ancient wartime code of honor that most people today have never witnessed.

During 1781, charismatic and ruthless military leader David Fanning built a following of almost one thousand loyalists and made a name for himself in North Carolina. His brazen actions included a raid on the Chatham County Courthouse, an attack on the home of patriot leader Philip Alston in Moore County, and the capture of nearly two hundred patriots, including Governor Thomas Burke, in Hillsborough. Mid-year, Major Craig made Fanning a provincial colonel in command of all loyalist forces in Randolph, Chatham, Orange, Cumberland, and Anson Counties.

Revolutionary America was far more diverse, culturally and religiously, than what most students learn in high school history class. The most famous Jew associated with the war was financial broker Haym Solomon, an Ashkenazi Jew from Poland who helped fund the Continentals. From the number of congregations in existence at the time of the war, there must have been many Jews in America. The goals of the Congress appealed to most Jews because they'd been persecuted for centuries elsewhere in the world. For more information on this blend of culture and religion, read my article on the topic. http://www.suzanneadair.net/2014/07/09/religious-diversity-in-america-during-the-revolution/

Many people believe that testimony from slaves in court during the American Revolution wasn't counted, as the fictitious Uno fears. Historically, it was up to the discretion of the judge to decide whether he'd consider a slave's testimony in a trial.

People have been dancing waltzes since at least the 17th century, thus waltzes aren't an anachronism in this setting. During the American Revolution, waltzes would have been similar to what Michael and Kate dance in this book (and what Sophie and David danced in *Paper Woman*), simpler than the grand Viennese waltzes that came into fashion in the 19th century.

In 1781, Third Street in Wilmington had yet to be laid out, although some houses like that of the Hoopers existed on what eventually became Third Street. Because it can be difficult to visualize the strategic military importance of a town with so few streets, I've taken the liberty of granting "official" status upon Third Street.

Colonial-era treasures in cities such as Boston and Philadelphia are well known, but few visitors to North Carolina realize that some houses and geographical features from the time of Craig's occupation remain intact in the historical district of Wilmington. A gem in the city's colonial crown is the house at Market and Third Streets. In April 1781, Lord Cornwallis stayed there while resting his troops. The British general described it as "...the most considerable house in town." The Burgwin-Wright House has been beautifully restored and is open for tours.

Dramatis Personae

In order of appearance:

Michael Stoddard—officer of the King stationed in Wilmington, North Carolina. Lead criminal investigator for the Eighty-Second Regiment.

Henshaw, Jackson, Ferguson, and Wigglesworth —King's men.

Clayton—British Army surgeon.

Alice Farrell—wife of tobacconist in Wilmington.

Kate Duncan—owner of White's Tavern, sister of Kevin Marsh.

David Fanning—loyalist colonel and militia commander.

James Henry Craig—officer of the King, commander of the Eighty-Second Regiment.

Nick Spry—King's man, assistant investigator to Michael Stoddard.

Dunstan Fairfax—officer of the King, dragoon of the Seventeenth Light.

Jonas Hickory—financier, business partner to Jasper Bellington.

Anne Hooper—wife of William Hooper, signer of the Declaration of Independence.

Lavinia—William Hooper's slave.

Rachel White (aka Aunt Rachel)—aunt to Kate Duncan and Kevin Marsh.

Eli—cook at White's Tavern, cousin of Uno.

Adam Neville—scout, ranger, double spy.

Uno—Jasper Bellington's slave.

Mrs. Bolton—Jonas Hickory's housekeeper.

Tifton—Jonas Hickory's manservant.

Pearson—locksmith.

Lord Faisleigh—the sixteenth Earl of Faisleigh, Michael Stoddard's benefactor.

Lady Faisleigh (aka Lydia)—mother to Lord Wynndon (Geoffrey).

William Hooper—signer of the Declaration of Independence.

Alexander Maclaine—Hooper's associate.

Buchanan—King's man.

Smedes—wainwright.

Samuel Bellington—financier, business partner and nephew to Jasper Bellington.

Lord Wynndon—Faisleigh's heir.

Selected Bibliography

Dozens of websites, interviews with subject-matter experts, the following books and more:

Balderston, Marion and David Syrett, eds. *The Lost War: Letters from British Officers During the American Revolution.* New York: Horizon Press, 1975.

Bass, Robert D. *The Green Dragoon.* Columbia, South Carolina: Sandlapper Press, Inc., 1973.

Boatner, Mark M. III. *Encyclopedia of the American Revolution.* Mechanicsburg, Pennsylvania: Stackpole Books, 1994.

Butler, Lindley S. *North Carolina and the Coming of the Revolution, 1763–1776.* Zebulon, North Carolina: Theo. Davis Sons, Inc., 1976.

Butler, Lindley S. and Alan D. Watson, eds. *The North Carolina Experience.* Chapel Hill, North Carolina: The University of North Carolina Press, 1984.

Dunkerly, Robert M. *Redcoats on the River: Southeastern North Carolina in the Revolutionary War.* Wilmington, North Carolina: Dram Tree Books, 2008.

Gilgun, Beth. *Tidings from the Eighteenth Century.* Texarkana, Texas: Scurlock Publishing Co., Inc., 1993.

Hagist, Don N., ed. A *British Soldier's Story: Roger Lamb's Narrative of the American Revolution.* Baraboo, Wisconsin: Ballindalloch Press, 2004.

Hoffman, Ronald, Thad W. Tate, and Peter J. Albert, eds. *An Uncivil War: The*

Southern Backcountry During the American Revolution. Charlottesville, Virginia: The University Press of Virginia, 1985.

Kniep, Robert Charles II. "William Hooper, 1742–1790: Misunderstood Patriot." Ph.D. dissertation, Rice University, 1980.

Massey, Gregory De Van. "The British Expedition to Wilmington, North Carolina, January–November 1781." Master's thesis, East Carolina University, 1987.

Mayer, Holly A. *Belonging to the Army: Camp Followers and Community During the American Revolution*. Columbia, South Carolina: University of South Carolina Press, 1996.

McGeachy, John A. "Revolutionary Reminiscences from 'The Cape Fear Sketches.'" Essay for History 590, North Carolina State University, 2001.

Morrill, Dan L. *Southern Campaigns of the American Revolution*. Mount Pleasant, South Carolina: The Nautical & Aviation Publishing Company of America, Inc., 1993.

Peckham, Howard H. *The Toll of Independence: Engagements and Battle Casualties of the American Revolution*. Chicago: The University of Chicago Press, 1974.

Scotti, Anthony J. *Brutal Virtue: the Myth and Reality of Banastre Tarleton*. Bowie, Maryland: Heritage Books, Inc., 2002.

Schaw, Janet. *Journal of a Lady of Quality: Being the Narrative of a Journey from Scotland to the West Indies, North Carolina, and Portugal in the Years 1774 to 1776*. eds. Evangeline W. Andrews and Charles M. Andrews. New Haven: Yale University Press, 1921.

Tunis, Edwin. *Colonial Craftsmen and the Beginnings of American Industry*. Baltimore: The Johns Hopkins University Press, 1999.

Watson, Alan D. *Society in Colonial North Carolina*. Raleigh, North Carolina: North Carolina Division of Archives and History, 1996.

Watson, Alan D. *Wilmington, North Carolina, to 1861*. Jefferson, North Carolina: McFarland & Company, Inc., Publishers, 2003.

Watson, Alan D. *Wilmington: Port of North Carolina*. Columbia, South Carolina: University of South Carolina Press, 1992.

Discussion Questions for Book Clubs

1. What does author Suzanne Adair do to project an image of the Southern theater of the Revolutionary War in *Killer Debt*?

2. What did you learn about the Revolutionary War that you didn't know before you read the novel?

3. What role does the historical setting play in *Killer Debt*? How does Suzanne Adair evoke a sense of place? What role does nature play?

4. In a novel of crime fiction, the characters should be put in danger. What makes you worry about the fate of characters in *Killer Debt*?

5. For you, what is the most memorable scene in *Killer Debt*? Who is the most interesting character in the book? Why?

6. What is your reaction to the inclusion of real historical figures (book examples: Major James Henry Craig, Colonel David Fanning, William and Anne Hooper) as characters in a work of fiction?

7. In the 18th century, a code of honor during war dictated that certain courtesies be upheld between opponents. How did you react to the issue of William Hooper, signer of the Declaration of Independence, and the white flag party?

8. In what way has Michael Stoddard's concept of women been shaped by his first lover, Lydia? How do you foresee this changing?

9. Is justice served at the end of the story? Explain?

10. How would the use of modern forensics have changed the plot and outcome of *Killer Debt*?

11. How does Michael Stoddard differ from your ideas of what redcoats were like during the Revolution? In what ways does having a redcoat as a hero challenge your beliefs or teachings? Why do you feel that way?

12. What do you think happens to the characters after the story ends?

sThank you for purchasing this book. Word-of-mouth is crucial to the success of any author. If you enjoyed the book, please post a review on your social media (Facebook, Goodreads, online retailer, blog, etc.). Even a brief review is appreciated.

www.ingramcontent.com/pod-product-compliance
Lightning Source LLC
Chambersburg PA
CBHW031235120726
47905CB00002B/600